THE ANVIL CHORUS

Other Books by Shane Stevens

BY REASON OF INSANITY

RAT PACK

DEAD CITY

GO DOWN DEAD

THE ANVIL CHORUS

by

Shane Stevens

DELACORTE PRESS/NEW YORK

Published by
Delacorte Press
1 Dag Hammarskjold Plaza
New York, N.Y. 10017

LIBRARY OF CONGRESS CATALOGING IN PUBLICATION DATA
Stevens, Shane.
The anvil chorus.
I. Title.
PS3569.T453A84 1985   813'.54
ISBN 0-385-29384-4
Library of Congress Catalog Card Number: 84–23858

Manufactured in the United States of America
First printing

For Beate and Serge Klarsfeld
in awe and admiration

ACKNOWLEDGMENTS

Many have helped in the writing of this book, some by giving of their time and effort, others by their example and work. I thank especially Simon Wiesenthal, Werner Maser, Robert Sarner, Dr. Isadore Rosenfeld, Rabbi Alain Goldmann of Paris, Gideon Hausner of Yad Vashem, Jackie Farber, Lynn Nesbit, Dr. Wilbur Gould, Crystal Zevon, and the Criminal Investigation Department of the Paris Police and the staff of the American Library in Paris.

I am most particularly indebted to Lilli Kopecky, Aurelia Pollack and Ruth Elias. With indescribable courage and humanity they survived Auschwitz.

THE ANVIL CHORUS

BOOK ONE

PROLOGUE

April 6, 1975—Paris

The City of Light beckons all who come but for some, that light quickly dies.

Dieter Bock's turn came during the hour of the wolf, precisely at 4:29 of a wet and windy morning, in a gloomy *pension* on the Right Bank. It came to him in the form of a whistle, a sudden sharp hiss of forced air as the piano wire bit deep into his throat. The very last sensation he felt was the warm spill of urine splashing down his left leg. Dieter Bock died, like the others, in surprise.

A gloved hand reached out to crush a final cigarette. Someone sighed impatiently. There were still a few things to be done, traces removed, before the ordeal was over. The gloved hands grimly set to work as the lifeless body hanging from the ceiling pipe slowly voided itself.

Outside the room a solitary drunk staggered down the hall toward his own quarters, unreasonably angry at the world. Light from the single bulb did not quite reach his door and he loudly cursed the dark while fumbling for his key. He was quickly answered by even louder shouts from behind thin walls: a lout was all he would ever be, and foul-smelling too, a pig of an oaf, a *clochard* the *flics* would come drag away, and good riddance!

Silence soon returned to the floor, a heavy blanket of stillness covering soft steps of departure. No one was seen leaving the building and all anyone afterwards remembered of the time was that the drunk in 410 had been at it again.

The death of Dieter Bock, a former SS captain who'd spent three years in a German prison during the 1950s, received little notice at first, and this was seen by some as signaling an end to publicity over war crimes. It had, after all, been thirty years since the fall of Nazi Germany, and those who served it in a criminal capacity were older now, and would soon be dead. Bock, for example, was fifty-six when he died, and others of his ilk were dying all the time. Better to let nature take its course. It was a far different world and a more democratic Europe had risen out of the ashes of war. Painful memories were fading and deserved to be forgotten.

Yet, as it happened, Bock's death in this anniversary year created new interest in the search for Nazi war criminals. Strangely enough, it also served as the beginning of the biggest treasure hunt in history, and one which has left an awesome mystery that remains to this day.

In secret American State Department files, the Bock affair is coded *Anvil*. The West German government—and that of East Germany— know it as *Nibelung*. Austria and Switzerland still deny any knowledge of the matter, as does the state of Israel. And in France, where it all began all over again on that cheerless Parisian Sunday when Dieter Bock died between 4 and 5 A.M., it is simply called *L'heure du loup*.

The hour of the wolf.

The hour that the hunt began.

ONE

Everything is so easy for the young, who are not hampered by wisdom or experience.

"Suicide," said the youthful detective from headquarters, "plain and simple."

The two of them stood off to one side of the room, their words pointed, their eyes narrowed in that careful look all policemen seem to share. They had watched the corpse removed, the noose unwound; on the floor a chalk outline marked where the body had fallen. All the pictures were taken, the information noted. What more could be done with suicide?

"Not so simple," suggested the tall spare inspector. He was older and wiser and had seen a few things in his day. During the Algerian war he had brought down a general who murdered two prostitutes. A *général* of the French army! He'd almost been shot for it but he finally won out. That was fifteen years ago when he himself had been young and full of piss and vinegar. After that nothing fazed him, but he knew he'd never make it beyond inspector. He had made important enemies instead. "Not so simple," he repeated now in reflection.

"What's that?"

"Everything." The inspector sighed, shook free of reverie. "This," he said, pointing to the pipe above their heads.

"He hanged himself."

"With piano wire?"

The youthful detective remonstrated. What else could it be? The *gendarmes* who found the body reported the door bolted from the inside; they had to kick it in. See! The bolt was still hanging by two screws, the latch on the doorjamb flung halfway across the room by the force. And the windows were also locked from the inside, which meant he was alone when he got on the chair and stuck his head in the noose. He had to be.

The inspector sympathized with his young colleague but facts didn't always add up. He'd once worked on an obvious murder victim, shot at close range with a missing weapon; obvious, that is, until he discovered the victim, for insurance reasons, had rigged the gun to a rubber inner tube that jerked it up the chimney after it was fired. Death was never accidental, and neither was life. It always sought new ways to scheme.

Noise erupted from the hall, feet climbing stairs, and then voices, low murmurs growing louder until two thugs finally cleared the doorway, government agents in blue suits looking for all the world like a pair of bankers. The next moment a third man swept into the room, Supervisor Junot of the SCE. He did not look pleased.

The Service de Contre-Espionnage handled internal security for the Ministry of Defense, often in direct competition with the internal surveillance unit of the Sûreté Nationale, which bothered the Service not at all. Mistrust was its stock in trade and its agents were very good at their jobs. So was the head of Sector 2 who now faced those in the room with obvious distaste, his practiced eye searching out the inspector.

"Suicide?" It was almost a command.

"Murder!"

César Dreyfus silently watched the haughty face at the door run through disbelief and suspicion before softening finally into caution.

The report of Dieter Bock's death had quickly reached SCE headquarters on the Rue St-Dominique in the military Seventh district. His name was on a low-level security list of those to be observed periodically, persons who were perhaps not troublesome themselves but might become the occasion of trouble. In Bock's case, his Nazi past could conceivably lead to acts of revenge disturbing to public order.

Paris police used all such security lists and since Bock's name had a Nazi designation, Junot's Sector 2 was immediately notified. Their expertise was the Middle East, primarily the activities of the Palestinian groups, and of course the Israelis. The Nazi past was a ghost no longer seen or felt but still their responsibility. His responsibility.

The police, meanwhile, continued their methodical search of the dead man's effects. Some papers had been found, letters and receipts, and in the closet a metal box with twenty thousand francs. Robbery was not the motive, as César had already guessed. Hanging usually meant revenge.

Junot called him aside. "You must realize this is a matter for my office."

"Unless it's murder, yes." The voice was soft, almost mocking.

"They had to break in."

César nodded in agreement.

Eyes studied him, testing. "And how does one leave a room sealed from the inside?"

"It can be done."

"But was it done?"

"Yes."

"Show me."

"Look behind you," César said, pointing.

The supervisor turned, perplexed.

"The door." César pinched the bridge of his nose in nervous gesture. He wished they would all disappear, all the blue suits from the SCE. Maybe then he could get back to work. The clues were here, something, anything. What he needed was time—and a little luck, always that. In the corner of his eye he saw the young detective edging nearer, curious.

"I don't understand," Junot said irritably. "What does the door have to—"

César indicated the barrel bolt hanging off the frame. "The screw holes are set at a ninety-degree angle downward." His finger circled the holes he'd found earlier. "With enough butter rubbed on the bolt, the barrel will slide down into the latch by itself, like—this! All it takes is a slam of the door."

He produced a small screwdriver from his jacket. "Also, the bolt is new. Notice it's been scratched to make it look used, but the holes are fresh."

They reset the screws and covered the bolt with lubricant. It worked each time, the barrel catching onto the latch.

The room was sealed.

César smiled at his youthful associate but the supervisor was not satisfied. All he'd seen was the presumption of evidence, nothing more. Where were the hard facts, the proof of murder?

"Where?"

"It's only a beginning," César conceded. "More will come."

"Indeed!" Junot roared. "Then again maybe he put the bolt on so he could rot in here; just look at this place. Or maybe he wasn't crazy at all. Maybe there's insurance that doesn't pay off for suicide."

"Maybe anything," César protested, "but just the same we know he was hanged by someone."

"He was hanged," Junot said with finality. He rubbed his hands together, suddenly full of animation. The voice of authority. "That is all we know, Inspector."

César understood the supervisor's motive, of course; he could hardly be fooled after fifteen years. The usual information without responsibility. What annoyed him was that Junot knew he knew. And didn't care.

"Piano wire." Junot looked out over the room, shaking his head. "What will they think of next?"

He motioned to his men; they were leaving. Then back to César, a mouth of friendly teeth. "We'll work together on this, *mon ami.* Exchange ideas."

Now it comes, César thought. We do the dirty work and they get the credit like always. Or even get away with worse. Government security had its hooks so deep, the police themselves couldn't function properly half the time.

"A pity, something like this." Junot laughed. "With the world so different now, I mean."

"He was SS," César muttered. They were Hitler's special killers, everyone knew that. "Surely you remember the SS, *Monsieur* Supervisor."

Junot closed the notebook in which he'd been writing. "Death, always death." He sounded like he enjoyed it.

Junot's men were already in the hall, their heavy steps booming on the ancient boards. César thought they had looked familiar, one of them anyway. A shooting some years back.

"My conclusions remain open—for the moment." Junot replaced the notebook in his breast pocket. "There, that should satisfy you. Now that I've acceded to your demands you may continue." The pen went behind the handkerchief.

"Demands? What demands?"

"That body, this so-called murder. You've finally got what you want, *nicht wahr?*"

"What do you mean?" César asked with mounting anger.

"A Nazi war criminal hanged? That should have its appeal. One of you finally chasing one of them."

"The man is dead if you remember."

"There may be others, more of them for you to bring down in righteous revenge."

César wasn't sure that he had understood the supervisor's remark. "Am I being accused of something?"

"Only of excess eagerness to deal with this matter in your own way, without proper supervision."

"Supervision from your office, you mean."

"My office will set up the necessary authority with your superiors" —Junot bristled with power—"so there'll be no misunderstanding. I want to know all developments as they happen."

"Naturally," César said dryly. "Even before they happen."

Junot overlooked the remark; he had made his point. "Let us part as patriots of France"—it was pronounced as even de Gaulle never had—"and President Giscard d'Estaing."

"And the Prefect of Police," César sneered in spite of himself.

Thugs and killers, he murmured to Junot's back. Political cutthroats. Yet maybe political crimes needed cutthroats like Junot. Or was he starting to think like them? He could feel the hate rising again and he hated that, too. Everything had suddenly turned to shit. Even the sun was gone. In the car the blue suits waited for their boss. They wondered if that bastard upstairs had recognized them.

Junot also had doubts about the inspector. The man was too scornful of authority, like so many of those people. He had to be watched. But all else seemed to be in order, he told himself on the way to the car. If Bock's killer turned out to be an Israeli, he needed to know; he couldn't see any of his Arabs killing a Nazi. And if it was just the maniac next door, well, that wasn't his worry. Leave it to the Jew upstairs, serve him right. He should've got his a long time ago.

César watched Junot's black Peugeot pull away, saw it burst into flames, big blue balls of fire that lit up the pale sky. He hoped he'd never go blind; his whole fantasy life lived through his eyes. The next moment he glanced at his watch, forgot to note the hour and had to look again. Almost lunchtime, the worst part of the day. Too early to eat and too late to change. César usually spent it working at his desk or lying on top of Catherine Deneuve or a constant virgin who opened only to his touch. It was all the same, him too. He came alive after lunch. Something to do with the spin of the earth or the shape of his ear. In the room his men still searched.

"About a week," César growled in exasperation. "Let's see if we can do better than that."

He sent someone to talk to the other tenants, another was already with the concierge. Then there were the neighbors, the shopkeepers and petty officials, the newsstand, the café on the corner. A man's whole life could be learned from his block. His public life anyway, and even some of his private and if not, then that would tell them something too.

"All the tenants or just this floor?"

"Both."

Let him figure it out. César was beginning to feel he'd make the morning.

"At least a week, maybe more," said the voice at his elbow. "Hard to tell in that condition."

The medical officer had returned for his raincoat. April meant rain since he was a Breton who knew weather was more important than geography. Twenty years in Paris made no difference. He still wore his raincoat in April and May. During the summer he only carried it on his arm. But he was good with knife and needle.

"We'll let you know tonight."

"What time tonight?"

"Sometime tonight."

After the coat came the hats, a half dozen at least. Watch caps, ski hoods, mostly dark, all used. César quickly went through the other clothes: jacket, shirts and pants, underwear, gloves, shoes. And a half-dozen hats. Obviously they had a purpose. To conceal—César stopped; he had trained himself well. *Nothing was obvious.* "Always be suspicious," he mumbled and returned to the hats. That many might mean disguise. He would have to find out.

Things were looking better, he had to admit. His mind ran over the points of interest: 1. Hanged with piano wire. That was positively baroque. 2. The door bolt. Showed planning and imagination, maybe even contempt for others. A possible flaw? 3. The money. Too much of it. From where? 4. The hats. 5. Junot and the Service. Fifteen years was a long time to wait.

"Someday," César had said everyday for fifteen years.

One of his men found the newspapers under the bed, three days running of *France-Soir.* The last date was April 5.

The Nazi, what was his name?—César reached for the folder, found it: Dieter Bock—didn't work so he probably bought his newspapers nearby. He sent the man around the corner to learn what time Bock picked up his paper each day.

If he did, César thought. Or were the papers another plant, like the bolt? They knew what they were doing, these people.

What people? Who said more than one? Careful.

Someone asked about lunch.

"In the neighborhood," César said. "Talk to everybody."

At the table he was joined by André Sauter from headquarters; young and bright and on the way up, his career in front of him. Unlike César's. André was spending a month in each division, to study procedures. He had a lot to learn.

"A man with millions of enemies and few friends." César let the letters fall through his fingers onto the table. "Hanged with piano wire and left to rot. No claims of credit, no clues. Nothing to show motive. What would you do?"

César wasn't sure himself. Not about what to do, that was easy. Dig into the past. But this time it could mean more agony, more guilt. All that was long ago, so many years and nightmares were behind him. He didn't know if he could handle it again, or even if he should. Only that he would. He had to.

An Oedipus in a house of mirrors, Reba had once said of him and his police work.

André knew what *he* would do. It was simple, as always. "Follow the money."

César looked at him with sudden interest. "And Junot?" he asked when André didn't continue. "What would you do with him?"

What he wanted was a gut reaction, to see if the boy had more than brains. He was right about the money, though; twenty thousand francs was too much for someone on pension and living in squalor. But it was the crime that concerned André, not the politics. He didn't intend to get in anyone's way. Junot was just doing his duty, he supposed.

"You'll go far," César laughed. "Yes you will. Only be careful about cases like this. Sometimes they can get away from you."

"An ex-Nazi?" André was skeptical.

"I've seen it happen, so listen. We're going to discover all we can about this man Bock. Start with the money, as you suggest. Get his bank statements for the last year, then call Germany on the pension. What it was for, all the details. And a list of his friends in those years, anyone he knew." César turned back to the letters, looked up. "Do you know Rimbaud?"

"The poet?"

"Hardly." He clucked derisively. "Menard is my good right hand. When I'm not available, he's the man you see."

"Rimbaud."

"Menard."

César spent his lunch reading letters and sorting out receipts and travel folders. The receipts were mostly from Nice and Lyon within the past year. In the same box he found Bock's marriage certificate dated 1970 and notice of his wife's death in 1974, folded in an envelope with a picture of them staring into the camera. Of more interest was the second photo of a group of middle-aged men in suits. César didn't recognize the others; on the back he printed Bock's name and three question marks. The letters were mostly real estate ventures; Bock apparently expected to make money and move. Or did the move come first? His passport was blank so at least he hadn't left Europe recently. But where was his *carte d'identité?*

There were only two personal letters, both in German. One told of the death of a mutual friend in Vienna, a tragedy. The letter was dated January 18 and signed Gerd. The other was a note from Berlin reminding Bock that one final task remained, after which his promotion to the rank of *Sturmbannführer* (Major) was assured. It was dated March 16, 1945, and signed by Heinrich Himmler—

César didn't think he'd be able to keep it down. Sweat poured from his brow, his hands ran rivers. He couldn't seem to catch his breath. Himmler's face covered his mind, sealed his eyes. Behind them lay images of marching black boots, swastikas and SS insignia. Suddenly he was running for the bathroom.

The boy believes he is a man. He has seen them come for his parents, hides in terror as they are dragged away, hears their screams; he cries when they are gone. Then a dead body turns up and they are back in his mind. The inspector hoped this time to set the boy free; he saw himself as both avenger and accused, and probably doomed. But he would first get the others, all of them.

It's more than one, César thought, convinced now.

Afterwards he read through the letters again, making notes this time. The real estate offerings caught his eye, all expansive landholdings in the same country. Why Spain? he wondered. The Middle East would be more comfortable for ex-Nazis. Or Morocco or South Africa. But Spain was in Europe and that made it attractive to people who didn't like to leave. Bock had spent three years in prison rather than leave Europe.

They were back from lunch, in better humor on bread and wine. The Nazi picked up his newspaper at 8 A.M. everyday of the week. He skipped around the papers, getting different ones on different days. Sometimes he wouldn't show for a while and then he'd say he was traveling.

César had the parameters of Bock's last hours. The concierge saw him come home alone at 10 P.M. on the fifth. He didn't pick up his paper at 8 A.M. on the sixth. "Now let's see if we can pinpoint it."

The bolt would've needed a sharp slam of the door to catch. He sent a man to check the surrounding tenants again, looking for a loud crack on the previous Saturday night. Anything was possible.

The report on Bock from the neighborhood was mixed. Nobody saw much of him so he was considered dependable. On the other hand, he wasn't trusted because nobody saw much of him. What was he up to? He'd lived there a year and always paid his rent on time. There were few visitors, a woman occasionally.

All of which meant no one knew anything about him. He had no known enemies in the neighborhood; he spoke French with a German accent so he had no friends either.

The fingerprint expert arrived, annoyed at being called last. What good was that? In a murder he should be first.

"Some talk of suicide," César explained, calming him. Anyway, all he wanted was the door around the bolt and the area of pipe that held the noose. And the noose itself if anything could be done with it.

"The noose?"

"It's piano wire."

The fingerprinter hadn't been told. His interest perked up.

"Not that there's a chance in hell," César grumbled. "Even amateurs know enough to wear gloves today."

He was finished with the room. It would tell him nothing more.

"Everything on the table goes to the office," César said to no one in particular.

"This is my short day," complained someone feeling guilty about something.

"Then hurry."

The other two detectives smirked knowingly until César announced he needed two volunteers. There was nobody else left.

One of them would show the hats to manufacturers to date the styles. Fashion changes could reveal when they were bought, possibly even where. The other man would seek out hardware firms to check on the door bolt.

"Don't come back until you find something." César decided that was too vague. "Or until tonight."

He returned to the table for Bock's wallet. It held four hundred francs, a calendar and a pass for a local *boîte de nuit.* César put the pass in his pocket, tossed the wallet into the transfer box.

"Anything else?"

"The gun." It was found wrapped in a wool scarf on the closet shelf, a Walther PPK pistol. "And those few books there."

"That's the James Bond gun," Clément whispered.

César hardly ever went to the movies; they ran on cause and effect while real life was mostly chaos. But he'd seen a Bond movie once by sheer accident, tailing someone. Clément was right. Bond used a Walther PPK. César looked at the pistol, saw Bock holding it, using it. He was James Bond, killing those who would harm his country. Invincible, never making a mistake. Except one—he got old. Maybe he turned bad when they lost, had to be eliminated. So why wait thirty years? The question killed César's fantasy. He wasn't in the movies where it always came out right even when it was wrong. Bock wasn't Bond; he was a Nazi. And James Bond didn't kill him, either. They did. César saw them in shadow, faceless forms beating the two figures, heard the woman scream—

"James Bond," Clément repeated.

César shook his head, glanced at his watch. "There is no James Bond," he said irritably on the way out. "Just the rest of us."

* * *

César had two quick stops to make. He swung the Renault around the Place de la République, past the statuary, coming out of the circle onto Boulevard Voltaire. Traffic was moderate and he weaved in and out with grim satisfaction. He'd been cooped up for three hours with little light and less air. Or maybe it was just that the room itself hadn't told him enough, not nearly enough. Coming to the Boulevard Richard-Lenoir junction he jumped a lane and sped straight ahead. Releasing tension.

The inspector knew his business. After eighteen years of police work, fifteen of them chasing those who might have committed homicide and detecting those who did, he had come to know the banality of murder and the weightlessness of motives. None of which stopped those who saw permanent happiness if only this one or that were removed. Nor was he unaware of how murder had become a political tool. A lone terrorist with the right language, the wrong passport, an automatic and money could board the European Express in Ankara and emerge in Paris with precise directions to a specific location for an assured shot at the target, all planned in Beirut or Baghdad or Moscow. The thin line between murderer and hero had virtually disappeared. Intuition told César his murderer-hero was no local maniac or vengeful Jew. In the dark at the moment, he also knew that the search itself would become the candle.

The Renault slowed near Place Léon Blum, César's foot pumping the pedal. People scurried across the square. He veered left, coming up behind the main police station for the Eleventh district, and pulled into a reserved stall that clearly read NO PARKING. Seconds later he was up the steps and through the glass doors, heading for the third floor and Identification.

Each of Paris's twenty districts keeps files on those in its area who've had dealings with the police; these are usually housed in the main station of the district. In this case César hoped the locals would have something to add to the flimsy report he'd received from the Sûreté. Dieter Bock was a former SS officer who had served time in prison for war crimes. But he was also a man who ate and slept and had a woman now and then and perhaps some trouble with the police, or maybe reported some trouble. Anything.

There was nothing. In his year on the Rue de Malte, Bock had not been involved with the law. His dossier—kept because of his past—noted that the SCE would provide additional information. César didn't think Junot would provide a thing.

Bock's file had been sent down from his previous district, the nearby Twentieth; he was required to notify police of any change of address. César looked in the folder. Bock had lived there for four years with his wife after they moved from Germany in 1970. The folder contained only one report, a burglary of their apartment in March 1974. No disposition. And no picture, which was unusual.

He called the Twentieth station on the Place Gambetta. The ID section had nothing on Bock. His file went to Place Léon Blum when he moved.

Did they remember a picture with his file?

Hesitation, voices. Then: Yes, there was a picture.

César explained the problem. "Would anyone in the Twentieth know Bock from years ago?"

"Not likely. You should try the substation nearest where he lived."

César talked to the sergeant at the substation. Would he see if any of his men knew a couple named Bock? Husband's name: Dieter Bock. They lived on the Rue de Pali for four years. If anyone remembered them, a call to headquarters would be appreciated. Inspector Dreyfus, Homicide.

Twenty minutes later César was at his second stop, a short walk from his office. He descended the two narrow flights of stone steps as he'd done on so many Fridays. At the bottom, close to the level of the Seine, his eyes picked out the brooding shadows of the hexagonal crypt, the stark granite chambers and iron-barred windows, the funeral urns and finally, the tomb of the Unknown Deportee. Once again he slowly read the names of the concentration camps hewn into the rough stone walls, beginning with Auschwitz, and as always his eyes filled with tears long before he finished.

He was in the Mémorial de la Déportation behind Notre-Dame, which commemorated the two hundred thousand French citizens—almost half of them Jews—who were deported by the Nazis for slave labor and then exterminated in the camps. Among them were César's parents, kidnapped by the Gestapo on a Friday in 1942. He was never to see them again and on each Friday of his life César bared his grief, and his guilt.

So it was on this Friday of the finding of Bock's body that César finally arrived in his office at 4:15 where he found a dozen messages waiting for him, most of them marked urgent. The next moment the door opened. It was Menard Rimbaud.

"Looks like we're in for it," he began. "Dupin wants you."

César quickly went through the messages. Only the last had meaning for him. "Upstairs?"

Menard looked glum. "The war office."

It was almost a whisper and César raised his eyes. "What about the SCE?"

"They won't release Bock's file without a request from the director. It's on his desk now."

César had expected as much. Each service guarded its information with unholy zeal, often jeopardizing other investigations.

"Bastards!" Menard said.

"You read the Sûreté report?"

Menard made a disdainful sound. "Not even good background. Too many holes."

"Exactly." César dialed a number. "We're going to cover those holes. Given half a chance—" He spoke briefly on the phone, turned back to Menard. "I've already started some lines of inquiry."

César hurriedly filled in his assistant. He should blow up Bock's face from the group photo and run off a few prints right away. Somebody must've seen him on his last night. He came home at ten. Too late for shopping and too early for entertainment, which left dinner or business. Someone should know. "He paid the rent that afternoon. He was around."

Menard was also to make prints of the other three in the picture, try to identify them through Interpol. They might have criminal records.

On the way upstairs César put the twenty thousand francs in the division safe, the sergeant signing it in. Bock's gun went to Ballistics.

César wanted anything they could tell him. When? Yesterday, or at least today.

He settled for tomorrow. But in the morning. *Bien!*

* * *

The war office was on the fourth floor, an enormous enclosure with sculptured reliefs running the length of opposite walls. On them were depicted every official and public building in Paris, every center of communications and transportation terminal, every waterworks and gas plant and power station. Everything that could be attacked or blown up or seized. All major traffic arteries were detailed, all intersections and bridges and tunnels and railway lines. And over everything, on a celluloid overlay with red grease-crayon lines, was every possible place in Paris where roadblocks could be set up, crossings closed, access denied. The diorama, and its computerized system linking security forces in the area, had been built in the wake of the 1972 Munich Olympics disaster, an emergency command post for instant mobilization of police who suddenly saw themselves at war with a mobile enemy bent on terrorism. Where once they had been responsible for the control of crime, they were now expected to insure the safety of the city. In the war office they plotted their strategy, and it was here that Chief Inspector Dupin, the Homicide division commander, sat surrounded by gleaming instrumentation. He had a rapist-killer on his hands and was in no mood for a troublesome inspector, especially one like César.

"We're still sifting the Marie Pinay suspects," César said, referring to another case. Had he been called for that? he wondered. He always tried to anticipate around Dupin.

The chief inspector grunted impatiently. Someone whispered to him and he rose to follow the man. César relaxed; much of his work required waiting and he did it well.

When Dupin returned César stood while his superior glanced over some papers. Finally he looked up. "This Bock thing. Any trouble?"

"No more than usual," César answered with the expected ring of confidence. "No sir."

So it was the Nazi, he thought.

Dupin grimaced. "We all know the quality of your work, Dreyfus," he said sarcastically. "What concerns us are the unusual circumstances here." He indicated a chair. "The man's past, for one."

César remained standing in front of the desk. "It might be the key to his killing." That sounded too definite. "Only a hunch," he added quickly.

"And what about your own—background? Any problems regarding this investigation?"

"None whatever," César lied.

Dupin shifted in his seat. "At three o'clock this afternoon we got a call from the ministry, tactfully suggesting the SCE be kept informed of any progress." The eyebrow raised. "It was more than a request."

"They have a dossier on Bock, meaning there was some interest in the past. We know he worked for West German Intelligence."

"Could this man have been up to something here in Paris?"

César would try to find out.

The chief inspector was worried. The SCE? He didn't like that at all.

In the corridor César ran into the fingerprinter, whose name was Hugues. He had gone over the door and pipe. Wiped clean. Thin wire could not sustain prints, of course, but might pick up lint or even a hair.

His noose had nothing. Sorry.

César gave him the envelope that had held the two photos of Bock. Would he examine it? People always touched envelopes. The piano wire went to Metallurgy.

Back at his desk César listened to André talk about Bock's money: 120,000 francs, deposited in his account over the last year at the rate of ten thousand a month. Always in cash. A week earlier Bock withdrew twenty thousand, undoubtedly the money found in the closet. That was on April 4.

While André talked César carefully removed the collected items from the transfer box. He made room on the bookcase and placed there the travel folders and other papers and the few books. The personal letters he kept on the desk with his notes.

Meanwhile, said André, Bock's pension from Germany came to fifteen hundred francs a month, the checks sent from West Berlin. This was evidently what he lived on. The Berlin Border Protection Brigade, which issued the checks, would say nothing until officially notified. But they were curious about how he died.

César's office was a hectic assembly of chairs and filing cabinets. In a corner by the windows squatted his massive mahogany desk and

behind it the wooden swivel chair with the leather armrests that had
long ago lost their look. A beaten couch sat in the opposite corner.
The two windows faced north overlooking the Rue de Lutèce, and
from them César could gaze onto Place Louis Lépine and the flower
market in the square. The flowers always helped, especially when he
had to listen to excuses.

". . . without their cooperation, naturally I could learn nothing
more," André was saying.

César turned into the room. "Good try," he assured the detective.
They would have to approach it another way.

"He gets a steady ten thousand which he banks. Saving to go
away, probably Spain. Then suddenly he takes out twenty thousand,
maybe for a trip to see if he likes it. But he's killed." The move was
obvious. "Check reservations to Spain. Also Portugal, a few letters
came from there. Any time after the fifth, trains and planes."

César would handle Germany himself.

For the next ten minutes he spoke to contacts in the Bonn police,
confirming that the Berlin Border Protection Brigade was a front for
West German Intelligence and sometimes used as a money channel
for clandestine operations. An incoming call cheered him further.
The hats were recent items, and available in France.

* * *

César listened to the pathologist discuss the autopsy report he held
in his hand. René liked his work and didn't understand why the
inspector hesitated to visit his domain. After all, they both dealt with
the dead. The toxicology labs, the cutting tables, the refrigeration
room—each had a soothing effect on the nerves, as far as he could
tell. If hell was other people, as René believed, then surely he was in
heaven.

Bock's body had been photographed, weighed, measured and
washed; an ID number on a manila tag was wrapped around the
right big toe. Afterwards René had scalped the head and taken off
the top of the skull with a vibrating Stryker saw. Next came the
brain; following examination he'd removed it, and opened the abdominal cavity with incisions from the shoulders. After sawing
through the rib cage he removed the organs and viscera, leaving the
body an empty shell. Once examined and dissected for microscopic
analysis, these were returned to the cadaver by René's medical atten-

dant who then sewed up the skin flaps. Fibrous material went into the empty skull, the top of the skull bone refitted and the scalp sewn back.

Dieter Bock was ready for viewing.

César declined the invitation, as always. René's subjects were just bodies without people. Who needed them?

"But you really should. This one is special."

René was always saying that.

They sat in the medical examiner's office. To César it looked like the autopsy room, almost as sterile.

"Not much here," he complained, "even for a prelim."

"Not much to go on, you mean. You should've got there sooner."

"He didn't call us in time."

Bock had died horribly, more like a man strangled slowly than hanged. The neck had finally snapped. Decapitation came much later.

"The body was mostly dehydrated. Imagine?" René seemed fascinated.

"No blood, no urine, no stomach contents." César was an expert at deciphering clinical language. "How'd you do the drug screen?"

"The liver. One-nine-five-zero grams."

There was no new evidence in the report. Unlike a shooting, where bullets might be recovered and arguments laid for manslaughter or murder, Bock's death was known. He had been hanged. What César sought were little oddities that could turn into leads. Dead bodies often held surprises. He found two.

Bock had been badly injured in the groin. He could not function as a man but he still sometimes brought a woman to his place. César wondered what he did with them.

The other surprise answered a question about the murder itself. Why didn't Bock fight back? He wasn't unconscious or it would've taken four men to lift him into the noose, and he showed no bruises on the scalp. There was only one possibility: drugs.

"Alcohol!" César had said when he decided it was murder.

"Succinylcholine chloride!" said René, beaming. "We found traces in his tissues."

"Lethal?"

"Very. It stops your breathing by paralyzing the diaphragm." He snapped his fingers. "You're dead in seconds."

"I mean in Bock."

"Just enough to make him helpless. It's a muscle relaxant. Vets use it on animals."

"Never heard of it."

"Nobody has." The pathologist leaned back in his chair. "Good thing too. It's the perfect murder weapon. Acts fast and looks like a heart attack. If people knew about it, they'd be dropping like flies."

"Dropping others, you mean."

"But why hang him?" René asked. "A little more succinylcholine chloride and poof! No one the wiser."

César shrugged. "It was supposed to be suicide but they got too cute." Either that or the piano wire meant something. Or was he getting too cute now?

"I'll tell you one thing." René leaned forward over the desk. "Whoever did it had to know a lot about chemicals, and a lot about hanging, too. This was no amateur."

"You know a lot about chemicals. Maybe you even own a piano. Where were you last Saturday night?"

"Where were you?" René came around the desk, a folder for the report in his hand. "I'm not kidding. He knew what he was doing."

César got up to leave, prepared for the worst.

"I have something to show you. A young girl, disemboweled with a sharp rock. Really special."

René never gave up.

Fingerprints was on the second floor, a long musty room smelling of dusting powder and iodine fumers and silver nitrate. Along the walls stood endless rows of sectional files bulging with prints on yellowed cards. Brushes and atomizers were everywhere. At the far end of a slim metallic table Hugues sat on a stool in front of a comparison microscope. He looked up as César approached.

"You're not going to like it," Hugues groaned.

"Let me guess." César forced a smile. "Ghosts." He hadn't expected anything, really; the man obviously wore gloves. Probably didn't even go through Bock's papers.

"Worse!" Hugues handed César the envelope. "It's been soaked in gasoline." He made a face. "Your man knows what he's doing."

The second time he'd heard that; César hoped it was just coincidence.

"Nothing?"

"Gasoline dissolves oils secreted by the skin. No oils, no patterns." Hugues gestured helplessly. "Nothing."

Less than nothing, César told himself. Maybe another plant, something in the envelope. But what?

The report on the piano wire was waiting when he got to Metallurgy: high-grade steel, high-tensile strength, 0.80 percent carbon.

"Where's it from?"

"Hard to say. France, Germany, maybe Austria. Hard to say."

"No markings?"

"Here, look for yourself."

More of the same awaited César at his desk. The door bolt was a type available anywhere in France, including around the corner from Bock's *pension*. No help there! But at least they had the time of death fixed. The old woman across the hall heard a door slam about 4:45 Sunday morning. She usually got up at five to feed her cats but the drunk in 410 had awakened her earlier with his shouting. She thought it was him slamming the door. Was she sure it'd been last Sunday? Most certainly; she went to church afterwards. And what time? About 4:45 as she said. Even her cats woke up.

Dieter Bock had died between 4 and 5 A.M.

L'heure du loup, the hour of the wolf.

A lone wolf, César thought, beginning to get a feel for the man. He stayed to himself, confided in no one, depended on no one.

Whatever Bock's work had been, César suspected he did that alone too.

TWO

The Marais quarter was north of the Place de la Bastille, an intricate maze of narrow streets whose decaying mansions once housed the Parisian aristocracy. It was here that the Knights Templar held sway in the thirteenth century and the kings of France lived until the sixteenth; here that the Bastille was stormed and the French Revolution begun. Over the centuries many groups had taken root in its three hundred acres. One of these, the Jewish section, was not too far from the Ile de la Cité and police headquarters.

César turned right on the Rue des Rosiers, moved slowly past shops with Hebrew painted fascias, and parked halfway down the block. The building he entered was of gray stone and like its neighbors severe in line. Upstairs he followed the curve of the corridor to a rear apartment where Yishay Kussow waited for him.

The two men greeted each other as friends. In truth, Kussow was César's only Jewish friend. Not that he avoided them; he just seldom had occasion to run into them. Or made the effort.

"A long time," César said.

They sat in a room lined with books and drank tea as Kussow wiped his glasses with newspaper. "So! Your work prospers?"

"People still die before their time," César admitted.

"My congratulations."

Yishay Kussow with his sense of drama. A lifetime of learning looted in the fires of Europe. Head wrapped in knowledge. Eyes that smoked of pure reason. Half mad and a reluctant skeptic, Kussow was a German Jew who would never go home again. César had once helped him and now they always spoke in German whenever they met. And always about César's work.

"An SS captain was murdered."

"SS?" Kussow hadn't heard. "That sounds more like justice than murder. Simple, swift. Almost biblical. But you're wondering if any of us would do it."

"A Jew from here, yes."

An elaborate shrug. "The younger ones might if they brooded over what they've been told all their lives. But they're not brooders anymore. They're all dancers now. They dance all night, I've seen them. And not the hora. Pagan dancing, probably Christian—"

"How about the Israelis?"

Kussow stretched out his arms. "I'm a simple scholar. What would I know of worldly things?"

"He was killed not too far from here," César added, absorbed in the quest. "Hanged with piano wire."

"Piano wire?" The sudden gasp of air could be heard across the room. "And you say he was SS?"

"You think there's a connection?"

"What I think"—Kussow let out a huge sigh—"I think you do not want to look for Jews, my friend. What you want is a German."

"German?"

"You were too young to remember—" The older man settled further into the couch and closed his eyes. "It was 1944 and Hitler's generals knew the war was lost. What else could they do? They plotted to kill him and sue for peace. A half-dozen attempts were aborted for one reason or another, something always went wrong. Then on July 20 the bomb went off. But that devil survived to take his revenge. The army was purged, over five thousand executed."

"I know all that," César protested.

"Do you?" Kussow returned to wiping his glasses. "Then you must also know that almost a dozen of the leaders—generals, important men—were hanged. Hanged with piano wire from meat hooks. They even took movies to show the butcher in Berlin."

In the apartment nothing moved and time stood still as two men sat lost in the past. César's voice, when it came, sounded strangely distant.

"Who did the killing?"

"Who else? The SS!"

* * *

It was after six when César got back to his office. The close-ups of Bock and the others were waiting for him. So was Menard. Interpol had no file on them, nor did the Sûreté central records. They probably were German, maybe even former SS officers, and he would get on to the Bonn authorities in the morning.

César pulled the letter out of his pocket, looked at the signature again. Gerd. In his excitement he'd almost forgotten to show it to Kussow who quickly pronounced it Bavarian, likely from the Munich area. The writer had mentioned a nearby lake. The next step was the Vienna connection. Someone named Kurt had died there on January 10.

A few calls later César took one from André: Bock had not made any reservations for Spain or Portugal. (So I was wrong, César thought.)

It was for Austria.

"What?"

"Linz. Last Monday, the seventh."

That was the third time Austria had come up. What would Bock want there?

On the stairs César drew in his gut and buttoned his jacket; it wasn't often he was called up to the director's office. Paris itself had no mayor yet, though each district claimed its own chief executive and city hall. The Paris Prefect supervised the city's affairs and the Prefect of Police took care of public order; under him were the head administrators of the several police agencies and under them the directors of the various departments, one of which was Criminal Investigation. From the director the chain of command flowed through his deputy to the commanders of the different divisions. To most professionals Paris police headquarters was the hub of the universe, virtually a separate service of the French national police force. In the matter of responsibility, the director answered only to his administrative chief who listened only to the Prefect who spoke only to the Minister of the Interior. It was rumored that since the death of de Gaulle, the Interior Minister spoke only to God.

The director did not like to be kept waiting. In his view of virtue, punctuality was next to loyalty and he measured his men by their sense of time. Unfortunately for César, punctuality was next to impossible. Though he constantly looked at his watch, he never noted the time. Which wouldn't have helped anyway, since his watch had been five minutes slow for the past six months.

The occupant of the corner office studied the antique clock on the wall as César was ushered into the room, then quickly returned to his reading. César took this to mean he wasn't late.

After a suitable interval the director raised his eyes, the reading lamp reflected in his gold-rimmed glasses. He exhaled loudly through his nose, a sign of displeasure. "You are not early," he announced.

César said nothing, stared at the mouth since he couldn't see the eyes. The director wasn't angry, he decided after a moment. Still, people in disfavor were sometimes known to get the DT's—deliberate transfers—around him. The best approach was absence, César had long ago concluded. Yet here he was.

"Your request for the SCE dossier on this man Bock is denied." The lips hardly moved, as though words came out already formed. There was a startling resonance to them. Like music, César thought. But jarring all the same.

"May I ask the director his reason?"

"Specifically, in the interests of national security." The phrase had a resounding ring to it and caused the speaker to smile. "We have been informed the release of this information would endanger a current operation."

"What operation?" César asked.

"That," answered the director with genuine regret, "I'm afraid we are not permitted to know."

César hesitated, not sure how far he should go. "This murder," he began, "may have wider implications."

The director's mouth tightened at the corners. "Exactly what does that mean, Inspector Dreyfus?"

"Bock received large sums regularly for the past year, almost certainly for something he was doing now, some covert activity. If his murder is connected to that—" The inference was clear. They had to know what Bock was doing.

Did the SCE know? Were they themselves involved?

"Involved in what?" The mouth tightened even further.

"I don't know," César answered truthfully.

"We can do nothing," the director declared. He gazed once again at the antique clock.

Menard had tacked a print of Bock to the bulletin board and was hurling metal darts at it when César returned, disappointment etched on his face. A bad blow, agreed. But not fatal, César kept saying. Bock's past was the key, but which one? He had three: the immediate past in Paris, his work for the West Germans, his Nazi years with the SS. The best bet was Paris; people usually were killed for something they just did. But Bock's work in West Berlin must have made him some enemies. And the manner of his death obviously went back to his SS days. (Except for the obvious fact, César constantly reminded himself, that nothing was obvious.)

"Which one?" he demanded.

Menard didn't know. He flung a dart at Bock's head. Should they look at him again? He lived in Cologne with his first wife when he went to prison in 1954. For what? The German court only specified him guilty of complicity in SS killings.

"Meaning?"

"We don't know what he really did in the SS." (Another dart!) "After prison he surfaces in West Berlin security and in 1968 he's out. Again we don't know what he did there." (And another!) "Then in 1970 he turns up in Paris and is killed five years later. Still *again* we don't know what he did." Menard threw the last dart. "Is it because we're not supposed to know certain things? Like why our own people protect him now?"

In his mind's eye the young man saw them. Both women had been hacked to death, butchered. It was Algeria again and suddenly César was back stalking the murderer who was also a general. And well-protected.

"The point is, we don't know," Menard insisted.

"Yet!" said César, reaching for the darts.

At 7:30 and a dozen dart games later they still didn't know, and César sent Menard home to his family. A henpecked husband; César found that incomprehensible. Menard would go up against killers but was afraid of his wife. Or was it just fear of being alone? That César could now understand, too late. He put the darts away and folded a print of Bock's face in his jacket pocket.

* * *

The Paris sky was a river of light. César drove east on the Rue St-Antoine until he turned up Boulevard Beaumarchais. He soon reached the nightclub. Le Chat Botté was not unknown to the police; the drinks were usually weak and the women even weaker, especially around tourist time. He showed the pass at the door. When were they given out? On Saturdays, their busiest night. Good for Sundays and Mondays, their slowest. The colors were changed every week. César put the pass back in his pocket. Bock had been in the club on his last night.

Inside he ordered a wine and showed the bartender Bock's face. It looked familiar. A woman was called over. Did she recognize him? She laughed. *Monsieur Pistolet.* Not a regular but stopped in enough to be known. A pervert, besides a *boche.* How? Some of the girls would know. One was summoned. Ahh, the man with the pistol. Only he was not a man, you see, he couldn't do what they all do. She giggled. So he used this black pistol he had; he would rub the jelly on the long part and then put it inside, you see, and move it with his hand back and forth—

"Unloaded?"

"Mais oui!" She looked at César as if he were crazy.

"Did he hurt any of you?"

"No, no. Very gentle. It excited him. After a while he would stop, not too long. But he paid plenty, you can believe me." She turned to the older woman for support. "A thing like that, the pistol—"

César asked about Saturday night. Yes, he was in. That was usually his day. Stayed an hour or two. He left early, she remembered that. Maybe around ten. Alone, yes.

"Did any of you ask if he—"

She giggled again. *"Naturellement!* We all asked him, I can assure you. And more than once." The police were all going crazy, she was convinced of it now. God help the country!

Another girl recalled a few weeks back the *boche* had told some of them he'd soon be rich, but men were always telling women that.

* * *

César parked the car in the Hôtel de Ville section and sauntered over to the Seine and sat by the bank, staring across the silver water to his office. In the foreground was the flower mart he viewed from his windows. On Sundays birds replaced the flowers and César often strolled among the stalls and shops in the square. He would probably do that tomorrow. No, the next day. Go see the birds and think of Bock. What else was there to do? Reba was gone.

Around him Paris was turning from gold to glitter as the evening sun changed to neon glow. Everywhere lovers met and made vows. It was a time of celebration.

Alone in his office, César worked on his notes of the Bock murder. He would make out his report in the morning, before too many other things piled up. But what did he have? A dead Nazi with a friend in Munich and three others in a photo. With secret money and secret files. Who planned on Spain but booked for Austria. Who said he would soon be rich. Who used his gun for sex.

On the other hand, they knew when he died. They knew his murder was carefully planned. They knew where he'd been on his last night. They knew he came home alone, which meant he knew his killer well enough to let him in afterwards. And they knew some people didn't want them to know more.

Summation: They didn't have a single lead worth a damn. They'd have to keep digging into his past. Try to dig.

The only certainty was that Bock's death was not an isolated act. César had seen victims killed with every imaginable weapon, but hangings were rare. They required extraordinary strength of purpose. Murders mostly were spontaneous bursts of carnage carried out by people of below-average ability who spent the rest of their lives in regret or self-deception. They killed because they couldn't cope, which was hardly the mentality needed to hang someone. Even César had never seen anyone hanged with piano wire.

"Have you?" Tobie stood in the doorway radiating enough cheer to rout César's gloom. An ambitious man who spent his life chasing thieves, the polished inspector dressed like a Minister and dined at Maxim's. Naturally he was not married. "I asked if you have eaten."

Food for Tobie was as air for others. No, not food. *Haute cuisine. Truite à la meunière! Tournedos Rossini!* He doted on classic simplicity and its stunning subtleties.

"Many times," said César, who always made light of Tobie's presumed invitations to dine. They usually ended in orgies of *foie gras,* doubly sinful to César who believed eating in public was obscene enough.

"Then let me guess. You've got an ex-Nazi you're glad is dead." It was not a question. "And you wonder if you can flush out more."

Does everyone know? César wondered.

"You want to watch this one." Tobie's smile lit up the room. "Nazis can bite even when they're dead."

"Are you saying something?"

"Only that some people might be more susceptible to their bite than others."

Tobie Maton had many talents and a wide circle of friends, most of whom told him what he wanted to hear for he wasn't afraid to return a favor. Marvelously intricate, he thrived on intrigue.

"You, for example. With your special circumstances"—he always referred to César's background in an oblique way—"you could become too emotional in this matter of Nazis, might not see all the realities involved." Tobie's voice leaked concern that didn't register on his smooth features. "It's always the political aspects in these things."

César heard the warning. "And what are they?"

"I merely say they exist in this case of yours. These are strange times when yesterday's enemies are today's friends, *n'est-ce pas?* Men I put away now work for intelligence. It's all crazy." Tobie slipped off a glove. "Who knows what fresh horror tomorrow brings?"

César watched his good friend button his topcoat.

"Careful, they still remember Algeria," the robbery inspector added softly on the way out, "and Laffage."

César stared at the closed door, seeing nothing. Beyond his windows the sky soon lost the last light in the west and darkness stole over the land like a thief in flight. In the room the solitary figure sat in the dark of his own mind.

Algeria. General Laffage . . .

The woman lay naked on the bed, her head resting on a pillow placed against the grimy wall. In the gloom of candlelight she gazed at the tall athletic man undressing near the door, watched him fold his pants carefully over the chair. A French gentleman, she thought scornfully, which meant a smaller tip. She sighed, knowing she'd have to work hard with this one, use her pelvis, moan and gasp, fake pleasure at his every touch. Try to squirm whatever extra money she could out of his tight fist.

Her customer crossed the dingy room and motioned her onto her stomach. An old pervert, she groaned as she rolled over. Still less of a tip. Just her luck! She felt his body slump between her legs and she tensed for the initial thrust, her eyes closed, her face nestled into the pillow.

Absorbed in her act, waiting for her cue, the prostitute did not sense the man's arm slowly reach down over the foot of the bed. Moments passed and still she felt nothing, not even his hands on her buttocks. A voyeur, she decided miserably, now certain there would be no tip at all. In which case she would give him no performance, yes, and damn little satisfaction either if he didn't hurry up. She had men to meet and money to make.

As she was about to turn over and remonstrate, she felt a slight pressure against her vagina. Not a pervert after all, she breathed thankfully and tensed her body again and opened her mouth to moan and as the pressure increased she suddenly felt a warm rush beyond anything she'd ever experienced and her mouth slowly widened in a silent scream as a hand pressed her head into the pillow and held it there while the military sword plunged and tore through her abdominal wall. Impaled on the sword, her body soon shook itself free of life.

Ten days later a second corpse was found, another prostitute. Only her face had been left untouched, its waxen mouth agape, the glazed eyes wide with horror.

It was March 1960. A young Paris detective, in Constantine to bring back a French Algerian fugitive, was asked by authorities to look into the pair of particularly brutal murders. Just for the few days he was in town, to give them the benefit of his experience; his commander had approved the request. A week later César was still in Constantine but he'd unmasked the killer, Brigadier General Homère Laffage of the army's psychological warfare service.

That night the youthful detective told the general of his mass of evidence.

"It is conclusive," he reported to the superior officer, and when the latter said nothing, blurted out, "enough to have you shot."

Instead, Laffage threatened to have *him* shot, even pointed a pistol in his direction.

"You know nothing," he warned the Parisian detective. "This is a different kind of war and they were the enemy."

"They were women."

"Who carried bombs."

"In bed?"

"You have no authority," Laffage said in dismissal, "no Frenchman in Algeria will listen to you."

He was right. When César presented his evidence to local officials, they turned their backs. He took the matter home to Paris and pressed the issue from there. Everyone advised him to drop it but he was young and foolish. He was also right. A month later the general was relieved of his command and soon shot himself.

Afterwards César learned that Laffage had been the army's liaison with the SCE in Algeria, still politically tied to France and under the jurisdiction of the Defense Ministry. In fact, Laffage had led much of the early secret war against the FLN, first in the Algerian *bled* and later in the cities, and was something of a hero to those in the SCE. His own contact there had been a young Gaullist fanatic named Henri Junot.

The relentless detective was suddenly hated by men with long memories, men of power not only in the Service but in the police hierarchy who maintained close relations with the government security agencies. They didn't like the suspicion César had brought down on them, a suspicion that the police couldn't control their own. They would not forget, and they'd see to it that he did not forget either. He wasn't one of them, anyway. What was he but a damn Jew?

César snapped on the desk lamp. Had he finished his notes for the report?

There wasn't much, he said to himself.

Give it time, he heard himself say.

The call came in at 9:20 P.M. The inspector glanced at his watch, which read 9:15, without realizing that he would remember this moment—the wrong moment—for the rest of his life.

"*Alors?*" César grumbled. "What now?"

He picked up the receiver.

* * *

Ballistics was at the end of the corridor past Microscopic Analysis and Serology.

A metal alarm door guarded the entrance but everyone used the fire exit next to a stairwell, and it was through this doorway that César now hurried to meet a smallish man with shocks of white hair and a penchant for thorough examination and explanation. His name was Félix Pégouret and he was excited.

Félix showed the three spent cartridges to César.

"These all have a class designation of 9mm auto ammunition with six lands and grooves with a right twist. This is characteristic of bullets fired by very few weapons," Félix explained. "But the casings have marks on their bases which tell us that the gun used to fire them also had a loading indicator."

He smiled, took a deep breath.

"There's only one gun that fires 9mm ammo and has both a loading indicator and a barrel with a right twist that leaves six lands and grooves to the right on the slugs." He pointed to the automatic on the table. "The Walther PPK."

Félix picked up the pistol César had left with him. "For months we've been matching the slugs against every PPK that came in. Not many did, of course, it's a very special weapon. But none matched, until now." Félix returned the automatic to the table and gently laid the three spent cartridges next to it, one by one. "They all came from your gun," he whispered loudly.

César was already sweating. "Where did you get them?"

Félix reached for a sheet on his desk. "The first was a Swiss banker murdered six months ago. The second from a Belgian industrialist in December. And the last was the British diplomat in February." He looked up. "You remember that one; got him right in front of his apartment house on the Avenue Paul Doumer. Shot once in the forehead, like the others."

"All in Paris?"

"No, no." Félix consulted the sheet again. "The first was in—Nice, the second in Lyon."

"Why were they sent here?"

"But we are the best in France." It was not said as a boast.

César didn't need to check the dates when Bock was in Nice and Lyon. Or what he did. Were there other bodies the police hadn't yet tied to Bock's gun? César was willing to bet on it.

All of a sudden the inspector knew a lot about Bock's business.

Not only what he did in France; what he'd done for the West Germans, and for the SS too.

It was a lone wolf's work, as César had thought. But who hired him this third time around? And then fired him?

It was almost ten when he returned to his office. He opened both windows, took off his shoes and lay on the couch against the far wall. The room was still disordered despite the nightly cleaning. A wilted flower drooped on the bookcase; César didn't know its name. He went by color and usually pointed to what he liked. Red was his favorite, red and yellow.

He lay there feeling sorry for himself. He didn't know about flowers or even about people anymore. Reba was gone and there was no reason to go home. At least he knew that. He closed his eyes, an arm curled round his head, the legs jackknifed into his stomach. He would never see her again, never again feel her warmth or share her dreams.

In his own dream César was standing with Dieter Bock, who showed him the Walther.

"When do you wear the gun?" he asked.

"Only when I need it."

"How often do you need it?"

"All the time."

The gun boomed—

In his solitary cell by the Seine, the inspector sat up the rest of that night spinning stories of how he would slay every Nazi in sight. He would protect his parents. He would find Bock's killers, the other killers. All of them, one by one. He would free the boy. In his fantasies he was the Jewish avenger. He was the plagues of Egypt and the angel of death.

And as always, he was the hunter. An ancient race.

THREE

The inspector hated Saturdays, especially from April to September. Most of the backup branches for Homicide kept only skeletal crews over the weekends, not only in Paris but all over France; other countries did much the same. Which is strange when you think of it since most spontaneous homicides—those unplanned or not involved in the commission of a felony—are committed between Friday night and Monday morning.

By 8 A.M. César was at his desk, working on his report for the division commander. He had spent the night on the couch lost in thought, sleeping fitfully between bouts of fantasy that he was Inspector Maigret saving the honor of France. Coffee and a croissant at a nearby café had refreshed him enough after sunrise to return to the real world of the battered typewriter and Bock's remains.

Curiously, Bock's death had occurred on a weekend. Was it just a coincidence? César wondered. Or did the killers know about the reduced manpower? Were they part of a paramilitary group? The SCE? West German Intelligence? Another country's security section? Even—*sacrebleu*—the police department itself? Suddenly anything was possible.

He had quickly realized that the discovery of Bock's business changed everything. No longer was he just SS, a page of history. His gun had been used to shape recent events; the slaying of the British official was proof enough. That meant political investigation and government interference. Questions of national security might be raised, the case taken away.

Political assassination, as César knew, was the Pandora's box of modern civilization; nations denounced and employed it, statesmen feared and plotted it. The paranoia of conspiracy was everywhere and governments lashed out fiercely against any threat to their rule. No defensive action was considered too excessive, and so secret agencies thrived and espionage grew. Spies and counterspies, agents and double agents, disinformation and disappearance: all of which had nothing to do with the concept of crime and punishment that drove César.

Simply a matter of right and wrong, he believed. A sense of justice, and inevitable retribution.

The inspector held no illusions about the murder on the Rue de Malte. His limited authority would probably get in the way of internal security; the shadow government, as with everything that fed on fear, was itself paranoid and there were several branches that could lay claim to Bock.

The SCE was the biggest threat. Any number of ex-Nazis worked for it, primarily in the Mideast and Russian sections. Why not Bock? He could've been a double agent—possibly still working for West Germany—who was discovered and eliminated. César had learned that at least two of its top people, including the head of the Western Europe sector, were Nazi collaborators during the German Occupation.

Nothing infuriated the political police more than talk of their role under the Nazis. César knew it was mostly one of close cooperation. They helped round up thousands of Jews and dissidents who were sent to concentration camps like Drancy, on the outskirts of Paris. And they conducted similar outrages in unoccupied France and even in Algeria, where French Jews were stripped of their citizenship.

When Himmler finally ordered all Jews in France deported to the east, the political police acted vigorously. Indeed, it could've been no other way since they were part of the Vichy regime which had systematically persecuted the Jews from the very beginning of the Occupation.

But that was history and the political police had a new image of protecting the republic in a time of unrest and terrorism. They kept the trains running, the wine flowing; to do so they needed men like Bock. Even César could understand that a Dieter Bock was part of the price. Now he was dead. Had the price gone up?

The SCE—Junot's Sector 2—would increase the pressure to take over the investigation. That was not what César wanted and he began to make his plans.

* * *

For the next two hours César plodded through details of the case, closing with an observation he believed accurate:

"In light of our leads—and the discovery of three more murders, and still others I expect will be assigned to the deceased—the continuing investigation might proceed more expeditiously if not transferred to security agencies with wider duties."

César did not look for his words to carry any weight with his superiors; action required reaction. With time and a few breaks, that would come. Meanwhile, his view was on record. They wouldn't want to be caught wrong with him right. All had a vested interest: themselves, their careers. The police brass might lay their lives on the line but never their jobs.

After finishing the Bock report César turned to other cases, making notes and filing papers in folders. The phone, when it rang after ten, startled him. A *gendarme* from the Twentieth district who remembered the Bocks on the Rue de Pali; his sergeant had asked him to call in to headquarters.

Quite right, said César. How well did he know them?

Just in passing. He'd been in their home once, a burglary about a year earlier. The usual things taken: tape recorder, camera, some cash. And a box of pictures.

"Pictures, did you say?"

"Family stuff. He laughed it off but the wife was indignant."

"What was she like?"

"The quiet type but strong-willed, if you know what I mean. Had her own mind, I should say. Still, she was a lot younger than her husband."

"How about him?"

"Didn't work, far as I could tell. Couldn't have had much money from the looks of things. A real shame. He moved out right after the accident, can't say I blame him. Soon's he got the money, I guess."

"Money?"

"Insurance; some kind of policy she had. I don't think it was too much. The agent came to the station for the accident report."

"Which company was that?"

"I think it was Frenchlife."

"Anything else?"

"Not really. Did I mention the glasses?"

"What glasses?"

"In the burglary. They took her eyeglasses. Can you imagine? Didn't matter, though, a week later she was dead."

César debated calling Frenchlife. On a Saturday morning? He dialed anyway, got through immediately. Wasn't that unusual? Working Saturdays, I mean? Not at all. We're a growing company, open every Saturday until one. Can we help you?

He finally got to the right claims agent. Yes, he damn well did remember Bernadette Bock. Fell from her fifth-floor apartment about a year ago—hold on!—thirteen months, to be exact. He had the file in his hands. Thirty thousand francs went to her husband, Diter Bock.

"That's Dieter."

"What?"

"Dieter. As in beat her."

"Damn funny names Germans have. But interesting you should say that because at the time we suspected Bock did even worse to her. Only there was no proof so we had to pay up."

"Proof of what?"

"That he was home when she fell. If she fell."

"How long was the policy in effect?"

"Almost a year."

"Hardly your typical insurance fraud. Why the suspicion?"

"There wasn't any until we got a call claiming murder. Naturally we had to look into it."

"Did the caller have a name?"

César took it down as Menard came into the office. He'd been told about the murders linked to Bock, César phoning his home earlier. He wasn't surprised. All that money had to mean something covert. Why not murder? It was a growing business. What Menard did find strange were the victims: a banker, an industrialist and a diplomat. What was the connection? And three different nationalities, too. That smelled like an international conspiracy, the kind of spy stuff Clément was always talking about.

César agreed. Bock could've been just the tip of the iceberg. But where did the ice come from? If it was their own waters, they'd feel the pressure soon enough.

What about the victims, anything there?

Clément was already on his way to Nice and Lyon with Bock's picture. He'd identify Bock at the hotels he used, check out the receipts.

Meanwhile, Menard was to work through Zurich and Brussels on their backgrounds. There was a thread somewhere and they would find it.

"How about Germany?"

Menard cleared his throat. "Not all their men are working today, naturally. I wired the prints anyway but Bonn didn't sound too confident."

"Germans like being conservative. Except when they're being Nazis, of course."

"Their point is that if Bock's three friends were SS, they either served their time or were never wanted. Otherwise they wouldn't be so dumb as to get photographed."

"Maybe they didn't figure to be recognized after thirty years," César said. "The German state prosecutors only have pictures from the 1940s."

Menard frowned in disagreement and César studied him. In thirty years he'd know that face no matter what. Menard was right.

"Maybe they're wanted for something more recent."

Neither man considered that a strong possibility.

"I don't expect much from Bonn," César said suddenly. "They'll show it around, though, which might loosen up the Border Brigade. But we'll probably have to get the Three Musketeers another way."

The other way was through a dead man named Kurt and a letter writer called Gerd. César had already started inquiries in Vienna regarding deaths on January 10. He'd also asked the Munich prosecutor's office to check their SS lists for someone named Gerd who might have worked in the legal area or Ordnance.

Nothing mysterious, he assured Menard. A graphologist friend had pronounced the writer someone who probably worked with figures in an organized structure. A controlled imagination, not a risk taker, with a high opinion of his abilities.

"It's worth a try," César said.

"Not much more," protested Menard who didn't think much of handwriting analysis. Or the Vienna police for that matter. They had several times botched inquiries of his, once actually led him astray. It was something about the Austrians; they seemed too set on themselves, as his mother used to say. But then, he was from the Loire. The inspector came from Strasbourg and spoke German fluently, so he could probably handle them better.

"Those travel brochures in Bock's flat?" César pointed to the stack of folders on the desk. "Not one of them from Austria."

"The reservation could've been a plant," Menard suggested. "If he knew someone was after him, he'd reserve for anywhere in case of a check. Then go to Spain at the last minute in another name."

"Someone was after him," César said, "but he didn't know it. He let the killer in that night. Also, how would he cross the border? He'd need another identity card."

"Not impossible in his line of work."

"Exactly." César's brows raised in thought. "Exactly," he repeated.

He fished out his phone book, dialed André's house. A stranger answered and he verified the number with the operator. He dialed again and got André on the third ring.

César was curious. Why had André checked reservations to Austria when he was told only Spain and Portugal?

He hadn't.

What's that?

It was just a coincidence. He checked Germany as an afterthought because Bock was German. But reservations people must think of Germany and Austria as the same since they speak the same language. When they did one they did the other, and Linz came up.

"Or maybe," César said, "Bock was routed through Germany on purpose." He looked at Menard. "Maybe that's what someone intended all along."

Menard sat stunned as he listened to the inspector give instructions on the phone. It was the strangest command he had ever heard in his dozen years with the Criminal Police. César wanted André to see if Bock had used his reservation.

* * *

Steely Martian tripods, rubber over the doorframes, wide-angle lens, flood lamps and dollies met his eye. Lead-lined sinks seemed to surround him. He suddenly saw the infrared world lying just outside of visible light, felt the longer wavelengths leaping at him, their thermal fingers insinuating. Devoid of darkness, he had nowhere to hide. Was he discovered?

"It's like I told you on the phone," Sebastian was saying. "Your man came later to the group. The other three form a set with no breaks in the composition. They're authentic." He rubbed his soft hands together enthusiastically. "A good job, actually. Whoever did it knows what he's doing."

Photography too, César thought. Chemicals and fingerprints and now photography as well. Not to mention piano wire and sealed rooms. What else?

"Of course, it doesn't compare with what we can do."

"Of course."

They were in the reproduction department in the old city barracks part of police headquarters. The walls were white to catch the light; everything seemed bathed in space.

"What do you know about laser photomicrography—the amplification of electromagnetic waves in the visible spectrum to get pictures of magnified images?"

"I once owned a box camera," César said.

"Electronic photomontage?"

"I'm still listening."

Sebastian led the way to a long table covered with prints and magnifiers. He was chief technician in the lab he'd built into the best in France. Forensic photography was his passion and he was an expert on camera traps.

"So much for the technical." He sounded disappointed. "Basically what I did was to screen the photo to the right of your man and bump the edges up to higher magnifications. Eventually I found a slight vertical line between him and the next figure where the edges became ragged. Depth analysis showed the densities were different;

so was the shading. Nothing that can be seen with the eye but it's there."

"What's there?"

"A composite print."

"They were different pictures," César said.

"Obviously." The photographer gleamed with professional pride. "From the measurements I'd say your man was in the other by himself."

"But why?" César asked, thinking furiously.

"Only two possibilities. He was supposed to be part of their group or they were friends of his."

"No, there's a third," César offered. "He was used to replace someone else in the picture."

A door slammed nearby; voices were heard.

"On the other print you gave me of Bock—was that his name?— and his wife. Nothing out of the ordinary there. Your standard 35mm close-up taken in the past six months with a home camera."

César didn't think he'd heard right.

"Did you say six months?"

"Not much more. Light yellows, you know. Your picture's fresh." Sebastian frowned. "Something wrong?"

"Plenty. Bock's wife died over a year ago."

* * *

César talked to the detective who handled the British diplomat shot in February. "Your report mentions a Palestinian terrorist group."

"The Popular Front for the Liberation of Palestine. But anyone could claim a kill afterwards. Happens all the time."

"You didn't believe this one."

"Not really, the job was too professional. The man just walked up to Stiles and shot him once in the forehead. Apparently the gun was concealed in a sling he wore for his arm." The detective's voice held a note of admiration. "In the usual terrorist attack there's little subtlety or imagination. This one was different enough to make me think there's more to it."

"In your report you say the killer vanished without so much as a trace."

"Easy enough to do. The apartment house is near the corner, two doors in. He could've pulled off his ski cap and sling, turned the corner and disappeared."

"Any chance of a car waiting?"

"Not that we found. The Avenue Paul Doumer's heavily traveled at that hour of morning. Wouldn't have been much trouble to lose himself in the crowd."

"Heavily traveled," César said, "yet no one even got a decent description."

The detective shrugged. "Too sudden, too fast. His cap was down, the coat collar up. People were stunned. You know the routine."

* * *

In the bleak room Supervisor Junot read the confidential message, quickly called central control. "Will the general be available today?"

"The general is on official business outside the ministry. He is expected to return on Monday." Which meant he was home for the weekend.

"Inform his office that Supervisor Sector 2 urgently requests an audience. . . . Yes, Monday will have to do, won't it?"

He slammed down the receiver. Idiots! The civil service was falling apart. Nothing but idiots on the phone. He flexed his fingers, trying to calm himself. Not only the phones but all around him. He was surrounded by imbeciles.

His face drawn in anger, Junot picked up the single sheet and glanced through it again. Impossible! Three murders in the last six months were the work of an assassin who was himself murdered within the past week. Police had the weapon used in the killings of a Zurich banker, an industrialist from Brussels, and a British diplomat.

Junot resisted the temptation to crumple the paper and hurl it from his sight. What good would it do? That fool Dreyfus had discovered more in one day than his own idiots could in six months. Six years!

Damn the Jew, Junot thought grimly. And damn Dieter Bock too. Who the devil was he? They had a file on him, of course—it was on his desk at the moment—but it merely detailed the man's SS background, his work for West Germany as a security officer dealing with refugees from East Berlin, and finally a move to Paris with his French wife. What in hell was he doing killing people now? Worse, why hadn't they known about him? As an ex-Nazi he belonged to them. Which was precisely what the general would scornfully tell him.

Junot stared at the blank wall, his anger turning to bitterness. Competition among the supervisors who ran the sections was often fierce. In recent months he'd lost an agent, Arab terrorists had staged several well-publicized slayings and the Israelis enjoyed a few coups of their own. None of which served his interests or those of national defense.

The Ministry of Defense was also the Ministry of War, of course, and this latter title perhaps best described the outlook of those who worked in its squat complex on the Rue St-Dominique. War was hell but it was their business as well, and the nation needed its military as much as the fist needed knuckles. In this anthropomorphic view even the gods had enemies, and peace itself was merely a time of cold war.

Junot was part of this netherworld and understood its workings. What he didn't understand was why no one in the Service knew anything about the Nazi.

Or had he simply not been told?

The Mideast supervisor folded the sheet of paper and slipped it into an envelope to be put in his safe until Monday. One thing was certain. The general would want him to take over from the police. Raymond Broussard, the Belgian industrialist slain in Lyon, had been one of his agents.

*   *   *

By 4 P.M. César had his answer. His hunch had worked out and he didn't like it one bit.

Someone using the name of Dieter Bock had flown Lufthansa from Paris to Munich on April 7, as the reservation called for. He used a false identity to get into France and Bock's identity card to return to Germany, so there'd be no record of him out of the country. He'd come to Paris, kill Bock and go back unseen.

"Back where?" Menard wanted to know. "He didn't use the rest of the reservation to Linz."

"He didn't need to go on to Austria." César's voice had defeat in it. "Our man's German."

German probably meant an agency, almost certainly West German Intelligence. The investigation would soon be taken away from him. It wasn't fair.

"Not fair," César growled through clenched teeth. "Bock was mine." He slumped farther in the chair.

"But why'd they kill him?"

"Maybe he got too greedy," César said, distracted. "Or maybe he just got careless. How the hell do I know?"

He had banked on Bock being killed by ex-Nazis in France. It was his one chance to get back at them, lay the demons to rest. Or even by the SCE, he might've been able to do something there. But West German—

"We don't know for sure it's them," Menard said, wanting his boss to feel better. "So far it's circumstantial."

"Let me tell you something about circumstantial evidence." César remained burrowed in his chair. "A man enters a house, steals the valuables, then burns it down. There are no witnesses. The next day he's stopped with the loot and a liter of gasoline. His clothes smell of fire and his hands are burned. Only his lawyer would call that just circumstantial."

"This is no burning house we have here."

"Maybe it is, and we're in it."

"There are other explanations," Menard pressed.

César peered at him through tired eyes.

"And other questions, too."

"For example?"

"Why use Bock's name to go back when that's the last thing the killer should want?"

"I wish I knew," César moaned. "It doesn't make sense."

"And no picture in his police file. Does that make sense?"

César admitted it didn't. At the moment, anyway.

"Or the SCE keeping their dossier from us?"

"It's happened before."

"Or our own people covering up for Germans. Has that happened before?" Menard shook his head vigorously. "None of it makes sense if it was a West German operation."

The chair moved as the inspector nudged forward.

"You see?" Menard spread his hands. "Other possibilities."

"I'm listening," César said, starting to get his wind back.

"Suppose the whole trip was a fake? To throw us off if we ever got that far."

"Someone went," César objected.

"Could've been anybody. One of the others you keep talking about."

"A false trail. Go on."

"But not the killer. He stays here."

"Why?"

"He's French or lives in France."

"A German who lives in France. Good."

"Same for the others in the group."

"But he works alone," César urged.

"So he goes himself to Munich as Bock and doubles back."

"Using his own identity!" César was becoming inspired again. "Or maybe still another fake so he can't be traced."

"By nightfall he's back in Paris," Menard continued excitedly, "and Munich's just a plant."

"Why Munich?"

"Why not Munich? It's Germany's third largest city, big enough to lose anyone. Bock's probably a Bavarian name, lots of them live there."

"Who made the reservation?" César prompted.

"He did. In Bock's name to match the identity card. You said the reservation was confirmed, so he knew there'd be no trouble."

"The reservation was confirmed but he had to leave a phone number with the airline."

"So he makes one up. They never call back anyway."

"Except the number he left wasn't made up."

Menard's eyes popped open.

César slumped back in the chair. "The number was Bock's house."

Menard's eyes snapped shut.

In the café they stared moodily into their wine. Life was shit and so was the detective business. You had to follow people around, clean up their mess. Shitcleaners, all of them! Some were just better at it than others. They were no good at all.

Tobie found César sitting alone, Menard gone home.

"You solve the Bock case yet?"

"Not yet."

"I remember this friend of mine who sought something he

shouldn't have. When he found it"—Tobie sniffed his glass—"it changed his whole life."

"What did he find?"

"Death."

The two friends sat in stony silence, César with a refill and Tobie on a recommended Pouilly-Fuissé.

"How'd you find me here?"

"I was looking. When one looks, one finds."

César promised to remember that.

* * *

In the heart of Paris, at the head of the Seine, stood the Sorbonne. No other seat of higher learning was so grandly influential; in its halls and galleries gathered those who would plumb the past and fathom the future, students of the spoken word as well as the written, whose endless debates spilled over the surrounding boulevards, giving the section an intensity that charged the air and raced the blood. This was the famed Latin Quarter, and it was here that César had come to learn.

Walking over from the café, the inspector carefully threaded his way through throngs of students on the Boulevard St-Michel, the babble of voices strangely harmonious to his cosmopolitan ear. A grim girl in battle denim thrust petition and pen at him and he automatically signed, hoping it didn't advocate the end of the world. Intimidated, he quickly turned the corner onto the Rue des Ecoles and found himself on the edge of protest.

A group of students stood by a cart filled with smashed wine bottles; their voices loudly called for the government to end the invasion of foreign wine since French growers couldn't sell their own stocks because of the cheaper imports from Italy, Spain and North Africa. Near them was another group with signs demanding the government stay out of foreign wine affairs. The cheap imports were all they could afford.

"French wine!" screamed the first group.

"Cheap wine!" yelled the second.

No one budged and they kept repeating the slogans between swipes of red or white, French or foreign. The wine war was an emotional issue that gripped the nation; only days earlier a mob had raided a warehouse in Bordeaux and destroyed ten thousand bottles of Spanish imports. The war divided the country and there were those who even foresaw the fall of France unless it was settled quickly.

"French wine!"

"Cheap wine!"

The mood was one of calm tension. Everybody hoped the war would soon end.

"Cheap French wine!" someone suddenly shouted from the crowd. Everybody looked annoyed. That was not the issue.

Moving behind the crowd, César worked his way around the statue of Montaigne that faced the Sorbonne entrance. The next moment he was in the main courtyard and turning left down a hall, then right into the Galerie Richelieu. From there he followed directions to the linguistics laboratory, where he found the graduate research worker standing over a phonetic chart. Bathed in white light, immobile, she exuded silent energy. When she moved finally it was with a flow of motion that struck César as inordinately sensual. Even the glare of the fluorescents could not dull her youthful beauty and César wondered if he'd made a mistake.

"Come," she called out as her hands continued their movement. César watched her smooth the chart under the magnifying glass, adjust the sprockets and turn up the illumination. The light skimmed off her skin like pebbles on water and he saw the delicate blue veins that laced her arms. Her long slim fingers bore no rings. A work of art, César thought. Even more, of life. She reminded him of Catherine Deneuve. At his approach she looked up, her eyes curious.

"Inspector Dreyfus, I assume." Her voice was musical, Parisian. "We meet again."

"Have we met before?"

"In another life perhaps." She smiled with her eyes. "There are so many lives, one can never be sure."

"In that case it's good of you to see me on such short notice, this time around."

"I didn't know I had a choice." She said this pleasantly, watching him. "But of course I want to help if I can."

César had expected someone quite different. Jacqueline Volette's record showed a graduate student who knew a half-dozen languages and held a research fellowship at the Sorbonne. What it didn't show was her vivacity and spontaneity.

"You mentioned my sister on the phone. Have you discovered anything new about her murder?"

"That's why I'm here," César said quietly. "To ask why you think it was murder."

"Because her husband killed her."

"So you told the insurance company. But have you any proof?"

"Proof?" She laughed, a dry hollow sound. "Isn't it a little late for that?"

"Have you?" he persisted.

Jacqueline Volette was twenty-six and never married. Her career, César supposed as he waited for her answer.

"Only a feeling," she admitted finally. "But I know he pushed her out that window. Dieter Bock is a killer."

"Dieter Bock is dead."

César watched her eyes run through the emotions to anger. She had wanted him executed.

"How—"

"He was murdered."

That was better. Poetic justice. He'd killed her sister; now someone had killed him. But wait—

"You think I did it." She felt for the chair. "Mother of God!"

"Did you?"

She treated the question seriously. "I could have," she said. "A year ago I could have."

"Exactly."

Jacqueline Volette shuddered, her hands gripping the armrests. César knew she would have a bad night of mourning, the memory revived. He had no choice. If she knew anything—

"I know nothing." The voice was flat, distant. "It's over, isn't it? They're both dead."

"Not over yet," he told her.

She didn't think she could help. How?

"Did your sister say anything before her death? About Bock, I mean. Anything at all?"

She shook her head helplessly. "Bernadette loved him."

"She was twenty years younger than him. Was it love, or something else?"

"Does it matter now?" Impatience, then a sigh. "My mother was very young when she had my sister; the man soon left. Ten years later she married and had me but my father died when I was four. Bock was like a father to Bernadette, I guess. The father who would never leave."

César suddenly saw how Bock remained married despite his injury. Instead of husband he was the surrogate father to his wife. But did he kill her?

"Tell me about your sister's eyeglasses. Did she wear them all the time?"

"Eyeglasses?" It took a moment for her to adjust. "Only in the house, for close work. Bernadette was terribly vain about her looks."

"So she had just the one pair."

"Except they disappeared right before—" She pressed her lips together, breathed deeply. "Bernadette was having another pair made when—" She began to cry softly.

César kicked himself mentally. Jacqueline Volette had been right all along. Her sister was murdered. Bock had her glasses stolen in a fake burglary, then edged her over to the window and pushed her out. She probably knew too much about his business. He'd get rid of her and get the insurance money at the same time, enough to set himself up again.

"I'll be fine now, really." She fumbled in her handbag.

César didn't tell her the truth, not yet. He still had to make certain.

Dieter Bock had committed the perfect murder but he'd needed help. According to the police report, he was out with his wife when the burglary occurred. That meant he hired someone, a thief. And César knew just the man to find him.

Before he left, César showed Jacqueline Volette the photograph of Bock and the woman who was supposed to be his wife. Jacqueline did not recognize the woman, had never seen her before. Yes, she was positive. But why had he shown her the picture? César didn't understand. Because of the woman, obviously. To make sure it wasn't her sister. Only the woman? Yes, she was supposed to be his wife. Whose wife? Bock's wife, of course. César pointed to the photo, and as he did he began to get the strangest feeling—

"But *Monsieur Inspecteur,* the man in the picture—"

—that there was something awfully wrong here—

"—it is not Dieter Bock!"

FOUR

April in Paris and a party as well. Playful guests oozing oohs at the drop of a name or the lift of a lash. Bottles of champagne carefully designed to loosen women and tighten men. The animal heat of bodies. Shouts, slips, suggestions, the spontaneous overflow of powerful emotion. *Voilà!*

César stayed close to Tobie Maton, his host. In such surroundings he felt himself a fish out of water, a beached whale on this Saturday night of his life in which his wife was gone for good (ex-wife, César muttered mentally, *ex-wife!*) and Bock apparently not gone at all. By comparison Tobie seemed solid, his life secure.

They had known each other for almost twenty years, these two, rising together through the ranks, two out of thousands, a pair of policemen called up to become detectives in the Brigade Spéciale, eventually making inspector, one in Homicide and the other in Robbery. Now there was nowhere else to go, no more room to rise. At least for César.

Naturally Tobie made it first, with his connections. An ambitious man, not lean yet hungry. A barracuda, as some saw him, or even shark. No matter. Some wise investments allowed him to shop on the Faubourg St-Honoré, serve his guests caviar and quail, and live in splendid isolation in the center of town.

The house stood on the Place des Vosges, one of dozens of rose brick and white stone maisons that formed a square of interior courtyards and gardens. Victor Hugo had lived there, as had Georges Simenon a century later with his Parisian detective. At parties, Tobie would throw open the *volets* and point proudly to the pavilions of the past; stories were quickly repeated of the thief who became a churchman and the churchman who became possessed, of the king who died in a joust and a queen who lived in the dark. The Gallic God favored, it seemed certain, swift changes of fortune.

"Peace and privacy!" Tobie announced tersely at the window, his back to the noisy throng gathered in his salon. "All a man could ever want." He slapped at his ample midriff with both hands to indicate a sense of *joie de vivre*. Behind him they slapped at his end table laden with delicacies, and the sidebar with its silver buckets.

Outside the moon slowly fell until it dangled precariously above the treetops.

"An ominous sign," Tobie proclaimed. "A low-riding moon means more bloodshed."

They were on the flagstone path that led to the center square and the great marble statue of Louis XIII on horseback. César was convinced the equestrian pose held meaning for him; he often saw himself astride a fierce Arabian charger, bearing down on the enemy and battling evil at every turn. His Lawrence of Arabia fantasy, which he wisely kept to himself. Or was he just another Don Quixote tilting at windmills? This Bock affair could finally unseat him, defeat him, and then all the kings of France couldn't help. Not even his good friend who knew everyone.

Good food, good wine, good women. A French husband could be fined only thirty francs for adultery, but a wife might get two years in prison. Served them right, César told himself smugly. And wondered why he'd thought of it. In all their years together he had never been unfaithful to his wife.

Tobie was urinating on the flowers in his most careful manner, slowly, luxuriously, spreading his flow as far as possible. A budding *jardinier,* he believed the chemicals were good for the soil. Nature wasted nothing. *Très bien.*

"So what do you think of her?"

"Nicole?"

"Oh, that one. She's more your type."

"Ah, Cécile."

"You approve then." Finished, he felt almost mystical. "And why not? Charm, beauty"—he glanced at César—"and a body to match. If she were a flower she'd be a bouquet by now. Sex is no laughing matter to her, I assure you." He pulled out a blue box of Boyards, tore open the cellophane. "A lot of women are like that today. Only one word to describe them." He shuddered in anticipation. *"Formidable!"*

"She's got rings on her fingers."

"And time on her hands, thank God."

"Wedding rings."

Tobie laughed, pushed back the cover and lifted the silver paper. "I forget you are divorced. Suddenly you see marriage differently, no? But you'll get over it." He offered the box to César who declined.

They walked in silence toward the far end of the square, to the fountain where they sat on the rounded stone edge of the pool. At such times César felt surrounded by order and history—and quite alone in the world.

Tobie lit the brown rolled cigarette; the smoke was pungent, a spiral of fragrance. "And the investigation?"

"There are problems," César admitted.

"You're taking too much on your own."

"It's my case."

His host snorted in derision. "Only by default." He fixed his eye on César. "Nobody in your division would touch it now; too much could go wrong. The only reason you still have it is because they don't know what to do with it. The political police are involved up to their snouts, and God knows who else. You can't win."

"What would you suggest?"

"Play politics and let the gutter rats fight over it. The thing'll sink fast, wait and see. You probably have enough to do that right now. If not, plead your special circumstances. These are animals who killed your parents. How could you be objective?"

"Bock was a lone wolf, as you say I am. Maybe it takes one to catch one."

"Bock is dead."

"Maybe not." César took a deep breath. "Maybe he's still alive."

Was his life so empty he needed to form a bond with the unspeak-

able Nazi? César wondered. Loneliness is almost endurable when one
is not quite alone.

"Even better," Tobie said softly. "Emotional involvement. Dupin
would have to release you."

"Dupin?"

"He made division commander by learning how to survive, didn't
he? We're all civil servants in criminal investigation. Him too. And
the first rule in civil service is, Never stick your neck out. Give him a
good reason and you're off the case, or else he shares the blame if
anything goes wrong. It'll be in the files. Who kept you on after a
formal request? He did. So he won't. You're too independent, anyway, too full of surprises." Tobie shook his head sadly. "Besides, he
doesn't trust you."

"You never worked Homicide." César was curious. "What's all
this about Dupin?"

"Nothing really. Just while you were out sick that time, a house
thief I was chasing got himself blown up over in the Nineteenth;
some tenant who'd been robbed twice rigged a radio with explosives.
Your people saw murder."

"Hardly."

"Not so fast. The tenant was a petty crook himself, one I used for
information here and there, and he knew the deceased. Anyway,
Dupin saw it my way and we worked out a deal so there'd be no
charges."

"How did my name—"

"You were part of the deal. I was supposed to get you to cooperate
more, you know, one big happy family. The usual shit."

"Apparently you didn't succeed."

"I didn't try. I just said that to get the poor bastard off."

Tobie hunched over Dupin's desk sorting out secret agreements?
The man was full of intrigue. "Are you trying now?" César asked.

"Only to save you, *mon ami.* You're the best they have, even if
they don't know it. But this thing"—the voice took on a conspiratorial tone—"could cut very deep. Then what? You'll say you're investigating a murder, true. But they'll claim you're endangering national security. Deals will be made and soon *you'll* be investigated.
After all, you wouldn't be under suspicion if you were blameless. The
department won't stand up for you, either; the brass and political

police piss in the same pot, and they've waited a long time to get even. You'll be lucky to serve seven years in Santé."

"You exaggerate."

"Not by much. See Hugo's house there"—Tobie pointed—"it's a museum now, but think back to the captain framed by the government and sent to Devil's Island before Hugo helped him. And he was army, not merely the police—"

"It was Zola."

"What was?"

"Emile Zola helped the captain. Not Victor Hugo."

"Forget history. What about that local inspector who was told of Syrian threats against the pro-Iraqi paper on the Rue Marbeuf there? When the bomb blew they accused him of ignoring information that could've saved lives, even though he claimed he'd passed it on. But meanwhile, he lost everything."

Tobie nodded happily, a chess master revving up. "French justice, you see what I mean? Not for us, anyway. Go it alone and you'll lose every time but involve others, this one, that, and there's a chance. At least go through the motions. Everybody seems to know that except you. Except," Tobie emphasized, "you! And that I don't understand." He frowned in thought. "Remember what the German general said when he burned one building after Hitler ordered Paris burned to the ground? *'Beschützen deine hinter, so weit als das Gesicht reicht.'*"

"Cover your ass," César said, smiling, "as far as the eye can see."

"Precisely."

Tobie smoked in silence as César broached the favor he needed. A minor burglary in Bock's apartment on the Rue de Pali a year back. Not much taken, no disposition of the case. What he wanted was to talk to the thief. Just talk, no threats. Surely with Tobie's connections he could find the man. "Would help a lot," César added.

"Hopeless!" Tobie groaned in defeat. "Half mad and full of iron nobility. No wonder you remind me of de Gaulle." He crushed the cigarette under his heel. "Vatel too. A great chef, but *proud?* One day Louis XIV ordered him to prepare a state dinner; everything went fine through the soups but when the sole didn't arrive in time Vatel naturally committed suicide, impaled himself on a steak knife. Later someone asked Escoffier what he would've done, and he said he'd have taken the white meat of young chickens and made fillets with them. No one would've known the difference." Tobie's body shook enthusiastically. "He was right, you see. The point is, he was right. You can always learn something new."

The host started back, César following in a daze. If he lived to be a hundred, he'd never understand gourmets. Madmen, all of them. It was their concentration on food, itself a sign of derangement. He saw nothing wrong with his own belief that man was meant to eat alone, preferably in a darkened corner of a locked room.

But the madman was right about one thing. You can always learn something new, even about people you've known for years. Who would've suspected Maton of making deals with Dupin?

* * *

They returned to the party of wine, women and men. Nobody seemed to have missed them.

"Cécile must be upstairs in the gallery," Tobie whispered at the sidebar. "I should really go and comfort her."

Did he mean as a friend, father, confessor, lover? To help her, advise her, screw her? All of it, César decided. A man of enormous appetites. And devious.

"She's insatiable, you know. Quite insatiable." Tobie set down his glass. "Her last lover was Pichôt. The sculptor? By the time he returned to his wife he was a wrecked man, and good for nothing." The host paused to see if César was properly shocked; choice gossip demanded suitable outrage. "She was forced to take a lover herself. Two, in fact, though I imagine the second was just to get even for—"

"But we have been searching *everywhere* for you," Nicole announced breathlessly, rushing at them from the hallway. "Hungry, that one," Tobie had warned him. "The eyes of a beggar and the thighs that trap."

"Cécile's admiring your art." Nicole placed her hand on Tobie's arm in a feminine gesture of urgency. "Is he really a private detective?"

"That would be Kayser," Tobie said, nudging César. "You should meet him—from Zurich. Knows his Nazis; might be able to help you."

"No more shop talk," Nicole cooed and squeezed herself closer to César as their host rushed off to find "the love of my loins."

"A terrible man." She gazed hungrily at the fleeing back.

"A ladies' man," César said, refilling the glasses.

"Oh, you men," Nicole pouted. "Our most harmless flirtations are condemned while your virtue is never questioned—or even suspected."

César laughed in spite of himself. "Apparently Tobie's virtue is that he's a libertine; worse! He fancies food as well as women."

"And you?" Nicole raised her glass.

His eyes met hers, held. "And you?" César asked.

Her painted smile reminded him of a Gauguin he admired. The same sensual mouth beneath pools of innocence that gave her face its smoky ambiguity. Will she? César, knowing women well, decided Nicole was the kind who won't.

"Libertine, me," she sighed. "I have always absorbed the future best by eating it."

* * *

The nude woman lay on her back with her legs apart. She had a narrow pinched face framed by excessive ringlets of bleached blond hair. Her large breasts bounced and sloshed against sallow skin over the rib cage. The eyes were closed in ecstasy, the mouth open.

Above her, the man moved rhythmically in his lovemaking. His body was arched, the arms serving as pistons, the palms pressed into the mattress. He was tall and thin, his skin tightly drawn. The black hair shone, the forehead glistened.

"Must be in training," someone whispered.

"Obviously," said someone else, "but for what?"

They crowded around the huge bed, a dozen pairs of eyes transfixed into one gigantic orb staring at the straining athletes. Several heads moved even closer over the bed, peering at the position. The pace grew quicker, the woman's squeals louder. An elderly man with a pocket watch studied it in disbelief while others in the naked group nodded silent encouragement. At the rear a squat swarthy man touched a woman's thigh and she swiftly removed his hand. "Not yet, *s'il vous plaît.*"

"When?" he asked brusquely.

"But when they're done, *chéri.*"

The swarthy man shrugged, turned to another woman with his hand outstretched. Sexual sharing held his mind at the moment, and he saw no reason to wait any further. There were other rooms with eight-foot beds and blue bidets and mirrored walls, even mouthwash for those with a touch of *minouche*. This was, after all, a legal house of well repute where loving couples shared their sexual pleasures from noon to midnight seven days a week.

The public *partouze* was off the Place de Clichy in the residential Seventeenth district, a neighborhood of cobbled streets and closed courtyards. The house itself loomed like a dark combatant in some medieval mystery, its entrance gained through a massive iron gate. Beyond, a polished stone path twisted around the garden to the front steps of the three-storied residence. From its shuttered windows, the curtains tightly drawn, no light escaped.

Inside, the several dozen guests roamed from room to room, watching, waiting, participating as the mood moved them, their clothing hung on hooks. Bodies and positions changed, faces blurred, and soon all seemed a tableau of arms and legs and matted hair, wrapped in ribbons of skin. Almost all, for two of the men had more than angry organs in mind as they smiled and stared and stroked their way through the *partouze*, paying particular attention to the parlor floor of offices and private chambers for the more powerful and wealthy. There the musky smell of money was strong.

The squat swarthy man quickly spotted the office where the weekend receipts would be kept. A hundred francs per guest times hundreds of guests, plus the price of drinks. Operating expenses for the house. Payroll, protection, emergency fund, maybe more, all in cash. Also whatever valuables came from the occupied chambers. Another perfect setup.

"Looks good," whispered Nadal.

"Easy," Leduc agreed.

Combining business with pleasure, the pair was searching the site for a future robbery. Meanwhile, they were killing time until midnight when they had a robbery planned. It was an odd sort of job but with a guarantee of money and safety. What could go wrong?

* * *

The food was gone by ten so everyone was drunk by eleven, courtesy of the sure hand and swift feet of their host who repaired several times to his wine cellar.

"What happens to all this when you fall in love?" César asked as they searched the cellar for still another bottle. "Does she get half?"

"Only after I die." Tobie reached for a Romanée-Conti.

"Who gets the other half?"

"It dies with me."

Neither man considered such a fate even remotely possible. Tobie already loved his kitchen, with its double oven and separate sinks and eight-foot chopping block; the wine cellar was the other side of the gold coin. Together they were the fruits of his creative urge, his children. He possessed them entirely. What could ever come between them?

"Did I ever tell you about the Ponthieus?" The robbery inspector had a round unlined face of soft pink skin that turned remarkably red when he got drunk. "They were in love."

César decided that meant they were probably married.

"After a while Paul acquired a mistress he took on trips. Monique eventually found out and left him the next time he went on business, but first she raised the thermostat in his wine cellar to 84 degrees. *84 degrees!* By the time he came back, his wine was vinegar. All of it, thousands of bottles." Tobie looked like he was going to cry. "Nothing but vinegar."

"What did he do?"

"He killed her, of course." Tobie blew his red nose. "What else could he do?"

César didn't know. A wife who'd do that would do anything. His own wife'd never do that. Ex-wife. She would never do that to him. He had no wine cellar. César shook his head. He wondered if he was getting drunk.

"They called it justified but he got three years anyway."

A long time, César thought. Still, compared to—

"When he got out he got another wine cellar."

Upstairs again, César carefully threaded his way through a half-dozen groups in passionate pose, all arguing loudly. Someone handed him a drink. When he turned in thanks—no one was there. He slumped into a chair, bewildered.

She had her back to him but César spotted her immediately, the soft curve of the neck, the smooth taper of wings under the simple black dress. He was so happy to see her, inexplicably, that he lunged out of his seat. His hand touched her shoulder as she turned into him, startled.

"Monsieur?"

She wasn't Jacqueline Volette at all.

César strained his eyes to clear his head. Didn't even look like her; about the same age but—Probably one of Tobie's *putains* that always showed up at his parties. He murmured an apology, walked out of the salon. The disappointment in him rose and fell, he didn't know why.

"Never!" The speaker stood at the far end of the formal dining room, immersed in his own emotion. "To cut off one's ear—Ah, that is artful. A trifle Van Goghish, yet essentially artistic. A form of statement, yes? But to cut off *both* ears, and then the fingers and toes one by one—" He shook his head wildly. "Excessive, grossly excessive." His blood-red eye focused on the group. "It positively *reeks* of self-indulgence."

Voices whirred, the whine of a woman winning out. ". . . a history of artists using their bodies as protest." She bristled with youthful indignation. "What Pierre proposes is simply to raise the possibility of escalation if our demands aren't met."

"And Danton?" the man shouted. "Was he escalating when he lowered his pants and shaved his groin on the altar of Notre-Dame?"

"Purifying." The woman smirked.

"Comment?"

"Purification," she announced hotly, "is the first step in artistic protest."

"And the last?"

"You've heard of the Viennese artist Rudolph Schwarzkogler, who cut off his penis inch by inch—"

César reeled around and left the room foot by foot. A bell clicked somewhere in his head but he couldn't escalate the sound. Something to do with that last part about a penis. Had he heard right? He quickly finished his drink, headed for another.

They were still dancing, those who had given up talking. No one had given up drinking yet. César fumbled at the bar until he got what he wanted, though he wasn't sure what that was. Next to him a couple kissed so passionately he wondered to whom they were married, certainly not each other. Probably more of Tobie's crazy friends. César didn't like most of them; they all seemed so . . . free. He wished the kissing couple would go away, disappear. When they didn't, he did.

Kayser found him in the kitchen, slumped at the table, a slim silver server in front of him. To one side a huge glass-fronted cupboard laden with Buffon service reflected the room's métier, while elsewhere a petit-point fire screen rested gracefully beneath a collage of Picasso's and a George Sand watercolor. In such a *mise en scène,* César seemed somehow woefully out of place.

"Maton tells me you're handling the Nazi major who got himself killed the other day. I know a little about them; maybe I can help." Kayser walked around the other side of the table to get a better look at César. "You all right, Dreyfus?"

His head was a balloon bursting into flame and his throat burned like the Gobi desert. When he moved his arms they broke. It must be the coffee, he thought, taking another swallow.

"I'm arrogant enough to believe I'll survive," he rasped through numbed lips. "Barely."

Kayser sat across the table and savored the special Turkish blend, his nostrils flooding with aroma, his eyes on the inspector the whole time.

"Nazi hunting isn't exactly a popular sport these days." He poured himself a cup, careful not to spill. "No one takes them seriously anymore."

"But you do. You take Nazis seriously."

The Swiss detective shrugged elaborately. "I've had some dealings with them, money dealings. Is that serious enough?" He took a sip, blinked back tears. You could walk on it.

"When?"

"Over the years. Not as direct clients, of course." Another sip, thoughtful. "But I've met them, ex-Nazis, that is. Austria alone has a hundred thousand. Mostly good men who just did their duty, I suppose."

"Mostly, you say."

"I've come across a few of the others too."

"Others?" César was amused. "You mean the few bad ones who did more than their duty, killed more than their share?"

"You want more coffee?"

Peter Kayser, as César knew from Tobie, specialized in transfers of money from other countries into Switzerland—a form of smuggling —and the recovery of stolen goods. His smuggling activities were largely illegal since most nations had currency regulations curbing capital flight. Switzerland itself was a money haven with limited restrictions on incoming funds. A lucrative business, César thought, and one that ex-Nazis had long used. Ironically, Switzerland's strict banking secrecy laws, dating back to 1934, were originally passed to protect Jewish account holders from Nazi persecution.

But what was Kayser doing in Paris, and why his interest in Bock?

"More a case of mutual interest, as I see it," said the private detective affably. "I'm trailing a stolen painting commissioned by Hitler himself. It's valued at half a million francs."

"French?"

"Swiss."

The theft was discovered three weeks earlier and Kayser had traced it to Paris for his client.

"And your client's name?"

The detective just smiled.

César's head still pounded and he silently swore to give up coffee along with cigarettes. "You mentioned mutual interest."

"I thought we might work together on this, trade information. There could be a connection between the two."

"How?"

The Swiss leaned further across the table. "I've reason to believe the painting was taken by a young neo-Nazi group in need of money. My guess is—it's more than a guess, actually—they intend to sell it here in Paris to ex-Nazis or Nazi sympathizers." Kayser refilled his cup from the silver server, settled back in the plush chair. "Probably the same people you're looking for."

Maybe his head would never stop hurting. In that case he wouldn't give up coffee. Might even go back to smoking.

"See what I mean, Dreyfus?"

"It's possible," César offered.

"More than possible," snapped the Swiss. "It fits like a glove."

"Gloves come in different sizes."

"This one doesn't."

"But Nazis do," César said softly, "even different nationalities. They could be here in this house right now, even"—he paused, glanced around the empty kitchen—"right in this room."

Kayser's eyes narrowed into steel balls.

They agreed only to stay in touch. For his own part, César had no intention of telling the Swiss anything about Bock. The men he chased had money, no doubt, but the last thing they'd want was a life-sized portrait of their *verrückt Führer*. They were not exactly going public. Still, Bock had saved Himmler's letter all these years. Maybe they were sentimental, the old crowd. Could you be smart and sentimental at the same time? César didn't know. *He* certainly wasn't sentimental, not a bit, and he considered himself pretty smart, not too dumb anyway. Smart enough, at least, to doubt Kayser's motives even if his story checked out. Who could believe someone who made money moving money around?

Besides, who would trust a man who used only last names? The mark of a devious mind, for sure.

Just to be on the safe side, though, César decided never to go to Switzerland. They all spoke German, anyway.

Not only that; anyone could be a private detective in Switzerland, set up shop as a detective. No license was required. No license and no training, nothing.

Except maybe a magician's hat.

César wondered how Kayser knew Bock had been an SS major. His war record listed him as captain, and the only mention of major was in Himmler's letter. But he hadn't shown the letter to anyone. No one!

* * *

By midnight everything was bathed in drunken splendor. César sat in the downstairs bathroom and read hidden messages for help on the toilet tissue. He suddenly longed to be in the Foreign Legion, except there was nowhere foreign for them to go anymore. Only France was French, he mumbled, and standing alone—like him. Sitting alone. A wave of self-pity swept over him as elsewhere a dozen drunks still held out doggedly, determined to drink the house dry. When the two masked men arrived, the host was upstairs with Cécile.

"Wrong place," a nearby drunk giggled above the crunch of voices, "no masquerade here."

A gun butt cracked against his skull; toppling backwards, he smashed into an end table of glassware. Everyone sobered up swiftly as the other gun motioned them further into the main salon, men and women on opposite sides.

"What's this?" César, jarred by the crashing glass, stood in the open doorway.

"A party," someone snarled as a hand shoved him into the room with the rest. He saw the fear on their faces, the eyes filled with shock. It was all happening too fast.

"Undress," commanded the voice, "everything." The squat swarthy man held the pistol steady while his partner raced upstairs, returned with two couples. Tobie, in the lead, wore a bathrobe. "A robbery? Here?" He sounded offended. "You must be crazy."

"Shut up!"

In minutes everyone was stripped. Expert hands rifled through the clothing on the floor, the wallets and purses. Watches and jewelry were next, rings from fingers, bracelets and necklaces. One woman refused to give up a string of pearls and it was torn from around her throat. Another had difficulty removing her wedding band and was told her finger would be chopped off. Hysterical, she had to be slapped into silence.

"Who's Dreyfus?" The taller man held César's identification.

"I am." He stepped forward.

"A cop!"

Both guns were suddenly leveled at him.

"We don't like cops," Nadal said.

"What he means is we don't like them alive," said Leduc.

"Get dressed."

The money and jewelry were scooped into a canvas bag as César put on his pants and shirt.

"Hurry."

They were almost to the front door, César between them, when Kayser burst out of the kitchen, firing. His first shot tore away a piece of Nadal's scalp, spinning him around. He tried to rise and the second gouged out part of the lower jawbone. Blood and cartilage flew in all directions. The robber's hands jumped in reflex, clawing empty air. His body jerked backwards, the legs jackknifed underneath so that he seemed to be tumbling in space. His eyes were already glazing when the third heavy slug smashed into his chest and he sank without a sound, lifeless, the body a broken vessel spilling with fluid, the arteries running red onto the green rug.

Leduc was already out the door and gone, the money bag left behind, as Kayser pegged a shot into the dark.

Only seconds had passed, an eternity. In the room, trembling hands were reaching frantically for clothing.

His eyes narrowed to slits, César stared at Kayser's back for a long moment before turning his attention to the dead man. He bent down and pulled off the relief mask. It was a face he'd never seen.

"Know him?"

Tobie looked away from the phone. "New to me."

"I thought you know all the thieves."

"What thieves? These had guns."

César nodded. "So did Kayser."

"Good thing for you."

"Is it?"

"He saved your life, didn't he?" Tobie spoke briefly into the phone, hung up.

"He could've got innocent people killed," César grumbled.

"But he didn't."

"But he could have."

"That's not the same thing," Tobie snapped.

"So where'd he get the gun?"

The police took statements from everyone while the body was being processed for the morgue. Kayser had been in the wine cellar searching for a Château Simone when the intruders entered the house. Coming up—a cautious man, and silent—he'd heard them. Retreating into the cellar he found the pistol kept there for emergencies (which Tobie confirmed). As a private detective trained in firearms, he intended to capture the pair; it hadn't worked out like that. His only regret was that he didn't get the other man. César had been in the way.

"One dead and one gone," the duty inspector said to César. "You're lucky the Swiss was around. Could've been you."

From the emptied salon César watched the homicide squad finally leave. They had all the information needed: a justified killing of an armed robber. There still were times when justice was served, after all.

"Bedtime," Tobie yawned as César thoughtfully regarded his good friend. He'd been in the cellar a dozen times over the years; funny how he had never noticed the gun.

* * *

Heavy with wine, César had taken Nicole to his bed. Not his bed but a room in Tobie's town house. After a year alone, almost a year, he still could not bring a woman to his home. He had committed marriage in that apartment, the bittersweet fruit of nine years, and committed divorce. He could not yet commit adultery there, too. That it wouldn't be adultery any longer still eluded his troubled soul.

Married at thirty for the first time, César swore it would be the last. He was in love, a feeling he'd never known and now shared. No matter she was years younger, a postman's daughter from Nantes. His fantasies at the time, he remembered, were filled with lifelong desire and devotion. But the gods planned differently, and when she returned to her father's house, without child or husband, César knew she left without love as well. She could not have children, the result of a botched adolescent abortion, so she needed even more of him; more, he admitted, than he knew how to give. Or could ever give. Had he failed her? She him? Who was wise enough to say?

She had married another, a man she'd known in earlier years who ended her loneliness, a helpmate rather than a partner. It was well for her, and in the dark of his mind César knew that he had lost what he'd never really won, except in dreams.

Lying now beside Nicole, César marveled at the resilience of humans; they functioned, most of them, regardless of the agony to heart and head. A primeval ordering of nature, the will to survive. He met it constantly in his work, in both predator and prey.

Even in the Bock case, the triumph of the will was everywhere. In Bock himself since his Nazi days, in the political police protecting their sources and the Criminal Police pursuing theirs, in self-serving politicians and the self-indulgent press, in private citizens and public servants. Maybe even in friends. Why, César wondered, had Tobie brought Kayser to talk about Bock? How did the robbery fit in? And Nicole, was she in on it too? In on what? César didn't know.

His eyes searched her face. It was a lovely face, nothing more, nothing he needed. It held no answers for him.

"Promise?" A whisper.

"What?"

"Next time," she moaned drowsily. "Your uniform."

He had already told her that he never wore a uniform, in or out of bed.

"Buttoned," she murmured. "So I feel all safe and secure in the arms of the law."

"I see you like fantasy." He almost added "too."

"Mmm. What else can you see?"

"Only you," he lied, not knowing the truth. "You're as far as I can see right now."

His eyes seemed to close without his consent. The last thing he remembered was the wolf running, running after the man. As the wolf leaped, the knife flashed. Bock! But who was he, predator or prey? Or was he both?

FIVE

"—as usual full of surprises," Dupin was saying. "A man is found dead in a sealed room, an apparent suicide. You quickly pronounce it murder and soon three other equally mysterious killings are solved. Extraordinary." His tone suggested a deep distrust of surprise. "Based on evidence of the matching automatic and shell casings, a review of unsolved homicides by firearm has already begun, involving all units of the national police force. Thus far, two more bodies have been tied to the Walther PPK." Dupin scrutinized a sheet on his desk. "One from Marseille, a French engineer slain last August, the other a city official in Vichy a year ago. Which seems to coincide with your theory of this Dieter Bock being a paid assassin. The money received from unknown sources each month also support that theory, obviously."

The chief inspector's voice conveyed an unmistakable sadness and resignation, the very model of abused patience, and long-suffering. It was a pose more worthy of a gifted actor than a police superior and Gaston Dupin clearly was both. Active in amateur productions, his parts were invariably suited to his personality and profession. He preferred Racine to Molière.

"Other explanations are possible, of course. They always are. In this case, specifically, the gun could've been planted in the victim's flat; there is no direct evidence of ownership. The money could be from some past activity, perhaps going back to his work in West Berlin, which should prompt an investigation by their intelligence people, or maybe even French security. Certainly not the police; we're not equipped for that sort of thing. Still, the odds are with your theory and that I find disturbing. Also puzzling. A series of related killings like this probably means criminal conspiracy of a political nature. Yet no security service has come forward, beyond a progress request." The frown deepened. "How do you account for that, Dreyfus?"

"I can't," César said warily.

"Unfortunately, there is more. If I read your report correctly, the victim was not Dieter Bock at all but someone who resembled him closely—an unknown male picked expressly for that purpose. You then conclude that Bock himself was the killer and is now in Germany, having flown to Munich on April 7. Without any proof, using only your highly developed imagination"—Dupin sighed, regarded his subordinate—"you further suggest that the victim was hanged because hanging often distorts facial features; that piano wire was used to facilitate the decapitation, which would make precise identification even more difficult; that pictures of the dead man were substituted for those of Bock to insure recognition; that 120,000 francs were left behind to complete the deception; that Bock's personal effects were left for the same reason, that . . ."

César had spent Sunday at his desk working on the report, grateful for the empty office so no one could bear witness to his bouts of despair. Graphs, charts, lists, points of cross-reference, names, dates, places; a dozen times he gave it up as hopeless, a few specks of light in a sea of dark. Each time he returned to the task, driven by a desperation César himself could not explain. He was convinced his gut feeling was right. What, after all, was crime detection if not intuitive leaps across uncharted chasms? The Holmesian science of deductive reasoning was being handled in the forensic specialties, in ballistics and the other disciplines of modern criminology. From the tiniest fragment—a human hair, a piece of lint—evidence grew into a chain, but chains could not bind voids. Often more was needed than technology could give, something peculiarly human. César called it his spark, a leap of the imagination. Or was that merely another word for faith?

César knew only that the fragments in the Bock case were few, the leap great. The Nazi had committed murder to fake his own death. What was his motive? He had earlier changed his life-style. For what reason? And given up a small fortune since he would soon be rich. From where? How? He left a gun linking him to at least five killings, and receipts placing him at two of them. He left a letter that led to other people, and another leading to the past. Finally, he left a faked suicide almost anyone could see through. All of which meant he wanted his own murder discovered and identity as an assassin revealed. Why? César had to make the leap. He felt Bock testing him, even daring him.

". . . certain difficulties since the assumption of your report is long-range planning. To take just one example: the victim's sex wound. To fit the facts Bock had to pretend impotency with those he took home from the nightclub during the past year, which would make him a model of patience as well as virtue. It also means he'd have to be intimately acquainted with the proposed victim over a long period. The wound was an old one, and the kind men don't usually talk about. Yet here you are asking me to accept that Bock did all this and more, for reasons unknown, and in place of evidence you mention the SCE refusal to give up his file. Who would believe me if I believed you? What surprise would you imagine next? Criminal investigation is not concerned with political considerations anymore. You should know that; think of Algeria, the purges that followed. Our responsibility now is only with the accumulation of fact to find the guilty."

"And in this case?" César asked.

"Proof, Dreyfus, proof."

"That the victim is not Bock."

"For a start, yes."

"The fingerprints would confirm it—"

"Assuming they're on file."

"—which is why I need the authorization to contact West German Intelligence directly."

"Wouldn't he have thought of that?"

"He knew we'd take the body for his," César said quickly, "so prints didn't matter. We would've, too, I would've except—"

"Except?"

Except for Jacqueline Volette but César was damned if he'd bring her name into it yet. Suddenly he didn't even trust the police, at least until he saw how deep the Bock affair went.

"Too many little things," César lied. "Money, for one. He said he'd soon be rich."

"To women, which is what men do."

César blinked. Dupin was a notorious ladies' man and like such men, he believed everyone did the same.

"The gasoline-soaked envelope with the photos."

"Photos of the dead man."

"The reservation with the house phone number."

"Not impossible for someone to get."

"His wife's convenient accident."

"Accidents happen everyday."

"The theft of the eyeglasses."

"Thieves take anything."

"Bock's identity card the killer used in Munich."

"Passports and identity cards are falsified all the time."

César, desperate: "The missing photo in Bock's police file."

"A clerical error, statistically insignificant."

"That could be said about any of these."

"My point precisely."

"But not all taken together," César reasoned.

"There is no hard evidence." The chief inspector tugged at his moustache impatiently, his eye on the door.

"If Bock is alive," César said in a sudden sweat, "we could use him to pull down the Service, get back at them."

"Comment?"

The eye shifted.

"Bock's kills were political, you said it yourself. But they were solved without help from the political police, not even the use of their file on the killer. To them Bock is dead. Think of the publicity we'd get in the Palace if he was still alive—and we proved it."

"Specifically?"

"Two of the victims were French. To make sure French justice is served, regardless of the political aspect, I would demand the Service release not only Bock's file but all their files on ex-Nazis, some of whom may be linked to him. Their angry refusal should make us look even better."

César stared at Dupin, who no longer had his hand at his face.

Ever since the Munich Olympics, the SCE had been taking credit for terrorist information developed by police agents. More recently, it was involved in the wiretapping of a newspaper blamed on police.

"You must be mad; it's a scandalous suggestion. Infamous."

"Exactly."

"Think of the consequences to your career."

Having lost hope, César had expected a curt dismissal. Instead, he watched the chief inspector's eyes, saw the wheels beginning to turn. Turning.

"In police procedure, willful flights of fancy can only lead to disaster. Still, your theory about Bock is plausible in light of the oddities here. And you do have a feel for that sort of thing, don't you? If the West Germans confirm your belief, would you extend the investigation to all deaths attributed to Bock?"

César thought he was dreaming.

"Of course."

"Under certain conditions, authorization is possible." Dupin reached for the phone. "You will be informed."

"All of them," César shouted. Was this finally his chance to get back at Junot? "Their files are full of ex-Nazis."

"So are their ranks. Don't be greedy."

* * *

James Bond swung the Walther PPK around, slowly.

"Everything you can tell me," César said, handing the pistol to the Belgian arms expert.

The gunsmith hefted the weapon, almost lost in his huge hand, and examined its barrel. With a practiced motion he pulled down the front-end trigger guard and pushed it to the left, releasing the seven-cartridge magazine. César silently watched the Paris representative of Fabrique Nationale take the gun apart.

Baudrin drew the slide back with a slight lift until its rear end cleared the guides, then eased the slide forward over the mounting and off the barrel. Next came the stock, revealing all the lockwork parts. César marveled at the dexterity of those fleshy fingers, and smiled encouragement.

The gunsmith peered at the trigger connection. "First of all, it's not the James Bond gun. That's a 7.65mm and this is the heavier 9mm Kurz—more firepower. Other than that, it's the usual double-action blowback model with fixed sights." He squeezed the trigger. "Has a smooth light touch, good trigger pull."

"How old is it?"

Baudrin inspected the receiver and slide. "Prewar, certainly. No later than 1939 from the looks of it. There's the original spring-supported pin"—he pointed—"mounted in the slide above the firing pin as a loading indicator. Most of the war models had no indicator pins."

"It's not recent, then."

"No, Inspector. The manufacturer's stamping tells us that."

"Could you trace it back?"

"What are you looking for?"

"I don't know," César admitted. "Just a hunch it might've belonged to someone special."

"Nazi?"

"Could be."

"I'll tell you one thing. It wasn't Hitler's suicide gun; that was another model—and 7.65mm. Besides, it's documented in a dozen different locations."

"There's always Hermann Göring."

"Göring liked Smith and Wesson."

"How about Himmler?"

"SS Himmler?" Baudrin frowned. "He owned a presentation model PPK—this isn't it—but generally he hated guns."

César looked at Bock's thirty-six-year-old pistol. How many men had it killed? "See what you can do?"

* * *

The informant waited in the café, his hand wrapped around a glass of red. It didn't pay to look too drunk in front of the *flics,* and he'd already had three with his own money. Let the next be on the inspector, a man who liked a few drinks or even a few more. They'd never gone out together, mind you, but he could tell a drinker when he saw one. And a Jew too! He wouldn't think they went for the grape. Wasn't wine strictly Catholic? He took another sip and watched the streets, his livelihood. Choupon was paid for what he knew, and he knew enough to know his own limitations. He was small and ugly and had a clubfoot. Only his eyes were big; he could see a coin around the corner or a Jew inspector in the dark, like the one now crossing the street.

César sat down and pulled out a photograph.

"Looks like a thief," Choupon said.

"Was." César wrote Nadal's name on the back.

"Thievery often leads to violence like spitting on the street."

César wondered how many wines had passed those violent lips. "Nadal had an accomplice on his last job," he told Choupon. "I need to find that one."

"Where will you start?"

"With the dead." César handed over the photo. "Somebody must've seen him with a tall thin man who moves very fast."

"Tall, thin, quick," Choupon mused. "Not much to go on."

"He also handles explosives."

"That's better."

* * *

In his office again, César turned to Clément's report on his desk. The detective had followed Bock's trail to Nice and Lyon, where he stayed at the Alexandra near the railroad station. In Nice it was the Dorard, two blocks from the train. Room clerks recalled Bock from the blowup, or thought they did. (Strangers often saw small differences, César knew from experience, that acquaintances missed.)

Bock had spent two nights in each town, arriving the day before the killing and leaving the morning after. Receipts showed that on his first day in Lyon he visited the motorcar museum housing Hitler's personal Mercedes, then dined in the main café district along Place Bellecour. The bill indicated that he had a dinner companion.

The second day saw more sight-seeing and dining. A restaurateur thought he recognized Bock as the man who insisted on a receipt with the time noted, an unusual request. It was 9:50 P.M. The Belgian industrialist was shot three blocks away at 10:25.

In Nice the Nazi spent his time differently, going into Monaco the first day to play the tables at Monte Carlo. Afterwards he dined across the square in the famed Hôtel de Paris. Back in Nice he stopped in the casino on the Promenade where he seemed to have won; he tipped the night clerk a hundred francs for his room key. He was not alone. Was the clerk sure it was the first night? Didn't matter, he had a woman both nights. What kind of woman? What other kind were there for that?

The next day Bock walked around town; there were receipts from cafés and shops. The purchases were inexpensive: socks, soap, sunglasses, and miles of bandage. Enough to cover a convenient arm sling, as César now knew.

The only museum Bock apparently visited in Nice was the Masséna's collection of weapons; he had asked the hotel clerk for directions. Dinner was in the Negresco; the receipt did not show the time but a check of the number revealed it to have been between 8 and 10 P.M. The Swiss banker had been shot in his nearby hotel room at about the same time, though the body wasn't discovered until morning. By then Bock was gone with the wind, or at least the train, leaving no tracks. Except, of course, for a mountain of paper that included even railroad tickets coming and going.

To César that was imcomprehensible. In all his years of police work he'd never heard of such a thing. Professional killers didn't leave records. Yet Bock went out of his way to detail both missions— and then kept the evidence for six months! As if he had wanted to be caught, or at least intended his deeds to become known someday. Careful planning? Of what?

César went back over the report. Clément had covered everything, almost everything. One point was overlooked, now vital. Not his fault, really. How could he know it wasn't Dieter Bock he held in his hand?

The door opened and a face peered around the edge. Clément, sandy hair neatly combed, eyes too far apart in a soft face that showed no lines. "Busy?"

A favorite linguistic device combining curiosity, hope, impatience and challenge, that required instant denial or bad manners. Clément used it often.

"Just calling you." César replaced the receiver.

"The woman, naturally; you've read my report. Had I known about Bock I would've included all of it."

Clément Noyes was a seven-year man, four of them with César. His prickly defense postures annoyed, but César found him efficient if a bit strange. Every few months he found himself a new girl friend.

"You must understand I thought she was lying; it comes natural to them when the police are involved. Or at least exaggerating."

A year earlier Clément had fallen in love with a baker's wife. When her husband discovered them together two months later, he complained to César who gently reminded the detective that he was overdue anyway.

"You talked to one of them?"

"She was with him the first night. Claims to be twenty-five but adding five years would be more like it"—Clément had all the animosity of the rural French peasantry, from whence he came, for women of easy virtue—"and not at all attractive. Not to me, anyway. Or too bright either, like most of them. The others were impossible to find, though God knows I tried." His eyes went wide with earnest endeavor; the bushy brows gave the face a startled look. "Had I known how important—"

"What did she say?" César interrupted.

"Naturally I let her talk first. According to her account, Bock was demanding and quite impatient. When I finally protested she haughtily claimed to have been with over a thousand men, simply to show her qualifications, including the mayor, the chief of police and the entire magistrates bench. She insisted Bock was as good as any of them, and better than most police and politicians who talked the whole time. I merely repeat what she said."

"No injury?" César's voice rang with triumph. "No impotence?"

"Nothing."

It was not proof and it wasn't evidence and a competent commander could blow it away in a minute, but it did César's heart good. The first sign that he wasn't running wild.

"She was certain it was the man in the photograph?"

"My first thought. I hammered away at her until she described him in detail, right down to the shoulder scar that could've come from a bullet. She's sure it was the man I showed her."

"But that man is not Dieter Bock."

"Neither is the dead man who has no shoulder scar."

So it was Bock, as César knew it would be. It had to be. "Why do you trust this woman's identification?"

"Precisely because she was so positive about the picture. She told me the truth so I would think she was lying." Clément smiled his best smile of man's work well done. "Women like that, you see, they can't really be trusted."

* * *

The body was cold as ice.

"See for yourself," René said.

He pulled the plastic sheet farther back, down to the thighs, and carefully folded it over the knees. With an exaggerated motion he lifted the penis. The smooth skin glistened like marble.

César looked, nodded in satisfaction.

The pathologist deftly pushed the penis back into place next to the shredded testicles. Against the white thighs, the tiny dark spots on the vein suddenly stood out. César knew what they were: carbon deposits left by flame-sterilized needles. This Bock had tried to inject himself into sexual potency. René claimed it hadn't worked.

"So he was circumcised. What made you think of that?"

"A party the other night," César said. "Someone mentioned Rudolph Schwarzkogler."

"Do I know him?"

"You should. He cut it off inch by inch."

Walking away, César felt ecstatic. Right was right and he'd been right all along, by God and de Gaulle himself he was right. In Nice, according to someone who'd been in a position to know, Dieter Bock had not been circumcised.

* * *

Parisians hid their gold in safe-deposit boxes at neighborhood banks, a cozy convenience of civilization, but the nation stored its reserves in steel and concrete cellars sixty feet beneath the floor of the Banque de France next to the Palais Royal. An aide led César through a maze of quiet cubicles that exuded fiscal dignity. What to do Nicole? She wanted to see him again; they had shared a bed, a moment of passion. It was pleasant and pleasing and she obviously wanted more and so did he. Was there more? He couldn't shake his feeling of guilt, or at least shame. Maybe it was too soon. Other unfamiliar things were happening as well. A dead thief and a missing accomplice were somehow connected to Bock. The Nazi was still alive and seemingly important to Kayser. Against all odds, with his will fusing the pieces, the puzzle was taking on form.

At the end of the corridor César was ushered into a gloomy room of black walls and brown carpeting and ebony furniture, the biggest of which, a huge desk set in the farthest corner from the door, held the Deputy for Illegal Outflow, a giant of a man, balding, his face unmarked, the clothes funereal, the body bent over an infrared lamp, peering intently at something held between his beefy hands.

"Sit down." The deputy nodded absently to his startled visitor who was straining to see the room's outline—a rectangle free of shadow save near the lamp's eerie glow—and to find a chair.

The giant, delicately pale-eyed, his lids almost transparent, finally turned off the machine and favored the inspector with a smile.

"Light sensitivity?" César asked.

"Not so rare." His words boomed, claps of thunder in the bowels of the earth. "I just happen to have a bad case. Of course, it helps that I'm color-blind too."

César indicated the infrared lamp. They were often used to alleviate muscle injury. "Help any?"

"Only on the job," the government official laughed. "Infrared's good for reading letters in sealed envelopes, if they're typed on a carbon ribbon or written with iron-base ink." He shifted back in the oversize chair. "Sometimes we borrow a letter from people we're watching to see what they're up to. Your department probably does the same."

César decided not to mention that such a thing was illegal for the police. Government agencies were allowed anything, naturally. At least anything they could get away with.

"You said you wanted to know about smuggling money into Switzerland." The radiant smile again. "That could take months."

"I'd settle for the Swiss I asked you to look up."

"Dangerous, that one," the deputy roared, reaching for the file on his desk.

* * *

César opened the black folder at a nearby table and snapped on the shaded light.

Crimes of violence generated publicity but crimes of currency caused the government even more concern. Entire agencies existed just to curb money manipulation. Counterfeiting was punishable by life imprisonment; each bill carried a solemn threat of *réclusion criminelle à perpétuité.* Money smuggling was fought with draconian measures and even foreign bankers were arrested for violating currency regulations. Not everyone who smuggled money out of the country could be caught, obviously, so the emphasis was on those who did it for a living.

The inspector was impressed by Kayser's industry. He'd not only smuggled money into Switzerland by train, plane and car—but East Germans into Western Europe. No details were included for how this was done, though reference was made to the East German secret police. The Swiss had apparently bought some powerful connections before giving up that activity a decade ago. Moving money seemed to be much easier and safer.

Kayser's file listed some of his acquaintances in Paris, presumably businessmen for whom he'd transferred funds. Dieter Bock's name was not among them. César scanned the list, stopping at one he recognized. But Tobie Maton was no businessman. Or was he?

"Why'd you call Kayser dangerous?" César asked.

"In the days when he was handling people," the deputy said with a shrug, "some of his clients were found dead. Or worse."

"Worse?"

"Some were never found at all."

* * *

The initial report of the robbery investigation filled César with misgivings. There were a dozen men questioned, most of them from the criminal class, all friends of Nadal, but his accomplice was not among them. And Robbery had no record of their operation. Could he have teamed up with someone new?

"It looks like the other man was a pickup, maybe only for the one job," César told Menard. "Or maybe they just started working together, which doesn't help us any."

"I thought Robbery's got that."

"Doesn't mean we can't give them an assist, unofficially of course. Especially if it's connected to the Bock case."

"Is it?"

"They singled me out, didn't they?"

"Because you're a cop."

"Suppose that was just a ploy?" César frowned in thought. "Bock could've paid them to stage a robbery merely to get at me. That way it wouldn't tie into anything I was working on."

"How'd Bock learn you're after him?" Menard asked.

"I don't know," César said darkly.

"And what would it change? So someone else would go after him. Besides, Nadal's no killer."

"It could have been the other one, with him along to make the robbery look professional."

Menard's face wore a skeptical smile.

"Anyway, our man's into blasting," César announced, "which usually means mining or construction. There's not much mining around Paris so we'll check the construction companies and wreckers."

"Why blasting?" Menard was intrigued. "Where'd that come from?"

"The Marquis de Sade," said César.

"De Sade?"

"According to his friends, Nadal liked to stick firecrackers into people's bodies and light them. For a sadist like that, who better to team up with than a real dynamiter?" César pulled the phone book out of the bottom desk drawer. "Besides, his hands were callused and his clothing smelled of cordite. Cordite's a nitroglycerin powder for explosives, and the only work today that could make those hands is mining or construction."

"What about farming?" asked Menard, who had left the Loire for the big city. "He'd get callused hands there all right."

"Except he's no farmer."

"Farmers use dynamite," Menard persisted, "to clear the land."

"So does construction."

"Sounds more like demolition to me."

"Then check the demolition yards too"—César pushed the phone book across the desk—"while I go see a magician about Bock's disappearing act."

* * *

What good were clothes to the dead? In the morgue all lay naked finally, their bodies pushed, pulled, probed and plundered. There ultimate secrets were revealed, mysteries resolved, the past reviewed. Infrared spectrometry for this one, a radioimmune assay for that, or crossover electrophoresis or neuron activation analysis, all done on the bodies themselves, freed from false dressings of dignity which now belonged to others, garments to be worn again, to be sold or discarded or even sent to the Paris Musée de Technologie's Department of Fabric to be screened, catalogued and collected, perhaps even displayed.

Some of its research was criminal, a working liaison with police. A victim's jacket might need a history or a thread an origin, a button a manufacturer. In the department's listings were swatches of every fabric, countless clasps and zippers, endless garments; from them virtually any fiber could be identified, analyzed, traced. Founding curator Auguste Gauchet and his staff worked with the Leitz comparison microscope and miles of files. In regional cloth classification, his specialty, Gauchet was the final authority and so it was to him that César came bearing gifts.

"Bock's clothing." He put the packets on the desk. "The big one has everything from the closet. The other, more important, from the body."

As the curator reached for the smaller parcel, César roamed the room with his eyes. Nothing had changed. Display cases held history under glass: a sleeve from Napoleon's tunic, a brocaded shirt of Dumas *père,* several men's stockings from the court of the Sun King, a ball gown worn by Marie-Antoinette. Smaller artifacts dotted the walls nearer the windows, where a hardwood table groaned under animal hides. They, too, were fabric of sorts. Was human skin still another fabric? César wondered. Ilse Koch had made lampshades from tattooed skin in Buchenwald.

"Clothes are much like tattooes in a way, don't you think?"
"Pardon?"

"What I mean is, they brand a man," Gauchet said. "Stamp him into a mold, just like the skin art. Men usually wear the same kind of clothes all their lives. Did you know that? Sometimes even the same color and shade. They find what matches their self-image and they stick to it. Think of all the organized suit types you've known, the independent jackets, the casual sweaters and sporty shirtsleeves and reactionary undershirts. Even nudists make a statement about themselves so the list is depressingly long."

"Where do we fit in?" César asked.

The curator snorted, his version of a laugh. "There's also the chameleon. A subspecies obviously, the chameleon wants to wear all coats. His self-image is cloudy, confused. He survives by blending with others, often absorbing their outlook, even forming bonds of empathy. The hunter, for example. Apparently a model of self-reliance, his actions are really adaptive of others. A classic case of out-ward direction. His whole life is circumscribed by what he pursues, and he's always fearful that what he pursues is really inside himself." Behind the glasses his pale eyes surveyed César and the garments of a nomadic Nazi. César was certain they held a clue. Bock had lived in them and killed in them. A hunter himself, he'd washed his clothes in blood and shaped them in his own image. Could the cura-tor outline that shape? "Some small luck. Your man wore natural fibers mostly. Synthetics are made by machine so they're internally structureless. Harder to compare. We also have a better chance at the history with wool or cotton."

A killer had once left many clues, including clothes and match-books with phone numbers scribbled inside. The curator patiently traced the clothing, which led César to the owners—all of them innocent. The killer, never caught, had carefully picked everything out of garbage to confuse the police. And teach César that nothing was obvious.

"White cotton," Gauchet continued, "the only safe thing to wear anymore. So universal it's practically untraceable, and almost worth-less as evidence. If all the terrorists in Paris wore white cotton, half the population would be snow-blind." He smiled at the thought. "And the other half probably dead. Is your man a terrorist?"

"Not in a strict political sense."

"But you say he was SS."

"That wasn't just politics," César grumbled. "They were a crimi-nal conspiracy."

The two chameleons sat in silence for a moment, César brooding over the man who got away, the Nazi, his life, the world. Somewhere he'd heard that the world would end in ten days; that wasn't enough time. Across the desk the curator studied him.

"You're an inspector now. Any future in it?"

"Not for me, no."

"Any past?"

César shifted uncomfortably in his chair. "I'm still working on it," he admitted finally.

"Dreyfus is a Jewish name." It was said softly, matter-of-factly, with a faint nodding of the head. Men understood these things, some men. What could be done in such a foolish world? Gauchet sighed.

"All the clothes seem distressingly commonplace, except for the trousers worn by the dead man. Any reason for this?"

César could think of none. He had assumed everything belonged to Bock, at least while he was dead. But with him alive, *if* he was alive, anything was possible. The other man was obviously dressed when he arrived so the trousers should be his, and the shirt and belt and socks and shoes. Unless Bock wanted them for some reason. What reason? Why would—

"We'll find out," Gauchet insisted. He dismissed César's fitful conjectures about the packets. "Possibilities don't impress me, only physical evidence. The evidence here, of course, may mean nothing."

"Bock left these things behind," César stressed, "and I'm hoping you can tell me why."

The curator closed the wrappings; a plastic hiss echoed through the layers of fabric.

"Maybe even who wore some of them."

"Am I a magician?"

"An alchemist, Monsieur *Conservateur*. You can turn thread into gold."

Gauchet smiled, shook his head. "There are no alchemists, Inspector. Only men who deal in fact."

"The fact is," César said, "I need to know what the Nazi is planning and you can help me."

"In what way? I can't show you the future."

"Then show me the past."

SIX

The news from Vienna was good and bad depending, like so many things, on how you looked at it. Two men named Kurt had died on January 10. One was a Kurt Lammel who died of natural causes; he'd been a butcher and served in the *Wehrmacht* during the war. The other was Kurt Linge, a local lawyer who'd built a successful practice. He had also once been an administrative aide to SS General Ernst Kaltenbrunner.

"That's our man." César matched the photo from Vienna with the group shot. Linge was on the other end. "The SS connection to Dieter Bock."

The bad news was that his death had been an accident. Subject to dizzy spells, he'd fallen from his sixth-floor office window. César was hoping for something more dramatic; even a suicide would've helped. An accident was so neutral, so *accidental*. Still—

"Get all the details you can," he told Clément, "and some background on *Herr* Linge of the SS."

Zurich was next. Louis Girard had worked for the Swiss Credit Bank, mostly on foreign accounts. Just before the murder he'd requested a week off, claiming family difficulties; something to do with property in France. Two days later he turned up dead in Nice. His widow knew nothing of any property. The bank did the usual audit and came out short a half-million francs from one of his biggest accounts. Menard wasn't given the name of the account; Swiss banking laws made that impossible.

"Not impossible," César corrected, "just difficult." They would come up with a way.

On to Brussels. Raymond Broussard had worked with small companies that made electronic instrumentation, part of the new high-technology wave. He acted as a middleman, finding venture capital for plant expansion. His visit to Lyon was to have been for one night, a look at a suburban site for a possible deal. He never made it. The body was found next to a rented car in the hotel garage. His wallet and watch were missing, the pockets turned inside out, so police assumed robbery. Not unusual for Lyon, said Menard, or any big city for that matter. A damn good maneuver on the killer's part.

"The fine hand of the Nazi," César declared, catching the rising admiration in his voice and hating himself for it. Yet the man was good; he would not make many mistakes. Had he made any?

"Something wrong here." César reached for the report on his desk. "How'd Bock know where to find Broussard?"

"He followed him," Clément said.

"All the way from Brussels?"

"He's a professional."

"But not a sorcerer."

"The arrivals!" Menard cried.

César scanned the report from Lyon. "Bock arrived the day before the murder and left the day after. So," he turned to Nice, "he could not have followed Broussard who only got to Lyon the afternoon of his death. And you"—to Clément—"say the same for Nice. Registered," he found the place, "on the third and left on the fifth." César looked up. "Again the day before to the day after. But Girard had already been there for a day by then." A frown. "Conclusion?"

"He already knew," Menard declared. "But who tipped him off?"

"When we know that," César said, tossing the report back on the desk, "we'll know who hired him."

The rest was routine. Menard, tracking the group photo, had wired blowups and the dead man's fingerprints to the Landeskriminalamt, the German version of the American FBI, in Bonn. He'd already received a negative reply. The Bonn government itself kept no centralized record of former SS officers; each state used its own prosecutor's office for such matters. Physical descriptions of the men were telexed to the West German Central Identification Registry in Wiesbaden on the chance that one or more might be missing. Again, the response was negative. Interpol Paris also came up empty on the dead man, which meant he had no international criminal record. Finally, the Munich prosecutor's office, answering César's request, had no one on their SS lists named Gerd who could've worked in the legal area or in Ordnance. Another dead end.

Menard had also started on the latest known victims, Léon Theoule in Marseille and Emeri Prévert in Vichy. The only link so far was a 9mm bullet in the forehead. "The bastard must really like his work. Or else he's crazy."

César didn't think so. "More cold than crazy. To him people are just targets."

"But why only in France?"

Both men suddenly saw the possibility. Bock was a German who could have—

"Jesus!"

"Maybe not only in France."

* * *

The fingerprinter thought it might work.

"They've used it on forty-year-old postcards," he told César. "How old's your letter?"

Earlier César had sent Hugues back to Bock's flat for his prints. He'd lived there a year so he must've touched everything. With him dead, they weren't needed; the corpse's identity was known. Now that he was alive . . .

All it took was a lot of prints; the most prevalent would surely be Bock's. Could it be done? No problem, he was assured.

"The problem," Hugues explained later, "is too many prints. They're everywhere, except on the door and pipe where I already checked. Must be thousands of them."

Even Hugues was impressed. There were ways to do it, of course. But on such a grand scale?

The theory was simple enough. If you had too many prints to remove, get rid of them in reverse. Flood the area with prints, so many that clear single pickups were impossible. All you needed were two-inch strips of double-sided transparent tape and an ink pad.

After a party collect the prints from glasses and other hard surfaces by applying the adhesive tape to the object, then peel off the tape and wrap the strips around your fingertips, using the other side to hold them secure. Press your fingertips into the ink pad and touch things. Each change of strips should be good for at least a dozen sets, all of them smudged and a horror to technicians but prints nonetheless. That was the theory. In practice, as Hugues pointed out, Bock must've worked like the devil to flood his flat.

"The guy's good, one of the best I've ever seen. Who the hell is he?"

"One of the best," César repeated grimly, his mind elsewhere. If the public only knew half of what he'd learned in Homicide—the silent ways to kill, the undetectable poisons and untraceable weapons, the endless methods of concealment and infinite variety of disappearances, the countless number of natural deaths that were really murder—thank God retired detectives didn't write books!

"How old?"

César blinked, his mind focusing. There was one more way to get prints, a long shot.

"I'll know when I see the handwriting analysis."

"Hitler?"

"Himmler."

"It's worth a try," the fingerprinter urged.

* * *

After a dance session filled with whirling pirouettes, Nicole shared a late lunch with her best friend Cécile, the two of them feasting on tales of romance between nibbles of *salade russe* and Perrier. Soon they had extinguished old flames of the heart and were trading superlatives on the new. Cécile, married to a famous chef, was still seeing Tobie.

"A smooth talker," she insisted, "who swept me off my feet."

"And right into bed, no doubt." Nicole sighed. "The men, they have their way with us."

"More than once too," Cécile bragged. "Usually."

Both women laughed. The sun was shining, the salad superb. Life was good.

"César is also an inspector, you know." Nicole dipped into her *glace*. "But very gentle."

"Just like mine," Cécile reported. "He has seen a lot, that one." She smiled knowingly. "But he hides it well."

"My own inspector!" Nicole had often seen herself in the arms of the law: such strength and authority. And those stern blue uniforms all tightly buttoned. "Does yours wear a uniform?"

"Only in bed," Cécile prompted.

Nicole's eyes widened in fantasy, the blue-buttoned policeman hard against her soft white body.

"What's it like?"

"Pleasant," said Cécile who was two years older and had few fantasies left. "You should try it sometime."

Nicole had already called César once, didn't want to scare him off. Men were so fragile in some ways.

* * *

Junot arrived at the general's office in a sweat, as always. The general was a man of wide eminence and responsibility who governed all elements of the SCE, from information to termination. Intelligence probes vied for his approval, field operations required his consent. As chairman of the five-member staff commission—the infamous Colonels Committee from the Ministry of Defense—the general issued policy directives, planned agency strategy and, day to day, guided the covert activities of the seven sectors under his command.

On this Monday afternoon General Bordier was not amused. His desk was piled high with papers, a breach of order and discipline. Worse still was the incessant chatter of the telephone, a diabolical tool designed to subvert his sanity. He would take no more calls; nor would he allow himself the luxury of further anger. He was as always in complete control.

"Dieter Bock!" he roared from the shuttered window overlooking the garden.

Junot remained rooted to the spot, a point equidistant between the steel desk and the soundproofed door. Under his feet aluminized heat sensors felt his presence, the approximate height and bulk and even direction of his stance. Overhead the movement-activated TV cameras whirred incessantly, their globular eyes attached to retinas that recorded his image in linear microdots. The room itself was cavernous, a full twenty meters in length; toward its far end a bronze conference table seemed swept in shadow. At the windows gray bulletproof drapes ran on rails. A desk monitor continually scanned all approaches, while beyond the entranceway a magnetometer arch was supervised by armed patrols. Automatic locking devices controlled the door itself, a sheet of solid steel. There was very little wood in the room and even less warmth, though the general's smile was said to have turned rabbits into roses.

"The man was yours." Bordier wheeled round from the window and speared his prey.

The Mideast sector chief blinked nervously, his mind grappling with the meaning of his presence. Dieter Bock had killed one of his agents, Bock himself was now dead, the Service should investigate. A simple problem and an equally simple solution. So why had his appointment been moved up an hour?

"You should have watched him more closely; half your group is ex-Nazi or collaborator anyway. Instead, I am summoned to a morning report by the ministry—bad enough—and then made to stand the fool for those pigs in counterintelligence. They seem to know more about our business than we do."

"Does the general refer to the Bock case?"

"Obviously."

"Surely we must do something."

"We will do nothing." Bordier's eyes rested on his subordinate. "You will do nothing. There will be no further contact with the police. None. Is that clear?"

Junot nodded dumbly; it wasn't what he'd expected, not at all.

"More than simple jurisdiction is involved here," Bordier said, taking an expansive breath, "though luckily the police clearly have that." His smile flashed. "As you know, my dear Junot, your man Broussard worked for the Gestapo in Lyon for a time. Do you happen to remember who was head of the Gestapo there?"

"Of course. Klaus Barbie."

"The Butcher of Lyon, who now lives in Bolivia. Since this year is the thirtieth anniversary of the war's end, the government is feeling heavy pressure to get him back, pressure brought by the international Jews and—what shall I say?—certain liberalistic French elements. I am told negotiations are already under way. If they should succeed . . ."

Junot began to understand. "We wouldn't want it known that the Service employed one of Barbie's people."

"Such publicity," said Bordier, straightening a sheaf of papers, "would be dangerous to us. And to French prestige abroad. I'm sure you agree."

"But will the police fare any better from our point of view?"

Bordier sighed; his hands instinctively sought another pile. "To them it's a murder case so they're interested in the murderer, not his victims. They know it was Bock who killed those men, they have the evidence. Now they will try to find who killed him. That need not concern us. The Bock episode is over."

So were Junot's ten minutes. Relief flooded his mind as he quickly counted his gains. He'd anticipated strong censure for not knowing about Bock's part in the agent's death. Instead, he experienced only mild reproach and, even better, he was free of the odious Jew and his cheap detective tricks. There was some justice in a Christian world, after all.

"Following your orders," he began, "I will forcefully—"

"Forcefully?" Bordier looked up, his eyes hooded.

"Quietly break contact with the police," Junot responded after a moment's hesitation.

"That might be advisable," his superior hinted, the hood closing.

Junot made his customary obsequious retreat from the room and was turning toward the door when the general called after him, the lips curled cruelly and the soft voice full of scorn. "The Nazi did us a favor with Broussard, according to counterintelligence. You, of course, didn't know he was a double agent, did you?"

* * *

The prisons of Paris, like its sewers, were often buried in the very bowels of the earth; to César none seemed buried deeper than the cells of the Central Police Station in the basement of the Law Courts. The ancient stone steps beneath the modern facade slowly led the brooding inspector downward to the Seine. What was happening to him? All weekend he'd thought of Jacqueline Volette, her smile, the smell of her hair. A woman he had talked to only once! It was preposterous. Even in bed with another woman he'd been thinking of her, a thing he never did with his own wife. Obviously a case of nerves; Bock was out there and he was in here. Something had to be done.

On the second level César turned left into the corridor, past the airless offices, little cubicles of damp congestion, and continued across the front of the detention pens, the Seine slapping against the walls of his ears. Another twenty meters took him to the cell he sought. Inside, the Burgundian stood at the rear, a small man swearing softly, the punctured words bursting into measured rhythm.

"Lecoeur!"

The puncture sealed, its cadence broken. A head turned in surprise, eyes watching César enter the cell, walk forward, the step describing the man, the drawn face speaking loudly of grim determinations. Now Lecoeur, flecks of fear stabbing at his eyes, backed onto the cot and screwed himself down.

Bock would need a new passport and identity card in a new name for his new life; only a handful of expert forgers were known to be readily available. César began with Lecoeur because of his strong Fascist views as recorded in his file. He was also one of the few independents left; most were part of the Corsican underworld that controlled the forgery business in France. César didn't think the Nazi would go to them.

"Tell me about Bock," he growled.

"Another name?" The voice was sullen, worried.

"A man came to you for German credentials in the past few months."

"Why me? I'm retired."

"You're not retired enough."

A defiant shrug. "A man must live."

César nodded, sure of himself. "I want to know about Bock."

Lecoeur looked blank.

"You'll tell me sooner or later." César leaned over the cot, his face inches from the frightened eyes. "You know you will."

"I have friends."

"You have me." César reached down and pressed the piano wire against Lecoeur's neck, the thin wire of slow death, and tightened the ends so he would understand. "And I'll let you rot in here."

In the fetid cells beneath the Palais de Justice, where they put the petty criminals and prostitutes of Paris, the regimented routine of life went on. The inspector waited patiently, a man used to waiting, as the soft swearing continued into early evening.

* * *

No professional forger could be without cameras and paper stocks and forging instruments from metal pens to mechanical seals. In the Burgundian's secret greenhouse studio, César's men also found a small printing press, tintype watermarks, a variety of blank documentation forms and an assortment of facial props and cosmetics, along with a complete developing room. Besides issuing false passports and identity cards for most European countries, which required them of all citizens, the forger had apparently branched out to credit cards; plastic materials, embossing machines and hand-held molders were found as well.

Did Lecoeur want any of it back?

By then the forger was ready with his version of the truth. He didn't recognize the name but the photograph César showed him of Bock was similar to one he'd been given a month earlier to use in making German papers. Not the same man, mind you, but bearing a very close resemblance.

Had he made any extra prints?

Such a thing was unthinkable. A matter of honor, as the inspector must surely realize.

And the name to appear on the documents?

Otto Wirth.

At César's prompting, Lecoeur described his client. It was not Dieter Bock.

Did he remember anything else about the man?

Not really—except for the phone number.

He left a number?

To call when it was ready.

César hoped he hadn't heard wrong. Did Lecoeur say he remembered the number?

Mais oui. Numbers were part of his business. He could recall a dozen digits three months later. It was a thing with him.

César studied the little forger, who suddenly felt his honesty was being called into question.

"It was 278-20-40 extension 116. There! Go see for yourself. Félix Lecoeur does not make the mistakes."

Neither did César, who paid his bills on time, chewed his food carefully, and kept a list of special numbers in his desk drawer. He matched the new number to the list, his heart pounding.

His heart stopped.

278-20-40 was a central switchboard that routed all incoming calls to the proper personnel. The central switchboard belonged to an arm of the French government, an arm with an iron fist.

César saw it flexed.

The Service de Contre-Espionnage.

* * *

It was almost midnight when he turned into the Rue de Meaux and home. The vein with the weak wall behind his right kneecap pulsated so loudly he could hear it. A weakness becoming weaker every year, a defect of birth and not his fault. Small comfort. He would die of it, that was certain. The elastic stocking barely held it in, those few times he wore it; nothing really helped. If the smallest piece broke free and sped up the bloodstream, he'd be dead in minutes. Was life worth all the fear and pain, the unfulfilled ambitions and daily disappointments? Mostly the disappointments. The boy in him had seen only the forest, his to explore. Eventually the man saw the jungle. The rattle of death was everywhere, and the blind lion soon served the angry ants.

César hated when he felt like this.

The street had slipped into silence. Morning came early to Rue de Meaux, a neighborhood far from the Champs-Elysées or even Pigalle, and dawn found tradesmen already on their way. Soon shutters were opened, sidewalks washed down: a neighborhood of shopkeepers, like France itself. César loved it. On warm summer evenings there would be hundreds walking the blocks or sitting in cafés with friends. People knew one another and César knew them all, at least by sight. He'd lived in the area for twelve years, first on nearby Rue Bouret, then on Meaux with his new wife. She'd shared his enthusiasm for the blocks, a reminder of her own childhood in Nantes. They would stop in the butcher's for a nice piece of meat, perhaps pinch the vegetables next door to see if they were fresh enough. The café on the corner, the park close by; years flew, or stood still. Suddenly it was all gone, *fini!* What would he do now? Catch criminals, live alone, feel guilt, harbor grief, drink wine, taste joy, smell fear, and no doubt die of a blood clot.

Past the middle of the block at the end of a row of white-faced brick, César's house sat in shadow like a medieval battlement. Reaching it, he silently pushed through the door and trudged wearily up the stairs to his flat on the third floor. Above him the carpenter's family slept fitfully while the tenant above them, a confused widow whose husband had recently died, slowly swallowed an accumulation of pills.

Inside, César snapped on the light and the television, turning the tuner to a dead channel. What he needed was the static of a blank screen, a kind of white water that washed away other sounds and left him numb. Since his wife's departure the static had become a close friend, a drug driving his fantasies and drowning out memory. Even a filter that freed his mind for work.

That was the best thing about the detective business: it gave you plenty to think about. You might not always discover the truth, but at least you started out knowing everyone was lying. In the beginning César had been bothered by this denial of reality, later learning it was only a denial of truth. Generally, people were very realistic in their reasons for lying. He'd simply confused truth with reality. *Eh bien.* He was young and innocent; it took Algeria to teach him, and fifteen years of watching people at their worst.

He sat on the sofa and stared at the angry screen, an empty glass at his side. It was a black-and-white set of little merit; color seemed a fad not worth the added cost. All his fantasies were in black and white, and all his dreams too. Was it because of the gray world he worked in? César wondered.

There was a lot to think about in that world.

He unlaced his shoes, stretched out on the sofa, the drone of white water slowly filling his ears, his eyes, his mind. After a while he thought he saw the face of God. Reaching out, his fingers touched Jacqueline Volette's breast. It was throbbing with life, the penis hard against his hand.

In the room the SCE silently took their pictures. He would deal with them later.

SEVEN

French justice was largely caught with its scales down during the German Occupation. Under the Vichy government the regular police routinely cooperated in the roundup of Jews, often working closely with auxiliary police troops like the notorious *Milice* or even German occupation forces, all of them preserving order by presuming guilt, intently flushing out supposed spies and saboteurs alongside hapless Jews who were herded into the hunger and exposure of concentration camps, giant hives buzzing with the steady drone of death, monstrous cellblocks and ghastly perimeters that led inexorably to the east.

When the end came some police groups rebelled, turning on the Nazis and their collaborators. In Paris the police struck back on August 19, 1944. In the bitter fighting at headquarters, scores of policemen were killed in the courtyard where emergency trucks and black detective cars usually parked.

"Only one"—Menard counted the cars—"two, three today."

César walked briskly across the courtyard, as he did most mornings, taking the long way into headquarters yet undeniably the right way to his office, a journey full of substance and shadow much like his work.

"Trouble ahead." Menard gauged the temper of the day by the

number of available cars, and less always meant more. "Must be a full moon out there."

"We'll know soon enough," César grumbled on the stairs. "Meanwhile let's push Vienna. His business associates, bank records, everything." He had awakened his assistant at 6:30 with the startling observation that both Bernadette Bock and Kurt Linge had fallen out of windows. Just coincidence? The inspector didn't believe in coincidence. Under the Napoleonic Code, any two similarities were guilty until proved innocent. Menard, thoroughly French, agreed and silently wished he had César's vision. His wife, who merely thought César paranoid, just wished he would disappear, or at least get married again. He had lately taken to phoning her husband at odd hours.

Clément, also awakened early, was already in the office surrounded by books. At César's command he was to become an instant expert on the SS, specifically those close to Himmler. His most trusted men had used piano wire to hang the leaders of the plot on Hitler's life. Was Bock there? He had to be there. "Find him," César told Clément who spoke German and liked mystery.

After that, he was to learn about Nazi art. He would visit dealers, talk to experts. Eighty percent of the European art market filtered through Paris; original oils of Hitler might be noted. A friend on *Le Monde* had given his detective the necessary introductions.

Which left the temporary André, for whom César had a very special job.

"And us?" Menard asked when Clément had gone.

"We work." César stretched at his desk; his day had actually begun at 3 A.M. with someone banging on his door. The widow on the top floor had left her own door open, most unusual. When the back tenants came home from a party they naturally investigated. *Mon Dieu!* She was dead. They ran for the inspector downstairs. César found her barely breathing, rushed her to the hospital. An obvious suicide attempt; doctors were hopeful. César was not; she had nothing to live for. He knew the feeling.

Sleep was gone, of course. Home again after five, he'd sat on the sofa mulling over the living and the dead. It was getting harder to tell the difference. More victims were being found, maybe even in Austria and Germany. He clearly had to go on. He was, after all, an inspector of Criminal Police. And an Alsatian Jew whose father claimed kinship with Captain Dreyfus, another Alsatian Jew drummed out of the French army and sent to Devil's Island. Was it all madness? César wondered. Just the hour, he'd told himself.

At 6:30 he had reached for the phone.

. . . and caught it now on the first ring. It was the supervisor of translators in the Ministry of Foreign Affairs in Bonn. Bernadette Vitry had worked there for two years.

"Started with us November '67 and left in January '70 to get married. A good worker in a sensitive area. Her fingerprints and photograph were on file at the time; not anymore, of course." A pause. "I'm sorry to hear of her death."

"Ever meet her husband?"

"Never had the pleasure."

César decided not to mention that Bock was a Nazi. He was talking to Germany.

"Any pictures of the wedding?"

None he recalled. It was in Cologne, a civil ceremony. At least she sent none, and German law didn't require fingerprinting for marriage. If there was nothing else . . .

"Danke."

They hadn't really expected to get anything from Bonn or even his second marriage. His first wife wasn't much help either; she'd thrown everything out when she remarried. Her photography business at least explained how Bock knew pictures. The rest of his specialized knowledge could've come from the SS and his Berlin Border days.

"Still no photo," Menard said in exasperation.

That didn't bother César; Bock resembled the man he'd hanged. What they needed were the Nazi's prints. The Cologne prosecutor's office didn't have them; they'd moved ten years earlier and things got lost. The German prison where Bock stayed didn't have them; a fire in 1960 destroyed most of the records. (Could Bock, by then a government agent, have set fires and got things lost?) And the original SS files were missing, presumably stolen by the Russians or Americans in 1945.

Which left only West German Intelligence.

César turned to his wall map of Western Europe. It stretched from Britain to West Berlin. Everything east of that was the heart of darkness.

"You'll be informed," Dupin had said. They were always saying things like that: You'll be informed. But don't hold your breath.

"The brass," Menard rasped, "they're just like lawyers. There was this undertaker who screwed all his female corpses? Necrophilia wasn't in the criminal code back then so we charged him with rape. Would you believe it? His smartass lawyer stood before the judge and argued that corpses weren't people anymore so they couldn't really be raped. The bastard got him off too." Menard still smoldered at the miscarriage of justice. "Later I heard he was handling more female bodies than anyone else in town."

"Don't tell Clément. It would just confirm his suspicions about women." Actually it was César himself who'd been having some misgivings lately. Of the country's 80,000 uniformed police, less than two hundred were women; of its 1,800 commanders, only sixteen. In Paris there were very few women in the Criminal Police, none in Homicide. Obviously unfair yet César didn't want it changed. Had he always felt that way? Or was he harsher since his wife left?

With Menard gone to pump Marseille and push Vienna, César called in André to prepare for Zurich. He was the brave new breed of detective, technically trained in any number of languages including FORTRAN and COBOL. "Follow the money," César repeated and wished him a good flight.

At the open window César looked down on the riot of colors overflowing the cast-iron stalls. It was good to be in Paris, and would be even better if things worked out. They wouldn't, of course, never did. He had to try anyway, keep trying. It was what he did best and so he loved it. Or had he already killed the thing he loved? Did he ever love her? He wasn't sure anymore. Weeks earlier he woke up screaming her name, holding her close to him, embracing her. When he turned on the light—she was gone.

Now it was the SCE he wanted. They held the key to Bock's present just as West Germany had the key to the past. If he could shake them enough, they might drop Bock's file in his lap.

Dupin had already reassigned the rest of his load except for Marie Pinay. So they were listening. Or were they just giving him enough rope?

* * *

You think it takes guts to stand up for what you believe is right? the SS leader asked César. That doesn't take guts. What takes real guts is to stand up for what you know is *wrong*. Day after day, year after year. *That* takes guts. Only the master race had it, he claimed. You're right, César said, and pulled out his pistol and shot the *Reichsführer* in the forehead. Bang! Trying to do what's right when everything goes wrong.

* * *

César saw his arm reach out to stop the ringing in his ears. A local *mec,* full of irritation.

"You wanted one of my girls?"

"A talk."

"It's tourist time, you know how busy that can get."

"Not too busy, I hope."

"Where?"

César named a time and place and was assured the prostitute would be there.

A dozen calls later he got the one he'd been waiting for. Over the years Julien Briand had detected many Hitlerian forgeries, from whole diaries (inconceivable since Hitler dictated everything) to individual letters of release from concentration camps (not a single one ever authenticated). By the 1970s the science of detection had progressed to fluorescence under ultraviolet light, to moisture meters and rudimentary electric grid microscopes. It was getting easier to find the fake.

The Himmler letter was real.

In his cluttered office on the Boulevard de Strasbourg, Briand ran enlarged copies of a genuine Himmler document and César's letter on a screen, told César to note the natural flow of writing in each, the inevitable slight variation of most characters, even those easiest to reproduce: the *e* and *o.* He viewed the spacing and the pressure exerted by the writer on each character, all of it not too carefully consistent. The grained paper, green ink and bold-tipped pen had also been examined, and matched the time and geography of the letter: Nazi Germany, 1945.

As for Himmler's handwriting, it was rigid, precise, controlled, a man fearful of mistakes and contemptuous of others, mean-spirited yet given to sudden bursts of largesse, respectful of authority while resenting it. In Briand's view, a classic paranoiac mired in anal regression who was meticulous in his personal habits and who hated his father and loved-feared his mother, clearly shown by the slight rounding of sharp points in some of his characters to resemble cartoon versions of women's breasts.

César fought down his queasy stomach. Himmler was dead and Bock still alive; his energies had to be directed toward the living, and the letter might help him get there.

Lunch was soup and a sandwich. If food had to be eaten, let the punishment be swift. Bread and meat disappeared together, soup flushed everything out. *Gott sei Dank!*

* * *

The meeting was brief and to the point. Not once did the director look at his antique clock.

Dupin saw it as a golden opportunity. The SCE had been at their backside for years and more recently at their throat. Something had to be done, unofficially of course. The Nazi might be the answer.

The director winced. He did not like declarative sentences.

"But can Dreyfus be trusted? We all know what he is—that is to say, how he is."

"Whatever else he may be," Dupin declared, "he's a good detective. If this Dieter Bock is alive, Dreyfus will find him."

"And the SCE? Will he cooperate in using whatever he finds against them?"

"He needn't know," Dupin emphasized. "His only concern is with the investigation itself. That's his revenge for his parents."

After glancing at the director, Dupin added: "We'll monitor everything he unearths, including any Service files. And, of course, if Dreyfus should fail after such an unprecedented maneuver . . ."

The director finally agreed. He would talk to the administrative chief.

* * *

César stared at the two files in the metal drawer. Bock's was growing daily, filling up with reports and technical data; more than half the drawer was already consumed.

The other file, thin as a pressed flower, needed only waiting. The label read Hôtel Rio for the squalid building on the city's south side where the murder occurred. Marie Pinay was no Jacqueline Volette, nor was there anything to command the attention of a Dieter Bock. Uneducated and lonely, the fortyish Marie spent her days in drink and her nights with anyone she could find. The list included most of the neighborhood men, several of whom were missing. Among them was a local eccentric who'd apparently gone fishing for salmon in the sewers of Paris. Since the Paris sewers ran for 1,800 kilometers, César had not sent anyone after the salmon catcher who was expected to surface soon. He could hardly wait.

Glancing at his watch, César dialed Nicole's home. She answered, breathless as always.

"I'd like to see you tonight," he said after the preliminaries.

"With your uniform," she giggled, "as you promised."

César reluctantly agreed.

"I can be there at nine."

"All right. About nine then."

"I'll be there."

"Inspector?"

"Mademoiselle?"

"The uniform. Don't forget."

He heard the giggle again as she hung up.

What was happening to him? César didn't know. He hadn't called a woman since before his marriage. Was it love? He couldn't be in love, it wasn't that kind of feeling. Not like what he'd felt for his wife, and even that was over. Was it over? Yes, no, he didn't know. But the hurt was leaving and something else was taking its place. It had felt good being with a woman again, the physical part. Was this what was left? All César knew for sure was that he had an erection.

* * *

In his office César returned to putting Bock together again. Most of the parts were still missing but at least a shape was beginning to appear, though one could not yet make out the devil. Bock had planned his move for a long time and had some important help. What that move was, and who helped him, were not clear but César's instincts told him more was involved than simple assassination.

Alors! Dieter Bock was alive and César hoped to make it official soon. Bock had used the nightclub girls as proof of his impotency, which meant he had his victim picked out at least a year. The girls never saw him undressed; for real sex he used a local prostitute but not too often, so there'd probably been someone steady in his life. The street girl had recognized him, maybe, from the photo of the *gendarmes,* told her *mec.* But something was different—César understood. Could she describe him? She could, right down to the scar on his shoulder. Voice? French with a German accent, same as the girl in Nice. It was Bock, back in business for a year while he built up credibility for his death. Why? César knew only that he had to keep the reins.

Alone in the room, he sat staring into space while his imagination battled the shadowy demons and hideous shapes. He listened to the screams, heard the maniacal laughter. Was that Bock's voice? His own?

An assassin goes back to work, in itself believable. But then, realistically, why would he suddenly stop? What purpose does his disappearance serve? How could that make him rich? Or put another way, what evidence was there for anything beyond a spy's game between security agencies? A political contest of deception and death, as Tobie had said. In which case, why was an inspector of police weaving an elaborate plot out of something that didn't concern him? To get back at the SCE, show them he hadn't forgotten? Or the department, prove they made a mistake in writing him off? Or the fact that he was a Jew, a late burst of ethnic pride in the face of a Nazi? He felt guilty on all counts.

Or suppose it was none of these? All there, to be sure, but suppose he had subconsciously decided to create, out of his loneliness and despair, a whole mythology of good and evil—much like Wagner's *Ring* operas—to flesh out his empty existence. Was he really so paranoid that he could invent a diabolical scheme going back thirty years by the force of his own will? An obsessive fantasy real only as long as he pursued it?

Then why wasn't the SCE pushing to take over the investigation?

* * *

When Tobie tapped on the door, César's face was still screwed into a quizzical frown. The noise pulled him back to earth and he quickly reached for some folders on his desk.

"Here's one you'll like," Tobie said, sitting down. "President Giscard d'Estaing and Premier Rabin meet over the strained relations between France and Israel and Giscard d'Estaing says, 'Suppose we start with something noncontroversial.' 'Like what?' Rabin asks suspiciously. 'Just some statistical data you might find interesting,' answers the French president. 'For example, did you know that among the two million Arabs living in France are several thousand trained pilots, even more tank and weapons experts, hundreds of military engineers and rocket crews, thousands of—' 'If you don't mind,' the premier says, 'could we go on to the controversial issues? I'm willing to promise . . .' "

"Sounds like me and Bock."

"Hear from Kayser?"

"He called before."

The robbery inspector's gaze took in the open filing case with the Bock material. "You and him going to work together?"

"In what way?"

"I don't know; something about a picture he's after that could lead you to Bock. Didn't he tell you?"

"Let's say it's possible"—César chose his words carefully—"that he didn't tell me everything. Besides, he's got nothing to trade."

"He saved your life, for chrissake."

"So you already told me."

Tobie laughed. "You're a cold bastard. How's Bock going, anyway?"

"Nothing yet. What about Nadal's partner?"

"Same thing. No one knows him."

"You think there's a connection?" César asked.

"With Bock?" Tobie's brow tightened.

"To get me out of the way."

"How would he even know about you? He'd need someone—" Tobie sucked in his breath, his eyes sudden pinholes of surprise.

"Someone here"—César finished the thought—"to keep him informed."

Tobie shook his head in disbelief. "You're nuts," he said.

"Am I?"

"But he's Swiss."

"They're three-quarters German."

"A private detective—"

"Who smuggled people out of East Germany," César said, "when Bock was working the other side. They could've met along the way."

"Kayser?"

"Why not?"

Nobody spoke for a moment. Then: "Why would he kill Nadal if he's working with Bock to get rid of you?"

"Maybe that was the plan—for him to kill Nadal to make it look good while the other shoots me. Only something went wrong."

"Like what?"

"How do I know?" César bristled. "Maybe Nadal's partner got scared, thought it was a double cross. Could be he didn't know about Kayser."

"Could be you're nuts too."

César was reaching and his face showed it. But the tight fist in his stomach told him the Swiss was involved in more than stolen art. How much more?

Tobie mistook César's uncertain expression. "This is nothing to kid about," he growled.

"Who's kidding?"

* * *

The Bonhomme Fils demolition yard was in the Thirteenth district at the bottom of Paris. Here for all to view were the remains of a changing world, from iron beams and wooden doors to marble mantels and stone floors. Every day hordes of people descended on the land to buy bathroom installations or complete facades of Renaissance châteaux, all secure in their visions of restoration.

César skirted a trove of oak timbers and followed a sandy-haired youngster into a low building, with Menard in the rear.

"The manager's waiting for you," said the guide.

They passed a nest of narrow offices that ended in a room of white walls and wide windows, a space incredibly cluttered with demolition debris. From his desk, the manager greeted them with transparent eyes.

"You're sure it was dynamite?" César began.

The manager nodded. "Been around the stuff most my life."

"Tall and thin, takes quick strides." César closed his eyes in reflection. "Moves his hands very fast."

"That's the one."

"Tell us what you can."

He'd been wary from the start, something about the man's looks.

Furtive, always gazing around. Short on patience, too. What he wanted was to sell some dynamite, a full box, actually; said he needed the money to leave town, a job somewhere. He didn't seem impressed that it was against the law. This was a demolition yard, wasn't it? Well then, wasn't dynamite used to demolish? The manager had carefully explained that they tried to salvage things, not blow them up; little dynamite was actually used. To which the man replied he had more than just the sticks.

"More?"

"Claimed he also had five hundred meters of detonating cord, a shithouse full of explosive primers and at least a hundred blasting caps." The manager grinned. "That's when he pulled out a few of the sticks from his pocket. Right away I saw he knew what he was doing. There's a certain way to handle the stuff, you see. You either know it or you don't."

Menard cleared his throat. "On the phone you said you questioned him about the dynamite."

"What little I could, you understand. I wasn't about to tangle with a shooter like that."

"Shooter?" It was a hiss.

"What do you mean—a shooter?" César asked.

"He told me he'd worked a mine up north, that he was a shooter in some mine up there. That's the guy who plants the charges, then shoots it. Some days they'd shoot a hundred shots on a shift." The manager's eyes grew luminous with excitement; dynamite and demolition were part of his life. "The shooter sets the charges in the mine wall and then runs a wire to the battery a safe distance away. Then he just hooks it up to the battery and blows. Bang!" A hand slammed the desk.

César glanced at Menard. It was what they'd suspected, what he had suspected. A dynamiter.

"Anything else?"

"Nothing I didn't say on the phone. When you called about dynamite, right away I thought of this guy."

"He didn't say he'd be back?" Menard asked.

"Didn't need to. I wasn't going to buy."

"Or where he was going next?"

The manager shook his head.

"Somewhere else he could sell it, maybe?"

"Not legitimately."

Then it's the criminals or terrorists, César thought. The underside of Parisian life, the side Choupon worked best.

"But you got a good look at him."

"Good enough."

* * *

Menard and his wife lived in a two-story frame house on the edge of Paris that bordered a stream in back and a street in front filled with animals and children looking much alike; three of them belonged to the Rimbauds, along with two dogs and a sleek cat who usually perched on a tree limb high above its enemies. The tree was at the rear of the tidy garden and sloped gently toward the stream. It was Menard's favorite spot and here he sat with César under the leafy branches, while the steaks sizzled on the nearby outdoor grill.

"Peace and privacy, that's what the country's all about," Menard said as he gazed at his neighbor in the next plot of land. "Peace and privacy."

César watched the neighbor carry a portable saw to the worktable rooted on his lawn; just what every suburbanite needed.

"I've tried to keep the place like I found it, nature's way." Menard poured more wine into their glasses. "Except for the garden."

"Best on the block." And tended solely by Menard's wife.

The two of them sat in lawn chairs, stripes of green-and-white plastic wrapped around aluminum tubing. César stretched his long legs on the grass, a country pose. Once a month he had dinner with the Rimbauds; Menard believed everyone needed fresh air, and in that sense his boss was deprived. Menard's wife believed César more depraved. Hadn't his wife left him? Didn't he dote on blood and death, spending all his hours on the job? Well, and what else was that but a ghoul of some sort? She prayed he wouldn't infect her husband.

The neighbor's electric saw suddenly whirred, a deafening noise louder than a jet at a hundred meters. Menard leaned forward, agitated.

"He's at it again."

"Man's way," said César, who liked noise. "Build and destroy."

The machine whirred on, slicing wood like salami. Menard closed his eyes in despair.

"Sounds like the Etoile at rush hour."

Menard glared at César. "Only happens when I'm out here," he muttered darkly.

"You could always arrest him." César rummaged his brain for an applicable law. Disturbing the peace? Splitting wood on Wednesday? Except this was Tuesday. "How about incitement to riot?"

Menard kicked at the grass under his feet. "It's not funny."

"More than you know."

"Not if you lived here."

God forbid! César told himself. He recalled La Fontaine's fabulist jingle about a *rat de ville* and a *rat de champ*, which neatly divided men as well: the city dwellers and those who lived in the country. Neither really understood the other, which didn't matter as long as each understood himself. César estimated a night in the country to be worth two in hell, and once a month was all he could handle. Where was the *electricity?* he murmured, dozing off to the whine of the saw.

* * *

Nicole led César into the living room filled with divans arranged in a radial fashion like the petals of a giant sunflower, with a clutch of cushions at its heart.

"My late husband," she cooed, "believed a reclining position was good for health as well as business. He was in funerals."

The room reminded César of an enormous mushroom sucking everything into its maw.

"We reclined as much as possible, of course, but he wasn't very good at it." Nicole stretched out lazily among the flowers, a nest of silkworms in her mouth. "Not good at all."

"Has your husband been dead long?"

"Divorced," Nicole said softly, a web of spiders in her eyes. "But that's the same as death for a man, don't you think?" She sounded hopeful.

César gave her a dark look and changed his mind. There was no malice in her, just lack of feeling. Many people were like that, most. Was he like that? Certainly not; he cared for people, a lot of them. Who?

"And your bedroom?" he asked irritably. So he was traditional, nothing wrong with that. Beds had heads and feet and sides you could get out of. What could you do in a Venus's-flytrap?

"I'll show you," Nicole said, the hiss of snakes in her voice.

With girlish glee she bounced off the divan and set out to find romance, or at least the bedroom. Roots sprang from her loins, branches leaped from her limbs. She began to feel moist.

"Fuck!" she shouted in spontaneous joy. No longer would she feel the dry death or smell the formaldehyde. "Fuck!"

"Love," suggested César, embarrassed. He didn't like the graphic descriptions that made sex seem so mechanical.

The fuck machine stopped. She had to remember to control her exuberance around men, who scared easily.

"Comment allez-vous?"

"Pas très résistante."

Moments later she burst into flames.

EIGHT

Nothing was worse than chaos in a world seeking order; some found it less frightening to believe in hostile conspirators than to face the possibility that no one was in control.

Assassination conspiracies were well-known to the Criminal Police who handled the endless reports of killings committed by sinister forces. Even more numerous were those who saw themselves as the instruments of destruction; murder, or the report of murder, drove them to the police. All had to be heard and investigated, at least acknowledged. Leads, they were called, or perhaps just cranks but who could tell? Not César as he listened politely to the businessman explain why he had to kill Dieter Bock.

"Too dangerous to live," he announced majestically. "Nazis come and go like flies on flesh but that one had secret powers. I tried to warn you, tell you what was coming but no one would listen to me. Statistically I was alone."

The businessman, whose data had revealed to him the existence of a gigantic conspiracy, worked as a government statistician. Espionage was his passion and he lived in a world of sodium morphate–induced heart attacks, methyl bromide poisonings and sulfuric acid disappearances. Through his conspiratorial lens he saw a world controlled by a small cabal, Nazis, aided by such diverse groups as the

French army, the Bulgarian secret police, the fashion industry and the World Wildlife Fund. Each day in his diary the statistician warned future readers of the danger and alerted them to the latest Nazi trickery. The PLO was a Nazi front, but so was the Israeli government; most French politicians were programmed through Nazi mind control. There was even a plan to vaporize all Parisians.

"Bock was working on the vaporizer, almost had it finished when I finally found him. He wouldn't be talked out of his mad scheme. The Parisians were devils and had to be destroyed, and after them came the Jews and Corsicans and then teen-age German girls. Statistically I had to kill him, don't you see?"

"And the vaporizer?"

"It disappeared before my eyes."

Vaporized, no doubt.

Other reluctant killers had gratefully confessed equally startling stories. Some were agents of foreign intrigue, a few worked for even darker powers. Only one did it on his own, a cripple who'd been seeking the Nazi on the streets of Paris for most of his life.

"And why not? Time means nothing when you thirst for vengeance. You take the south, the Italians, they'll wait forever to get their revenge. The Greeks too, and the Cretans. My mother was from Crete, you didn't know that. Well then, don't I have her blood? I've waited over thirty years to get the bastard who crippled me like this, seeing his face every day and dreaming of him at night. How'd it happen, you want to know. In the war, of course. Right here in Paris I was in the *Maquis,* doing a dangerous job when this Nazi captain came up and shot me in the spine. Just like that. But I swore I'd get him someday. Let's be honest. There's enough trouble in the world without more Nazis. Did you know they're recruiting midgets to sneak in under the radar when they attack Russia? You didn't know that, did you?"

* * *

By midmorning César was back on Bock's trail. According to West German police, who'd been sent the ballistics material through Interpol, nobody had been shot in that country with the Walther PPK in question. Which meant, as Menard saw it, that Bock confined his killing to France. So he probably worked for a French security agency. Good news.

Not necessarily, César protested. Only the gun was eliminated, not the man. Bock could've killed in other ways in other countries. In fact—

Vienna. Kurt Linge's body had landed on a car roof three meters from the side of the building. A very pronounced arc for a six-story fall.

"Ever hear of such an arc for that distance?"

Menard had not.

"Accident victims usually don't land more than their own height from where they started, even closer. Yet Linge arcs out to three meters before he hits the car. Why?"

"He was pushed."

"By someone he knew, someone who stood with him at the open window."

A murder made to look like an accident. Just like Bernadette Bock's body, which landed over two meters out. Or maybe even a murder made to look like a suicide that authorities happened to rule accidental.

"The killer couldn't control that," César said.

What killer?

Bock's suicide, Linge's accident. Who was next?

César thought he already knew.

In the police list of Linge's friends and associates, a Franz Straus was noted as having died on February 13 of an accidental gunshot wound in his home near Salzburg. Salzburg was not far from Linz, to which Bock had booked his escape flight. He didn't fly there but he could've gone another way from Munich. Was Austria more than just a blind? To César the western part seemed an extension of Bavaria which nurtured Nazism. In fact, the whole Nazi nightmare came out of that area; even Hitler was a Bavarian Austrian, born near the German border.

As for Straus, César had spoken with the Salzburg police who were sending the investigation report and a picture. No, they were not entirely pleased with the accident verdict and yes, there was some talk of suicide.

Meanwhile, did the homicide inspector know of the man's past?

He did not.

Then he might be interested in hearing who Straus was.

The homicide inspector had held his imagination.

Franz Straus was an alias for a Gestapo chief named Max Baur who'd fled Austria in 1945 to escape possible prosecution by the Allies. During the war Baur had been Gestapo boss in Linz.

César felt his imagination slipping away.

In the dark of the room now he hurled the dart at Bock's head. The next moment Menard threw the last dart and went back to work, leaving César with the information on Bock's newly discovered kills. Theoule was a brilliant metallurgical engineer who was also a bit of a satyr around Marseille. He paid heavily for his lifestyle. Where he got it was a mystery until the talk turned to industrial espionage. He was fired from his sensitive job but not arrested, not enough proof. Soon he was destitute, then he was dead. Prévert, the Vichy official, seemingly cared only about keeping his town the biggest spa in France. His father, however, had been a member of Marshal Pétain's government during the Occupation.

César scribbled two quick questions on the pages: Who was Theoule thought to be selling to? And was Prévert's father still alive? Trying to find a link, a connection—which was what criminal detection was all about.

* * *

The Minolta Montage was designed to turn eyewitness descriptions into arrests. César escorted the demolition yard's manager to the small office behind the line-up room and seated him in front of a large television screen. Waiting for them was an operator with thick glasses and nicotine-stained fingers.

"We're running a little late," the operator groused.

"Then let's begin."

César quickly explained to the witness what he'd be doing. "Building a face piece by piece, from pictures of different parts. Picking out what you recall."

"Where's the police artist?"

"Behind you." César indicated the television cameras at the room's rear. "They'll feed you photos and hold whatever ones you select."

"It works?"

"Better than any freehand sketch of a suspect," César assured him.

The system consisted of several small television cameras feeding into a single screen. By drawing from a collection of stock photographs spanning the range of facial characteristics—head shape and size, hair and features—the operator could vary selections in front of the cameras to produce an electronic composite on the screen.

Seated in the dark now next to the witness, César closed his eyes and toyed with the possibility that the composite image would turn out to be Bock himself. It was a hopeless projection, obviously. The suspect was taller, thinner, younger. He had no German accent, was surely French. Bock's son? Nephew? Protégé? Nothing seemed to fit, no leap was possible. Which left César only the probability that Bock had hired the shooter to get rid of him. But why a public killing? The man knew dynamite. Why not simply blow up his car? Because he had no car. Then the police car he used. No good; it changed. Then his front door, his mailbox, his refrigerator. Why not? César had no answer, except for Kayser; the Swiss was part of it. Wasn't he?

"Was he?"

"No, hatless."

"So you got a look at his ears," said the operator.

On the screen the montage was almost complete; only the lower chin and ears remained. Ten minutes later the face was finished and peering out at César. A wide low brow, the cheeks pinched, the nose angular. A northerner, he decided, possibly even a Walloon.

The lights came on.

"Satisfied?"

The witness shook his head. "That's him."

"I need prints." César turned to the operator. "Fast."

"Fascinating," said the manager.

"Even better when we get him."

"We already have him," the operator said in a bored voice.

"What?"

"This is the second time in a month he's been identified."

César wondered if he'd heard right.

"It's true. He raped a young girl in her home while robbing it. Tied up her parents, then took her into a bedroom where his mask came off. Guess he got a little excited," the operator said dryly. "Or maybe he figured she was so young she wouldn't be looking at his face at all. Anyway, she saw him good. Robbery's got the composite print upstairs somewhere."

Not only the print, as César quickly learned, but even his name:

Jean Leduc, wanted in Belgium for armed robbery. Born in southeastern section near the French border, a Walloon. The accompanying information also noted his work as a miner and his experience with explosives.

But why would Bock hire them to take him out? César wondered. Leduc hadn't killed the girl so he wasn't a murderer, and neither was Nadal.

Back in his office César took calls from André in Zurich, busily charting the Swiss banker's money trail through the computers and learning he'd been heavily in debt, and Clément in Versailles seeing a collector of Hitlerian art familiar with the painting allegedly sought by Kayser.

The last call before the noon hour was to Jacqueline Volette's office at the Sorbonne. César had things to tell and others to ask, none of which mattered except to him. He wanted to see her again. When? Now, hopefully. Sorry, he was told, she'd already left for lunch on the Eiffel Tower. The restaurant was on the second deck, 115 meters above the manicured lawn. Paying the eight francs, César rode up the hydraulic elevator with tons of tourists and felt himself strangely alone in the crush of bodies. On the observation platform he looked out over the hundred square kilometers of Paris; everywhere indolent air softened the stone spires. The restaurant itself seemed bathed in sunlight, a silken strand of hammered gold. Jacqueline was seated at a window table. Her eyes were bright with energy and she moved her hands in splendid animation. When she laughed her body arched like a bird in flight. César watched her raise her glass, fingers barely touching the stem, swirl the wine with a deft circulatory motion that revolved her wrists, pure poetry, steady the flow after a moment with tightened forearm, and slowly sip, eyes wide. She was Mnemosyne and all the mythic muses, the memory of mankind but mostly of the imagination. Lowering the glass she pressed her lips together appreciatively, and Peter Kayser returned the smile.

César, unnerved, surrendered his view, his dream in ashes. Fool, he told himself, blind stupid fool! He should have known better; romance was only for those still alive.

On the way down César saw his Paris in flames. Even the stones were smoldering.

* * *

He ignored the pigeons in the park, brooding over the nature of man and his inherent criminality. It was all in the genes, obviously. Limpid pools of building blocks lying there undetected, slowly shaping cells into little pickpockets and thieves and murderers. Detectives too. They were just the other side of the coin, seeing evil all the time, hearing it, becoming intimate with it, even comfortable. Namely, life was shit. You had to eat and sleep, both a waste of time. Then you evacuated what you ate and slept all over again. Incredible! If he wasn't already an agnostic, he'd find it hard to believe in a rational god. Evil, after all, was everywhere. Yet without evil he would be useless, impotent. Wasn't Bock merely his reflection? César was certain that someday his battle with Bock would be seen as a religious struggle between good and evil.

* * *

The director lunched with his administrative head, who had already spoken to the Minister of the Interior.

"You agree, then."

"Of course."

"If this Bock is alive, his Service file will be seen only by you and your division commander."

"And the inspector conducting the investigation. Dreyfus."

The administrator nodded gravely. "Unfortunately."

The waiter refilled their glasses from the silver bucket.

"An excellent vintage, this."

"The best private cellar in the city."

Both men sipped carefully.

"You know of course, if he should succeed—"

"Who?"

"Dreyfus."

"Ah."

"If he should succeed"—the director fidgeted in his seat—"it would mean a promotion, if only to buy his silence in the matter."

"That is one way," said the bulky man with bushy brows. "Yes. How's your *onglet,* by the way?"

"Very good, actually."

"Good, you say."

"Very good." The director dabbed at his plate. "What's another way?"

"*Pardon?*"

"You said that was one way." He looked up. "The Dreyfus affair."

"Oh, that." The administrator seemed distracted. "I merely meant promotion works only if the man's more interested in doing well than doing good." He finished off the final forkful, determined. "Perhaps I'll try the *onglet* next time."

"Do. It's excellent."

"Is it?" The administrator motioned for the menu. "Your man seems a bit radical, wouldn't you say?"

"Who's that?"

"This Dreyfus."

"Very." The director sighed. "Full recognition after all these years—" His voice trailed off.

"He's a long way from success."

"Let's hope."

Both men drained their glasses.

"Did I tell you I shot four finches over the weekend?"

"Did you? What weapon?"

"A Flobert, .18 caliber. Got each of them through the eyes into the base of the brain. Any dessert?"

* * *

Three-meter laser machines, eerie blue lights suspended in midair, rubber eye guards, heat lamps and cooling systems came into view as César entered the room. He'd come to the Interpol administrative office on the Boulevard Gouvion St-Cyr to witness a miracle. Space-age tools were going to give him fingerprints—had already lifted them—that hopefully belonged to SS Captain (Major?) Dieter Bock. The prints were on a letter written thirty years ago.

"Before this," said the technician, "we couldn't find anything more than ten years old. Now we're already up to forty."

Interpol's secretary general had agreed to put the Himmler letter under the laser, first in Paris, as a matter of practicality. The international police system depended on local enforcement agencies to flesh out its files; if Interpol Paris was the informational brain, and the other national bureaux the spine, then the police in the member countries were the nervous system that transmitted the data. César had fed Interpol many times and now he needed a morsel in return.

"Your letter has two different prints." The technician handed César the blowup of a thumb. "From the front, with a matching index finger on the back. That exerts the most pressure when you hold the paper." He pulled out another blowup. "This thumb's from the top of the letter."

"Old?"

"Definitely."

César shook his head in wonderment. "A miracle, as promised."

"And there's no contamination of evidence, as with chemicals or dusting powders."

The laser bathed the prints in blue light, picking out the amino acids from the body deposited by the fingers. Even rubber gloves were no longer protection since amino acids penetrated the gloves and became visible to the laser. Washing the hands didn't help, nor did soaking the gloves. Amino acids were forever.

There was only one way to beat the machine.

"Don't touch anything," said the Interpol expert, "ever again."

The homicide inspector was given a pair of eye shields and shown the laser in operation, a proud papa showing off his *Wunderkind*. It reminded César of a space movie he'd seen on television, cops and criminals amid electronic gadgetry. Fascinating and frightening, but he had to admit the results were spectacular.

As the blue light faded into the cooling system, César removed his eye guards. The room became earthbound again.

"Interesting document." The technician returned the Himmler letter. "I couldn't resist checking the prints with someone who has all the big Nazis. Hope you don't mind."

César studied him, unsmiling. "And?"

"The top thumb matches the writer."

Himmler, the SS superboss and second in terror to Hitler himself! The enormity of that terror suddenly hit César and the letter slipped out of his grasp. He was in the presence of great evil; it was palpable, he could feel it. A religious war, with justice only part of the spoils. There was also vengeance.

The technician caught the letter, laughed. "More prints," he said in mock dismay, "for the next generation."

César apologized, the shock of Himmler. That left the other

thumb and index finger. Were they Bock's? They looked like Bock's. César felt himself getting giddy; lack of sleep, no doubt. He placed the letter in the envelope with the blowups.

"Remember, Inspector. Touch nothing."

"I'll do my best," César promised, and left without shaking hands.

*　*　*

The Ottoman Empire was in the Odéon area north of the Boulevard St-Germain, a stretch of streets bearing the names of eighteenth-century French dramatists. The restaurant came divided into the east bank, ruled over by a regal blue Burmese called Racine, and the west bank under the paw of a haughty white Persian named Corneille. The door fortunately was in the middle and from it hungry patrons could make their *choix du jour,* secure that neither thespian would upstage the other during business hours.

César entered his favorite eatery and slumped down at a table in the east. Several west regulars greeted him despite the disapproving glare of *le chat blanc.*

"The *coq au vin,*" whispered the waiter.

César ignored Lelouch since all he ever ate was the onion soup *gratiné* but Lelouch usually persisted in naming the day's delights out of sheer perversity. He was the proprietor's brother-in-law. In his prime he'd worked the whole floor, a younger man in faster shoes, but eventually had settled in the east where he drove the regal Racine crazy by reciting neoclassical drama. The west was handled by the proprietor's sister-in-law, who also handled Lelouch since they were lovers for twenty years. Their mates accepted the odd arrangement, one facing east and the other west, for the sake of the restaurant. The proprietor, with four other brothers and sisters, accepted anything.

"Forget the soup," Lelouch said.

"In that case, bring me a bowl."

"The cheese was grated the wrong way." Lelouch rolled his eyes in despair. "Left to right."

"Then put it in from the other end."

"What other end? The bowl is round."

Cosme Lelouch of the trick memory, a sponge soaking up everything in its way like a great white whale sucking in water. When Lelouch pulled out names and dates, César saw a top hat and rabbits.

"Tell me about Linz under the Nazis."

"How about Minsk under the Cossacks?"

"Only Linz," César sighed, "in Upper Austria."

"Hitler's favorite city," Lelouch hissed. "A port on the Danube, mostly industrial. Hitler had plans to rebuild it with an opera house so he could listen to Wagner. Naturally he first built a concentration camp nearby."

"Any trouble for the Gestapo?"

"Less than other places. Austria wasn't exactly a conquered country, and Linz gave Hitler a hero's welcome when the Nazis marched in."

"So no reason for killing Gestapo now."

"Killing Gestapo?" Lelouch no longer flinched at César's abrupt questions, even fancied himself solving murders by proxy. "Sounds more like pest control. When does this take place?"

César shrugged it off. "Who'd want anything like that?"

"Almost anyone waking up after thirty years with homicidal views. Or take any tourist."

"Tourist, you say?"

"You've never been to Linz," Lelouch clucked. "Not much to do there."

"I'm impressed. You think it's tourists, then."

"Do cabbages sit with kings? But if you're asking, I'd say what you want is a late sleeper with a long fuse. Either that or someone with pronounced touristic tendencies, probably American."

César ate his soup in silence. Talking to Lelouch always gave him food for thought, and sometimes a headache.

Over coffee and aspirin, César found himself telling Racine all about this involved scheme to get Jacqueline Volette to Venice.

* * *

Choupon sat in the chair by the window, his clubfoot tucked back under the bent leg as always, the other leg straight out and resting on its heel. He felt it made him look bigger. Choupon liked anything big. The only big things he had were his eyes and he used them like shovels.

"You're sure it's Leduc?"

"Sure." Choupon gazed at the empty glass, his eyes hot coals.

"Still in Paris." César suppressed a smile. "That means he hasn't sold the dynamite yet."

"Tomorrow for certain. He's meeting his contact tonight; the talk is a German radical group. Not that he cares who he sells it to, I suppose."

"But you didn't see him yourself."

"I trust my sources." The Boot sounded offended. "So should you."

César apologized. He was right, of course. Trust nobody. Still, you had to trust somebody or you'd never make the end of the day. And who better than an ugly cripple with sharp eyes that saw only money? What did he gain by lying? Maybe more money. What did he lose?

"Leduc is acting like someone's after him."

"I'm after him."

"No, someone else."

César leaned back and fantasized Bock coming after Leduc for failing, and him getting both of them; except Bock would come after him instead. No, it had to be one at a time, with Leduc first. He suddenly felt distant, his life without logic, his only language the name Bock, the Nazi Bock, keeping up the pressure . . . The thought held him, made him think of his parents, which made him feel worse. Feeling guilty, he turned his thoughts back to Bock.

"Tonight, you say."

Beyond the café were the homes and lairs of three million people, at least one of whom wanted to leave, a rat trapped in a maze of stone and steel hemming him in while the hunter slowly advanced, always a step behind though only his shadow showed, a huge black cloud that grew and grew until there was nowhere to hide.

César knew the feeling.

* * *

At his desk the inspector stared at the names on the blackboard:

Emeri Prévert – Vichy, April 12

Léon Theoule – Marseille, August 17

Louis Girard – Nice, October 4

Raymond Broussard – Lyon, December 18

Henry Stiles – Paris, February 26

And beneath them, the beginning of another list:

> Kurt Linge – Vienna, January 10
> ? Max Baur – Salzburg, February 13

César played with the dates, the time spans and totals. Except for a double period between the first and second victims, they were slain roughly two months apart. Five victims multiplied by two months each equaled ten months, but Bock had been paid for twelve. Conclusion: someone was missing.

The second list left nothing to conclude. Bock had finally taken his kills beyond France. The method was different, too. Accidental death. Only César and his nemesis knew better.

The hunter looked at the director's memo again, fondled it, folded it, felt the amino acids in his body flow into his fingertips, fusing his prints onto the paper, forcing his identity, his will on the authorization that promised to open the lock to *Herr* Bock. One lock, one door, one foot on the right road.

In the morning he would contact West German Intelligence for Bock's prints, with the department backing him—just as far as his neck and as long as he won.

At seven o'clock Menard joined in the celebration, called away from home. "We're going to get him," César had said on the phone. "I feel it."

Menard's wife felt something too, anger, and firmly resolved to put her foot down. Her husband had to be home in one hour. And if *Monsieur* Inspector Dreyfus didn't find a woman soon, she'd send for her sister from Avignon who'd just buried her second husband, and then God help him!

Menard tacked the authorization memo on the bulletin board and let César win two games of darts to honor the occasion.

"Once we have the prints we'll get Bock's file," César said after the first win.

"And then we'll get Bock," he said after the second.

"How many more must I win?" he asked after the third.

In the café they raised their glasses, joyful.

"To crime," said César.

"And criminals," echoed Menard.

"Some criminals."

"A few."

"Just one, really."

"You'll get him."

"On my parents' grave."

Tears came suddenly to his eyes, the words more than the wine. His parents had no grave. They were murdered in Auschwitz, their bodies burned in the crematoria.

Through his adolescent years César dreamed of finding their killers, becoming a hunter of murderers. When he finally did, he discovered there were many murderers, more than he'd realized, more than he had ever imagined. They were everywhere, in every walk of life, looking just like everyone else, and so his quest turned into a calling, his job a profession. But the dream never went away, or the nightmares either.

Over the years César had trained himself to sleep as little as possible.

* * *

With Menard gone home he went on to Smith's, curious about Linge's SS connections. An aide to a general! The bookstore was on the Rue de Rivoli near the Louvre, a famous browsing stop that had been turned into a Nazi propaganda outlet during the war—a Parisian outrage—with the upstairs tearoom used as a German officers club. Searching the sections, César sped through half of history before he found himself in the time of terror. The next moment he found Ernst Kaltenbrunner.

The man was a caricature in polished boots and swagger stick, who also happened to be a homicidal maniac. He happened to be dead as well, hanged at Nuremberg. What interested César was that he came from Linz, of all places! As SS security head Kaltenbrunner shared responsibility for the Holocaust. Adolf Eichmann, an SS lieutenant colonel who handled the logistics of extermination, answered to Gestapo chief Heinrich Müller who answered to Kaltenbrunner who in turn reported to Himmler who took his orders from Hitler. César quickly discovered that not only Kaltenbrunner but Eichmann, too, came from Linz, Müller from nearby Bavaria, Himmler from Munich not far away, and Hitler himself from Upper Austria whose capital was Linz where the young Adolf went to school. Then there was the Gestapo boss of Linz, Max Baur, who later settled in Salzburg, and Linge from Vienna and Gerd from Munich.

César flexed and went back to his browsing, fascinated by the remarkable geographical coincidences. On a borrowed sheet of paper he plotted the places, with Vienna on the right and Munich to the left. In dead center loomed Linz. What did it mean? Bock wasn't from Linz; he was a German from Cologne. But he surely went to Munich from Paris. Then where?

Using the index in William L. Shirer's *The Rise and Fall of the Third Reich* he raced through the Kaltenbrunner pages, his eye caught by a passing reference:

Some fifteen members of an Anglo-American military mission—including a war correspondent of the Associated Press, and all in uniform—which had parachuted into Slovakia in January 1945 were executed at Mauthausen concentration camp on the orders of . . .

Who else? César thought grimly. SS General Ernst Kaltenbrunner, who said at his hanging he loved his German people. And apparently loved to kill the rest close to home. The concentration camp at Mauthausen was just outside Linz.

César left the bookstore feeling he'd found his parents' killers, at least the hierarchy. Hitler, Himmler, Kaltenbrunner, Müller, Eichmann, all dead as far as he knew. But there were still the others: those who pulled the triggers, dropped the gas, closed the locks, opened the ovens, bulldozed the bones. They were everywhere, in every walk of life, looking like everyone else. There were thousands of them.

There was one.

*   *   *

The Parisian night glittered with blue diamonds set in clusters of constellations. Everything was bathed in zodiacal light.

César drove slowly by the Louvre on his way to the rendezvous. Most of Paris was a museum to the past and the greatest of all was the Louvre, enormous beyond belief, whose endless corridors could carry you to Carthage or imperial Rome, to the studios of Rembrandt and da Vinci, or even back to the beginning of Babylonia with a block of black basalt on which were inscribed the laws of Hammurabi. At the moment César was concerned with laws more recent, especially one forbidding the police to enter situations of extreme danger without adequate backup. So why hadn't he told headquarters?

He had his pick of answers. The city bureaucracy was a vast network of forty thousand civil servants spending an annual budget of thirteen billion francs in dozens of departments and divisions, one of which was the Criminal Police. Why cost them still more? Or perhaps Choupon was mistaken, even lying. Wasn't he a drunk? Or maybe there just was no one to trust.

Unsatisfied, he decided to splurge on the truth. He wanted to get Leduc on his own to show Bock that he was not like the others, that the chase was real and relentless—and capture inevitable. If he could get the Nazi rattled, he stood a better chance.

But just in case the chase *wasn't* equal—and the outcome different —he hadn't even told Menard, who had a family and a good life.

Tiens! César growled, annoyed at himself. Life was no wrapped package, but chaos that came without warning. Who could control it?

He drove into Montmartre, up the highest hill in Paris, past the white Sacré-Coeur basilica, turning finally on Rue Chaptal where he eased into a darkened space and cut the motor. This was close enough to the theater since police cars were often recognized. A young couple glided by, his arm around her waist, protective. They reminded César of his loss. He quickly locked the car and hurried down the street, heart thumping, his eyelids snapping with excitement.

The Grand Guignol presented plays of heavy horror, followed almost immediately by light comedies. César walked in on the horror, a scene of murder and dismemberment and bloodcurdling screams. A railroad switchman is visited in his lonely station late one night by a passing man and woman, who bring liquor. They all get drunk and have an orgy; the switchman awakens just as the crack express thunders into another train. He failed to throw the switch! Guilt-ridden, the two men decide that the woman is a witch and so they douse her with gasoline and burn her at the switch before throwing her charred remains onto the tracks below. As the railroad worker turns happily absolved to his confederate, he sees the man sprouting horns. It is he who is the devil! Come to collect not only the woman but the switchman as well; but first the tortures of the damned . . . Amid all the bloodletting and screaming, his eyes already filled with the spectacular stage effects designed to terrify, César found a seat at the rear of the small theater. He would wait, a patient man used to waiting for devils like Leduc.

At the close of the usual bedroom farce involving someone hiding in the closet, César saw his man moving down the aisle as the audience spilled out; the witness had been exact in his description. He followed as Leduc exited with another man, watched them get into a nearby car. He ran to his, caught up to them at the corner. A short drive took them to a shabby block of rooming houses at the edge of Montmartre. They entered one—even poorer than its neighbors— toward the end of the block, a street of thieves and drab women with sour looks. César parked a dozen lengths ahead, worked his way back. The two men had already vanished into the gloomy interior and César followed.

The ground floor twisted toward the rear, a long hallway beneath a canopy of crumbling plaster. A naked bulb spread grotesque shadows across grimy walls. César swept by closed doors reverberating with Algerian music, mournful dirges that trembled on the brink of meditation. He didn't see Leduc or his contact, nor did he sense their presence. They had disappeared.

At the hall's center, rickety stairs spiraled upward into darkness. Footfalls echoed from above, the clippity-clop of prancing feet, and César flashed back to the theater and the sound of cloven hooves. Grand Guignol?

He tensed in the stairwell as a shadow descended, became substance, then scurried through the hall, an animal's gait, the hooves beating a tic-tac of hasty retreat. A thief at least, César told himself. Or else a laborer hurrying to his nocturnal job; what else could these people get? He cursed his imagination, a two-edged sword that cut left and right, heaven and hell both.

At the first landing he put his ear to the doors, searching for sounds, sensing demons on the other side. Darkness filled his mind, a sinner seeking light. He was certain they hadn't slipped by. A crash brought him to a rear door, paper thin, and the mumblings of a drunk. In the despair of desperate lives, drunks came and went. And so did killers.

The third floor yielded little but garbage and broken glass. Starting for the top, one foot on a squeaking step, he heard a door open behind him, the room at the foot of the stairs. César spun around to see Leduc peering out, his mouth open in surprise. Before he could react, César sprang forward and grabbed for his hair, slamming his head into the door. Leduc staggered as César pulled the head down and brought his knee up in one swift motion, catching the dynamiter under the chin. The body sprawled backward into the room like a blown-out window. A kick in the groin kept it down while César searched the pockets. There was no gun.

"I have it."

The German radical stood by the sink in the room's far corner and regarded César with disappointment. His face had an arrogance to it, a Prussian's face. In his hand was the weapon that belonged to the man on the floor. Leduc, dazed, didn't move.

"It's him I want," César said, trying to sound authoritative. "Not you." He showed his police identification.

"And what I want?" asked the German.

"That goes with me too."

The man's eyes didn't flicker.

"You've done nothing illegal yet," César pressed in a reasonable tone. "You're still free to go."

The Prussian pursed his lips, studying César, then shrugged in acceptance and turned toward the door.

"The gun stays here."

The Prussian smiled, a half-sneer, and broke open the revolver and pushed back the bullets which he shoved into his pocket. "A fair trade," he remarked and threw the empty gun on the floor.

From the window César waited until he saw the German leave the building and get into his car. Moments later he found the dynamite tucked away in the closet with the rest of the explosive materials. They could pick it up afterwards; what he wanted right now was to get Leduc to headquarters.

Using the empty gun for emphasis, César shoved the still-stunned dynamiter out the door onto the stairs, clutching him by the coat collar. Around the bend they trudged down to street level, the last flight, a step at a time—three, two, one, passing the hall light when the first shot struck.

César felt Leduc's body go limp. In the same instant his gun hand jerked up to smash the bulb; too late, the second shot ripped away the left side of the face. In the blackness César hugged the floor, Leduc's blood spilling over him. The killer was at the rear of the hall, invisible until the gun barked a third time, a brilliant tongue of flame that spoke of resolution. The slug splintered the wall inches above César's head; it was meant for him. He waited, defenseless, unable to move as the seconds spread over his body.

Expecting the killer to rush him, César saw instead a sudden split in the dark, then another, cracks of light coming from both sides of the hallway, sunlight on a dead moon. In the orange glow he watched the demon's eyes melt into vapor before the rear wall parted and swept the demon away. As Arabic strains filled his ears, the inspector's mind grasped the essential fact that he was not dead. His life was a miracle, a favor returned.

César pushed himself up, soaked in blood, and embraced the terrified Algerians.

NINE

The articulated figure was covered in blood-splattered clothing that gave it the look of a Guignol scarecrow.

"Inspiration and perspiration," the curator declared. "We implore one while we explore the other." He patted the mannequin affectionately and gestured to César. "Papier-mâché, literally chewed paper. More than fifty meters of it, tightly woven into a pulp material from which we mold arms and legs and trunk, then cover them with the clothes of the dead usually full of knife rends or bullet holes." Gauchet's laboratory, kept cool to protect the fabrics, felt uncomfortable; César wished he had worn a sweater. "For you they might determine the weapon's angle or trajectory, maybe even the victim's position immediately after the attack. Would he have fallen this way or that?" Gauchet rubbed his nervous hands together enthusiastically. "I use them to see how the fiber withstood the onslaught, to gauge the pressure and force, the diameter of broken ends, the direction of loose strands. Everything holds clues. Nylon tears while wool rips; some attacks would require brute strength, others—You begin to see. An hour's study could clear a room of suspects or even pinpoint the guilty."

"And Bock?" César asked.

"Strange, that one."

"In what way?"

"There are two of them, at least."

"Two, you say?"

"Either you haven't told me everything, Inspector, or I've just told you something. I don't think I have. Do you?"

"There's a strong possibility," César admitted, "that the dead man—"

"—is not your Nazi." Gauchet grimaced. "You can make it a virtual certainty. The clothes in the closet did not belong to the corpse. If he is your man, then the killer put them there. I find it easier to believe they belonged to this Bock, which means the corpse—"

"—is someone else."

"Suppose you tell me about it."

César did not understand. Both men had the same build, as well as facial resemblance. How could—

"Simple." The curator positively glowed with complexity. "The clothes in the closet were right-handed."

Had the inspector heard correctly?

"And those on the body left-handed."

Afterwards César confessed to a certain incredulity, but at the moment all he could feel was annoyance at Gauchet's little joke. With Bock on the loose . . .

The curator assured him it was no joke. Most everything in life had a left or right bias, and so did clothing. Shirts, for example, showed more wear on the right cuff and armpit for right-handers. In pants the belts were put through the loops from opposite ends depending on the bias, and the buckle loops would reflect the appropriate wear. Shoelaces were crisscrossed differently; shoe heels were worn more on the favored side, as were socks and underwear and the pockets of jackets. Even tie knots were slanted differently.

It was easy for an expert to tell one from the other. Bock was right-handed, his victim was not.

As for Bock's clothing, strictly synthetics off the rack. Except for a pair of Bismarck boots made in Düsseldorf in the 1960s from leather lasts no longer in use, and a scarf still in excellent shape. The finest pure wool; under a microscope the dark brown dye showed a distinctive pattern common to German manufacturers of the 1930s, many of whom went into production of military goods after 1939. Such wool scarves came to be especially favored by the elite of the SS in the early 1940s, much as the *Luftwaffe* had adopted the Isadora Duncan silk scarf some years earlier.

"Which means Bock was someone special."

"Almost certainly."

The dead man's clothing was mostly cotton of good quality and poor design, the kind turned out by the eastern bloc. Inside the shirt were laundry markings invisible to the eye, a process in wide use. The pants were quite different, fine gabardine with layered cotton panels at the crotch. New and expensive.

"The reason for the panels," Gauchet continued, "was obviously to enlarge the appearance of the sex organs, though why anyone would want this I don't know."

César didn't bother to explain the owner was impotent and needed ego boost, or that the cotton protected the penis after painful injections.

"Especially since he was sexually active."

"What?"

"Semen is highly fluorescent under the microscope, you know."

César closed his eyes as the room began to reel. It was impossible.

"—even though semen stains can be removed by laundering," the voice whirred, "and in this case they were, but the sperm cannot"— emotionless and dry as dust—"sperm stays, unless there's been a vasectomy in the family."

Gauchet's humor.

The dead man was onanistic or liked intercourse with his pants on, according to the curator. The only other possibility was rape, where the clothing of the rapist and victim normally showed evidence of sperm regardless of any quick cleaning.

César swore silently at René Camors. The injections worked. Either that or Bock had switched pants. But why would he want to wear the—

Why else?

The victim's pants were identification! An invisible marking, a magnetic stripe in the lining, almost anything—and that meant he was involved in security, too. Someone Bock knew, maybe even worked with. He had the gabardine pants made especially for his victim—probably the same kind he wore, panels and all—then used them a few times himself like a frugal German.

César let out a deep breath. That narrowed the world quite a bit. The SS? Too long ago for this level of technology. The West Germans, a possibility. Or the people Bock worked for the past year . . .

"You said the shirt had laundry markings."

"Nothing special. Every country has its own system."

The curator saw César's meaning, returned to the lab desk for the data sheet and walked it over to a card catalog at the end of the aisle. Inside was the coded history of the world's soap opera and it took only a moment to match the markings on the data sheet, an intricate combination of numbers and letters that César hoped would point him in the right direction.

"East Germany," Gauchet hissed.

* * *

"You're sure about that?"

"Sure as a bullet."

An apt expression, César thought. Especially since the bullets were the same.

"Not the same gun—"

"Obviously not."

"—but the same kind."

"9mm."

"With six lands and grooves with a right twist—"

"Which is rare, you say."

"And loading indicator marks on the casings, which makes it unique."

"Only the PPK," César said.

"The only one," Félix agreed.

Germans didn't tolerate failure, César reminded himself. "And wielded by the same hand," he droned.

"That remains to be seen, doesn't it?"

At César's insistence, René had quickly dug the two bullets out of Leduc's body and sent them to ballistics for immediate comparison.

"It's him," César urged. "I know it is."

Comparison hadn't taken long, since Félix knew exactly what to look for. "See for yourself," he'd said to César who swiftly spotted the similar right-hand rifling and characteristic markings on the slugs from the earlier killings and those used in the latest shooting. Both came from Walther PPK's.

Bock. The Nazi was back.

* * *

From his tangled office on the third floor, César spun a growing web of interlocking strands that stretched as far as Vienna in the east to London in the west. Henry Stiles, the British attaché shot in February, almost certainly had other duties as well since nobody at the embassy would tell César anything. Vienna, meanwhile, had sent a list of firms Linge used in his law practice. Four were from Munich and Menard was getting names in each.

Closer to home he'd run a quick check on Jacqueline Volette after seeing her with Kayser. She'd been born in a small town about thirty kilometers from Paris.

"Not exactly in town," the local informant told him. "Back then it was more rural; a lot of people lived on the outskirts like Jacqueline's mother. Little plots of land, dirt poor."

César hated himself. How could he do such a thing? He'd still been bothered by her Parisian accent and her sister's fluent German, true, but there was more to it. Jealousy? How childish. Well, and what else did he have to do with his emotions? Nothing stood still. If you didn't use them, they would start using you. Only the dead slept soundly.

"Want to know about her sister?"

"Already know about her sister." He thanked the *gendarme* and replaced the receiver.

When Tobie popped in, César was erasing a question mark on the blackboard. It had been in front of Baur's name.

"Next you'll be cutting out paper dolls."

"Better than cutting them up."

César surveyed his work. Baur was under Linge on the second list of victims and César now put a question mark under Baur. Who was next?

"You seem to have this thing for questions," Tobie said.

"Is that so?"

The Salzburg police had sent the accident report. Baur shot himself with a Steyr 7.65mm pistol while cleaning it, not easy to do. The Steyr was primarily a self-defense weapon; to kill yourself with one, you had to bypass some simple precautions. But Baur was known to be careless around guns. The bullet had traveled upward through his throat; he'd been seated and presumably cleaning the loaded gun with the barrel pointed directly at him. César didn't believe it. Accident simply sounded better than suicide to those left behind, and the police knew nothing of Bock.

"That thief you asked about?" Tobie frowned. "Nobody knows a thing."

"But it happened," César protested.

"Would you say I know the thieves in Paris?"

"Pretty much."

"Then take my word for it. There was no theft."

"Meaning?"

"He did it himself, or someone close to him."

César blinked at the odd thought. "Bock had no one close to him."

"Maybe you just haven't found them yet," Tobie said on the way out.

Brooding, César returned to the pictures on his desk. Baur's photo from Salzburg versus the group snapshot from Bock's flat. Baur was next to Bock with Linge on the other end. Three down and one to go. César hoped Gerd was still alive.

* * *

The murder weapon. Gunsmith Baudrin had fashioned a history for César—starting with its manufacture at the Carl Walther plant near the Buchenwald concentration camp—but the bottom line was its destination. The *Wehrmacht* had the Walther P-38, which replaced the Luger as the German service pistol, and the *Luftwaffe* liked the Walther PP, the standard police pistol. Ranking officers often had their sidearms festooned with elaborate scrollwork. In the SS little could be done since Himmler hated guns. Their holsters held weapons. Well then? An unofficial consensus developed among some SS officers who began to carry the PPK, especially in the security service headed by Heydrich and then Kaltenbrunner. Designed to be concealed, the PPK was used by the *Kriminalpolizei,* the detective branch of the German national police force. And wasn't the SS protecting the security of the German nation?

Bock's PPK, one of several hundred in that lot, arrived at the SS headquarters in Berlin on December 14, 1939, some three months after the attack on Poland and the start of World War II. Nazi Germany would soon conquer the world and the Third Reich would last for a thousand years! Millions were in uniform and more were coming. Who could stop them? Especially those clever young men of the SS. They would rise in the ranks, and as they rose more doors would open to them and perhaps one day a senior officer would present them with a special weapon to show they were among the chosen, one of the boys, the men of the SS. Or maybe they would kill for it.

Had Bock killed for it? César wondered. Or had his killing begun after he got his own PPK?

Subsequent records of weapon disposition were destroyed or lost but Bock's gun did not have the coding system which went into effect in 1940 so the 1939 shipping and receiving dates were judged reliable. There was a single engraving on the PPK, indicating one owner. It was Baudrin's educated guess that Bock, unlikely to engrave a gun in his business, was probably its second owner. Since the weapon served as a prized possession, it was assumed the previous owner had been killed. Between 1940 and 1945 the average length of service for those SS officers who died in duty was eighteen months, which would put the gun in Bock's hand sometime in late 1941.

Baudrin pronounced it in excellent condition, seldom fired. That seemed reasonable to César since Bock practiced on people. He himself hadn't fired a gun in ages. What was the sense? He was a hunter of men, not their judge or executioner.

Would this time be any different? Should it?

Distressed, he traded his office for the flower mart downstairs to await West Germany's reply. Along the several dozen stalls everything was to be seen and sold. To this end merchants made mysterious moves, rolled their eyes and repeated words of encouragement as people passed. At the edge of the square, two men stood in silent gaze as someone swiftly turned away to escape notice. Too late.

"Dreyfus!"

The word bounced off tree and plant to become a vine around César's waist, binding him fast. Dupin, the taller of the two, led the way to his side.

"Jules, I'm sure you know Inspector Dreyfus from Homicide."

"Doesn't everyone?" The ministry official had pencil lines for lips, bluish and very hard.

"The price of fame."

"And well-deserved, too."

"*Merci.*" César half-smiled and glanced up at his windows but Dupin would have none of it.

"We don't meet like this often enough. People doing the same work"—he turned to the ministry official for support—"should get to know each other, develop better rapport. Isn't that how most cases are solved? Cooperation! Surely you know that, Dreyfus."

"I should be getting back," César pleaded.

"And spoil this chance meeting? Nonsense." Dupin steered the two men before him like a ship's pilot, past the flower stalls and over to the courtyard of the Hôtel-Dieu. "Who knows? Joining us might solve all your problems."

The courtyard fed into a series of gray corridors that stretched into the bowels of the old city hospital. At the end of a tunnel lit by blue overhead bulbs, an elevator was waiting to take them to the fourth floor. There, more twists and turns led them past a guarded gate into a large foyer of tufted couches and leather chairs. The deep pile carpeting reflected a brilliant red beneath the mirrored walls and above all loomed a centerpiece in cut glass, a crystal chandelier soaking up shadow, its electric candles on fire.

Dupin guided them to a circle of chairs. His manner was gracious, voluble, almost deferential to César. A steady stream of good fellowship shone from his eyes. He smiled at the look of discomfort on César's face.

"You didn't expect such luxury in a hospital."

He eased himself into the folds of the lounger. "It's not the luxury that counts but what it brings: privacy and a place to unwind." He leaned over to César, the voice soft as a whisper. "Ministers, magistrates, people who make important decisions, they need somewhere to relax with their own kind, try to work out solutions to problems."

Moments later they were ushered into a vaulted dining room of dark wood and sterling silver. Flowers flooded the corners and at the rear oaken tables groaned under the weight of fresh fruit and the finest cheeses. On the walls beautiful women leered out of gilded frames.

"German generals," Dupin hissed at César, "built this. They wanted to dine away from the conquered masses but near city hall and the police. You know the Prussian aristocracy."

They were seated at an end table with a military man well into his

first course of chicken *mousseline* in Madeira sauce. César, who liked
a mustard sandwich for lunch, feared the worst.

Dupin introduced General Bordier of the SCE.

"Dreyfus? I've heard the name."

"The Bock affair," Dupin suggested softly.

César smiled as the general measured him carefully. The ministry
official seemed content to talk between bouts of food but he had the
eyes of the girls who worked the Champs-Elysées and could see into
a man's wallet at twenty meters. When the waiter filled his wineglass,
César reached for it resolved to watch his ass as far as the eye could
see, especially those eyes. *Pass auf!* he told himself.

"Inspector Dreyfus expects to get proof of Bock's rebirth soon,"
Dupin boasted, "and then it's on to the files."

Food was brought—oysters with spinach and mussels *marinière*
and buttered leeks—and placed in front of César. How he longed for
a stale croissant! Or even a way out. Such surroundings were obviously for important men who made important decisions, alone or
otherwise. What had he to do with them? He was just trying to catch
someone who kept on killing.

"To Thursday," Dupin raised his wineglass, "because it will soon
be gone."

"The past must be buried," the ministry official said, glass in hand,
"to make way for the future."

"To Friday, because it will soon be here." The general took a
swallow of Cheval Blanc.

"Those who revel in the past are doomed to repeat it," the ministry official continued. "You can't steal Marshal Pétain's bones from
the Ile d'Yeu and bring them to Paris, as those fanatics did last
year—"

"Two years ago." Dupin beamed.

"—and expect that to change what happened. You cannot punish
the dead."

"Or persecute the living," the general added quickly. "Too many
of our people are doing that."

"Revenge," the ministry official announced solemnly, "is merely
another name for murder."

César imagined they were talking about the Klaus Barbie publicity
in the newspapers. Barbie, after all, had been head of the murderous
Gestapo in Lyon; he had sent thousands to their deaths, including

Jean Moulin, the legendary *Résistance* hero. Even so, the political police were not anxious to bring him back from Bolivia for trial; too many embarrassing questions of collaboration could be raised. Nor were the ministries happy with the prospect: Barbie had worked not only for the Americans but also for West Germany after the war, and present French interests were not served by harassing an economic and military partner. It was primarily the Palace that pushed for his return on this thirtieth anniversary of the war's end, goaded by some mystical sense of moral outrage even though they'd known of Barbie's whereabouts for at least a dozen years—

"Surely Inspector Dreyfus could help us."

César blinked, found all eyes on him.

"We were wondering," the general intoned, "how far one should go for the sake of justice."

"The Bock case, for example," rasped the ministry official. "If it could harm the government, would you stop?"

"Would it harm the government?"

In the vaulted room waiters flitted silently by, bearing racks of lamb and rounds of roasts while obsequious stewards tended the wine.

"Dieter Bock turned himself in to us last month"—the general dabbed at the corners of his mouth with a linen fold—"and we began using him as a double agent. When we heard he'd been killed, we naturally assumed the East Germans had found out." He replaced the linen next to his empty plate. "If he's alive, on the other hand, it means we were duped. That could prove most harmful to the government at this time. With the Butcher of Lyon all over the papers, here we are recruiting a Nazi."

Why had Bock done it? César mused. How did such a move fit into his plans?

"Now you come along," the ministry official said, "and want to nail him for some political killings. And one of them—Raymond Broussard—was a double agent Bock killed to show us good faith on his part." He sounded offended. "Of course, we can't be sure anymore."

"It's the politics they're interested in," Dupin said dryly. "They naturally don't see it through the eyes of a police inspector."

César thought furiously. The important thing was holding on to the Nazi.

"Didn't Bock marry a Frenchwoman," he asked, "and then move here from Germany?"

"Of course," the general exclaimed, "a French citizen."

"And she worked for Bonn," the ministry official declared.

"So how could the government be harmed"—César made every effort to sound his most reasonable—"if the police seek a German national who murdered his French wife, a former employee of West Germany?"

In the silence César assured everyone that he had a good case of circumstantial evidence. Foolproof, actually. Yes, he was certain. Bock had killed his wife, as well as several men in Austria and at least six in France. But: "Only one is needed for pursuit."

"His wife."

"Yes, General."

"The man hanged instead of Bock. Do you know his name?"

"Not yet," César lied.

"Or his nationality?"

César lied again.

Settled, the intrigue shifted to sex, as always, especially sex in high places, and talk of movie stars, until the meal was over and César released. "They're satisfied," Dupin told him outside, "for now." And left him standing alone among the flowers where he'd been found. César tried to fight the feeling that it was all planned but somehow he failed.

* * *

Ballistics was alive with rumors: a cache of weapons had been found in Clichy that included some exotic devices. They could hardly wait.

César gave Félix the crushed cigarette box he'd taken from the table in front of the ministry official, who had bent one side into the other and then folded over the ends. An unusual method of destruction. Yet César had sat in Tobie's kitchen a few days earlier and watched Kayser do the same thing.

"Menard was asking for you," Félix said.

César, already on the phone, pointed to the cigarette box. "Tell me about it."

Menard sounded excited. His check of the four Munich companies doing business with Linge had paid off; one of them was an accounting firm that went back twenty years. The owner's name? Gerd Wilhelm Streicher.

"Good so far."

Better than that. Baur's wife remembered a few more of her husband's friends. One was a Gerd from Munich; she didn't know his last name and he'd never come to the house. But she knew his occupation. He was an accountant.

"Gerd Streicher," César said. He lived in the Munich area and worked with figures. Julien was right again, and so was Kussow.

Menard had already talked to the Munich police who were checking their files on Streicher and would call back. César was torn between warning him and setting a trap for Bock. What if he was wrong? But suppose he was right? He told Menard to warn Munich. They should get to Streicher fast.

Félix returned with the cigarette box opened. "I assume you saw this somehow related to weaponry, and you were right. It's an old Nazi trick. German cigarettes came in these presentation boxes and during the war they would use them as delayed action fuses; later the Allies picked it up." He carefully crushed the box in the same way. "When it's tightly balled and a hole made on the bottom"—he punched a small hole with a scissors point—"the lit match is inserted, so"—and placed the match inside the ball—"and the gasoline bomb or whatever's to be ignited is set above, or nearby, and another fuse draped over the box." He turned to César, smiled. "As deadly as a missile's heat sensors. Watch."

It took two minutes for the box to blaze. When it did, anything near would have blown. A homemade delayed fuse.

"Almost everything's a weapon if you know what to do." Félix swept away the ashes with his hand. "Everything."

* * *

César wound his way back to his office in the other wing, wondering how long his luck would last. A woman he wanted, the first to replace Catherine Deneuve in his fantasies, was connected to Bock and Kayser. And the case, which he'd seen as his salvation, was turning instead into a political time bomb that could blow up in his face. César could feel the danger; what he couldn't feel was any regret.

* * *

He was staring at the blackboard when the call came through again from West Berlin, a contact given him earlier by Kussow who knew many people in many countries. What he had needed was information about the East German secret police. Specifically, if they were missing an agent, someone who might have been in East Berlin in the sixties when Bock worked the other side of the wall.

Not surprisingly, the answer was yes. A Stasi agent named Herbert Reimer was missing for almost two weeks and presumed dead or defected. The secret police were changing codes and classifications just in case.

At César's request his contact had made further calls in West Berlin—175 kilometers inside East Germany, a tiny island in a red sea—to learn more about *Herr* Reimer, whose description closely matched Bock's. There was some talk of a groin injury.

Bitte?

Seriously wounded in the workers' riots in 1953.

Impotence! César had found his body.

Reimer, the contact now reported, went west in dozens of identities over the years. His expertise was in repatriation of East Germans. In the sixties he worked in East Berlin, mostly against West German agents probing the wall's weaknesses. Often such men got to know each other; they shared the same interests, after all, and operated in the same restricted environment. Normally the atmosphere was *leben und leben lassen;* some even became double agents.

Reimer a double agent? Bock was a better bet, César decided. Or with both in Berlin they could've begun to accommodate each other, take turns at winning. From there anything was possible, even going back out of retirement. César wondered how Bock had got the East German to Paris. "Where did Reimer go after Berlin?" he asked.

"Never really left. In 1970 he got off the firing line, made a group head. Then last year he became operations officer for special security—external espionage."

"Big job?"

"Not the biggest."

"But enough to control agents?"

"Some agents."

So Reimer goes up to boss and Bock goes back to work. César fought an impulse to laugh. He'd been seeking earthshaking conspiracies and found only a couple of friendly spies helping each other to a good thing, at least until Bock found better. César saw himself slipping. Some hunter! He couldn't find a woman when he needed one. How could he hope to find a man?

"Reimer's section was responsible mainly for West Germany and France," the contact said.

"Austria?"

"Odd you should mention Austria."

"How so?"

"One of Reimer's men was recently killed there, Max Baur. Ever hear of him?"

* * *

César stayed in the café until he saw snakes on the wall. When he got back to the office, Clément was in his seat and he stared the younger man to the couch before crumpling into the chair himself. The wine had split his left hemisphere from his right. Or was it just his headache? How could Baur do this to him? If Linge and Streicher were agents too, then Bock's kills were political and had nothing to do with the past or with him. All he had was Bock killing his wife and he'd lose that in a minute.

Defeated, César searched for snakes again and found one slinking on the couch. "Do your worst," he demanded, "but make it good."

Not all that bad, to hear Clément tell it. After the war Nazi art was worthless, then in 1970 collectors took another look and prices began to rise. Kayser's stolen portrait was from the midthirties, Hitler in his chancellor period. It had hung in Himmler's office during the Nazi years. Afterwards it disappeared until 1957 when it surfaced in a Hamburg curio shop; nine years later it appeared in Munich, part of a private collection. Then in 1972 the huge painting was offered for sale and bought anonymously through a gallery. Clément's Versailles informant believed the owner was probably an American or West German financier. They liked to buy in at the beginning of those things.

"Why American or West German?"

"They're the only ones who still take the Nazis seriously."

"Maybe others are still too afraid."

"After all these years?" Clément didn't believe it.

Too young, César told himself. What did he know? "Your man have any ideas about the supposed theft?"

"He thinks it's a publicity stunt to raise the price before selling."

"An anonymous collector who hires a private detective to search in secret?"

"He calls it reverse publicity. If nobody knows about something, soon everyone will be asking for it."

César stared at his detective.

"I admit it sounds strange," Clément said defensively, "but you should see his house. The guy must know what he's doing."

"This big collector of yours, what's his specialty?"

"Drainage art."

"Drainage art?"

"Toilets."

César flushed him out and went back to work, relieved. Every homicide squad needed one lunatic. But the lunatic was right about Kayser's painting not being stolen; he was after something else.

A quick call. "What could the Swiss want with—"

"Too late," Menard groaned in César's ear.

Someone in the Munich police had recognized the name and checked back. On April 8 prosperous accountant Gerd Wilhelm Streicher was killed in an accident on his farm near Altomünster, thirty kilometers north of Munich. He had somehow got caught in his baling machine. The mutilated body was discovered by his wife when she returned from shopping; her husband had been alone at the time of the freak accident.

César suddenly remembered his mother's warning about strange men who put little boys in big sacks and carried them away, never to be seen again. The same thing was happening to ex-Nazis. How many did Bock have in his sack? How many did he need? César turned to the blackboard, the second list. Under Baur's name he scrawled Streicher's, and the date. That made three. So far.

The rain had just started, a steady hum against the windows, washing everything clean. Across the Place du Parvis, the square from which all distance in France is measured, the cathedral of Paris bathed in warm spring water.

Notre-Dame. César often stopped in to sit silent, surrounded by eight hundred years of stone and glass, his imagination soaring. Here were kings crowned and presidents mourned. He saw them all; heard the great bell Emmanuel, its tone so pure it cured the deaf. Seated staring into space, he felt strangely moved each time, moving in mind, leaving a body bound by desires, floating free of worldly ambitions.

Across the square the April shower fell softly on César's world. He blamed himself for Streicher's murder, for not having caught a man whose face he'd never seen. Maybe he should have been a farmer like his foster father who could fix anything. Catch anything, too. Now he'd lost his wife, his prey, another victim—maybe soon the case. What did he know anymore? He should've been a farmer. At least he knew you don't fall off a baler.

Menard came by to commiserate. Something he could do?

Short of shooting him, César couldn't think of a thing. Munich was sending Streicher's photo but he knew it would match the last man in the group. So where do they go from there?

"How about Marseille?"

"If Theoule was selling—"

"He was or he wouldn't have been killed."

"According to the prosecutor's office, if he was selling"—Menard liked complete thoughts, right or wrong—"the talk was East Germany or Czechoslovakia. He probably tried to blackmail his contact after he got fired and ran out of money. Threatened to give the police names."

César would've bet on it. "And Vichy?"

"Prévert's father is dead almost ten years."

"So the killing can't go back to the war."

"Not unless Bock nursed a grudge all this time."

"We're dealing with murder for profit, not a Corsican vendetta." He reached for the map of Bavaria and Upper Austria bought in the bookstore. "Stay on it. There's a thread somewhere."

"Think we'll ever find him?"

Menard watched the inspector move a magnifying glass over the area between Munich and Linz, the major Nazi redoubt that came complete with concentration camps on both ends.

"Soon," César answered.

TEN

Intelligence work was often less a form of business than a way of life. Cleverness, stupidity, idealism and raw courage were tempered only by urges of envy and self-destruction. Danger was everywhere.

The West German *Bundesnachrichtendienst* rose like the phoenix out of the ashes of defeat and by the 1950s was fighting off the Russian bear. In 1958 the intelligence agency employed Dieter Bock; in the early 1960s Klaus Barbie worked for the BND, which found itself by the end of the decade locked in battle with waves of radical youths and zealots of every stripe. After the 1972 Olympics disaster, the agency was revamped and given additional powers and duties. One of these was to be more receptive to the requests of other governments, even the French.

"Inspector Dreyfus?" The connection was clear.

César checked his watch. The Germans were punctual as always, a frightening rigidity. This time he could barely wait. Fighting anxiety, he had speared the phone on the first ring.

"Guten Tag." The voice was smooth, devious. César looked out the window to make sure it wasn't night. ". . . *fünf minuten nach drei. Es tut mir leid."*

Even late, the news warmed his French soul. The thumbprint and index finger on the Himmler letter belonged to Dieter Bock. He was alive and another man dead! West German Intelligence had no record of the dead man's prints. Did the inspector know who he was yet?

César told them his suspicions and asked for anything they might have on Herbert Reimer.

"You say he was Stasi?"

"Apparently."

"And found in Paris. Interesting, *nein?*"

As for Bock, he'd been a BND field agent from March 1958 to November 1967 when he received a shoulder wound in the course of his duties. Four months later he applied for disability retirement and was released on partial pension in May 1968. Most of the decade he spent in West Berlin with a BND subcontractor (the Berlin Border Protection Brigade). There he debriefed East German refugees and countered attempts to return them by the East German secret police. It was a messy business and Bock evidently did his work well.

"Was he ever suspected of being a double agent?"

"Never."

"Did such people sometimes get friendly with those on the other side?"

"It happened occasionally. Mutual respect, mostly."

"Or mutual aid?"

"Ich verstehe nicht."

"Taking turns to make the job easier."

"A few did that, *ja.*"

"But not Bock."

César knew the BND wouldn't admit anything. Bock and Reimer had split the workload, maybe even done some business on their own. They'd been silent partners, and close enough for Reimer to hire Bock when he wanted to get back in; come to Paris, too, when Bock called. What was the excuse? Money, certainly. From where?

There was no photo in the BND files. Whenever an agent terminated, his pictures were immediately destroyed to prevent discovery and possible reprisal to himself or his family. Bock had returned from the dead without an image in the world.

* * *

When André staggered in from Zurich, César was still digesting Bock's brazen plan. Did it begin even before he rejoined Reimer, this time on the same side? *(Had* he rejoined Reimer? Nothing was obvious, César now reminded himself, and two sources were needed for any information.) Bock was infinitely patient but was he really that clever? Could he hold everything together that long? Was he alone?

César shook his head in annoyance. Of course he was alone. This wasn't Nazi Germany; Hitler and Himmler were dead. All Bock had to do was take one step at a time, from killing his wife to killing himself, courtesy of Herbert Reimer, and the plan would unfurl like a flag. What plan? Whose flag?

André didn't know about anything but Louis Girard and that was plenty. Hoping to make a killing, the Swiss banker had made some bad business ventures instead. To pay for them, he'd stolen money from his bank. More specifically, from one of his accounts, a large account, an account over which he had a large amount of control. How this was possible would require a strict reading of Swiss banking law, André was told, but the ingredients included a commercial account owned by a holding company through several interlocking directorships and a trusted bank officer with power of attorney.

César's contacts had allowed André to tap the computers of a Zurich credit concern and a bank ratings firm, which led to other industry computers tracking data on multiple listings and phantom funds. The money trail was not easy to follow; hiding ownership had become very sophisticated. The editor of a financial newsletter, who owed César a favor, and a government official were needed before André unwound the web. At its core was Olympic Imports, a satellite of Tech-Tele Systems which was a Liechtenstein corporation with strong financial ties to Deutsches Industries.

Deutsches Industries, as André soon learned, was the official trade arm of the Export Bank of the Deutsche Demokratische Republik.

East Germany!

César grabbed for the phone, muttered to Menard. Right now, yes. Waiting here.

He turned to André, tempted to kiss him. Instead, settled for a smile. His second source. Onward!

Based on the tracking data, Olympic Imports funded monies to a half-dozen countries in Western Europe at irregular intervals. Sudden heavy infusions were common. Obviously such activity was not cyclic and did not follow normal business practice.

"Which makes it a front," César guessed, "for bankrolling intelligence operations in other countries."

Front or not, the Olympic Imports account was sizable. Usually kept at more than two million Swiss francs; yearly disbursement was over a million. It was Girard's largest account, the one from which he chose to steal.

"But why run?" André asked.

"Panic, probably." César couldn't help feeling sorry for Girard. "He called his contact and confessed, not knowing how ruthless they were. A meeting was suggested in Nice, where Bock found him."

They went over the details again, confirming César's view that Bock worked for Reimer before killing him. By the time Menard called back he was beginning to feel better.

"You were right. Olympic Imports is here."

"Where?"

"Boulevard Raspail."

"And that," César said expansively to André, "is how Bock got his ten thousand in cash every month. Left on a park bench right here in Paris by a Stasi agent out of Olympic Imports." César rubbed his hands together in satisfaction. Life was good after all.

"Did I mention Peter Kayser?" André asked.

His hands flew apart like glass striking stone.

"I don't think I did. Anyway, his name came up on the computer in one of the deals that soured on Girard. His reputation is not good."

Mankind was without prisons for thousands of years but suddenly there were not enough to go around. France, for example, had 36,000 prisoners with room for only 30,000—and more were coming in every day. César wondered where they would go. Or if Bock would be among them.

"A private detective in Zurich." André sounded interested.

César stared down at the lifeline running across his palm, unable to gauge its length amid the creases of joy and sorrow etched into flesh. Was he ahead?

"Some people get born right the first time, like the Swiss." André ran his steely eye around the office, missing nothing. "The rest of us get to pretend a lot."

Strangely, César was thinking much the same thing. All of a sudden he didn't feel so confident. Bock was slipping beyond his grasp, spinning out of reach. He might not hold it together, might even lose control. Or was that just more imagination? He was certainly clever enough to follow the scent. Even André was impressed.

"The Nazi never expected to have his cover to East Germany blown."

"Or maybe he did." César patted the top of his head where the hair was thinning along the crown. He wondered if his father had ever worried about such things. "Back to Bock," he growled, waving André away.

The photo from Munich lay on his desk. Gerd Streicher was the last man in the group, as César knew he would be. The three friends of Dieter Bock—before he killed them—and a dead secret police agent. Now all belonged to the file.

The phone again, Félix reporting on a sixth man slain with Bock's PPK. "Strasbourg this time. Last June but they just got around to comparing the ballistics. Same style as your man, one shot in the forehead. A description, too."

"Good?"

"Bad."

César studied the name on his pad. Paul Dussap had been a leader of the *Résistance* during the war when the boy was living on a farm outside the city, hidden there after his own parents were deported to Auschwitz. He remembered the name, memorized them all. Dussap and the others were fighting the hated Nazis.

Now they were back—only there were no more Nazis. Just the East Germans, and Dieter Bock.

* * *

"Six victims in a year," Menard exclaimed when he heard the news. "It's like those operas that complete a cycle."

"The Ring of the Nibelungs."

"Germans are very methodical."

"Except there's only four operas in Wagner's *Ring*."

"That's almost six."

César liked the phone. It was fast, convenient, and you could always hang up. Still, Menard was right in a way. The cycle had been incomplete until now.

When Menard entered the office, César was at the blackboard writing Dussap's name between Prévert from Vichy and Theoule of

Marseille. "We won't find any more for this list," he said over his shoulder. "Bock was a good German."

It was the other list that caught Menard's attention:

Kurt Linge – Vienna, January 10

Max Baur – Salzburg, February 13

Gerd Streicher – Munich, April 8

César replaced the chalk. "What's missing?"

"March."

He rounded the desk to his chair. "Like most of us, Bock worked out his own rhythm for doing things." Sat down. "Even murder."

"A man a month," Menard murmured.

"On this one, yes."

"Which means he has less time to kill."

"Or more men."

Murder was easier to commit than prove. For conviction the victim had to be dead, the killing legally murder, and done by the person charged. A corpse usually helped.

"What now?"

"Find the March body."

Menard looked at the cities listed: Vienna, Salzburg, Munich. "Not in France," he said.

"Germany." Where César always knew it would be.

"Or Austria."

"That too."

"But how?" Menard, on the couch, crossed his legs and jiggled his foot to focus frustration. "We don't know where to look. It could take weeks to go through all the accidental deaths, months. What would they search for?"

"What else? An ex-Nazi." César was convinced Bock's plan went back to the SS. Linge, Baur, Bock, all were SS. Even Streicher was in the civilian section of the SS; he handled figures, like money.

"Could still take forever."

"If the German police do it." César rummaged in the desk drawer. "But how about a Nazi hunter?"

Menard's ears popped open.

"People who track down Nazis wanted for war crimes, like they did with Eichmann that time."

"Who you got in mind?"

"Someone I read about, a married couple actually." He unfolded a newspaper clipping, glanced at it. "They might be able to help."

"From where?"

"Right here in Paris. He's a French Jew whose father was killed in Auschwitz; his wife's a German whose father served in the *Wehrmacht.*"

"Not exactly your normal couple," Menard said.

"Nothing's normal when you talk Nazi." He handed the clipping to Menard.

"What's this?"

"Tells about them. A few years ago she went to Bolivia demanding Barbie's expulsion and before that she slapped the German chancellor who'd worked for Hitler, right in public at an election rally in Berlin. I think he lost. Then the two of them tried to kidnap a Gestapo boss back to France for trial, symbolically anyway, and landed in a German jail."

"But can they find a dead Nazi for us?"

"If anyone can." César dialed for the operator. "Still so many around we'll probably win."

"Suppose he wasn't wanted?"

"Then we lose."

* * *

The Sorbonne was crowded, as always. César stood with Jacqueline Volette in a court garden filled with impossibly straight rows of flowers that faced the falling sun. The garden itself was a perfect square cut from Italian stone, with graceful paths and noble statues. A gentleman's walk meandered through the cultivated beds of reds and yellows, vibrant colors that barely matched the flame César felt at his side. Even in anger she smoldered with conviction.

"This woman who visited Bock during his year on the Rue Malte," César urged, "had your hair, your eyes, even your smile. The concierge recognized you right away from your photograph."

"What photograph?"

"Your file here at the university."

"Is that a crime, then?" Jacqueline demanded of César. "Have I broken a law?"

"I kept asking myself why you would go to someone who did that to your sister," he answered, "but I already knew."

"Knew what?" she snapped. "So I visited him."

"More than visit," César said sadly. "You and Dieter Bock were lovers."

Jacqueline Volette stepped back, folded her arms, pressed them against her bosom in a defensive gesture.

"You were lovers when your sister was alive."

Her face had a Mediterranean cast to it, long-lashed and almond-eyed, a generous mouth. The hands were arabesques carved by Cellini. He felt as if he were watching Venus come to life.

"We were lovers, yes." Her voice was defiant. "But not then."

"When?"

"After." Her eyes looked boldly at César. "It started a few months after he killed Bernadette."

"He forced you."

"I went to him, thinking I could trap him into admitting he'd killed her. I was ready to do anything to get his confession, make him pay."

"You were hysterical."

"I was desperate."

"The police—"

Jacqueline scoffed. "Who would listen to me? Even the insurance company paid off."

"So you go to a murderer, demand he confess." César shook his head in bewilderment. "You expected the SS to suddenly plant roses instead of graves. But he didn't, of course. What did he do?"

"He gave me a drug that first time, I don't know what. I was helpless." She held herself firm against the shudder that ran through her. "After that . . ."

"He threatened you."

"Yes, no. Not threats. It wasn't like that." She licked her lips. "He talked to me. But the more he talked, the more I seemed to lose my will. It was what he said."

Her eyes widened as her skin flushed involuntarily. César watched her face harden.

"He said I'd really hated my sister and was glad she died, that I'd always wanted him but never had the courage to admit it while she was alive." Her voice grew hesitant. "At first I thought—he's trying to hypnotize me, I'd heard of that before. But then I began to think maybe there was some truth in it."

"That you hated her?"

"That I wanted him. Or else why would I have gone there? Maybe I was just using her death as an excuse. I didn't know anymore. I still don't."

Jacqueline Volette frowned, waiting. The red ribbon around her neck accented the shock of white that showed above her ruffled blouse. She smelled of azalea.

"So it went on all these months," he heard himself say.

"I thought constantly of killing him, dreamed of it, and yet went when he called."

"You still hoped," César tried again, "that you could get him to confess."

"No, Inspector. By then I thought only of saving myself, I can assure you. But I couldn't, don't you see?"

"Why not?"

"How can you run from the very thing you want?"

Her eyes melted into his, a transference of feeling rather than truth. César knew the feeling since he had it himself, felt the pain spread slowly through his body. Obsessed, he was no longer free.

"Then Bock left," he stammered, as if she didn't know.

Jacqueline nodded. "He told me that he was leaving France for good."

"But you begged him to stay."

"I accepted he would go. How can I explain it? Sorrow and joy, they are sometimes the same thing."

"Did he tell you where he was going?"

"He is not the kind, that one."

"Would you tell me if he had?" César asked.

"He killed my sister."

Jacqueline Volette looked away, out over the garden. Shadows inched across the flower beds, dimming the colored bulbs. She looked away, but not before César caught a glimpse of the fierce ambition that made her reject marriage for a career in a man's world. He laughed at his own blindness. It was money that moved her, not men. An obsession was a temporary trap.

"Where do you think he went?"

"He knows people in Cologne."

"Yet he flew to Munich and then disappeared," César explained patiently, "leaving behind 120,000 francs."

Jacqueline Volette leaned into César's hot glare, her eyes startled pools.

"Not only that," he said gently, "there's a Swiss detective named Kayser who's after him. Would you know anything about that?"

César watched the roses on her cheeks darken into crimson folds.

* * *

"Are you familiar with Flaubert's work?"

"Only *Madame Bovary*."

"A genius," Tobie sighed. "They say he was concerned with style as much as content."

"Sometimes style is everything," Menard suggested.

Maton had stopped by César's office, found it empty, and went around to Menard's.

"Not only that, he concealed his own thoughts and feelings to get complete objectivity in his work. Why can't we do that, I wonder."

"Maybe writing stories and chasing criminals aren't the same."

"Of course they are," Tobie said. "Flaubert studied the lives of his characters with strict scientific observation, just as we must do our suspects."

"Meaning?"

"The shooting the other night. Bock is obviously after César, thinks he's getting too close." Maton paused. "Now if I were studying my suspect scientifically, I'd say the Nazi was dangerous right now. A wounded wolf."

"And you're worried."

"Aren't you?"

Menard ignored the question; worrying about his boss could be a full-time job in itself. "And you think César's not taking Bock seriously."

"Not seriously enough."

"What would you do?"

"I'd give it up," Tobie said emphatically, "or else get all the help I could."

The comment caused Menard to smile. "You know the inspector—"

Maton nodded. "A loner, unfortunately."

"Besides, he's not sure it was Bock the other night."

"What's that?"

"I mean, he is sure in a way. But like he says, why would Bock hire a couple of amateurs for a cop killing?"

"Probably couldn't get anyone else," Tobie offered.

"Maybe," Menard conceded. "Still—"

"Has he got any other suspects?"

"Not really. Just a feeling, I guess."

"A feeling," Tobie said, distracted.

"Those leaps of the imagination he's always talking about."

"I just hope they don't get him killed one of these days."

"Anyway, all the facts point to Bock," Menard said brightly, "and especially now that he's back."

The inspector went over to the window, gazed at his reflection in the glass. "Where's César?"

"The Prince of Darkness?" Menard imitated the movies' Bela Lugosi. "Come, children of the night—"

"You don't know."

"Me?" Menard slipped on his jacket. "All I know is I have orders from headquarters to be home in a half hour. Or else."

* * *

From the Cité the lights of the Left Bank looked like so many smears on a Surrealist canvas. While zealous officials restored the Marais and prettified Passy, the Left Bank tended to its commerce and culture in a babel of tongues. César, troubled, wandered through the crowded quarter until he stopped in the Deux Magots for coffee.

The café was busy but César saw no sign of Camus or Bardot. At the tables men preened and women pouted and everyone pumped exuberance. He watched a nearby couple hold hands, the boy's finger tracing her liquid blue veins. He'd often done that himself as a youth with slim-waisted girls, skimming their skin with his, causing little shudders to caress the eyes. He recalled the first time he touched a girl that way, her arm, the soft smooth inside of her arm, so very long ago. Suddenly it was Strasbourg again and she responded to his touch, there in the field by his foster parents' home. She was love and he was life in a time when everyone was happy, the terror gone. A golden time, a year, a day, that moment. Where was she now? César didn't know. Where was he?

The couple was gone when he looked again. In their place sat sight-seers in purple sunglasses, while nearby a table of young *littérateurs* loudly denounced everything written since the Middle Ages.

Directly in front of him a girl in jeans carefully counted her coins. Her fingers were streaked with paint, the nails bitten. At her side an empty cup testified to a lengthy stay. She was alone and not pretty.

"This will take care of hers, too." César pointed to the girl, handed the waiter twenty francs. *"Merci."*

He made two more stops on the way home, a glass of wine in each. The cafés were good for sitting out moods, even creating new ones. In his life César had created many moods in many cafés, and some identities too. All were lost in time, all but the hunter. He'd failed to exorcise that one. *Eh bien.* Life was littered with failed identities and the grave was in everybody. He would play the hunter until his turn came. It didn't occur to him that others might have failed in exactly the same way.

Rue de Meaux. The ancient street dozed in darkness, the way old men slumber between bouts of memory. It was the fashionable dining hour for the wealthy who gather in great restaurants while hordes of workmen huddle in homes like gaggles of geese against the coming of dawn.

César, indifferent to night and day, turned his corner wearily. Down the block a black Peugeot hummed discreetly, its headlights off, the steering wheel gripped by steady hands. Despite the dark the driver quickly spotted César and eased the car out of its stall. Still no lights shone.

At the intersection César began to cross. A dozen tired steps, two dozen, to the end of the brick and home. *Ende gut, alles gut.*

Strasbourg bothered him. Why kill Dussap, a war hero?

Jacqueline Volette bothered him even more.

In the distance a two-ton missile hurtled toward its target. Stones crackled underneath. The moon was lost behind leaden clouds and even the white brick gave no light.

At least they'd finished with Vichy. Prévert had sold some papers from his father's years in the government to East Germany, doubtless acting for the Russians who favored such things. They paid the price and then repaid Prévert for his treachery. According to César's source in the internal surveillance unit of the Sûreté, the papers had been fabricated by Prévert *fils* for money.

César was halfway across the intersection when the car broke the darkness at twenty meters.

Instinct turned his head, saved his life.

A split second.

Sound filled his ears as adrenaline shot through him, pushing his body pumping blood stretching muscle, blind movement building momentum, *moving,* legs churning arms reaching heart pounding. Bursting. Too late. Too far. Can't—

Must!

César arched his body—an albatross in flight—and dove into the hood of the parked car as the killing machine swerved to snare him and smashed into the side searing César's heels.

He landed on his shoulder, soft flesh splitting, his head tattooing metal bouncing across the hood, his body tumbling out of control over the other side falling finally to the pavement like a spinning scarecrow. Senseless, he hardly heard the roar of engine racing off.

Pain glued him to the ground. He felt himself shaking with fear, and excitement too. Bock! César whispered savagely. Back in Paris, adding another accident to his list.

César tried to pull himself up, failed, fell backwards against the front wheel. He sprawled there, seeking strength for the coming encounter.

Above him, stabs of light began to show behind shades. Tiny teeth in a friendly face.

César waited.

ELEVEN

What did Parisians know of Paris, anyway? They lived with it, shared its sun and milked its moon, all three million of them, *mais oui*, but there were limits. No true Parisian, for example, ever climbed up the Eiffel or cruised down the Seine on the *bateaux-mouches* that left daily from the Pont de l'Alma on the Right Bank, their decks alive with tourists. On this Friday morning César, nursing his wounds, sat quietly by the rail, watching the shore and seeing Dieter Bock.

Martel slipped into the next seat. "The best meeting place in Paris," he began agreeably. "No one speaks French."

"Let's hope we do," César said without turning.

"If it's about Bock."

"And Junot?"

"You mentioned Bock on the phone." Martel rested his arm on the back of the bench and studied César who wished he were elsewhere. The man beside him headed the SCE's Western Europe sector. Worse, he'd been a Nazi collaborator during the Occupation. He was, after all, in the political police and had just been doing his job according to the laws of the land at the time. For doing it so well he was rewarded after the war with work where his contacts would best serve France. Like maybe now, César thought. The man was a ferret.

"About a month ago," César said, "you had German papers forged in the name of Otto Wirth."

"Did I?" Martel's face was a blank.

"You even left your extension number with the forger."

"How careless of me."

"Not careless," César corrected. "You meant to leave a trail so if anyone followed, they'd look for Wirth. That was to be his public identity."

"Whose identity?"

"Bock, of course. You already had another set made with the new name he would actually use."

"Why would I do that for Bock?" Martel asked.

"Because he turned himself in to the Service through you."

Both men stared at the water. Around them people took pictures, held hands, scolded children. Another boatload of tourists passed and César wondered how he looked to them. Did they see the high cheekbones, the searching eyes of the hunter? Or was he beginning to appear the prey?

"We won't pretend, you and me, eh?" Martel smiled, his head bobbing like a balloon tossed onto the waves. "I knew Bock from the war."

"How well?"

"Well enough, I can assure you, César."

"Inspector will do."

"As you wish." The smile disappeared. "Now you want me to help you, tell you what I know."

"Doesn't that cut both ways?"

"But not always equally."

"An uneasy answer," César said.

"Then let us wait, *Monsieur* Inspector, for the easy questions."

They came soon enough, as even César had to admit. Martel first met Bock in 1942. His impression was that the man had few friends, but was he not German? He liked the French, though, had an appreciation of the Gallic temperament. Bock believed, for example, that terror tactics wouldn't work in France as they did in the eastern countries. The French, he insisted, wanted to be considered intelligent at any price so the obvious method was to win over their philosophers and writers by maintaining an air of cultural activity. This was largely done and in 1943, at the height of the German Occupation, more books were published in France than in the United States.

Did Martel know if Bock had anything to do with this policy?

Possibly in a minor way, since he'd originally been attached to SS headquarters in Berlin.

Bock was in Paris on his second visit when Martel met him. He'd been sent to observe SS methods in the field and had already seen Lyon. An industrial giant, Lyon was a center of resistance and a new Gestapo boss, Klaus Barbie, was using repressive measures. Bock thought Barbie a good policeman and strategist but without common sense, and reported this to Berlin.

Had Martel seen the report?

Certainly not. He was just a liaison for Bock's visit to Paris and knew only what was said in idle conversation.

Bock had found Paris delightful the second time around. Despite some wartime shortages, the city glowed with vitality. Cafés and cabarets were open, the theaters and music halls, the restaurants, racetracks, museums, libraries. Newspapers were printed, plays produced, movies made. The Sartres of the land published their books with the Nazi swastika seal of approval. Collaboration was the national policy and Paris the nation's capital, and everything was as always for the French very practical. When Bock finally left for Rouen he vowed to return someday.

César was interested in the dates. When did Bock leave Paris?

Around the middle of July.

On June 28, 1942, Eichmann arrived in Paris with Himmler's order to deport all French Jews to the east. On July 16–17 nine thousand police, aided by four hundred *Milice* auxiliaries, rounded up thirteen thousand Parisian Jews and herded them into a sports arena before they were shipped east to be butchered. It was the blackest chapter in French police history; one César could never reconcile with his position as a policeman and a Jew. Nor was he helped by the knowledge that the Paris Police Department had given its card file with the names of 150,000 French Jews to the Gestapo.

There was no evidence linking Bock to Eichmann or the police raids, but César now used his presence in Paris at that precise time as still another nail in the coffin he hoped to seal. The man had become a symbol and the search a crusade.

Was there any significance in the dates? Martel wanted to know.

César shook his head, quickly asked about Bock's first visit to Paris. Did Martel know anything about that?

Only indirectly, from what Bock and others said. The *Résistance* was just starting then, pushed and prodded by de Gaulle's Free French movement, and the underground had yet to begin operating out of the Paris catacombs. By the end of 1941 the lights were going out all over the world. Things were changing for Bock, too; he was now on Himmler's personal staff.

It was December in Paris and Bock had come to kill Janos Skoda, the Czech resistance leader who'd fled a concentration camp and marched across half of Europe fueling the fires of opposition. Everywhere he went he made fools of the SS and Himmler wanted him dead.

César knew of Skoda, of course, a charismatic figure who instilled courage and hope in those under Nazi domination. His example had prompted the slaying of Reinhard Heydrich, Himmler's protégé and true architect of the Holocaust. While people like Gandhi were advising millions of Jews to commit mass suicide and the Pope was promising eternal rewards, Skoda was telling them to fight. Fight or die. And when the last Jewish resister in the last burning building in the Warsaw ghetto was finally murdered after twenty-eight days of fighting tanks with knives and sticks, the furious and ignominious SS troops found the name of Janos Skoda on one of the few remaining walls.

But they never found him, said Martel, not in all of Paris. The Gestapo couldn't locate him and Bock couldn't kill him, and soon Bock returned to Berlin and Skoda was gone.

Gone where?

To Casablanca.

He escaped Paris and went on to Marseille and Oran and finally Casablanca, which was under Vichy rule as part of unoccupied France. There he met a British agent who got him to Lisbon and then London, where he helped organize the underground.

For César, it meant that Bock had failed. He was not perfect.

But why had he been picked to kill Skoda?

Surely the inspector understood. Some of those on Himmler's staff had the killer instinct.

And Bock?

Perhaps he had the most.

César looked out over the water as the *bateau-mouche* glided serenely up the Seine, his mind's eye seeing the snap of Bock's gun. Late 1941—and the Nazi had become a paid assassin with his own PPK, just as the gunsmith had said. He'd killed for the SS, for West and East Germany, and now finally for himself. His latest victims were out of the inspector's jurisdiction, but all the boy could see was the beast in Berlin commanding Bock to kill his parents. César saw the cruel smiles, heard the venomous voices.

"Kaputt gemachen!"

"Jawohl, Reichsführer."

"Quel dommage!"

César's head snapped round to Martel beside him, smiling.

"What a pity, I said, that Bock didn't find Skoda here in Paris. Who knows? Things might have turned out differently."

César tried to control himself. "What about Junot?"

The smile soured. "I want him dead."

Had he heard right? The inspector's eyes flashed red. "We are not the political police, *Monsieur* Supervisor."

"Junot's been told to go after Bock. If you find him first, I get what I want."

Thugs and killers, César reminded himself, but how else could it be? Conflict and war were their business, and the nation needed its secret police as much as the hand needed fingers; in their view peace was an illusion even within the agency itself.

"Why didn't Junot know about Bock?" he asked. "It should've been done through his sector."

"Can't you guess?" Martel's grin returned. "Junot's on the way out. He never was one of us, anyway; even in Algeria he was a Gaullist when we were for the OAS. Now that de Gaulle is gone—" He glanced at César. "He was always an outsider in the Service, much like you with the police—being a Jew, I mean." Martel laughed. "I just want to give him a permanent push."

"So you get the Middle East sector, is that it?"

"Why not? Western Europe is the intelligence center for the Mideast anyway." He crossed his legs, craned his neck. "Shall we enjoy the ride?"

The boat slowly passed police headquarters.

"I'll find Bock," César said suddenly, "for my own reasons."

The supervisor nodded. "Any assistance I can give—"

"You can start with the photograph."

"Comment?"

"You took his photo from the district police file because your boss didn't want us to have any pictures of him." It was César's turn to smile. "You brought it with you because you need me to find Bock. The general doesn't think Junot can do it."

César held out his hand.

The glossy finish was faded. He cradled the print in his sweaty palms, his knees glued together lest it fall through his fingers. After a while he stared downward, down into the face of the devil.

It was 1945 again and Dieter Bock was twenty-six years old, tall and handsome in his black SS uniform. A superior Aryan specimen. His eyes were as deep as the Danube and ice blue, his mouth was a thin bloodless line carved out of Teutonic timber. The face spoke of strength and purpose. César sat amazed at how little of the human heart could be seen through the skin. Was that why aboriginal tribes carved out the hearts of their sacrificial victims? To touch the truth at last?

Even more amazing was Captain Bock's SS uniform. It bore the rank of major.

* * *

He'd been lucky. Battered but no bones broken; the shoulder would heal and so would his scalp. The doctor prescribed five days rest. César compromised with five hours sleep. At 6 A.M. Menard called. Was he all right? César silently vowed never to call anyone again before seven.

By eight he sat on his office couch, softer on his bruised body, and listened to Clément describe Himmler's inner circle after 1941. There was the usual assortment of generals serving as personal aides but the *Reichsführer* seemed to favor Kaltenbrunner's Security Service and the Gestapo; they held the reins of the Jewish extermination campaign, his special project. As he saw less of Hitler, who regarded his police duties as necessary but socially unacceptable, Himmler increasingly turned to those involved in the Final Solution, as if his successful efforts there would return him to the Führer's hearth.

With the July 1944 plot on Hitler's life, his loyal henchman had his final moment of glory as his SS killed over five thousand, sent another five thousand to concentration camps and broke the back of the German General Staff. By then the assembled killers around Himmler were highly experienced and one of them, an executioner named von Schirrmacher, was given the job of hanging the leaders in the most barbarous manner. The colonel did his work well. They were slowly strangled with piano wire suspended from meat hooks.

A stab of fear shut César's eyes. Von Schirrmacher? Could he have been wrong from the start? Where was Bock?

According to Clément, Bock apparently had nothing to do with the hangings. His name didn't appear on any records.

Suppose Bock was already dead, César agonized, and everything a false trail to Reimer? Meant to lead an idiot like him back to Bock, who would never be found, leaving the real killer not even suspected. Von Schirrmacher! Or was this still more of Bock's planning?

César sank deeper into the burning couch, felt his skin searing, heard the glutinous pop of tissue exploding. Could anyone fashion such a triple-cross and succeed? *Mon Dieu!* Could anyone rob the Bank of France?

He would have to run a two-pronged investigation, the second searching for Schirrmacher who was never caught. César's mind raced the possibilities as Clément ran down the list of SS elite in France, few of whom were ever brought to trial even though hundreds were known by name. Ernst Heinrichsohn, who gave the orders for deportation, was a mayor in Bavaria. Alois Brunner, an Eichmann lieutenant who deported 24,000 Jews from Drancy, the concentration camp on the outskirts of Paris, was a respected German businessman, as were Kurt Lischka and Herbert Hagen, who ran the French deportation machinery. The chief of SS in Toulouse served as a magistrate in Baden Württemberg and the head of the Paris Gestapo was a high official of Lower Saxony, while the Lyon Gestapo boss Klaus Barbie supplied arms to Bolivia . . .

"And Bock?"

"Listed on Himmler's staff, an aide."

"That's all?"

On second thought it seemed reasonable, since killing was not an acceptable job classification. Von Schirrmacher had been an aide, too.

* * *

Dupin himself brought the SCE file. Returned from his river ride, César was on the phone when his superior walked in with Bock's green folder. "No one else" was all he said. César wondered where the gracious manner went, or even the good fellowship. The chief inspector was all business. "Any questions?"

By lunchtime César had some answers. Bock had turned himself in to the Service in March, admitting two kills: Broussard the double agent, and Henry Stiles, who secretly managed funds for British intelligence in Europe. Stiles had embezzled large sums from his covert funding accounts and then claimed the money went for buying secret police in East Germany, which compromised several Stasi agents and demoralized others.

The file also detailed much of Bock's SS background. Coldly efficient, he'd quickly risen through the ranks; by 1942 he was one of Himmler's exterminating angels, largely used to discipline those who stood in the way of the state. His discipline took only one form: he killed them without remorse. When he was convicted in 1954 of complicity in SS crimes he was given six years, of which he served three years and eight months.

For his SCE keep Bock agreed to spill what he knew of East German security; he also promised to deliver an important Stasi agent who wanted to defect. Bock had a plan. He'd send word his cover was blown and Reimer would be sent to get him out. Once on French soil, he'd report to the Service. Instead, he killed Bock—or so it was thought until César came along. Now it appeared Bock had plans of his own.

César couldn't blame them for wanting to bury the file. They had been badly used. Reimer didn't want to defect; if he did, he could easily have found a way. Bock had killed six, and he hadn't mentioned the dead in Austria and Germany. Nor did he name Olympic Imports as the local Stasi pipeline. Bock told them just enough of East Germany's activities and nothing of his own. When he supposedly was slain, they panicked and declared his file's disclosure would compromise an SCE operation. But there was no operation; it had died with the patient.

César felt elated. He knew more about the man than anyone. What Bock wanted was to have the French and German intelligence agencies aware of him, and César was beginning to see why.

* * *

Who were the Jews but killers of the Christian God? At the infamous Wannsee Conference outside Berlin in January 1942, Nazi leaders drew up plans for the murder of ten million European Jews. With Germanic thoroughness they presented a country-by-country listing of Jews to be deported to the extermination camps, the first of which—Chelmno in Poland—was already in use. Holland, for instance, had 160,800 while Norway claimed 1,600 and Albania only 200. There were 742,800 Jews in Hungary, three million in Poland, two million in Russia, and another 2,994,684 living—but not for long —in the Ukraine. In Greece there were 69,000; Switzerland had 18,000; Spain 6,000; Britain 330,000. In France, where many had already been deported, there were still 300,000 Jews to be murdered and Eichmann had promised to give it his personal attention. Six months later he kept his word . . .

César spent his lunch hour in the deportation memorial at the foot of the Cité, dutifully explaining to his dead Jewish parents why he was involved with nothing but Germans lately. It was the Bock case. Bock was himself a Nazi who'd worked for both Germanys and was there again, had been anyway. César fingered his scalp. He'd have to be more careful; Bock might try again. Was it Bock? Why should the Nazi care about one hunter when others would surely pick up the scent?

The dutiful son mumbled the names of the camps over and over, his Friday litany to the dead. During the war 8,000 Italian Jews were killed in the camps and 85,000 French Jews. Was it because France openly collaborated and complied with the Nazis? Whenever César had such thoughts he reminded himself of the 642 inhabitants of the village of Oradour-sur-Glane who were slaughtered in retaliation for the death of an SS battalion commander. Almost seven hundred French men, women and children for one Nazi!

Back on his couch César spoke to West Germany. The BND had given the dead man's prints to the Stasi, told them of the body in Paris. It was Reimer. East Germany was upset, already in touch with French officials regarding the unprovoked and brutal murder of one of its citizens, a harmless retiree on vacation.

"Were they told it was Bock who killed him?"

"As the inspector suggested."

"And they denied any knowledge of Bock."

"Of course."

"But they couldn't deny the money link to Zurich."

"They said they would look into it."

"Meaning they'd change it."

"Quickly."

So César had something to trade if he moved fast. Bock didn't tell the Service about Olympic Imports because it would've tipped the Stasi that he'd crossed over. He counted on them thinking he was slain by French agents who learned of his role, and the French believing he'd been killed by East German agents for his double cross. Or even both of them suspecting West Germany of the deed. Anything, as long as each thought one of the others did it. Bock had turned himself in to the SCE to set up a reason for his own death. *Bon!* But why all the show for the police? Why leave everything behind in his flat?

* * *

At 3:15 Chief Inspector Dupin met with General Bordier and his aide. Inspector Dreyfus, it seemed, possessed vital information concerning an East German spy network in Paris, information withheld from them by their double agent Bock. If they did not agree to his request he would turn his report over to the appropriate ministry officials, which would greatly embarrass the Service and pave the way for other security agencies to gain power.

And the inspector's request?

The names of all ex-Nazis working for the SCE in France.

At 4:30 the Service agreed.

By 7 P.M. French security police had raided the Paris office of Olympic Imports on Boulevard Raspail and seized its records. The company's bank accounts were impounded, its assets frozen, and proceedings begun to expel key personnel on spy charges. President Giscard d'Estaing warned that the espionage activities could seriously affect relations between the two countries. A proposed visit to East Germany was abruptly discarded.

At SCE headquarters plans were laid to terminate the service of all ex-Nazis in its employ, at least those included on the Dreyfus list. They'd outlived their usefulness, anyway, and dismissal could be blamed on the regular police.

* * *

"What made you change your mind about Dreyfus?"

"Have I changed my mind about him?"

Curious, the director of the Criminal Police sat in his corner office and pumped his Homicide commander.

"You made his outrageous proposal to the SCE sound like life and death, when we could have just ordered him to tell everything he knew. A week ago you would've thrown him out of your office."

"A week ago I didn't see what I'm seeing now."

"And what is that?"

"Dreyfus." Dupin frowned, uncomfortable with his new thoughts. "He's bringing back some glory to the police department, some real criminal investigation. And not just stopping at the door of the political police, which is all we ever do anymore in these matters."

"That might be true," his superior acknowledged, "but the danger—"

"The danger, *Monsieur Directeur,* is that we try to stop him."

The director, a political animal, shifted in his seat as he sensed the wind beginning to blow from a different direction.

* * *

César, still at his desk, had pinned Bock's SS picture to the bulletin board. A hundred times he stared at it from the couch, focused on it a few feet away, peered at it through his magnifying glasses. He'd been using them the past year or two against everyone's advice. Go see a doctor, they said; cheap glasses would ruin your eyes, especially the kind that magnify. But what were a doctor's expensive eyeglasses? Just magnifying glass that cost ten times as much and didn't change a thing. Dieter Bock would still look the same.

César caught Bock leering at him and he turned away. When he looked again, the Nazi was smiling. And why not? They not only shared the same obsession—the hunter and the hunted, locked in fearful embrace—but they now shared the same passion as well.

Except Bock had already tasted his, and César never would.

He raised the dart in a toast—

"To Jacqueline!"

—and flung it at Bock's head.

TWELVE

Answers are always so simple once you know them. For days César had been bothered by Kayser's calling Bock a major. How'd he see the Himmler letter unless he knew Bock? But he didn't. What he'd seen was the photograph of Bock as an SS major, the same photo now on César's desk, and Martel showed it to him. They had felt each other out on Bock, according to the SCE supervisor, meeting once. Yet how did they meet? Martel was a former Nazi collaborator; Kayser knew many ex-Nazis. Did they have a mutual friend, someone still in the shadows? Martel claimed Kayser got his name from people in the intelligence community. Wasn't that obvious? Which was what worried César.

As for Bock being an SS major, even unofficially, it meant he had fulfilled Himmler's condition in the letter, done the one last deed at the end of the war. A killing, no doubt; maybe settling old scores. Who did Himmler hate that much?

"Who?"

Clément didn't know, not specifically. Himmler hated everybody around Hitler, felt they'd poisoned the Führer's mind against him. Bormann for one, always standing behind Hitler and keeping others at a distance. Göring was another, vain, brutish, filling Hitler's ear with grandiose schemes that excluded the SS. They were all guilty in Himmler's eyes, the whole entourage; all had conspired against him.

Bormann was the only one not accounted for. Could Bock have killed him right at the end? César now wondered. A bullet to the head and a hand grenade in the mouth would be all it took.

In the more recent conspiracy against Linge and Streicher, a look at their activities showed no links to East Germany. In fact, both belonged to political groups demanding the unification of Germany under western influence. Linge had strong anticommunist views. Streicher, the accountant, even denounced an East German decree requiring citizens to register their typewriters with the police, probably on the theory that calculators could be next.

Clément's conclusion: Hardly the types to be Stasi agents.

César had to agree. Max Baur, a policeman at heart, was the aberration so Bock's latest kills were not political but part of a plan having to do with the Nazi past. All the victims were from the old days, with the necessary exception of Reimer.

Were others involved? Former Nazis? Neo-Nazis? César hardly dared hope. No direct evidence existed for any other involvement, and yet—was his intuition ever wrong? Many times, he told himself, knowing that wasn't true. False modesty was a sin of pride, and César was proud of his leaps of imagination. He intended to follow Bock back to hell itself.

* * *

Like Antaeus, son of Poseidon and mother earth, César grew stronger each time he was beaten to the ground. From a botched suicide he'd nursed the Bock case along until the department backed him, if only temporarily. Even the SCE had reluctantly fallen in line, checking on the fifty biggest West German financiers for Nazi pasts. Anything was possible.

Menard and André, meanwhile, delved into Austria for leads involving money and Nazis; Bock's plan apparently included all three. Whatever doubts César may have had about his direction were gone. The Nazi hunters had found the missing March victim:

"Hamburg, March 22 (News Bureau). Richard Hoffman, a senior sales representative for an international metals manufacturer, died of carbon monoxide poisoning early Friday morning when he fell asleep in his car after driving home from a party. Subsequent investigation revealed that *Herr* Hoffman was a colonel in the SS during the war, attached to Himmler's staff."

The Nazi hunters were told about a second wanted man, this one still alive presumably. His name was Richard von Schirrmacher and he also had been a colonel in the SS.

They found him, too—dead in Hamburg on March 21. An accident.

It was the same man.

* * *

Kussow held the photograph up to his glasses.

"This is him?"

"Dieter Bock in the flesh." César managed to sound pleased and disappointed at the same time. "Thirty years ago."

"They all looked like that"—Kussow kept staring at the face— "those same dead Nazi eyes."

"You're sure about the uniform?"

"It's authentic, an SS major."

"Which means—"

"The way he wears it, you'd think it was made for him," Kussow scoffed, "instead of just posing for the camera."

"So how do you know it wasn't?"

Kussow lowered the picture, pointed to Bock's chest. "All those decorations."

"What about them?"

"The Nazis were plagued with phony medals, especially the Iron Cross. Everybody was wearing one. He's wearing two, and they're both the Grand Cross of the Iron Cross. Your man really dressed himself for the occasion."

"Apparently." César studied the decorations. He saw a labeled Crimea Shield next to an obvious Tank Assault Badge; for all he knew, others might be a Sharpshooter's Pin and the Assassin Medal of Honor. Maybe Bock had won them all. "What's wrong with the Grand Cross of the Iron Cross?"

"Nothing much," Kussow noted, "except the only one ever awarded went to Reichsmarshall Hermann Göring."

* * *

The news from Strasbourg was startling. In 1956 Paul Dussap had been accused by his ex-wife of having secretly collaborated with the

Nazis. He dismissed her as a vindictive woman out to ruin him, but she had enough stories to cast doubt on his denials.

The most damning tale concerned a 1943 Gestapo raid on a convent whose nuns were hiding a dozen Jews. On the previous day she'd followed him to a barn on the edge of their farm, suspecting him of being unfaithful since he often left for an hour or two. At the barn she saw a German staff car so she waited in hiding; eventually her husband came out with a lone SS officer who quickly drove away. She said nothing at the time but a decade later, bitter at Dussap for taking a younger woman, she began repeating her stories.

César knew none of this. By 1956 he was already in Paris, a young man seeking his fortune. He loved his foster parents yet felt his own destiny lay elsewhere; perhaps the army, like his famous relative who died in the year he was born. Or the hunter he was born to be.

But what was Dussap's motive? His ex-wife said he hated Jews, claimed he was always cheated by them in business.

For the first time César saw the danger he'd been in as a boy. The man knew his foster parents, had seen him. A Jew? More likely he thought him just another French waif taken in, a common occurrence as the war went on. Yet the threat was always there, though his foster parents never spoke of it. When they died in a 1967 fire, César cried the same as for his real parents. After the war he'd returned to using his own name but from the Fauchons he took a sense of justice, now sorely abused. Nothing in the police report from Strasbourg led to Bock, at least for the moment.

All he could do was get the names of the Jews in the convent raid and try to find a connection. Either that or forget about Dussap's treachery and Bock's bullet. He couldn't do that anymore. One man would've had him killed as a boy, and the other was trying to kill him now.

* * *

Proverbs aside, luck did not come to him who looked, Clément insisted, but to him who looked again. Half the previous day was spent in a Jewish museum going through wartime photos, searching for Himmler at work. He was seen inspecting SS troops, marching in Nazi parades, watching the slaughter of Jews, holding his young daughter Gudrun and saluting Hitler in his Wolf's Lair headquarters, none of which served the present need. With nowhere to go,

Clément sifted the pile again—and there he was, seated in his office with Hitler hanging on the wall right behind his desk.

In the galleries few knew of the portrait, none its owner. A dealer in folk art had an idea who might be seeking it, just an educated guess really.

Did César want to hear?

East Germany, Clément gurgled into César's glare.

The communist government was trying to recover treasure looted from its cities during the war. Trunks of priceless gems, tons of precious metals, thousands of art works were being sought. Everything that had once reposed in homes and museums east of the border, including half a hundred aluminum crates containing paintings by the old masters.

"But oils of Adolf?" César asked.

"Maybe they're just greedy. Wasn't Himmler's office in what's now East Berlin?"

"Or maybe they're trying to corner the market."

"Not a chance," Clément scoffed. "America alone has five thousand paintings from Hitler's War Arts program in army camps and warehouses."

Greed or gold, East Germany was a good guess. Kayser could be working for them.

* * *

The French intelligence community was more of a tuning fork than a divining rod. In the days of de Gaulle the community ran hard to justify its existence, a justification never entirely successful at the Elysée Palace which had contempt for grown men playing at spies. De Gaulle's departure brought slow recovery to the various segments, including the SCE.

The agency's struggle to repair its image was aided immeasurably in those dark days by the British and West German intelligence communities having been equally plagued, Britain with its Kim Philby scandal and the Federal Intelligence Agency with the espionage trial of Heinz Felfe who headed its spy operations in Eastern Europe. By the seventies things had largely returned to normal, which for the Service meant reacting defensively.

The present problem was no exception. An inspector of police had uncovered an East German spy ring under their nose in the heart of

Paris. The political publicity gave him an edge, a bargaining position, only temporarily of course. For the moment they would humor him, his latest humor being a list of West German financiers with Nazi pasts. What harm could that do?

At SCE headquarters, Bordier sat in his second floor office and listened to his chief of operations discuss the list. Fourteen of the fifty had Nazi pasts, four of them deep involvement but three of those four had been politically helpful to the Service. Two still were, both enjoying close relations with the ministry. At that level—a gleam of jealousy appeared in the chief's eye—they all talked informally, of course.

Bordier glanced over the four briefs: Speer's armaments liaison, a radio propaganda director, the Foreign Office vice-consul, and a special assignments officer attached to Himmler's staff, the last two still helpful.

"How helpful?"

"Very."

In that case, suggested the general, there was no reason to subject them to further harassment at the hands of opportunist policemen, at best an irresponsible breed. Dreyfus would be given the twelve names with the final two held back for future evaluation. Perhaps a word to each of them would show the proper spirit of reciprocity, *n'est-ce pas?* There had been no indication of current Nazi activity.

"Absolutely not."

"Then let the Jew have his due."

* * *

Lelouch was buried in a newspaper when César sat down.

"Let me tell you how *Le Monde* will handle the end of the world." The waiter kept nodding at the print. "After the headline announces Nuclear Holocaust Destroys Earth, a subhead will report Traffic Snarled Almost Everywhere, followed by a box of white space with the caption Parliament Takes Extended Vacation." He lowered the paper, beamed. "The ultimate journalistic balance."

"Do you always read upside down?" César asked.

"Only between the lines."

César tore off the front page and fashioned it into a stick figure that he placed on the table. "A Swiss detective."

"At your age, paper police?" Lelouch surveyed the shreds in front of him.

"He's only a symbol."

"So's a newspaper."

"What would make him work for East Germany?"

"East Germany? Only a gun at his head."

"How about a lot of money?"

"To a Swiss that's the same thing."

"The East Germans are after treasure," César explained, "they claim was stolen from them during the war. You know anything about that?"

"Just what I read in the papers."

"But you read *Le Monde.*"

"Only the comics." Lelouch swept up the shreds from the table with his hand. "But East Germany. It's a sore point with them, has been for twenty-five years. In the war a lot of treasure found its way to Bavaria where all the big Nazis stayed, other parts of western Germany too." He threw the scraps on the floor. "Göring alone looted a half-dozen cities; he stole Dresden blind."

"Wasn't everything returned after the war?"

"When the Allies caught up with him in the final days, he'd left a freight train full of loot—a whole freight train!—at Berchtesgaden. Must've been worth billions." Lelouch shook his head in wonder. "Most of it never got back."

"What I don't understand," César said, "is how East Germany can claim ownership. They weren't even a country until 1949."

"Neither was West Germany."

"What's that?"

Lelouch smiled a row of yellowed teeth. "The French like to forget that its new ally is only a few months older than the east. So age has nothing to do with it." He picked up César's paper figure. "It's the cities themselves, like Dresden. They owned the valuables and want them back." Pulled it apart. "But a Swiss? That I don't understand at all."

"This one can smell money a mile away."

"You could grill a Swiss in garlic and he'd still smell money." Lelouch began to read the torn fragment. "What they need is an army of Corsican bandits. Or a couple of Jews."

"We're a couple of Jews."

"That makes three of us."

"There's only two of us."

"Marked down."

César absently tore off another page. "Then you don't think he'd be working for them."

"Who thinks anymore? But if I did"—Lelouch folded the remains of the newspaper, tucked it under his arm protectively—"I would look deeper."

"An individual?" César asked.

"If those are the only people you know."

* * *

Back at headquarters César called Kayser's hotel; his room had been reserved for two more days. He asked if the room key was in his box. It wasn't, but Kayser always left the key when he went out. So he was in.

Menard returned from checking Kayser's Paris schedule. He'd arrived on April 10, the day before Reimer's body was found in Bock's flat; flew in from Zurich, where he had an office. In the past week he had been monitoring the Bock case, talking to whomever he could. "Which means he's after more than a painting."

"He's after Bock," César told Menard.

"So he knows Bock is still here."

"Or he's trying hard to give that impression."

Paranoia? César wondered. What was normal suspicion? It would be nice to see a cow without counting the nipples.

"But why?" Menard asked.

"He could be here to shake anybody loose from Bock."

There was no information on Kayser's client either. East Germany or someone else? César could almost hear breathing in the wings.

Menard had his notes on Linz and Mauthausen but César was more interested in Switzerland at the moment. Kayser may have used the Hitler portrait as his cover, but cover stories sometimes had a way of paying off.

"Bring Kayser down for a chat," he told Menard. "It's time we talked about Bock, anyway. No, don't mention him. Just say we might have something on his painting."

"Want me to call him first?"

"No use scaring him off." He fished in the drawer for car keys—

"Be warm and tender, you know the routine"—handed Menard a set, and put another in his pocket.

"Back in an hour."

With Menard gone César luxuriated for a moment, his sore shoulder forgotten. Things were starting to fall his way. Think of it! Killer von Schirrmacher could have worked alongside killer Bock in the old days. Now thirty years later one kills the other. Incredible. And Bock himself; he could've still been working for the Germans, east or west. But he was on his own now, seeking something after thirty years.

César took a deep breath; maybe he was better than he thought, after all. When Menard came back, they'd have a quick drink to themselves. Lately he'd been going home when it got dark, which meant his wife was on the warpath again.

The investigation had turned everything upside down. Oddly enough it even occupied his dreams, a cleansing and ordering of the day's events. But what if he failed? He was making enemies again, and pushing people who would push back. He shouldn't be so suspicious, trust people more. What people? He could barely trust himself half the time. Motives were everything. What were his?

He picked up the phone and called Jacqueline Volette at home. "I need to talk to you about something important, now."

She hesitated. "Saturday evening?"

"It's important," he repeated.

Curiosity moved mountains, as every inspector knew. Who could refuse something important?

"Come," Jacqueline said. "It's the second bell. I assume you also have my address."

Tobie stopped by—"Always know where to find you on weekends"—and listened to César fill him in on Bock, some of it. The rest required answers.

"Why do you think Kayser's here?"

"Isn't it the painting he's after?"

César leaned back in his chair. "Is that what he told you? I'm just curious."

"Far as I know," Tobie said lightly. "But who'd trust a detective?"

"Did you know he's interested in Bock?"

"The thought crossed my mind."

"But you don't know the reason."

"Do you?" Tobie asked.

"I intend to find out. Menard's getting him now."

In the car he thought about Tobie's evasions. Sinister plots ran through his head. Maton was a Nazi. Kayser was Hitler's secret son. Bock didn't exist; the two of them were Bock. If nothing made sense, he was to blame—him and his suspicious mind. He was working on nerve and adrenaline, an addict reaching for one more thread, still another connection. Why didn't he take Tobie's advice and get rid of it; was that so bad? Dump it on someone else. Who said he was the best they had? He hated himself for doubting his own abilities—and suspected he was right. He was not an extraordinary man, as he'd once believed, not even a good hunter. He had too many doubts. Didn't he?

* * *

The Excelsior lobby was a relic of a gilded age—full of chaise longues and velvet plush and ornate encoignures—whose glamour had vanished. Only the elevator seemed not trapped in time as Menard ascended swiftly to the fourth floor and Kayser's room.

The hallway was an elaborate maze of mirrors and scarlet antique that accented the flecks of fool's gold on the ceiling. Ranks of servants tended to the constant cleaning that preserved the grand illusion; no hotel in Paris so pampered its past or gave its guests so much fin-de-siècle splendor. There was even a button that could be set to leave the door unlocked: perfect for friendly visits. Menard knocked loudly, waited, knocked again, finally called out Kayser's name. Eventually he turned the knob, tried the door; it opened.

"Anyone here?" He fought his impatience. "Hello?"

Receiving no reply, he widened the opening and entered the room. Lamps were lit, the drapes drawn. He passed through the foyer into the huge chamber. The bed had been made, wastebaskets emptied, ashtrays cleaned. In the spacious closet hung clothing; the parted doors held dressing mirrors.

No one was home.

Inexplicably annoyed instead of alarmed, the detective sergeant stepped farther into the room for a final look, his mind intent on returning to headquarters and home. He hoped the inspector wouldn't keep him too long; Saturday nights were spent with his in-laws who lived even deeper in the country. On the other hand, maybe he could use César as an excuse to get out of going at all. Wouldn't be the first time either.

A movement from the bathroom caught his eye, too late. By the time he saw the sling he saw the gun.

* * *

The house was on the Avenue du Maine. Nearing it César practiced his words, what he wanted to say. Why were men afraid to talk to women? Action was easier, only words terrified. Was it because women were space and men time? They were always in motion, doing things. Like talking to themselves before talking to women. You and Bock. You and Kayser. You and me. Did it matter? She'd see what he meant in his eyes, and what he wanted too. Yet he wasn't sure himself. The fantasy was safe, incapable of disappointing.

He pressed the bell, pushed open the door, through the hall and up the stairs to the second floor. She stood in the doorway.

It was a physical thing, seeing her suddenly like that. The breath simply left his body, a swoosh of air leaving a balloon, deflating his diaphragm and boiling the blood. The next second he sucked in enough oxygen to cough and his reddish skin faded to pink. César felt for the railing, tried to smile.

Was he all right?

Not really.

She led him into a room filled with soft chairs and thick rugs. César saw only how radiant she was: Arletty in *Les Enfants du Paradis* or Marlene Dietrich in anything. He was suddenly exhilarated, lighter than air and full of lust.

She was glad to see him. Was it about Bock?

Yes, no. It was Bock who had tried to kill him, run him down the other night. Dieter? She didn't believe him.

"But he's not in France. You said so yourself."

"So I was wrong."

Distracted, he watched her pour the wine. Could he go to Dupin and tell him the Bock case was not about murder but stolen treasure? Something that happened thirty years ago under the Nazis? Dupin would have his head. What was the treasure? Where was it? How did Bock fit in? Who else was involved? He didn't know, didn't have any evidence. They'd lock him up for impersonating an inspector. Murders in Germany and Austria? Weren't they accidents?

Suspicion fell on Jacqueline Volette. Had they talked, she and Bock? They would've had to talk. What did lovers talk about? Did she know of his past, his present? He was not the kind to tell. He'd used her while he waited. Had he dropped her when his wait was over? Her eyes were pale and very deep, a bottomless reservoir.

The treasure was a lock of her hair. The Nazis were planning to steal her head. If he could find them, he would save her. If she would tell him where they were.

When she sipped he saw the wine clear her throat, red on alabaster white.

"Tell me about Kayser."

"I told you the other night."

"Tell me again."

"He wanted to know where Dieter was." Jacqueline set down her glass. "Wanted him in on a business deal; they were old friends, he said. I told him I couldn't help. Dieter was gone."

"That was the only time you saw him."

"At lunch, the day you saw me."

"Bock mentioned your name the last time they were together."

"How else could he get it?"

César took a long swallow, closed his eyes. Why was he here? He did not care what Kayser wanted; it was probably all lies anyway. He didn't even care if Jacqueline Volette was lying, at least it didn't seem to matter when she was near. Just being with her was enough. He didn't understand it, had never felt like this. It was madness. Here he sat, wanting to keep the case going forever just to involve her on any pretext. Had he been doing that all along? Was it all just for her? Maybe he wasn't dangerously paranoid, inventing everything; maybe he was criminally obsessive. At this very moment he was ready to subvert justice itself for her smile.

"Did you ever love Bock?" he asked, and felt her sigh. "Do you feel anything now?"

"Nothing, something."

"What?"

"Regret. Shame."

But love? Never!

César drank from his glass, grateful for the momentary lull. Someone close to Bock took the things from the apartment, Tobie had said. Even his wife's eyeglasses. Someone close to Bock.

How little men knew of women, he thought. Here he was, a loser in love, a man fearful of life and hiding behind death, and now seeking still another in whom to invest his failure. She would not be so easily fooled, this one.

Jacqueline got up to answer the phone, a man's voice. "For you."

Headquarters.

"Dreyfus."

". . . a homicide at the Excelsior. Dead man identified as Detective Sergeant Menard Rimbaud . . ."

* * *

The hotel corridor was crowded with local police and startled guests craning for another glimpse; at the door's edge managers stood wringing their hands in grief, their eyes testifying that nothing like this had ever happened at the Excelsior. Inside the room the duty homicide squad was busy with its own routine. Menard lay on his back by the bed; his jacket was still buttoned. The bullet hole in the center of his forehead looked like flakes of ash.

César joined the duty inspector, who shook his head sadly. "I had them call you soon's I got here."

"Anyone see it?"

"The two in the corner." He pointed. "They were leaving their room when they heard the shot. The guy saw them as he walked out, waved them back inside with his gun."

"They get his face?"

"He wore a cap pulled low over his eyes. The only thing they saw for sure was the sling."

"Sling?" César's breath hissed.

"His arm was in a sling. Mean anything?"

"Could be."

"The way I see it he surprised Menard, maybe from the bathroom. Or he could've been over by the window. You can see the far end there's hidden from the door."

"Who found the body?"

"Everyone. He left the door open."

César stared at Menard, smaller in death.

The duty inspector rubbed a hand across his jaw. "Got any ideas on the killer?"

"Only his name. It's Dieter Bock."

César searched the room for signs of Kayser, anything to show he'd left on his own; he found only evidence of a hasty departure. His clothes were there and so was his luggage but César didn't think the Swiss would be coming back. Bock must've caught him by surprise too. But where was his body? César wondered. The witnesses saw only one man leave the room. So Bock killed Kayser elsewhere, then returned to the hotel. Why?

Someone had folded Menard's hands across his chest for transport. His face was still soft, as if he were sleeping: a warrior gathering strength. The look of death would come later, marbleized and polished, granitic. Menard would soon disappear, César brooded. Become one of René's bodies.

Probably 9mm, the medical officer had said. The same as Bock's PPK. He'd found himself another right arm.

In the car again César sought to weave his own fantasies of death and destruction, but all he could see was Humpty-Dumpty. Somehow he'd always known that Humpty-Dumpty was the story of a German boy who lost his virginity and grew up to become an SS killer who found his way. In his own grief and guilt, César wondered what God had in mind when He created the Germans.

THIRTEEN

The Paris police force was born on March 15, 1667, under Louis XIV, the Sun King, who expressly enjoined it to do its duty. Three hundred years later its members were still trying to honor that kingly command, *bien sûr,* but in a time, as some saw it, of exceptional stress. Others were more sanguine, preferring to see life simply as a stage on which everything had happened before. One of these was Dupin the Actor.

César trudged up the stairs to the top floor of the Police Judiciaire building on the Quai des Orfèvres and waited by the landing. The chief inspector soon opened a nearby door, smiled at César, a half smile, and led the way back inside.

"Too quiet in the office," he growled, "even for a Sunday."

The police museum was arranged chronologically, starting with the *ancien régime* and the Revolution in the first two rooms. The exhibits—intended to show the evolution of the Paris police—included legal documents and prison registers, uniforms and pictures, but the most popular displays were the various murder weapons. The *musée grise* was open to the public on Thursday afternoons and each week they lined up to look in morbid fascination at things touched by celebrated killers. The tools of murder.

"I come here often," Dupin said, "to remind me that murder's always with us. What about you?"

"Once, years ago."

"No more?"

"It kills the imagination."

"See what I mean? The historical perspective. Here, look at this." He pointed to a display case.

"What is it?"

"Read it," Dupin urged.

César squinted, stared at the scrolled letters. "It's Old French," he said after a moment.

Dupin beamed. "Probably about somebody's murder. And this." He moved down the row of cases. "Tells about the assassination of Henry IV in 1610 and how the assassin was drawn and quartered. They didn't fool around in those days," he added with a policeman's nostalgia. "Did you talk to Rimbaud's wife?"

"She wouldn't see me."

Dupin shrugged. "It's emotional. She blames you for his death. The two of you worked on the case, now her husband's dead and you're alive. Something's wrong. Others will say the same. In fact"— he lowered his voice although they were alone—"the feeling is you shouldn't have let him go by himself. Not your fault, of course. How could you know Bock would be there? Still, you were in charge. He's dead and they have you."

"That's not what bothers me."

"What then? Surely not guilt."

"Not that either."

"Ah, revenge. You must get whoever killed him." His eyes swept the musty room. "Plenty of it in here. Personal, political, all the same thing." Dupin sighed. "Revenge."

"Something else."

"What else?"

"I don't think Bock killed him."

"Really." Dupin gazed at the menu for Louis XVI the day before he was beheaded. Besides three soups and four entrées, the king was served several roasts and compotes, all washed down with champagne, Bordeaux, Madeira and four cups of coffee. That was lunch. The dinner menu was even more extensive. Nine months later Marie-

Antoinette lost her head without a bite of breakfast. And before lunch.

"I think it was Kayser," César said. "Something I forgot; he always left his key at the desk when he went out. How could Bock get in?"

"It's your story."

"Kayser intended to shoot one of us, seize the opportunity. He made himself a sling and surprised Menard when he walked into the room. On the way out he made sure someone saw the sling." César watched Dupin's eyes. "He wanted Bock to be blamed, you see. He even wore a cap like Bock. It was all planned."

"Bock's already up for murder. Why frame him?"

"I don't know," César admitted. "If Bock's back in Germany now, maybe they wanted to push us, make us go there after him. When a cop is killed—"

"You said *they.*"

"Whoever's after Bock. Kayser's client."

Dupin's face had worked itself into a skeptical frown. "It's not very plausible," he announced. "He'd have to sit up there and wait for you to call or knock on his door."

"Not really." César hesitated. "Someone in the department may be involved, too."

"In the department, you say?" Dupin absently dangled the museum key by its chain, borrowed from the curator. "One of us?"

"It's possible." César peered at his reflection in the clear glass. "Only a suspicion so far."

"Suspicion?" Dupin abruptly shoved the key chain in his pocket. "You were right about Bock being alive, it seems, and now you suspect a colleague of complicity in murder. There's a dangerous difference. I suggest you don't tell anyone his name unless you have proof. No one, not even me." He stalked past a display of garrotes. "I don't want to hear it."

A portrait confronted them in the antechamber: a brooding Dr. Joseph Guillotin, inventor of the killing device given his name. His small suspicious eyes followed the two men into the next room.

"A medical doctor, that one." Dupin grimaced. "He thought a fixed blade would be more humane than the executioner's ax. Can you believe it? Maybe he was right."

The guillotine had been in use for almost two hundred years, though heads rarely rolled in recent times. Capital punishment was losing ground, a grim prospect for many police agencies.

"Whatever comes next will be even worse," Dupin assured César. "What about the hit-and-run? Kayser?"

César didn't think so.

"You're ready to accuse someone of murder without proof, but you know he didn't try to kill you?"

"Until now I thought it was Bock."

"Suppose I tell you it wasn't Bock."

"Are you telling me it wasn't Bock?"

"Let's just say I've heard rumors of other possibilities."

"What other possibilities?"

"Nothing definite. When I hear more, I'll let you know more. In the meantime"—Dupin drew a sharp breath—"Kayser's after Bock, and someone in Criminal Investigation is helping him. In your theory anyway." He nodded thoughtfully. "So now you have to get them all. Rimbaud's death makes it personal, right? Just like with Bock. He killed your parents, symbolically at least, so that's personal too. You'll have to get them all no matter what, even though your motives could defeat you, and ruin any chance. So you lose your objectivity, maybe your life—even the case. For what? I didn't know Jews were such vengeance seekers. What happened to you people turning the other cheek?"

"We turned it six million times in the war."

"So did another six million Slavs and Gypsies and politicals, including two hundred thousand Frenchmen."

"Almost half were Jews!" César said heatedly.

"They all were French!" Dupin shouted.

Rather than face each other's truths, the Actor and the Jew walked in silence through empty rooms filled with worn uniforms and used weapons. Everything smelled of death.

"What I should do," Dupin grumbled, "is take you off the Bock case right now. Let someone else look things over, get some balance back." He glanced covertly at César. "That's what I should do."

"Maybe you should," César agreed, "but you won't."

"Why won't I?"

"You remember the Nazis, what they did here."

"So I remember the Nazis."

"So you know I stand the best chance of getting Bock"—César's voice was flat, without emotion—"precisely because I've made it personal. I know more about him than anybody."

César had to fight the feeling of invincibility such focus gave him. Total commitment was a beam of laser light that could cut through most anything. It was raw power.

But to what end? For what purpose? If the madman Hitler had not dissipated his power with insanities like racial purity, he might have won the world. César wondered if Dupin knew about that kind of commitment. His own father had been in the *Résistance*. One day in 1943 his clothes were sent to his home and nobody ever saw him again, alive or dead.

"All right," Dupin rasped, "for now you keep Bock. But if he's back in Germany, you can kiss him good-bye from here. Germans don't like to look for Nazis, never did."

"And my suspicion?"

"You wouldn't have called if you didn't want something. What was it? Let me guess. My help in a silent investigation of your police suspect, or at least my approval. Would make things easier. In fact, would make it possible. But you'll need more than words for that. The truth is, you've been lucky with Bock so far and now you have some important people on your side; they're beginning to see you in a new light. The embodiment of the true police spirit, that sort of thing. Using the powers of your office for the protection of the public. And, not incidentally, in the service of the department. It was you, after all, who made the SCE back down; if not for you the whole spy apparatus would still be running. Don't think the Palace hasn't been told of this. Really, your name is known. Now you come along with this notion of someone in the department. If you push the suspicion any further, it could ruin the rest for you. Pull you back to the old days and Algeria, even worse. Is that what you want?"

It was no use, none. César saw he'd have to handle matters himself. Rather than burn Paris, the German general ignored Hitler's command and surrendered the city intact. César stared up at the photograph of Von Choltitz arriving at police headquarters on August 25, 1944. Later the general was declared a *Mitläufer* at his denazification, which meant he went along with the Nazis but was not one himself. Imagine, not a Nazi. To César he looked content in the photo, as though he believed he'd done the right thing. Would he so easily have ignored the chief inspector, who was now in the museum's last room? César hurried to catch up.

"I'll find the proof on my own," he warned.

"Then I'll take action," Dupin grumbled, "but I don't have to like it."

"Regardless of consequences?"

"Only a fool looks at consequences before the problem. Your problem is you're filled with nervous energy and mistrust. Do you know the motto of Paris?" Dupin locked the dead bolt on the entrance door and pocketed the key. "It swims but never sinks." He started for the stairs. "Think about it."

On the way down César thought about the summer to come. More serious crimes were committed during the summer than any other time of year, with July the peak month. He wondered if he'd still be around in July. Half his world had fallen away; no one seemed to be who they were anymore. Even Dupin the Actor was strangely elusive. César didn't understand why Bock hadn't been already reassigned. He would've been almost relieved, for the moment anyway.

In the courtyard he suddenly felt himself at the center of a bullring, except he had no sword and there was no crowd. Only the bull, a black mass thundering toward him, its maddened eyes burning fiercely, the pinched face locked in a death leer.

Junot!

*   *   *

He searched Menard's office for everything on Bock before returning to his own, moving slowly. His wounds were shades of pink, his head still buzzed and the shoulder stung, all courtesy of the SCE supervisor. Funny how the mind played tricks, César thought; his had registered a glimpse of the face behind the wheel, then buried it beneath the shock. When the shock lifted, the face surfaced. It was Junot who had tried to kill him. And Bock? Was he back in Germany, after all?

César wasn't worried about the SCE supervisor trying again. Covert operations had their own rules: If at first you don't succeed, good-bye. Junot had failed.

Menard's report on Linz and the concentration camp at Mauthausen was unfinished. César sat at his desk, nevertheless, and buried his head in its horror. He had to keep going. The previous night was spent in drink and despair. Today he would work; only work would set him free. The very words over the gates of Auschwitz and Dachau: ARBEIT MACHT FREI.

Mauthausen had been built before Auschwitz, soon after the Nazis stormed triumphantly into Austria in March 1938. In the first forty-eight hours seventy thousand Austrians were arrested by the Gestapo from lists prepared by local Nazis, and Himmler hurried the completion of the huge *Lager* outside Linz. It was built, like most of the early camps, by a stone quarry; here the inmates, mostly Jews, were put to work hewing great blocks of building granite, which they then had to carry up the 186 steps of the quarry to trucks at the top. Incalculable amounts of stone were needed for the massive monuments that would turn Linz into Hitler's artistic capital. Later, when the dreams of the failed artist turned to smoke over the ovens of Auschwitz, thousands would die in the gas chambers at Mauthausen. Nearly two hundred thousand finally, great mounds of murdered bodies to be buried or burned.

Linz itself basked in Hitler's approval. From its town hall balcony he proclaimed the union of Germany and Austria; in its central square he patted the blond heads of blue-eyed children, living proof of his Aryan master race. For those millions not blond or blue-eyed, he held out hope. In the camps experiments were being conducted on inmates, such as injecting dye into the eyes to turn them blue. Unfortunately they all turned black, the color of death. But there were millions of guinea pigs so a startling discovery was always possible. And that was only one of many similar experiments! Hitler was supremely confident of eventual success and so was the city of Linz, which longed to outshine Vienna.

Max Baur, an Austrian police chief before the war, became Gestapo head in 1942 when Kaltenbrunner took over SS security; he wanted his own man in office in his hometown, and Baur proved equal to the task. He stayed to the end. The police in Linz still remembered Baur, some of them. Ruthless but fair, they had told Menard. He killed without mercy. Only obeying orders, of course. Baur himself wouldn't have hurt a fly.

The police mind, usually feeling itself beleaguered, was loath to denounce its own or reveal anything unless forced. César suddenly saw why Bock had left everything in his flat except his prints. He knew the SCE—itself part of that mentality—wouldn't tell the regular police he'd gone over to them, and so was slain as a double agent. He left his gun and receipts to lead Homicide to the killings, the Himmler letter to suggest he'd done the same for the SS, the group photo and Gerd Streicher's letter to show that others, now dead, were involved in some plot. All to make the police arrive at the same conclusions about his death as the security agencies. Bock knew none of them would reveal enough for any to grasp what he'd actually done. He was dead, which meant he was safe. Until he was resurrected.

César marveled at the German's complexity. A master tactician, his opponent; someone to be watched at all times, even though they'd never met. He chafed at the intimacy shared with Bock, an occupational hazard growing out of the intense concentration on his past and present. Did he have a future? It was easy for a Nazi to lose himself in Germany or Austria, hundreds of thousands had already done so.

Yet César fully expected to find Bock and be with him until he was executed. It was a matter of justice—and of retribution. Twelve million murdered, his biggest case. The homicide inspector didn't want the Nazi to think he was able to get away with it.

* * *

César took the stairs to the basement level where old police files were kept. The corridor was dark, half the bulbs burned out, and he forged ahead warily. Shadows threw up shapes on the wet walls. His paranoia saw only Inspector Maton, who held a party where a friend killed a thief. Demons burst out of the bricks ahead and grew before his eyes.

The corridor veered to the left to form a cavern carved out of stone. César continued across it into a second room, even larger, that housed hundreds of metal shelves holding dusty cartons. There were separate records sections in each division, but closed cases and those unsolved after a decade usually ended up in the basement where they slowly faded into obscurity. César nodded to the elderly clerk at the desk.

"What've you got for me?"

"Just what you asked for." The clerk made a disparaging noise. "I don't know why."

"Curiosity mostly." César took the file over to one of the tables in the corner.

The records morgue held thousands of old cases, some of them hundreds of pages thick. César leafed through the few pages in his folder while the clerk sorted out newly arrived cartons.

"Not much here," César groaned.

"What'd you expect?"

An answer, César told himself. Why was Nadal killed? Armed robbers in a town house were unusual enough, but to have one of them gunned down—

"Don't seem like much to me," the clerk suddenly announced, pointing to the file in César's hand. "Two thieves falling out? Happens all the time."

César agreed. But then one of them had his flat burglarized, and more than once.

"By his former partner," crowed the clerk. "So he stuffed a radio with dynamite and blew the bastard to hell the next time he showed up. How's that for poetic justice?"

"How'd he know about dynamite?"

"Probably worked in a mine; I remember the inspector saying something about that at the time."

Eyes snapped shut. Behind the lids a pale sky fell into the sea so that air and water formed a concave tableau on the horizon. At its edge the darkness disappeared.

"But it wasn't much of a case," said the voice. "I think he even got the thief off."

César opened his eyes. "Must've been a first for Tobie."

"That's a fact."

"Sounds like the story of Calvary," César enthused. "I see here the lucky thief's name was Gouze."

"Valentin," beamed the clerk. "Same as mine."

* * *

Valentin Gouze used to be Damien Thierry. Damien Thierry turned out to be Jean Leduc.

César ran through the list again, all Leduc a.k.a.—also known as —de Gouzel and a half-dozen other names. No wonder Robbery didn't have his Belgian record years ago; they thought him a local thief and hadn't checked other countries. Not even Interpol, which wouldn't have helped anyway. Leduc was small-time.

"Got enough?" The robbery officer felt annoyed; working on weekends was no fun.

"Enough," César said and shut the file on Leduc. Good thing someone checked further after the rape and robbery; this time it wasn't Maton's case to bury. But Leduc owed him for the earlier save. Had the debt been paid?

* * *

What would Menard say about it?

César sat in the café and thought of his assistant's reaction to the news that Inspector Maton knew Leduc. A coincidence? There weren't any, certainly not that kind. But the inspector could still claim it, Menard would tell him. There was no proof he knew the robber's identity. Both wore masks, remember.

No proof, yes, but at least an assumption. He should've recognized the voice, for instance.

And no proof he talked to Leduc before the shooting.

Maybe there was a witness.

Who?

Kayser.

What about the motive?

César made his leap. Kayser wanted his help on Bock, needed it, so saving his life would put him in Kayser's debt, get the Swiss what he wanted.

What did he want with Bock?

César didn't know.

* * *

The Munich gallery did not give out the names of its buyers, would not even consider such a request from the French detective. Their reluctance had melted, however, before the glare of their own police who interceded as a professional courtesy to the French inspector Dreyfus. César soon had the buyer's name in the 1972 sale of Hitler's missing portrait: Oberst-Haupt, a Munich maker of agricultural compounds.

The name meant nothing to him, a company obviously expecting the return of Hitler or the end of the world; he now tossed it back into the Bock file for Clément to check in the morning.

* * *

René insisted he liked to work weekends. "All the really interesting bodies come in then, the torsos with their heads tucked under their arms, the skeletons that have been skinned alive, the eviscerations and transmutations—"

The phone rang and César breathed a silent sigh of relief; he needed to know about Menard's autopsy, not René's fixation. "For you," said the doctor. "How'd they guess?"

"Left word I'd be pumping ghouls." César listened for a moment. "I'm pretty busy now," he told Nicole.

"Won't take long," she promised.

César deemed it a toss-up, turned back to René. "You were saying—"

"The real nut cases spend all week brooding on how they're going to do it; the more they brood the madder they get. This makes them think of even more sadistically creative methods of destruction and we see the results every weekend."

"César?" Nicole prompted.

"Faces flattened, scalps split, eyes gouged out, teeth snapped off" —René catalogued joyfully—"that's all standard stuff, what we call midweek work. By Saturday we're into the body shop violence. Have one right now"—he rubbed his hands together enthusiastically— "rips in the perineum extending so deep into the anus it made almost a common opening into the pelvis from the outside. Can you imagine the force required to do that? Not to mention the jagged object it took. Hard to believe."

Even killers needed fans to judge the caliber of their work, César supposed. Who better than a pathologist who lived vicariously?

"I'd like to see you," Nicole urged. "We seem to be good for each other." She hesitated. "Do you agree?"

"Certainly," César grunted, not knowing what to say.

"Ruptured the bowel, no easy thing to do." René grimaced for emphasis. "Penetrated fourteen inches, causing lethal trauma to the kidneys. Also a collapsed lung from massive injury and shock."

"Who was this?"

"And there were a half-dozen drugs in the body," René babbled, "even Halcion which stupefies. Did I mention that the testicles had been hacked off, too?"

"If you come over tonight," Nicole was saying, "I'll make you something to eat and then I'll make you something else. You remember how good it was last time?"

"I remember," César answered mechanically and glanced at the pathologist. "What about Menard?"

"An interesting development."

"Please," Nicole purred.

"Did you know dried blood and cocaine throws dogs off the scent? Or that you can kill a female by applying cocaine to her genitals?"

"Menard didn't have dry blood or female genitals. What is this? He was shot."

"Take the rectal orifice." René smiled. "If you jam a gun muzzle up there and then fire, the cause of death would not be easy to find. And if you use a plastic or fiber-glass bullet, it wouldn't even show up on X ray." He studied his nails. "Makes you wonder."

César turned to the window, receiver in hand. "I'm afraid I'll be really busy," he told Nicole.

"Later then, when you're free"—he felt her pressing—"I could wait up for you."

"Not tonight." He looked at his watch. "I've got things to do."

"Tomorrow?"

"Wonder about what?" he asked René, then softened his tone. "Yes, tomorrow. I'll call you."

"Life and death." The doctor's words had a dry hollow sound. "Mostly death, of course."

"I saw Cécile today. She was going with your friend, the other inspector?"

"Tobie Maton."

"No more," Nicole said. "I think he got tired of her."

"He's like that."

"Men," she moaned.

"Women, too."

"Did you know," René asked belligerently, "that more babies are born between 4 and 5 A.M. than any other hour?"

The hour of the wolf, César muttered, the same hour that more people died.

"What's that?" said a disembodied voice.

The balance of nature was everywhere; even life and death were a balance, and men and women. Was Nicole meant to balance him?

César tried to picture being with her but drew a blank. All he could recall was the sex.

"Tomorrow," he promised into the phone and broke the connection.

René rubbed his sideburns impatiently. "To go on, Menard was supposedly shot as the killer came out of the bathroom, a distance of at least ten meters. That would've been some shot—dead center in the forehead—the work of a marksman like this Bock you're after. Except it didn't happen that way. I found particles of burned gunpowder embedded in the skin around the wound. It was a contact shot, fired at almost point-blank range." He peered at César over his glasses. "Do you see my meaning? No special skill was required." The voice was a hush smothered in caution. "Is it possible someone wanted to make it look like Bock's work?"

* * *

Menard had changed from summer to winter, from a man full of life to a stuffed animal filled with fiber. César stood in front of the open casket and brooded over their years together. Two detectives working closely like that, partners in survival, it was like a marriage. They depended on each other.

Now César was alone again, his second divorce.

"I'll live to be a hundred," said the summer Menard, "and when I die it'll be a cold day in hell."

The inspector thought of the man.

"French is the language of love"—Menard had felt sorry for anyone who didn't speak French—"and Italian the language of friends and English the language of money."

"What about German?" César had asked.

"German," Menard explained, "is the language of animals."

César took a last look at the German in the casket. It was no one he knew.

* * *

After nine already. He dug into another batch of papers, slowly worked his way to the bottom. Menard's notes came next, among them a mention that Gestapo boss Heinrich Müller had been placed on a list of most wanted Nazis in 1973, which presumed he was still alive. César had wanted the essentials on the Nazi leaders he'd jotted down in Smith's bookstore, Kaltenbrunner and the rest. He thought them all dead.

The paper trail in a homicide investigation was endless, a ribbon of words binding hunter and hunted and often trapping both; César felt himself getting drowsy, his body running down from grief and lack of sleep. He would finish the pile in front of him and get a few hours on the couch. Jacqueline Volette came to mind and he spent his last energy pushing her out.

From Munich the police had sent copies of Gerd Streicher's desk calendar for April and May. There were only two entries in May, one of them a reminder of his wife's birthday on the third. The other was for May 7 and read: *VJ—13—Nibelung—Dachau R Au*. César had asked Menard to see what he could make of it. Apparently not much, beyond the fact that May 7 was the thirtieth anniversary of the war's end and the death of Nazi Germany. That and a scribbled comment about *Au* obviously being the abbreviation for Austria. But Dachau was in Germany, not Austria. And what would a former member of the civilian SS want with a concentration camp? That was the last place a Nazi needed now. César took a deep breath, closed his eyes to think . . .

A spider will not eat a fly that is already dead. The trick is to catch a fly and hit it just hard enough for it to lose consciousness, then place it carefully in the web. Not easy! César watched the spider spinning closer and closer, crawling inexorably toward its prey. He saw it loom over him, its head hideous, the anterior mandibles snapping open and shut, giant jaws reaching for him, touching him with viscous slime, the ferocious mouth full of froth, ripping, rending, *feasting*—until the spider web exploded in his face and the buzzing of the fly turned into the phone.

César watched it ring, a transfer of senses, his head silent on the desk.

"Inspector Dreyfus?"

"Yes."

"I call, Inspector, to tell you that I had nothing to do with the death of your detective."

"Who is this?"

"I wasn't even in France . . ."

"Bock!"

César gripped the phone long after the echo died in his ears.

FOURTEEN

The remains were enshrined under a sarcophagus of red porphyry, the oak coffin resting on a bed of green granite; in the oak lay a second coffin of ebony, within that two more of lead, then one of mahogany enclosing still another of iron. The tomb reflected the grandeur of France under the emperor who was finally exiled to Saint Helena in 1815 where he died six years later of stomach cancer, though Napoleon believed he was being poisoned. He was right. A hundred and forty years later, strands of hair cut at his death were tested for radioactive trace elements: the arsenic content was thirteen times normal. Napoleon had been murdered.

César stood with Bordier inside the vault. The general found it peaceful, a favorite meeting place near his office; the military mind, he laughed, and hoped the inspector didn't object. His gracious manner made him seem even more sinister, and César decided he'd probably killed Napoleon himself. With that maniacal type, anything was possible. On the other hand, what was the loss? Most prewar children, César included, grew up with the admonition to behave themselves or Napoleon would get them.

"He's dead," the general said.

"Who?" César feigned ignorance.

"Shot once in the forehead, just like all those others you've been investigating."

Supervisor Junot had been killed outside his home by someone who stood next to him and fired one bullet from a Walther PPK 9mm pistol; Bock had presumably secured another of his favored weapons and was back in business. According to Bordier, Junot had been hot on his trail since the murder of the SCE agent came to light. The Service would of course continue its investigation.

"Perhaps we could help each other," the general suggested.

César didn't believe a word of it. Bock was in Germany—had called him from there, César was certain—and Junot was dead, shot by some SCE thug. The political police lived in houses of ice and always smelled smoke; like some fireflies, they devoured their own. Junot might talk; he'd become dangerous to the organization, to the country. To them.

"We could exchange information, even work together."

Bordier had given César the names of all ex-Nazis employed by his agency; it was a partial listing, naturally, and did not include those Nazis still considered valuable. César was also given his list of top West German financiers with Nazi backgrounds. That was incomplete too.

"Would you care to view the body?" It was an oblique dismissal, though the general's smile turned the somber tomb into sunny Spain.

"I'll wait for the next one," César snapped as Spain returned to stone.

* * *

Choupon was telling César how the Prussian army marched on Paris in 1870, ringing the city with steel. "After a while there was nothing left to eat so the people started eating their pets and whatever strays they could find. Next came the zoo."

César called the waiter over; information cost money and the Boot was one of the best.

"Soon the restaurants were serving stuffed donkey head, elephant legs and bear chops, with consommé of cobra."

Drinking in public wasn't quite the same as eating so he ordered another round.

"After that it was roast rat and spider stew. By the time the siege lifted, there wasn't a rat left in Paris." The informant leaned forward. "No Germans either."

With the waiter gone, César pulled his chair closer to the table. "Now tell me the part about Jacqueline Volette and Kayser again."

* * *

His military relative was buried in the Montparnasse cemetery not far from Napoleon's tomb. As he entered the grounds from the Boulevard Edgar-Quinet, César had a view of tree-lined paths and sloping hills filled with crosses and columns that marked the dead. The stones stood gray against the green earth, a melancholy quilt beneath the yellow sun and blue sky. Inexplicably, César had never been inside.

"Captain Dreyfus?" he asked at the gate.

"Who?"

"Dreyfus." He spelled the name.

"In here?"

"Do many escape?"

"No one I ever heard of."

"Then he's still here."

"Never heard of him."

"You're the gatekeeper," César explained patiently. "Gatekeepers are supposed to know where the bodies are buried."

"Do you see how many are in here?" the old man sputtered.

"Is Alfred Dreyfus one of them?"

"When did he die?"

"In 1935."

"Down there." He pointed to the left, went back to his book.

Following the path, César soon began reading names. He expected a monument to the man, at least a temple to commemorate the injustice; what he finally found was much less. César wondered if the authorities ever really forgave Captain Dreyfus for being innocent. Or was it just for being a Jew?

Jacqueline Volette lived in Montparnasse near the cemetery. After talking to the dead, César waited to listen to the living. He knew her schedule at the Sorbonne, knew when she'd leave her house. Now at her approach he got out of the car. Her eyes did not greet him.

"Kayser," he said accusingly. "You saw him again yesterday."

The eyes went wide. "You had me followed."

"Watched."

"You had no right," she cried indignantly.

"Right!" He didn't believe it. "You could be involved in murder."

"I don't know what you're talking about." She turned away.

"I'll protect you all I can," César pleaded, taking a step after her, "but you've got to tell me what's going on."

"I am." She left him standing alone.

Driving back, César railed against fate for falling in love at his age. How could he? And to a woman like that. Like what? César didn't know, and that only made it worse.

* * *

André was sobered by Menard's death. The idea of dying on duty had never occurred to him. He was clever and well-educated and came from good family. Rapid advancement was a certainty, had already begun. But sudden death? André wasn't so sure anymore. He could've been at Kayser's door. César nodded, told him to concentrate on the work. Only work would keep them going. Austria, for instance. What had he learned?

César sat at his desk and gently prodded André, hoping he wouldn't freeze, forcing him back into familiar thoughts, into patterns, molds, the old *bequem und richtig*—what was comfortable and right. In this case, it was standard police procedure. Information, analysis, judgment. This happened and then that—by the book, until the book wasn't needed again; until the imagination could again leap across voids, grounded in logic. A delicate balance, the mind, infinitely devious and afraid of change, of oblivion, even of itself. A good detective, César reminded his charge, was a juggler keeping all exits in view and all possibilities in motion. Then like the hunter, he pounced.

What about Austria? Anything involving money and Nazis?

André, glum but game, went to his notes. In 1945 the Allies found five billion dollars in gold (an American figure) in the vaults of the Reichsbank at Regensburg, Germany. Most of it belonged to the Austrian government. Also at the end of the war, American troops seized a train loaded with Hungarian treasure in a tunnel near Salzburg. The billion-dollar hoard had been sent to the Nazis to prevent its falling into Russian hands. At about the same time, thousands of artworks were discovered in a salt mine between Salzburg and Linz.

The priceless find included six thousand paintings stolen from all over Europe for Hitler's private collection. Some, like Raphael's *Portrait of a Young Man,* were never recovered.

"All right." César fixed his eye on André. "The Austrian gold. Bock could've been in a group that stole part of it on the way to Germany. Or the Hungarian train; they might've taken whatever they wanted before the Americans arrived. Same for the salt mine. The most valuable art in the world, but some are still missing." He rubbed his hands together in nervous excitement. "Gold, diamonds, art—whatever—millions hidden away, millions! just waiting. Ten years, twenty, even thirty, waiting for the right time"—a bell rang but César's mind was racing—"and what better time than middle age? When a man wants security and luxury." He nodded in satisfaction. "It has to be," he insisted. "Bock and the others, they agreed to wait thirty years until everyone forgot the Nazis and nobody was looking. Now he kills them off and it's all his. It has to be," he repeated. "What else?"

André's final item concerned dozens of metal cases salvaged a year earlier from a Nazi bomber on the bottom of an Austrian lake. Divers who hauled the cases to the surface of Lake Toplitz found them full of forged British currency, millions of pounds, part of Hitler's scheme to destroy the British economy during the war.

Could Bock have been mixed up in that?

César didn't think so. Whatever treasure the Nazi had was real and negotiable. But the lake intrigued him; he fished out Streicher's letter to Bock mentioning a lake near Munich that reminded him of another in Austria. If Streicher were part of it, so were the others who died by Bock's hand. Were any still alive? César had his doubts. More than five or six would be too many to hold a secret that long. They didn't want to take any chances, could afford to wait; apparently time didn't debase the treasure so it wasn't currency. Linge already owned a law firm and Streicher the accounting business; Schirrmacher was a big executive and Baur retired. Only Bock was hurting so he decided to take it all. If another of the group was left, he'd be dead by May 7. This time César heard the bell. That was the anniversary of the Nazi fall. What better time to rise again?

* * *

Kussow told César about Dachau where every member of his family was murdered.

"—but only because you ask as a friend and a Jew. For myself, I have already seen the face of the devil."

It was the fall of 1942 and the so-called medical experiments by demented German doctors were in full nightmare. Castration, blood removal, unspeakable injections, skull splitting, bone grafting, lung rupturing, skin flaying, gas gangrene wounding, mustard gas burning, saltwater diets, slow starving, fast freezing—nothing was considered too bizarre. In Dachau, demons like Sigmund Rascher and Klaus Schilling ran wild.

"Rascher worked on a dozen experiments, a sadist like you've never seen. To Dr. Rascher only the pain mattered, and death always came as a thief. One day he got this idea for a two-headed dog, probably from reading mythology. You must understand that doctors in Germany were very educated men. Rascher thought a two-headed dog would be twice as effective for guarding the camp. Since the Dachau dogs were in short supply, naturally he turned to the only raw material at hand. That's what he called us, his raw material. Well, that's exactly what we were. Rascher figured if he could create such a dog, Hitler would welcome him as a great Germanic hero. Himmler too. Which shows you how demented he really was. The last thing those beasts in Berlin needed were dogs with two mouths to feed. The war, you see, was slowly going against them. But all Rascher saw was his new breed of Aryan superdog. What I'm telling you is true. He believed the second head could be grafted onto the host body by freezing it before dissection to keep its cells alive and then attaching it at the top of the spinal cord. The relationship would be symbiotic, of course, but the second head would function. Why not? Mengele was trying much the same thing with identical twins in Auschwitz, grafting parts of their bodies together. Rascher, even more maniacal, merely wanted to go all the way."

Kussow had seen his brother strangled at his feet, watched his mother and sisters walk into the gas chamber, heard the screams of his father being burned alive in a ditch. When he left Germany after the war, almost dead and half mad, he vowed never to return.

"And Dachau now?" César asked softly.

"I'm told Rascher's dogs still don't guard the gates."

Yet César knew the horror Kussow described was essentially true.

The cremation ovens were still there. In other camps the gas chambers and medical torture labs still stood. In May 1933—three months after Hitler took over the government—Kussow's family had watched a Nazi torchlight procession snake down Berlin's main street to burn Jewish books in a huge funeral pyre. Six years later they were burning Jews. Now Kussow no longer trusted the German mentality, his own as well. They had all somehow fallen from grace, and the nature of this fall—the crime and punishment—occupied his thoughts for more than thirty years.

César showed his friend the entry on Streicher's calendar. Maybe another German could help.

"What do I know of Germany?" Kussow protested. "The streets were red and the sky black. Does that help you? Of course not. All I see are colors, isn't that strange?"

He lapsed into silence.

"Colors," César prodded gently.

Kussow nodded in memory. "Tokele was white, like bleached bone. The two of us would sleep sideways on the bunk so we didn't fall off."

"Who's Tokele?"

"A Polish Jew who went to Palestine when the Nazis came, only he couldn't get in. They wouldn't let him in. Why not? he asked. Wasn't Palestine open to Polish refugees? Yes, they told him, Palestine was open to Polish refugees but only if they weren't Jews."

"What happened to him?"

"He was forced back, landed in the death camp with me. They killed him."

"I'm going to get them," César said with conviction.

"One Nazi?"

"Too small?"

"Too late."

"Just to show them."

"They'll think you're a crank."

"What's wrong with cranks? You need one to get things started."

In the tiny living room, paint peeled evenly around the moldings. Hairline cracks had spread like branching veins across the edges of walls. From the weathered wing chair César watched his host regard the paper with Streicher's words: *VJ—13—Nibelung—Dachau R Au.*

"An accountant, you say?"

"His own firm."

Kussow sighed. "In Germany"—he laid the paper aside, used a square of newsprint to wipe his glasses—"formal business training taught that memos were to answer the four W's: where, when, what, why. Anything else was excess. Looking at it this way, *VJ* could be the place for your meeting. A hotel, for example, probably in Munich since Dachau's nearby. Thirteen would be the time, in military terms 1 P.M. The writer grew up in a military age. As for *Nibelung*, it might be the subject of the meeting. Obviously a code word. Or else—"

"Or else?"

"—your mysterious memo is about Wagner's *Ring* operas, the Nibelung legends. Could be just a harmless music group; the opera season's begun. Why Dachau's in there and linked to Austria is unknown to me, but that would be the reason for the meeting." Kussow leaned back in the chair, closed his eyes for a moment. "Vier Jahreszeiten!"

"*Bitte?*"

"*VJ*—Vier Jahreszeiten. Once the best hotel in Munich, catered to royalty. It should still suit the fantasies of Nazis."

* * *

The kings of Bavaria once stayed at the Residenz in Munich, a lavish palace. When times changed, royalty took to the best hotels.

César said a silent prayer to Kussow. The new royalty was corporate business, which used hotels for meetings as well as sleep. The Vier Jahreszeiten had a room reserved on May 7 from 1 to 5 P.M. for a Munich manufacturer of chemical compounds. It was Oberst-Haupt.

There were no coincidences in life, just as nothing was obvious. César quickly dug the name out of the Bock file and got André on the phone. He wanted everything on Oberst-Haupt, including the real owners. Just like in Zurich.

What would Hitler's portrait have to do with Bock's treasure? César wondered. Nazi art had no millions in it, nothing worth all those dead. Hundreds of Hitler paintings were stored in his old party headquarters in Munich and nobody had ever tried to steal them.

"Couldn't give them away," the Munich authorities had said.

César called Clément into the office. He copied one of the words from the Streicher memo on a scrap of paper, handed it to the detective. "Whatever you can find."

"Nibelung?" Clément wasn't sure of the word.

"Opera." César shooed him out the door. "It's the season," he added by way of explanation.

* * *

A cathedral of leafy spires rose out of concrete along the Champs-Elysées. César surged ahead at a brisk pace, counting tree trunks to distract himself. Kiosks made the latest events seem colorful, the newest sensations almost inviting.

At the Place Clémenceau he crossed Avenue Churchill, with the Alexandre III bridge and the Invalides in the background. Flanking the panoramic avenue were the Grand Palais and the Petit Palais, colonnaded and friezed, where César had once cornered a killer. His stride a declaration of purpose, he rehearsed what he would say to his good friend. His fingers flexed nervously, the arms swaying in cadence to the staccato rhythm of his step. He skirted the square at the end of the park zone where Avenue Montaigne intersected, the couturier's gold coast. In the distance he could see the massive Arch of Triumph towering over the treetops. As groups of people passed by, he caught snatches of conversation—a complaint from this one, a denial from that. On the boulevard, true love stirred uneasily.

Beyond the park streams of cars, Renaults and Simcas angry as hornets, buzzed past bumper to bumper. A concierge cleaned the stone steps of a bay-windowed house, the water dark against the setting sun. Owners preened before their property, gushing satisfaction. Life was good.

To get to the restaurant César hurried up the wide thoroughfare, now a full ten lanes across. Airline offices, banks and automobile showrooms rose and fell at his feet. Suited men stood ready in hopeful repose, vacant smiles their badge of business.

Nearly there. Turning in to the Avenue George V, César soon spied the gilded facade of L'Escoffier. The building's style was Second Empire but its spirit strictly La Belle Epoque. Inside the lobby of glass and gold began the ritual of greeting and comparing; here were hearts broken, egos bruised. Beyond beckoned the dining space, several salons of uneven desirability awash with glitter. Everywhere mirrors shone, flowers bloomed, linen snapped. Velvet vied with velour, deep pile with gilt frame. A soft reddish glow insinuated all with suggestion of romance, love, conquest. Glamour.

Inside, César saw the tables filled, the upstairs bar crowded. Electricity sparked the air; the Parisian spring, it was said. Or perhaps the people themselves, rubbing together in careful and costly rite. Here gathered cattle kings and oil barons, landed lords, grand dukes, talented tax lawyers and gifted electronic embezzlers, vice-admirals and nuclear generals, and wonderfully dressed women of every persuasion to eat and drink and watch one another perform. Only so many horses on this merry-go-round. Whirl!

Tobie Maton, splendid in silk, sat at a corner banquette. He wore a pleased expression that contrasted with the flutter of hands, reaching for things. He finally settled on his cigarette box, drumming it lightly on the table when he looked up at César's approach.

César caught the flicker of hesitation, the single stab of pain that was there and gone before the face froze into a forceful smile. He slipped into the adjoining seat.

Maton let go of the box. "I'd offer you one but—"

"I'm still trying."

"And Bock?"

"Same thing," César said.

Maton sighed, drank from his water glass. César noted the position of the banquette, not a choice location. He wondered if the inspector knew he'd never be truly accepted by the moneyed crowd he so assiduously cultivated.

"I have a shot at the rainbow," Maton announced suddenly. "You could be my partner, share everything."

"You already have a partner," César said.

"Kayser? I can handle him."

"He killed Menard."

"Bock killed Menard."

"You called him that night," César pressed, "warned him Menard was on his way. Why?"

"Kayser's my connection to the money."

"And now you're connected to murder."

Maton lit a cigarette with a gold lighter. "Bock obviously showed up after Kayser left. Menard must've walked in on him."

"Bock's in Germany," César rasped. "It was Kayser all the time. He killed Leduc, too. Got him before he could talk."

"Talk about what?"

"How you and Kayser set him up." César shook his head in dismay. "Two men dead just so he could get to Bock through me, or thought he could."

"Death's pain"—Maton signaled the waiter—"shouldn't interfere with life's pleasure." Translation: he was hungry.

The waiter took his order while César sat like a stone. He had lost Menard because he didn't take Kayser seriously, and now he would lose Tobie because he had lost Menard.

"Kayser was offered a lot of money to get rid of Bock," Maton said when the waiter left, "too much for industrial espionage. So he did some checking." The eyes grew luminous, lit from within. "He says there's stolen treasure involved, Nazi treasure. I'm getting half to help him."

"Who's his client?"

"A German. Kayser didn't get specific."

"But he believed him."

"He believed his money."

"So with Bock gone and me no help, he did the next best thing," César said. "Made it look like Bock killed a cop so we'd run him down no matter where. He knew the Nazi wouldn't be taken alive."

"That's only your idea," Maton growled. "Where's the proof? You couldn't arrest him if you tried. Meanwhile, I'm offering you more money than you've ever seen to come in with us. Why not? After Bock's dead, we'll pick the German clean. We know it's more than industrial espionage. So do you. Didn't you mention treasure that night? We'll all come out millionaires."

César studied his good friend, who delighted in conspiracy and now conspired to even greater intrigue. "No," he told his friend.

"I need that money," Maton whispered savagely. "My investments are failing; I could lose everything. What do you say?"

"No!"

Maton recoiled as if from a blow. "Kayser said you wouldn't go for it but I had to try anyway. I thought I knew you better."

"I thought the same about you. Looks like we both were wrong."

"You don't want money?"

"Not like that." César glanced around the restaurant. "Not for this."

"It's the life I want."

"The price is too high."

The two friends sat in silence for a moment.

"And Kayser?" Maton asked finally.

"I'll find him."

"Then you'll have to come after me." Maton's eyes shrunk to red dots. "You're a relentless bastard, just like Bock. But I suppose you know that by now."

The blow struck home, something César had himself been thinking. He didn't like the thought. "Don't get in my way," he warned.

"You're already in mine."

"You'll lose," César said.

"Or you."

"One of us."

Maton nodded. "I think you should know there's someone else involved. Jacqueline Volette was Bock's helpmate, but now she's gone over to the German through Kayser. Does that interest you?"

"Why would she do that?"

"Why else? She likes money."

César understood the implications. "If anything happens to her—"

"Just what I was thinking."

Their eyes locked, two animals caught in the glare of headlights. After almost twenty years César saw for the first time the wolf raging behind the mask, ravenous, its jaws snapping, desperation etched in the distorted features. He wondered if Tobie saw the same in his.

"I'm a hunter." César squeezed around the banquette on his way out.

"Two hunters," said Maton.

* * *

A howling monster lumbered toward him, its silvery tail a mile long, the sleek skin transparent. People were trapped inside its serpentine body, a man entombed in its huge gleaming eye. Steely malevolence exuded from every pore. The screeching increased as the demon drew nearer, now shaking the night with noise, turning the very air to dust that swirled and settled on every surface. Steam, escaping, burst in angry billows on both sides.

César stood at the station's far end until the locomotive pulled out of the Gare d'Austerlitz with its trainload of travelers bound for the

Pyrénées, Spain and Portugal. A train buff, César had long dreamed of taking one of those special steam excursions to the sunny south. Steam or diesel, he never had and neither, he knew, had Dieter Bock. Not yet at least. César silently swore that Bock would never reach Spain.

The railroad terminal was on his way to the Thirteenth district police station on the Boulevard de l'Hôpital. When he arrived he was ushered in to meet Bovise, who fished for salmon in the sewers of Paris.

"Catch anything?" César asked pleasantly.

Bovise regarded the inspector as if he were crazy. "There are no fish in the sewers," he snorted, "salmon or anything else."

The suspect, it seemed, relished the role of neighborhood eccentric and spread the story by buying some salmon each time he returned from one of his expeditions. But he didn't expect the police to fall for it, as they evidently had. Were they all idiots?

In that case, César observed, his expeditions took him elsewhere.

Bovise couldn't say.

Why not?

He wasn't allowed.

Comment ça?

He was on a spy mission for his God in the other universe.

César's eyes narrowed.

Would his God mind if he told them what his mission was?

He shouldn't.

They'd find out anyway.

Bovise eventually relented. Years ago his God lost six substances found only in Paris outside the Maison-Blanche neighborhood where he pretended to live. He was sent to search for them.

Could he say what these substances were?

If he named even one his body would turn to stone, one-sixth of it.

Suppose he named them all, someone asked.

Bovise smiled knowingly. How did they think all those statues in Paris got there?

In the room eyes shifted, faces turned. Men glanced around, mouths tightly drawn. César heard himself sigh. He had a feeling they weren't going to find the killer of Marie Pinay, who lived in the Hôtel Rio and spent her days with wine and her nights with men. She had finally found what she sought, but César didn't think death was one of the things God had lost. And Marie Pinay had been turned to ashes rather than stone. Paint thinner was poured over her body and she was burned alive. In the car again, César had to fight the feeling that he was already stone turning to dust.

*   *   *

Quantum epistemology admitted of only two possibilities. The universe was either a series of random events and therefore largely unknowable or the product of a unified field theory as yet undiscovered. As a Jew in a Christian society and a police inspector in an age of violence, César was somewhere in the middle. He didn't think God played dice with the universe but he wasn't sure about poker.

For more than a week now, César—trying to bring order out of chaos—had been linking facts and fancies that all too often had only the most circumstantial connection. The result was a confusion of associations that had little basis in reality. Ducks did not come *au naturel* in a choice of flavors. Nor was Bock the conspiratorial breath behind every disaster since the Nazis. He did not, for example, drive French forces to defeat in Indochina or General Salan to rebel in Algeria. He probably didn't even cause earthquakes and floods.

César nevertheless returned to his office in the late night gloom wondering what Jacqueline and Kayser saw in each other. Was it Bock's body? Or his treasure?

On the way in he met the photographer, not for the first time since both men used their offices as second homes. Sebastian, unmarried, loved his work and César, sensing a connection, had begun to identify.

"My new lenses from Switzerland," Sebastian said proudly, waving a package. "And you? I see you're into gold now."

"Gold?"

"Don't worry," he grinned. "I won't tell."

As head of forensic photography, Sebastian was familiar with gold and silver usage in film and darkroom equipment. But what had that to do with César? He didn't understand.

"The memo from Munich," Sebastian reminded him. "I just got around to it." He fished in his pocket.

César had sent him a copy of Streicher's memo, hoping he might have an idea about the *Nibelung—Dachau R Au* part.

"Not a chance," the photographer confessed. "I never was any good at those things, too straight I suppose. Around here we just deal in reverse images." He smiled helplessly.

"You said gold."

"Oh that. Well, sure, but it's right on there." He handed the copy to César. "That doesn't count, does it?"

"Where?" César held the paper up to the light.

"Right there!" Sebastian pointed. He didn't speak German and never thought of Austria, but as a forensic photographer he dealt with chemicals all the time. "Didn't you know?"

"Know what?"

"*Au,*" he said softly, "is the chemical symbol for gold."

FIFTEEN

"Gold!"

Another piece of the puzzle, César told Dupin. Not diamonds or art but gold. Two books in Bock's flat were about gold. He didn't think of books when he prepared the stage for his death. A mistake? Or did he want the police to find even those? The man was a fiend.

"What gold?" Dupin had asked. "Where is it?"

César didn't know. In his letter Gerd Streicher talked of a lake in Austria so the gold was probably in a lake; a fitting parallel to the Nibelung gold in Wagner's operas, which came out of the waters of the Rhine. Streicher had mentioned the Nibelung in his memo.

Even so, who else would know about it? Someone was after Bock, someone who hired Kayser to kill him. Which meant that someone knew not only about the gold but about Bock killing the others.

César, pacing his office, saw the single possibility. It had to be one of those in on the original steal, one of the Nazis. Except they all were dead. Who said so? cautioned the inspector. January to April were dead, but there was still May—

He would know of the gold and the deaths because he was himself involved in both.

Dieter Bock had a partner!

His partner was the reason for Bock's trail, trying to stave off a double cross, or at least exact revenge through the police.

César kept circling the room. He'd been right all along, right from the start when he said there were others. Could he trust his leaps anymore? He'd made a bad mistake with Kayser. Now this. Either Bock made mistakes too, or someone was out there watching, waiting. Who? Like Bock, a Nazi. The sixth man, the one who was trying to have him killed by Kayser.

César sank into the couch and closed his eyes. All his fantasies began with Bock killing his partner.

He was beginning to identify with his prey.

* * *

The rain had begun at 10:30, drowning everything by noon. Sheets of windswept water slammed against buildings and cascaded onto streets. At headquarters windows were shut; after a while the walls started to sweat. Waiting by the deserted courtyard, César thought of Bock in Germany. Would the police pick up his scent?

A silver Citroën pulled into the yard and swung round to the grim entrance hall, hugging the curb. The passenger door opened for César, who ran the few steps with a newspaper shielding his head. Inside he shook his raincoat loose as the ministry official Jules gave a curt nod and returned to his driving, absorbed in the mechanics of movement. César sat back and listened to the rain on the roof. It sounded like the rattle of gold teeth in the mouth of a corpse.

Soon they swung into a government compound ringed by railing in the prestigious Eighth district and hurried up the center stairs. The minister's inner office was a model of eighteenth-century taste, in which its occupant performed his duties and held his meetings and sometimes even watched the rain from the huge terrace windows, turning as aides arrived with visitors. In the rush César had forgotten to bring his notes on the Bock affair.

"Minister, Inspector Dreyfus," the aide reported. César immediately felt the vast energy that gave off so little warmth.

The minister nodded in César's direction. His aide said, "The minister wants you to know how pleased he is with your uncovering of the East German spy ring."

"It came at an awkward time," said the minister, "with a state visit in the works."

"The minister would like to know," his aide said, "if you are planning to reveal any other spy operations in the near future."

"The assassin Bock seems to have acted only for the East Germans this past year," César declared truthfully. His eyes wavered between the two men. "As far as we know," he added quickly.

"How does a police inspector," the minister asked, "get involved with the operations of a foreign government?"

"The search for Bock led to an investigation of his past activities, which included political assassination. This required looking into the victims' backgrounds. One of them led to the spy ring."

"I would think that should be the province of the security agencies," the minister said airily. "Wouldn't you?"

No one answered; after a moment the aide said, "We are particularly interested in the SCE list of West German financiers with supposed Nazi backgrounds."

"Especially your reasons for wanting their names," said the minister. "Does that surprise you?"

"Naturally."

"Yet you don't bother to ask why?" the minister remarked. "Now, that does surprise me."

In the Citroën César was driven to the Boulevard St-Germain, where he walked around the corner to the café. The storm had passed, leaving only the barest drizzle. It would be a Parisian evening, he could feel it, an April sky full of promise. Behind the clouds sat the moon glowing with anticipation while in the far north the aurora borealis already burned brightly.

The sign over the bar told eloquently of man's million-year march toward civilization: PAY OR DIE. César sat at a corner table and watched Choupon finish his second wine.

"He's still here." César was sure of it.

"Or Germany"—the informant toyed with the empty glass—"chasing Bock on his own."

César shook off the thought. "He's got something else to do here."

"What else?"

"Something."

It wasn't love, César kept telling himself. He didn't love anyone, no one. Except Jacqueline Volette who told Bock about Menard's murder. It had to be her. So what was she doing with Kayser?

"Stay with the woman." César folded four hundred francs on the table. "She'll lead us to him."

* * *

In Germanic legend, evil arose through the possession of a magic horde of gold stolen from a race of gnomes called the Nibelung. Out of this came murder and pillage and all the crimes of mankind.

"I never saw such slaughter," Clément confessed. "Bodies everywhere. And they made an *opera* out of that?" He couldn't believe it.

But Wagner had, of course, four of them dealing with the Nibelung treasure and the tragedy that struck those who touched it. The treasure was gold, just like Bock's, and César now knew the subject of the May 7 meeting. *Nibelung* was stolen gold.

"Anyway, they're mostly myths," Clément said thankfully. "Gods and giants and dragons, supermen too. You know the Germans, all hung up on the supermen shit."

Except there was no gold in Dachau, stolen or otherwise. No treasure, only tragedy. So what was *Dachau R?*

"Maybe Hitler got his idea for the master race from them." Clément was impressed with the thought. "Those people have magic powers, like they were gods themselves."

Dachau R?

"Imagine looking into a mirror and seeing a god."

Dachau R?

"Too bad there's no mirror can do it."

Mirror!

"You know what I mean?"

Dachau R! Mirror!

"Inspector?"

Mirror—*Dachau R! Dachau R*—Mirror!

César spent the next hour alone at his desk staring at the blank bulletin board and seeing only his own thoughts. The idea stole over him slowly, coming as a blind thief in the dead of day. Something Sebastian had said about photographers, that they dealt in reverse images. Like mirrors.

Dachau R. Dachau Reversed.

What was the reverse of Dachau? Its mirror image?

César's hands trembled, sweat ringed his eyes. He pored over the Bock papers—where was it? when?—the bookstore, he was in the bookstore, Smith's, reading about Kaltenbrunner and the others, all of them from Upper Austria and Bavaria. The line stretched from Linz to Munich. He remembered thinking about the concentration camps, how the Nazis needed them. Dachau was built in 1933 near Munich, at one end of the line. Five years later Hitler took Austria and built another near Linz on the opposite end. César found the paper, held it, blinking away double vision from the sweat: Linz—capital of Upper Austria; 26 kilometers east—Mauthausen.

The concentration camp at Mauthausen. A granite quarry with its staircase of death.

* * *

"You told a story yesterday. Today it's my turn."

"So! Storytellers in our old age." Kussow raised his glass. "In wine there is truth."

"Words of wisdom."

"Said by Pliny the Elder two thousand years ago."

"My story's not that old," César conceded, "just around the time the Nazis decided to steal the world. It was going to be a lightning war, you remember, a blitzkrieg. At some point a group of SS, six of them, did a little stealing of their own. Gold! In Austria, by the Mauthausen camp. Maybe the Nazis used a cave near there for stolen treasure, the same way they put stolen art in a nearby salt mine. Anyway, our little band hides their gold in a lake, then they wait out the war. Years pass, a decade. Two decades. They're cautious men, successful. They used to be Nazis but now they're lawyers, accountants, executives, intelligence agents. They know about money, know gold's going to skyrocket in the next decade. Maybe their gold is still being sought; it could belong to Austria. Or maybe it's stamped in a way that taking even one bar would jeopardize all of it. They agree to wait a few more years while the gold doubles and triples in value. So it stays in the lake, a fabulous treasure. I'm not making this up. Then a year ago, one of the group—I don't know who he is yet—decides to take it all. But he needs help; the others must be killed off first. He's not a killer himself so he turns to someone who is: Dieter Bock. They would share the gold, just the two of them. All Bock had to do was kill the others, make it look like accidents so no one got suspicious. Bock agrees but it would take time; he needed a new life-style, identification. And he had to plan his own death as well, so nobody would suspect afterwards that he was still alive in Spain. It took him a year."

Kussow sipped his wine, carefully wiping the corners of his mouth with the cleaning cloth for his glasses. "And the gold?"

"Should still be in the lake. They were going to meet soon to get it out; it's the right time. But they're all dead now, except for Bock and his partner."

His host seemed troubled and César guessed it was the thought of a Nazi with treasure wrought from people's suffering. Such injustice had led Kussow to work for the creation of Israel after the war, where he defied the British and saw the birth of a Jewish state, the first in two thousand years. In the 1950s he worked for the Israeli Secret Service but by the end of the decade, ill and wanting only his books, he retired to Paris where César first met him and helped to keep him in France, so near Germany yet not of it. Somehow Kussow had survived the Nazis and lived to see Hebraic history made, and the religious enigma filled his mind like trapped helium in a hot-air balloon.

"There's something else," César said. "Bock's partner is already trying to double-cross him, have him killed."

"The way of thieves." Kussow regarded the inspector with a worried frown. "Your theory has a flaw in it," he suggested.

"Only one?"

"A big one. You obviously believe it's an appreciable amount of gold, millions. Assuming you're right, how would they get the gold out of Austria?"

"They won't."

"Was sagst du?"

"Someone else will smuggle it next door into Switzerland."

"And who will do that?"

"Someone who's been doing it for years, and who's now working for Bock's partner. A Swiss detective named Kayser."

* * *

Red buttons tripped off relays, the opening act. Keyboards were punched into programs. Disks whirred, sent spinning as electronic brains in Paris babbled to their cousins in the Ruhr. André had massaged the wheels again.

On the streets below, people celebrated the end of the workday

with snarls of fatigue. César, fresh from two hours on the couch, sat
at his desk and read the results.

The West German chemical industry employed more than three
hundred thousand workers in over three thousand companies. In the
past decade the industry, led by giants like Hoechst AG, tripled
production to reach a sales volume in 1973 of almost a hundred
billion deutsche marks. In this sulfurous sea Oberst-Haupt, with its
forty million, was a minnow.

At the company's helm sat Otto Francke, who also held a seat on
the directors board of Kaiser Systems which owned Oberst-Haupt.
Kaiser was itself controlled by a pack of financiers headquartered in
Frankfurt. Goethe Associates had offices near the Eschenheimer
Turm and listed Hans Weber as its chief operations officer.

César pulled out the SCE list of financiers with Nazi pasts. There
were a dozen names but no Weber or Francke. He'd hoped to learn
who purchased the Hitler portrait, and why; Kayser mentioned it
and he was involved with Bock. Disappointed, César dropped the list
back in the file with André's report. Another thread that led nowhere.

The phone was even worse: the widow on the top floor had again
tried her hand at suicide. This time she won—paraquat, a deadly
weed killer for which there was no antidote. She had swallowed
almost a half-pint and died nine hours later in unspeakable agony.

César threw down his reading glasses and massaged his eyes. For
each one saved, a dozen died. In Russia they drank themselves to
death; in America they watched television until their skeletons were
found by grandchildren. What was it Dupin said? Murder was always with us. So was suicide, self-murder. What a world! Or maybe
it was just him, too tired to think.

He locked up the Bock file and went to the nearest café and listened to a man who claimed nobody had left the earth and gone to
the moon. It was all a plot by the superpowers to drive the rest of the
world crazy. How did he know? Because the government said it was
true. César bought him a drink.

When he got back the night homicide crews were already at work.
A half hour later the informant called from the Canal St. Denis.
He'd followed Jacqueline Volette to the deserted area, where she
entered a building. What else could it be but to meet with Kayser?

What should he do?

Stay there, César said. He'd arrive shortly.

He took down the specifics, went to replace the receiver—pulled it back. Be careful, he added into the phone but Choupon had already hung up.

* * *

The young man sat in the same weathered wing chair and politely refused a glass of wine. He didn't indulge during work hours, a holdover from his years in Tel Aviv. Another time surely.

Kussow silently sipped his wine and stroked the Siamese cat on his lap, whose name was Shin Bet. His visitor had been startled by the name. The Shin Bet was the Israeli internal security agency, counterpart to the American FBI. He wondered if there might be some connection.

Kussow smiled; he'd been asked that more than once. The connection was rather involved, he reported, and better suited to another time over wine. He hoped his guest was not offended.

On the contrary, the young man was fascinated. Attached to the Israeli Embassy on the Rue Rabelais, he actually worked for the Mossad, the Israeli Secret Service. His duties were administrative and included the transmittal of information and directives. The communiqué he had brought to the apartment on the Rue des Rosiers came directly from Mossad headquarters in Tel Aviv.

After his visitor's departure, Kussow read the directive a dozen times looking for clues of intent. There were none. But was it desire or demand?

The French inspector of police, César Dreyfus, himself a Jew, must stop his investigation of the ex-Nazi Dieter Bock.

In the small rear apartment on the third floor, the old man with sad eyes sat in his chair and talked to his cat, telling it of the time when men gave birth to a new nation. And of the things they had to do.

* * *

The water dozed. At its edges sludge from discharge pipes streaked slick colors along the narrow banks, while behind the wharf the old slaughterhouses still filled the air with the stench of maddened beasts. Farther downstream where the St. Denis turned into the Canal de l'Ourcq lay the livestock market with its empty stalls and holding pens; for centuries the market was the true stomach of

Paris. In this moon's night, misshapen shadows reached out from solitary silhouettes to snare unwary insects or capture new ground.

On the opposite bank huge industrial sheds huddled, monoliths of some nether world; no scrollwork served to soften their angularity. Around the rim of the piers, flat-roofed factories hid among the disordered streets.

Kayser had lured Jacqueline. He'd promised her wealth to work with him, but César was certain the real promise was death. It would bring Bock into the open.

In the heavens candles flickered from metal wingtips.

César stood by the slaughterhouse. Deserted, it now reeked of menace. The crescent moon hung low over his shoulder, and in the wash of light rose the jagged spires of buildings. Where the door opened a crack, he slipped inside.

On the cluttered floor of the shed shone the moon's rays reflected through a skylight. César inched forward, surprised he did not see them, hear them. Where was the informant? Worried, he moved faster. Past the animal chute from which the beasts were hurtled into the lock for the hammer blows to the head, stunning, finally splitting. Passing the carving tanks, the cisterns for the blood; crossing a void, his mind in darkness.

Near the light's edge he came to the dressing area, the meat hooks on overhead steel tracks. On the final hook hung a steer. As César approached cautiously, the steer turned into a man and then a face. Choupon!—trussed up like a side of beef, the hook's steel claw buried deep in his back. Blood still spurted onto the stained and slippery floor.

Ahead of César a movement became a form, then the form split in two. César lurched forward, lost sight of someone in the shadows. The next second he saw Jacqueline sprawled on the floor. He rushed over to her, bent down. Her eyes were glazed; she'd been struck on the head.

"He said you'd come after her," a disembodied voice snarled. César spun around as Kayser stepped into the reflected light. "How dumb can you get?"

The PPK in his hand motioned César to stand up; when he did Kayser began to search him. César could feel the smooth bore against the small of his back. "Where's your partner?" he asked the private detective.

"That isn't necessary"—Maton came out of the shadows behind César—"he never carries a gun."

"Never?" Kayser didn't believe it.

"I knew if I told you about the woman," Maton said to César, "you'd have her followed, and then you would come running."

"She was just his mistress," César said helplessly.

"Mistress? Is that what she told you?" Kayser snorted in amazement.

"You should have listened to me," Maton said sadly. "I tried to warn you. Admit I tried. Let the case go, I kept telling you, give it back to them. But not you; you people always have to prove something. Just like Algeria, like always with you. Always the lone wolf. So now what have you proved? If you'd let go, Menard would still be alive and you wouldn't be standing here in a slaughterhouse." Kayser, nearby, took the bomb out of the satchel. "But you couldn't, I know. Your obsessive nature. I warned you about that, too, if you remember."

Maton covered him as Kayser placed the taped bomb on the floor by Jacqueline and ran the fuse to the wall. César watched him bend one side of an empty cigarette box into the other and fold over the ends and punch a hole with a penknife in the bottom.

"Even at the last minute I tried to save you," Maton insisted. "You know I did. I asked you to come in with us, offered to share with you. But you were too good for that kind of money, as if there's any other kind. No, you had to be pure. And for what?" He glanced at Jacqueline. "Even so, you couldn't save her."

"You save her," César pleaded.

"It's too late for that now," Maton declared. "Bock is familiar with explosives; I'm told it says so in his dossier. He'll be blamed for you and the woman. You remember what I told you about going it alone? The same goes for the Nazi. He'll be hunted down like an animal. The two of you are really the same, you and Bock. Too bad you didn't see that in time. Why didn't you see that?"

"Too late now," Kayser snarled.

César's eyes were on Maton and when he turned toward the voice he saw the gun, the glint of steel, the flash of fire. It all happened at once. His knees buckled. He seemed to be falling forever, walls whirling around him. The bomb, César thought. Pain seared his mind. He tried to raise his arms to protect himself and they burst into flame, sparks shooting out of the fingers. The room exploded into color, the color into texture. As the ground came up to meet him, he had the sensation of still more shots. Then steps.

He stopped falling.

"Amateurs!"

The accent was German.

César lay with his head sideways and watched the blood spill out of his mouth. One of his hands seemed to be pressed into his side, the fingers locked together. Everything felt wet. He rolled his head until he could look straight up, tried to lift it off the ground. It fell back the other way. Kayser stared at him, one eye a bloodless socket. César twisted his neck to peer past Kayser's body and saw Maton. His face was peaceful, a white backdrop for the gaping red hole in the center of his forehead.

Someone nearby bent down to the cigarette box and lit a match that went into the hole; a hand draped the fuse over it.

César felt himself slipping away, his eyes filled with someone he'd seen only in a photograph and in his dreams. Yet he didn't hear the bells. When you're going to die, you always hear bells just before death comes. Everyone knew that, César thought. But he heard only the gasping and wheezing of someone dying far away. He knew it wasn't him. He was not going to die.

In his ecstasy César saw himself lifted on the wings of angels and as they flew high in the northern lights, the sound of the wind was like all the beautiful bells of Notre-Dame.

BOOK TWO

SIXTEEN

Every breath was a knife in the heart. Barely breathing, the body lay like a turnip in the field, its thick roots attached to the mantle of earth. Through days and nights of fire and ice the roots nourished the body, fed it, cleansed it. When the body babbled, faces appeared. When it revolted, hands worked hurriedly. As the roots shrank the body seemed to grow, taking on color and definition. In time the body breathed again in remembered rhythm, and then one day it slowly opened its eyes.

He stared at the stretches of white, ribbons of light that swirled in space. Dazed, he bit his tongue, felt the sharp edge of life, a pyrrhic victory. His eyes sought the room's lines, now barely discernible in the hot glare. In his nightmares he had fought for death, struggled with those who would keep him alive, cheat him of peace, shackle him to pain. Not him, his exhausted shell; that thing down there, the husk that hovered between sheets, clamped to plastic prods, while he perched in the mind and waged war on his umbilical body. He'd heard the voices, seen the glances. Men in white and others wearing black, calculating, cautious, their eyes a reflection of concern. He didn't know who they were or what they wanted, only that they wanted him alive, and so he waited for them, looked for their faces and noted their reactions. Slowly their lips lost the grim tightness, and the lines at the edges disappeared. Eventually they began to smile and he noted that too. When their whispers turned to talk he left his perch and put on his cloak to become one of them again, recognizable and connected in memory.

Now he studied the ceiling, the walls. All was a stark blinding smear, a window of escape. But he couldn't resist, didn't dare; they knew what they were doing. Doctors knew everything. He'd been sick, shot, was getting better. He knew everything too.

"Bock," he mumbled at some point but no one heard.

Later he began to feel his body, the weight of an arm, a hand, its fingers; he ran them over his chest and abdomen. After that came a leg, the foot, the other. He was still in one piece.

His mind filled with Jacqueline. Was she alive?

"Dead," someone hissed inside of him but he knew enough to know the voice of the devil.

The next time he looked the white of the room had become a pale eggshell. Both windows were filled with glass. In one corner stood a small metal table, near it a chair. By the bed silver machines gleamed; a lifeline was still attached to his arm but he didn't think he'd sink anymore.

"Feeling better?"

He turned his head into the sound, the eyes straining to focus. A blur became a form, the form a man, a big man moving to the foot of the bed. Behind him the door remained closed.

"I told them you'd make it," the voice said. Hands gripped the rail, the knuckles bleached bone under stretched skin.

"How long—"

"Five days." A chair was pulled over to the other side of the bed. "It's Sunday, if you care."

"Sunday?"

"Morning. Want to talk?"

He closed his eyes, saw himself die. Alive again, he was in a room with sunlight curling round the drawn shades. He wondered if Dupin had been there all night, found it fitting that Homicide should be with him. He had no other family.

"If you don't, just listen."

The woman Jacqueline Volette had regained consciousness in front of the hospital's emergency entrance, the car's horn jammed to sound until someone came. César was next to her, dying or dead.

Through prints and dental work, the bodies found in the wreckage were identified as those of Inspector Maton, the Swiss Kayser and César's informant Choupon. All had been shot. Assuming Maton and Kayser were in it together, who killed them and blew the building?

César's eyes widened in answer.

"Bock!" he swore.

* * *

After Dupin left, he lay in bed watching the light grow stronger against the shade and thought of the woman Jacqueline Volette. The phrase had a nice ring to it, superfluous no doubt, and doubly descriptive, but still a nice ring. Did it also explain the mystery of what she was? Or how he felt? Just when he was certain he had the solution a pit opened and he tumbled downward.

When he awoke the solution was gone, washed away in a flood of light. Someone had raised the shade and the sunshine was a harsh slap. He tried to get out of bed but couldn't even sit up. With his free arm he managed to knock over a glass.

The duty nurse was adamant. "We really must stay in bed," she insisted.

He agreed if she would take off her clothes.

"And we mustn't get too excited," she said in her professional voice. "It's still daylight."

Maybe if she lowered the shade?

Afterwards he stared at the shadows on the wall, changing with the earth's revolution, and brooded on Jacqueline and the passing of time. She had raised herself out of childhood poverty and was determined never to go back. For such admirable ambition, she would've had to pay a price. Sometimes ambition can turn into greed.

But why did Kayser laugh at her being Bock's mistress?

Her story to the police had her lured to the area by Kayser's false plea for aid—she knew him as a friend of Bock's—then knocked out. She couldn't imagine what he wanted with her. Obviously she was a victim, just like their own inspector. Would he say differently? She knew he wouldn't.

* * *

At noontime another nurse came by to report dozens of calls about him in the past few days.

"You certainly are popular," she trilled.

All it took was a bullet, César thought. And then wondered why Bock had saved him. He decided it was guilt. France was conservative Catholic when it came to guilt. Why was it wrong to make love standing up? Because it might lead to dancing.

Except Bock was German.

César fought down his paranoia. The German probably mistook him for someone else, was waiting in the hall to finish the job. Did nurses have pills for paranoia? Didn't matter; he couldn't trust them anyway.

* * *

"Are you a religious man?" Eyes glanced over his chart.

"Not especially."

"You should be," the doctor said tersely. He took César's blood pressure. "Over the years I've seen many medical miracles. Yours is right up there with the best of them."

"Then why do I feel so bad?"

"Infection, blood loss, shock syndrome. None of it fatal anymore, though the infection's still a problem." The eyes peered under bandages. "You also have a wound that must be painful."

"So where's the miracle?" César winced, suddenly feeling painfully wounded. "Besides being alive, I mean."

Stool nodded soberly. "Without trying to scare you to death at this point, let's just say a very big bullet passed between your lungs without touching either of them, a miracle in itself, came within a quarter inch of your heart, miraculously struck no bones, severed only one blood vessel, and passed out your back between the ribs an eighth of an inch from your spine." He took a deep breath. "What I mean is, you have a hole going straight through you."

"Dangerous?"

"You were a step away from the angels, and dancing your way into heaven."

"What about the bullet?"

"I understand they never found it. All I can estimate," said the former army captain, "is that it was smaller than a 75mm cannon shell and bigger than necessary."

"And the hole?" César asked.

Stool restored the surgical dressing. "The body's another miracle.

Given half a chance, it usually heals itself. Naturally you'll have to stay with us a while, to clear up the infection."

"How long?"

"A week, ten days. Let's see what happens." His examination was finished.

"And you, Doctor," César pressed. "Do you believe in God?"

"Whenever I think of you, Inspector."

* * *

Afterwards César had a nurse bring him a calendar. It was an obvious reminder of man's mortality. He quickly discarded the March sheet and counted the remaining days in April, then turned to May. He'd never make it! There were only ten days left to May 7.

* * *

He was just a local detective sergeant working the Thirteenth district, nothing glamorous like the boys in Criminal Investigation, but he had an idea about the Marie Pinay murder. Inspector Dreyfus was the man to see and so Durac sat on this Sunday afternoon in the darkened room and talked quietly of the substance poured over the body before the match was struck.

"Paint thinner," he reminded César. "Yet the woman clearly hadn't touched a brush in years, didn't even paint her nails. It occurred to me the killer could've brought the thinner with him, which might mean premeditation. I checked around the neighborhood and came up with a couple of handymen who've had some painting jobs recently, and the curious thing is one of them hasn't been seen in weeks. He lives alone and seldom goes into the local bars, which is why you weren't given his name. We didn't know about him. Might be nothing, of course, but if there's anything I can do—"

"Find him," César growled.

* * *

In the evening Clément paid him a quick visit, sounding as if he were diagnosing brain damage. Not hopeless, just irreversible.

"Couldn't be worse," he sighed. "You should've called me for help."

"My voice didn't carry that far."

"At least you're alive, what's left of you."

"I'll be back in a week."

"Six months is more like it."

"Five days."

"So how do you feel?"

"I think I'd rather be in Marseille."

"That bad, eh?"

* * *

Two days later he still wasn't allowed out of bed. No phones either, too stressful. Only people were permitted, as if they were a source of peace. He was a police inspector so they were admitted even between visiting hours, at all hours. Crime must not be given any rest.

He had Clément put a pair of posters on the opposite wall with tape. Picture hooks were unnecessary since pictures were forbidden. He told the staff he'd arrest anyone who touched them; destroying private property was a serious offense. They told him the wall was public since the hospital was municipal. If he didn't remove the pictures, they'd have him arrested for defacing public property, equally serious. Clément took away the posters of dancing girls and brought two small framed horses that danced on the table next to the lamp. No one said a word.

The bulletin board went on the wall in place of the posters. It was stolen the first time he slept, and he told Clément to take the darts away too. At least he had a few holes to look at.

Menard was gone, and so was André. For May he would be in Robbery, continuing his education. He'd learned a bit about Homicide, maybe even that he didn't like it. A detective who thought overly of his own safety could be a danger to others. And so could someone who saw only the goal, someone reckless like him.

He could feel the rising despair. Helpless when he longed to run with the hounds, he was a child again, dependent on others for survival, at the mercy of those who could leave or be taken away without warning, never to return. The hospital was for him defeat, and he found himself brooding once more on the nameless fears of his youth.

In defense he raced riddles through his mind. Questions, cases, puzzles, always coming back to the present as the touchstone of his life. In his soul he knew there would be no other cases, were no other cases. *This* was the case that measured his life. This was the case. Bock was alive and seeking gold. He had left a trail for his pursuer because he couldn't help it; treachery demanded satisfaction even from the grave. If he went over, his pursuer would settle with his betrayer. That was why Bock had saved him. There was no escape, nothing else mattered. Now it was only the two of them, the hunter and the hunted. The Jew and the Nazi. In César's disordered mind, this was the greatest riddle of all.

* * *

They came at him in pairs, one in Wednesday's dawn and the other at dusk, men from the Internal Affairs division. Their job was to exorcise devils in the department. Root out malingerers and malcontents, which always meant the same thing: corrupt cops. No reflection on César, obviously, who had an exemplary record. To show their good faith, they smiled into the bed where he lay with a bad conscience.

"Friendship is a wonderful thing," the early pair told him, "and especially in police work. Builds character and regulates conduct, keeps it within acceptable parameters. Mutual responsibility, you see? The right kind of friendship can even save lives. Sometimes, though, a friend becomes alienated, starts thinking only of himself, his own benefit. He forgets about those around him. He becomes unreasonable. Might want his closest friends to cover up for him or even join in. Make them unreasonable, too. We know you're not like that. You want to be reasonable, don't you, Dreyfus?"

"I don't have any friends," César said.

* * *

The information on the dozen Jews betrayed by Paul Dussap wasn't good. Strasbourg police could find no record of their names and so nothing could be learned of their fate, though they undoubtedly ended in Auschwitz. César suspected Dussap had once betrayed someone now in power in East Germany; he reluctantly settled on that for the motive, without knowing the specifics.

The rest of the news was still worse, according to Clément. Prints on the May 7 memo were not those of Streicher at all but matched the ones sent César by West German Intelligence. They belonged to Dieter Bock.

* * *

The evening shift wore silk suits and carried gold lighters. César wondered where they got the money for such things on a policeman's pay.

"You should have reported your suspicions about Maton," one of them said while the other nodded gravely. "Formally, to the division. They say the ministry looks favorably on you now, meaning you could go a long way. Yet you protect killers."

"Killers?"

"You admit Inspector Maton was helping the Swiss detective Kayser," said the other. "We know Kayser was Bock's partner."

"Kayser was trying to kill Bock."

"Kayser was paying Maton to help them. Believe me, all the facts are known. We just want your verification."

"Of what?"

"Tell us about the slaughterhouse, what happened. We won't say anything about you. Only Inspector Maton concerns us. Did Bock and Kayser try to cut him loose? Was there a double cross? Was anyone else involved?"

"Anyone else?"

"He means anyone in the department who knew what was going on, beside you."

"I didn't know anything was going on."

Only the goal mattered. Any admission meant trouble since the silk suits already considered him guilty. Wasn't he suspected? Well! His guilt, however, lay deeper than conspiracy. Obsessional, it fed on whoever would lead him to Bock.

To Internal Affairs, Maton's life-style was now thought excessive, his financial records confusing; he had too many friends which indicated a fear of being alone, a sign of guilt; his unwillingness to marry was antisocial, a manifestation of contempt; his caliber of conversation proved philosophical intoxication; his record of arrests showed a success-ridden sense of values; he was an obvious alcoholic who hid his addiction in bouts of sobriety; he used informers for work and women for sex; he liked money. All this and more was known by the silk suits, who knew Maton was somehow involved with Bock.

César saw they knew nothing. Otherwise they would know enough to concentrate on Jacqueline Volette.

After a while the questions just bounced off his brain. They all led to the slaughterhouse: what happened there? Luckily he had been shot, heard nothing. Wasn't he conscious at all? Only of being carried away by angels, beautiful beasts weighted with wings of gold. Eyes closed, César pictured them looking like Jacqueline that first time he saw her in the Sorbonne, an angel. When he opened his eyes the two devils still surrounded his bed. Warding off their attacks made him listen closely to their hissing noises, and he suddenly saw that he hadn't really heard them at all.

"You're not interested in Maton," he blurted out, startled. "He's just a screen. I'm what you're after. You think I was the one helping Bock."

"We have the proof."

"What proof?"

"We found your bank account," one of them said.

"In Switzerland," said the other. "A hundred thousand francs in the past four months."

* * *

The next morning Jules appeared. Plastic smile oozing cold charm, the ministry official looked disapprovingly at the holes in the walls, the hardback chair, the enameled bed with César in it.

"The minister remembers you," Jules said. "He wants you to know how saddened he was by the premature report of your death." The eyes were beams of controlled emotion. "Naturally he's relieved you're alive."

"Naturally."

"Getting everything you need here?"

"Only what they think I need." César hadn't expected the ministry to send visitors. The idea bothered him.

"Rules and regulations," Jules sighed efficiently. He pulled out a typed sheet. "We didn't get a chance to compare those names the minister asked about due to your, uh, incident. Is this the same list the SCE gave you?"

The dozen names belonged to West German financiers with Nazi pasts, as attested by the SCE. César quickly saw the lists were identical.

"There's some talk," Jules confided, "that this Bock is chasing after gold. Any truth to it?"

"It's possible."

"They say it's Nazi gold. Stolen from the Nazis, who stole it from someone else." He took back the list. "Now who do you suppose they stole it from?"

"Nothing's definite," César said. He didn't think it was a rhetorical question, wondered in turn why the ministry should be interested in the possibility.

"Not definite, of course. Still"—Jules edged nearer—"if there were hidden gold, it might be difficult to assess ownership now."

"For keeping it, yes."

"There, you see?"

César couldn't tell if he was serious. The ministry would have access to information an inspector could never get, obviously. Maybe even going back to the war.

"Thirty years is a long time." Jules tilted his head for emphasis.

"There's no proof—"

"Of course not."

César strained to find the man's motives. His face was suddenly as soft as stone.

"It might be a matter of what country found it," Jules explained.

"The gold—"

"Doesn't belong to the Nazis. At least we know that."

"What gold?"

"The *Anvil* gold. Isn't that what we're talking about?"

Stolen gold, César thought; he was talking about the *Nibelung* treasure.

"You never heard of *Anvil,*" Jules sighed. "I can see it."

"By another name," César said quickly.

"What name?"

"Nibelung."

"Wagner. That's good."

"During the war." César fixed his face in a knowing frown. "A secret SS operation."

"The most secret," Jules added. "Personally approved by Hitler; only Himmler knew of it among the top Nazis. And Bormann, of course."

"The SS," César prodded.

"A few of the generals. Heinrich Müller himself was in charge of the group that handled it."

César nodded. "In Austria, by Mauthausen."

"You know about the project, then." Jules was relieved.

"I told you I did."

"The biggest gold steal in history." His voice held a note of awe. "From millions of Jews in the concentration camps, from the looting of their homes and shops and synagogues. All of it melted down into gold bullion. Think of it!" Jules could hardly control his enthusiasm. "And it went on for almost three years."

César frowned. "I'd like to have seen that smelter."

"By the time the Americans got there, it was destroyed. Vanished," Jules assured him. "The gold too." He shook his head sadly. "The Linz area was practically the last Nazi stronghold to be liberated."

"So no one knew where the gold went," César said.

"Everyone knew. It went into secret SS accounts in Switzerland to help its members after the war."

César remained silent and Jules abruptly broke into a crafty smile. "That's what everyone said, anyway."

César glanced at the window. Beyond it roamed devils dressed as humans, sent to earth for their sins.

"You've surely heard the rumors," Jules added. "Everything from South America to hidden salt mines."

"Rumors—"

"Are often true, especially in something like this. After all, no one saw the gold again. Or any records from Swiss banks. Still, it'd be hard to hide that much."

"How much?"

"A good guess is fifteen billion in today's market."

"Deutsche marks?"

"Dollars."

And worth more each day, César thought. Now with gold legal in America, it would rise like a rocket.

"You think Bock knows anything about *Anvil?*" Jules asked.

There was no doubt in César's mind; it was the same gold. Bock and the others stole some of it at the end of the war, hid it in the lake. Probably not too much or Müller would've missed it; just enough to make murder worthwhile thirty years later.

"He was on Himmler's staff," Jules urged. "He could've been involved in the project."

"What would they want with a killer?" César scoffed. "That's all he did."

"That's all they needed." Jules laughed nervously. "What do you think happened to the workers?"

César envisioned the slave labor from the concentration camp picked to work the secret plant nearby. He saw them smelting the bars out of stolen gold objects. He heard the rattle of the guards' guns. When workers wore out they were killed and others forced to take their place. César saw that too. How many dead workers for each ton of gold? No one kept records. The bodies were burned, the gold stored. At the end there were caves filled with gold bars, even beyond the gold teeth siphoned off for private accounts in Nazi banks and the gold watches that glutted German pawnshops. Then the caves turned into bank vaults in Zurich and nobody knew the difference. Nobody knew that some of the bars had been sunk in an Austrian lake, either.

"If Bock's after the *Anvil* gold," Jules hinted into César's ear, "think of the possibilities."

SEVENTEEN

They sat in the room violating oaths and betraying confidences. César wanted a name and Martel a guarantee.

"How do I know you'll do what you say?"

"Because I say it."

"And the pictures?"

"Yours, all of them." César held up the envelope of photos taken by the forensic photographer, an expert in camera traps. They showed the two men on a boat in the Seine, huddled in conversation.

"What'll that prove?" the SCE supervisor blustered.

"They've been dated by a qualified witness, which should bring suspicion on your head at home. Bordier will want to know what you've been doing."

"So we met accidentally."

"Not good enough," César jeered. "You know how they operate since you're one of them. You'll have to admit passing me information to get rid of Junot."

"He's dead anyway."

"Don't be dumb. He's dead and I have you talking about it."

"You can't prove that."

"Your general won't care. He knows the mess I can make. He's already under orders to play along with me. If I tell him about you, what will he do? You'll be lucky to live."

Martel's bushy eyebrows rose in protest.

"Let's say you did kill Junot, one of your goons. And let's say you were told to do it, without being told, of course." César understood the secret police mind. "There's only one man could order a thing like that. What would happen if I start waving pictures around?"

The eyes narrowed in thought.

"See what I mean?"

César was twisting the hook all he could.

"All right," the supervisor snarled. He was caught and didn't like it. "They should've shot you in the head."

"All right what?"

Martel looked at the wall. "I get the negative in three days?"

"Three days," César said. "And I forget about our little talk."

"I don't have to do this, you know. Fuck your pictures. I could get rid of you myself."

"Look what happened to Junot when he tried."

Martel shifted in his chair as if warding off a blow. "There'll be other times."

"And meanwhile—"

"What's your deal?"

"I need the name of the Nazi moneyman in Zurich. No free samples, the right name the first time. He'd be a lawyer with a lot of contacts and easy access to the big banks."

"Why would I know?"

"They're still your friends."

Martel licked his lips. Names were part of his business, never to be revealed. "I could strangle you with my bare hands for this, just for this," he fumed.

"I'm waiting."

"Dunant!" It was hurled out. "Ander Dunant."

"In Zurich?"

"On the Bahnhofstrasse."

"If you call him in the next three days, our deal's off and I start talking." César gave him the envelope. "You think about that."

The inspector turned away in shame. Sworn to serve the law and paid to catch killers, he was letting murder slip through his fingers.

* * *

Outside the room the sun rose higher, splashing light on the houses to the west. Everywhere the promised buds began to bloom. Next to the hospital a garden slowly blushed into color.

The phone rang, a test. It had taken seconds to install, after a lifetime of waiting. César held the world in his hand.

"You're strong enough now," the doctor announced at the bedside. "Just don't tax yourself too much or out it goes."

"The carrot and the stick?"

Stool smiled thinly. Strands of graying hair were pressed straight across his forehead to cover a widow's peak.

"Patients are oftentimes children," he said defensively.

"Self-indulgent."

"At least we tend to see them like that."

César understood. He sometimes saw criminals the same way, without moral conviction or sense of responsibility. Criminals and children and now patients. It was a small world.

"Anyway, rest as much as you can," the doctor said briskly, "and soon you'll be up and around. Then——"

"When?"

"Let's see in a few days."

Alone, César fondled the phone. Ugly, intemperate, shrill, it was his lifeline. He'd been tied to one and was now plugged into the other.

His first call was to Geneva, the second to Zurich.

* * *

"What do you think?"

"Could be."

Could be? When it was clear where the gold was? César sometimes wondered about Clément. A good detective but a daydreamer. Still, he had tenacity.

So did the inspector. "Let's look at it again," he persisted. "We know in Bock's paranoid imagination, life is full of hidden signs and everything has meaning. Linge fell out a window, as a man falls into the water and drowns. Baur was killed with a lead bullet; lead and gold are the two heaviest base metals and have always attracted each other. Streicher was ripped open as if by a shark of the deep, and Schirrmacher had the oxygen pushed out of him much as happens to a diver whose air is cut off. You see? Gold and water. Such symbols are important to Bock."

"It's possible."

César stared at the daydreamer, strangled sharp words. "Remember he killed a man a month. What is that but a symbol? May 7 marks the war's end, still another symbol—all of them signals to Bock. In that kind of siege mentality, traces are left everywhere, in every act, to cover every possibility of treachery. Nobody's trusted," César said, "and death is merely the final vindication of all his suspicions. Think of it. Bock left a trail to his partner from the start. And Kayser proved him right."

"What about the painting that brought Kayser to Paris?"

"It gives us the lead to Bock's partner," César exulted. "Someone from Oberst-Haupt. Now what do you say?"

"Could be," Clément repeated.

César bit his tongue. Who could expect passion in the middle of a hospital in the middle of the day? He tried again.

"The ministry says the gold supposedly went to the Nazi underground after the war, but they're not sure. I am. At least some of it is in a lake near Linz, somewhere around Mauthausen."

"How can you be sure?"

"Bock told me."

"What?"

"Him and me, don't you see, we think the same way."

César finally saw the surprise spread across the detective's face. Satisfied, he instructed Clément to dig into Munich businessman Otto Francke.

* * *

"The man is blundering into something he knows nothing about."

The Mossad general was exasperated; he preferred dealing with clear lines of good and evil. Israeli defense was good, its enemies evil. When attacked, defend. When terrorists struck, retaliate. Yet there was no clarity in this matter, no frontal assault or secret swipe. The past had to be protected, of course. But protected from what? A French inspector of police? Himself a Jew? It was ludicrous, and potentially tragic. Nevertheless—

"Suggestions?"

"He's in a hospital now," someone said, "recovering from a shooting. Perhaps a hit team . . ." The sad eyes stared straight ahead.

"That won't be necessary," the general declared. "We are not the Al Fatah and this isn't a question of national security so much as perception. How a nation sees itself describes what it is; the world respects us because we respect ourselves. That mustn't change." He studied the faces around him. "What we need here is to apply the exact right pressure. No more or less."

The four men in the room represented the leadership of the Israeli intelligence community, its various branches, meeting in secret session chaired by the chief of the Mossad, the Israeli CIA. The other members included the heads of Military Intelligence, the Shin Bet internal security agency, and the special section of the national police force. It was their conviction, shared by Israel's leaders going back to Ben-Gurion, that God's hand was in the making of the Jewish state. If it was the will of Allah that the Jews be driven into the sea, then it was God's will that they live in the land of their fathers. God's will and a strong standing army and a good intelligence network.

Such security committee meetings—conducted far from Tel Aviv's central area and beachfront—were always filled with pressing problems of judgment and analysis, but to the general the question now under review was particularly significant since Israeli Intelligence had been directly involved from the beginning, even before the creation of the state.

The talk was of the French, their air of superiority. "Especially the security services. But when they lost Indochina, they were all shipped to Algeria where they began making the same mistakes. Seven years later they lost that country."

"I thought de Gaulle gave it away."

"By then there was nothing to give; it was gone."

"Hopelessly chauvinistic, all of them."

"That's what they say about us."

"But the French police," a voice prompted. "Isn't that the problem here?"

"If you're police, you're either Paris or anywhere else. And if it's Paris you hope to wake up some morning in the Criminal Division."

"Why there?"

"Politically safe," suggested the speaker. "In the war, for example, it was business as usual; the division was simply absorbed under the

Nazis. Which is exactly what they did with the German *Kriminalpolizei,* who became part of the SS. If the Russians roll across Europe, I expect the same would happen. Criminal police are invaluable to any conqueror."

"Assuming there's anything left to conquer."

"This Dreyfus. He is in the Criminal Police?"

"An inspector."

"So he is also the political police."

"Strictly speaking, no. But as I say, the capability is there. Anyway he's protected."

"Not really," said the general. "He's still a Jew."

"It occurred to me"—the speaker removed his glasses for emphasis—"maybe something could be done with his kinship to Captain Dreyfus."

Around the table eyes widened at the mention of the famous French Jew accused of espionage for Germany and sent to Devil's Island. Theodor Herzl covered the treason trial for a Vienna paper and was so shaken by the Dreyfus Affair that he began thinking in terms of a new Jewish consciousness; the result was his book *The Jewish State,* which led directly to the founding of the modern Zionist movement and ultimately Israel.

"With a background like that—an army captain finally exonerated and made a hero, out of which came a direct link to the birth of Israel—this policeman must surely see himself as someone special, perhaps even a reincarnation of his illustrious forebear. Aren't the police paramilitary? Maybe we could use that. If he harmed his people through his work on the Bock case, he would tarnish the name."

"An interesting idea"—the general spoke softly as always—"to go with what we've been able to learn about Dreyfus. It seems our French police inspector is himself part German."

* * *

For lunch he had soup and creamed corn, his first day on real food. It tasted even worse than he recalled. Only the ice cream felt good and he made a point of asking the nurse if he could be put on bottled chocolate. She giggled when César handed her the tray.

"I'm serious," he stressed. "All they'd have to do is water the cream and widen the tubes."

"Want me to suggest it downstairs?" Her cheerfully lopsided face had become a fixture in his days of delirium, a barometer by which he'd gauged his own puny efforts at life. "They still remember your posters."

"Do you know who stole the bulletin board?"

"I'm not allowed to say."

"Did you?"

"Not me."

"Then it was someone else," César said wisely.

"You'll be going home soon." The nurse plumped the pillows. "Leave it behind."

"The future's what worries me. If I stay here much longer, I'll end up on Devil's Island myself."

César didn't believe Internal Affairs would destroy him. They wanted to, of course, since their sole duty was destruction but he wasn't going to let them. Someone set him up because he was getting too close. To what? It had to be Bock. Four months ago he activated his plan by pushing Linge out the window.

With the nurse gone César paced at the foot of the bed, holding onto the railing. The dizziness soon cleared. Four months ago he didn't know about Bock so the bank account had to be some form of trusteeship, with his name added later. That meant letters from him. To get them he'd have to act like his prey, do what Bock did.

Seated by the window now, César looked out at a man consumed by despair. The man stared through vacant eyes, a reflection of himself. He was a fraud, professing ideals he no longer practiced. At least Bock was true to his murderous desires: born to be raised in some medieval court where flourished the art of cloak and dagger, a modern Macbeth, resolute and irrevocable, while he—What was he but a poor Hamlet? A man unable to decide, and full of moral ambiguity. He was losing all the beliefs he'd lived by; they were slipping away from him, even his respect for justice. He felt himself a criminal, dealing with devils, and the feeling frightened him. He was vulnerable again.

Except for the leaden image on the glass the world outside was reassuring. On the afternoon streets people hurried along familiar paths, the daily journeys of measured lives. Young evergreens lined the hospital's approach, shrubs of slender needles, while cars in heat exuded all kinds of effluvia and emanations invisible as truth. Lost in space, César began to fit Jacqueline Volette's lies into place. Inexorably the lies led straight to Dieter Bock.

* * *

"I'll tell you about running the division," Dupin said. "Efficiency is the killer. Next year's budget depends on last year's results, just like any business. Right now capital punishment's an issue so they're pushing homicides. Other years it's robbery or maybe spitting on the street; arrests are made in whatever's hot, you know about that. Or crime categories are juggled. Statutory rape is lumped with the real thing, wife beating becomes assault—that sort of thing. Politicians get the figures they need, the public reads the results it wants and everybody's happy. We're doing our job."

Dupin gazed at César's reflection in the window. The image was unclear.

"But we pay a price. The better we do our job, the more visible police power becomes. This frightens a lot of people; they don't like to think of all that power, so there's a backlash. While they praise us they're looking to cut us down. Anything comes along, they'll jump on it. Gives them a chance to strike a balance between their needs and their fears, healthy for them but not for us. You see?"

César nodded, wondered where this was leading. Dupin always had a bottom line.

"That brings us to the second problem: image and morale. We're always in the public eye and it never blinks when it comes to us. Others can do wrong but not the police. It makes sense in a way. Who would catch us? Which is the whole point. We have to catch ourselves; any scandal is ten times worse if we don't get it first. A detective goes wrong and we all look bad, but at least we flushed him out on our own."

He turned into the room, speared César with a look.

"That's why we watch things a little more than most people. A man lives beyond his means, we notice it and begin to wonder. Usually it's legitimate income from family, wise investments, a wealthy wife. We should all be so lucky." He smiled at the thought of his own handsome wife, from a landed family. "Corruption is almost always the issue and that's bad enough, but anything violent like murder— Well, it's the kind of trouble we don't need. I hope you agree."

"Of course." César saw ahead, the bottom line. "So Tobie Maton—"

"Was buried with full honors of an inspector killed in the line of duty. Why not? He was after Kayser, suspected of stealing artworks to be returned for reward. He followed the Swiss to the slaughterhouse where he was slain by Kayser who was in turn killed by his partner Bock in a falling-out over the woman Jacqueline Volette."

"And me?" César asked, intrigued.

"You had the Volette woman watched in connection with the Bock case. She'd been lured to the area by Kayser who intended to kill her—possibly he regarded her as a negative influence on Bock or maybe it was just jealousy—but you interceded and were shot. Before Kayser could finish her off Bock arrived and killed him, then torched the building to get rid of the bodies. He saved you for unknown reasons, and the Volette woman because they had been related."

"How come I'm not suspected of killing them all?"

"You would be," Dupin admitted, "except for the woman. She saw Kayser shoot you."

"I thought she was unconscious."

Dupin shrugged. "You know how women are, they weave in and out. Plus you never carry a gun. We found yours in a desk drawer. It hadn't been fired in years."

"So why did Bock save me?"

"How the hell do I know? I can't think of everything."

"Internal Affairs thinks I'm Bock's partner, or at least helping him for money."

"That's Internal Affairs," Dupin growled. "They've got their own axes. You just keep on with Bock. Your work's been brilliant so far, even dedicated. See? I have faith in you. Even more, I trust the department. No use to deny that Bock would make us look good in the presidential palace." He edged nearer the bed. "Now what about the money in Zurich?"

* * *

"While other girls dreamed of marrying millionaires," Jacqueline was saying softly, "I dreamed of becoming one."

She sat near the open window, the afternoon sun falling across her lap, her slender hands illuminated in the shafts of light. The door to the hall was closed, no noise reached them. Her eyes were wide with anticipation, the lids a perfect expression of her thoughts. She smoked a silver cigarette.

"You were going to tell me about the slaughterhouse," César prompted. "Why you went there."

"Money," she said defensively.

"Whose money?"

"Kayser, of course." She made it sound so obvious, the most natural of things in the circumstances. Shouldn't he have known?

From the bed he ran his eyes around the room, then back to her. She seemed somehow out of place, a photograph in a collection of negatives. Her coat was draped casually over the chair by the table lamp; that, too, looked like it belonged elsewhere, a rich blue, and fashionable.

"What were you supposed to do for the money?"

"Betray Bock." Her eyelashes fluttered. "Kayser knew I was desperate."

"Are you?" Her eyes followed his to the coat.

"Looks deceive," she snapped, "just like people." He felt the electricity across the room, heard the crackle. "Do you know how much my graduate fellowship pays, how little? It covers the costs and nothing else. How long do you think a woman would last on nothing?"

César didn't understand. "Your clothes, the apartment—"

"Gifts. From Dieter," she added as an afterthought.

"He's been good to you."

"Very good."

"You were with him because of the money," César pressed, grabbing at straws.

"Money is a sign of love to a woman."

"You mean he bought you." The voice registered disbelief. "Is that what you're saying?"

"No, that's what you would say. Money buys, yes, but it can also heal, and bring back feeling."

"So now you have feeling. Did he buy that too?"

"If he bought me, I wouldn't be here." She crushed the cigarette in annoyance. "But I didn't come to talk about myself."

"What then?"

"You."

Had he heard right? He'd been heartened by the prospect of her visit, and curious as well.

"Me?" he asked. "Why should I interest you? You have Bock—"

"It's you I'm trying to help."

"Help me? How? I'm trying to stop him." César frowned in confusion.

"Then let him go. He saved your life, as you saved mine."

"He saved my life but he's still a killer."

Jacqueline smiled into his frown. "The killings are over. He promised me."

"Promised?" César felt rising anger. "I should let a killer go because he saved my life, and promised not to kill again. What kind of inspector would that make me?"

"A very good inspector, and human."

"Why would you care one way or the other? Tell Bock to let *me* go, and give himself up if it matters so much to you."

"I want both of you to stay alive, can't you see that?" She shook her head in dismay. "Does it surprise you? The two of you are very much alike, you know. Surely that hasn't escaped your notice. I was hoping you would listen to me, your heart—"

"Did he send you?"

"See what I mean? He would've asked the same thing. So suspicious, always wanting the worst." Jacqueline's eyes flared. "No, he didn't send me. I just thought it would be nice to have you both live. But I see that doesn't interest you. You've got some fierce plans of your own, no doubt, and scores to settle. Men like keeping score," she said sadly, "and avenging honor. That's so important, and you all do it so well. I had an idea you might want to try something different, you seemed the type."

"I'd like to do what you ask," César said helplessly, "but I can't."

"I understand. Honor and duty are more important than life." She stood and drew near the bed. "You go on back to your war now," she said gently.

"And you?" He watched the lithe animal, apprehensive.

Jacqueline scooped up her coat on the way out. "Oh, I'll probably marry a millionaire," she said over her shoulder.

* * *

René paid César a visit after dinner. He had something special to show the inspector.

"No young girls turned into flypaper," César pleaded. "I'm not strong enough yet."

"Nothing like that," René assured him with a smile. He pulled out a handkerchief that had been tied at the ends to form a basket, opened it carefully. "How about these?" he demanded proudly.

César fastened on two small objects ridged like peanut shells but dark, a reddish black that almost glowed. They were attached by a thin strand of something that could've been petrified wood, but wasn't.

"Came off a twenty-year-old who was then stabbed at least a hundred times."

César blew air through his nose. "Is this what I think it is?"

"They are," René beamed.

"In your handkerchief?"

"It's silk."

"All right." César saw no way out. "Who did it?"

"Homicide doesn't know yet. But get this. They were sewn into his mouth before he died. Sewn! With needle and thread, while he was still alive." René couldn't believe it.

Revenge rather than sex, César decided.

"Tell them to look for a muscular female who hates lips." He blew air again, a beached whale. "Or else maybe the relatives of a sexually assaulted child who lived nearby."

The phone rang. For René, the lab.

He pivoted to César with his hand over the speaker. "Guy died last night in the sack, right on top of her. The Sweet Death."

"In German they call it *Blitzkurier,* the quick messenger."

"Quicker the better if you ask me."

"So what's your verdict?" the voice whined through the phone.

René blinked back to reality. "It's got to be heart attack or else hydrocephalus elephantiasis," he muttered impatiently.

"What's that?"

"Water on the brain brought about by stampeding elephants."

The voice turned suspicious. "There were no elephants in the house," it huffed.

"Must be heart attack, then."

René gingerly restored the silk handkerchief to his pocket, glanced at César. "Now that I've shown you mine, tell me yours."

"Tell you what?"

"What you're doing with the woman," René pressed. "What else?"

* * *

"Letters," César had said to Geneva, "authorization forms, bank signature cards, anything. *Documents.*"

He'd once helped a man, part of police procedure. Not the written part—invisible, unsaid. Develop contacts, help them to help you; just don't get caught helping them.

The man moved to Geneva, knew others, friends. He had a friend, too. His friend needed something in Zurich. Delicate, yes. And right away.

Nightly cleaning crews—like garbage collection—were an important part of underworld management. Things were always needed from locked office buildings, and someone was always available with the keys.

On the seventh floor of a building on the Bahnhofstrasse, midway between the lakeshore and the central station, filing cabinets were being opened . . .

"So how's Paris?" César's friend had asked.

"Going down the Seine, like always. And Geneva?"

"Half French and all Swiss. They're crazy."

"How's that?"

"They eat money and piss perfume. Every birth is virgin. Swiss men can climb anything but their women. All chocolate is vanilla; the rest is French. Swiss watches are made by gnomes and the gnomes are made in Italy. William Tell used to jerk off in the snow. The greatest thrill in the world is jumping off a mountain without skis. France sucks and Germany can't. A Swiss girl can open your fly and find a wedding ring. They're so crazy here they think the rest of us are nuts. So how's Paris?"

In the office, papers were being pulled . . .

César had received another visit from Internal Affairs, the silk suit pair. They had not changed suits; only the shirts were switched to confuse him. They sat at the foot of the bed and stared at him through the bars.

"You're guilty," one of them declared. "We have copies of your correspondence, everything, which will be shown at your departmental trial. It's more than enough to disgrace you. The least you'll do is end up in Santé. We are here to offer you a way out. Confess now and resign from the force. If you resign there will be no trial, no disgrace. No one will know. We don't like to wash our dirty linen in public. We'll even let you keep the money. Agreed?"

"I'm innocent," César confessed.

"Then how'd the money get there?"

Just what Dupin had asked, César reflected. How quickly heroes fall. "There are ways," he said. Another Dreyfus case?

* * *

At 9 P.M. Nicole came to him. Openmouthed, she gazed down at her patient with murmurs of appreciation.

"You look good," she gushed. "For being shot, I mean. Did it hurt?"

"About the same as childbirth, I guess."

Nicole giggled. "How would you know about childbirth?"

"Why? Does it hurt more?"

"How would I know?" Her husband, the undertaker, had not wanted children until they were ready. Nicole thought that meant when they were dead.

"Nice uniform." César brushed the white sleeve. "Yours?"

Nicole slipped her hand into his. "I wore it when I helped my husband in the embalming room."

"You must've helped him a lot."

"More than he ever knew."

Nicole carried a chair over to the door, propped it under the knob. At the window she raised the shade and lowered the lamp. "The moon's much better," she whispered.

"For what?"

"For what I have in mind."

In the soft beams Nicole removed her uniform and panties. Naked, she stood before him like Joan of Arc at her trial. Judge me, screamed her body. Take me, snapped her eyes.

"You're going to be disappointed," César said, hearing her. "I can't move much."

"You don't have to move much."

Her skin was silver light. Her hair brushed her shoulders with burnished gold. She knelt on the bed, the covers pulled back, and raised her body slowly above César and gently impaled herself on his penis, her breast touching his, her graceful arms enfolding him like the wings of a dove.

"César," she cooed.

"Jacqueline . . ."

"Pardon?"

César opened his eyes, saw an angel, not his. What was wrong with him? She was everything he needed.

"Nicole," he murmured. But she was not everything he wanted.

EIGHTEEN

The next morning César was moved to another room on a lower floor. He was doing nicely, they all agreed, and would soon be going home; meanwhile, his room was needed for someone really ill. "Might die," a voice warned him. Best not to make a fuss. If anything went wrong—César wondered if they'd said the same when he was brought in. A miracle, the doctor called it. Were they disappointed? No one was ever neutral about the police. A shame, since he was the perfect patient.

"The real reason," Stool said later on his rounds, "is that you're a pain in the ass—their words, not mine. You hang pictures, demand phones, refuse food, make holes in walls during the day and in women at night, a good sign, by the way, but not to them. You don't fit into their holes—a square peg—so naturally they're not going to like you." He smiled to show César that somebody liked him. "Even collectively you're a mess, too many of you marching in and out of here, they tell me, especially the last few days. What's going on?"

"I am. When?"

"Not yet."

Briand found him on the second floor in a smaller room. "Or maybe it's just there's no furniture. Could also be the paint's peeling and the window's barred. What'd you do to deserve this?"

"It wasn't easy."

"Might be a whole new form of therapy."

"How's that?" César asked.

"Show patients it could always get worse."

"So show me."

The May 7 memo found in Streicher's office in Munich matched the handwriting on a bank signature card in Paris. They both belonged to Bock. His prints were on the memo because he wrote it.

"You can see it clearly," Briand said, "on the capital *D* in his name and the word *Dachau* in the memo." The graphologist showed César the blowup comparisons. "Also the small *c*—notice how the upper curl starts with a dot like a period—and the *i* and *e*. The slant is the same, too. That's important. Letters can be traced but getting the same slant in free style is damned difficult." He turned to another blowup. "Here's a sample of Streicher's writing from the letter he wrote to your boy. Compare it to the memo. Very different."

For César it was confirmation that Bock had a partner connected to Oberst-Haupt, and the two were going to meet on May 7 in a Munich hotel, presumably after all the others were dead. But who was the victim for May? Were any left?

"I'll leave these with you."

Traces again, to repay treachery. As an inspector César had never come across such a controlled killer; everything was forced into a pattern so rigid it became ritual. In the obsessive methodology, he suspected, was the refusal to be surprised. Or cheated.

Briand set the blowups on the bedside table as César watched and thought of Bock, who'd left his prints on the memo. His plan hadn't worked. He was being hunted, and the hunter now wondered about an alternative plan. Or was failure part of the ritual, too?

"Why'd you call me here?" asked the graphologist.

"To see your results."

"You could've got that over the phone."

"I said I wanted to see them."

"There's a difference?"

"I already knew Bock left the memo for me."

Briand brought his chair closer, sat on its edge. "Something's on your mind. What is it?"

César told him about Internal Affairs. "A hundred thousand

francs tucked away in Zurich, and all I have to do is confess. They even gave me a deal." Just thinking about it made him angry.

"What kind of deal?"

"It's a frame," he snapped. "Someone wants me out of the way."

"Who?"

"Someone."

His bed was raised in front; early models worked on gears and springs, with a handle on the back. César reached under the mattress, brought out a plastic pouch.

"The evidence," he muttered. "Open it."

Briand removed the rubber band and doubled it over his wrist, worked the latch free. His fingers withdrew a green folder.

"Read the name at the top."

"Dreyfus, César."

"The papers for the frame."

"How did you—"

"No questions." César shook his head. "All you know is I gave you some documents to examine. My signature's on each. Look them over and tell me what you find." He frowned. "It better be forgery."

"When do you need this?" Briand rifled through the sheets.

"Yesterday."

"How about tomorrow? No, it's Sunday. If I can. Otherwise, Monday."

"What time?"

Briand laughed. "Police! All you know is today." He returned the folder to the pouch.

César wobbled out of bed and wove to the window. It was open. He stared through the bars at the center wing, a pile of dirty brick. "Someone's got influence," he revealed. "Internal Affairs wouldn't sweat like this if it was just routine. They're getting pushed hard."

"What's the interest in you?"

"Has to be Bock, at least for an excuse." His voice sounded tired, defeated. "They're really after me this time."

"Algeria?"

The inspector nodded. "You're a Zola man," he said. "An officer accused of being a German spy and—"

"Dreyfus!"

"—a Jew?"

The graphologist shook his head in disbelief.

"Why not?" César went back to bed. "It happened before."

"Things are different now."

"Not that different." César hoped he wasn't catching Bock's paranoia. "You think I'm overreacting?" he asked.

"I think you're worried," Briand said, slipping the rubber band around the pouch, "and need a rest."

"Remember, Julien, this is just between us," César pressed. "No one else until we know."

"Agreed."

"My life's in your hands."

"In that case, let me get you out of this room."

* * *

The two of them spent lunch in the dispensary: three walls lined with machines that dispensed all the fast food needed to get sick enough for the hospital. The other wall had tiny tables for those who ate their fast food slowly. At one of them César gulped down his daily dose of soup and pudding while Clément feasted on potato chips.

"Sugar," César said between gulps—

Clément nodded, hoping to become detective sergeant; from now on he would listen to every word.

"—is the leading cause of violent behavior."

A smile spread across the detective's face. The inspector had a theory.

"They did a study in one of the prisons? Took away everything with sugar and put in fruit and natural juices and popcorn, things like that. Right away the assaults dropped twenty percent and the disciplinary problems almost fifty percent."

"What prison was that?"

"Not only assaults," said César, "the suicide attempts went way down and so did the threats."

"Sounds like Marseille. They do a lot of talking there."

"Even the vandalism fell off."

"You think Bock was into sugar, then."

"Bock? What about him?"

"All those killings," Clément said. "He was probably eating too much ice cream."

"Are you crazy?" César regarded his assistant. He had to admit

Clément was strange at times. Bock was killing people because he ate too much ice cream! Where the hell did he get that one? Must be all those women he frequented, César thought. Who would trust a man who couldn't settle down with a good woman?

"So how'd you wind up with a room like that?" Clément asked.

"I think they're trying to tell me something."

On the way back César listened to the time Clément's brother made a scarecrow with a gun in its hand. It was in the Midi and the crows were so vicious they attacked passing planes. So many were shot they came to recognize rifles so his brother put an old German Luger from the war in the scarecrow's hand. It had a hair trigger that went off if a crow came close. "Made him famous, too; everybody heard of the farmer who potted the pricks with a pistol. For a while, anyway."

"What happened?"

"One day the Luger ran out of bullets and they stole it."

"How'd he know it was the crows?"

"Who else would want anything German?"

In the room again César exercised by the window while Clément reported on Francke. The man was elusive. Apparently came out of nowhere to head Oberst-Haupt in 1969. Before that he was a kind of industrial soldier of fortune, working in African states with incipient revolution problems. He'd help governments tighten control over heavy industry, mostly energy and metals.

An adventurer with an angel behind him.

A troubleshooter, anyway. Didn't spend much time running the firm; daily business was left to others, while he traveled around. Earlier in the week, for example, he was in Paris.

Doing what?

Clément didn't know. He'd got his information from the woman who handled the travel arrangements, posing as a credit card examiner. A computer error no doubt, happened all the time. Where was he staying in Paris?

At the Meurice.

"What about his war record?" César asked.

"Again, elusive. A lieutenant in the SS assigned to special duty at headquarters for most of the war."

"Nothing about what he did?"

"Just a thought."

"Anything."

"To stay in Berlin," Clément reflected, "near Himmler and all the SS power, he'd have to be very popular or protected. Maybe doing something special." He made a face. "Francke doesn't strike me as the popular type. Too secretive, if you know what I mean."

"Something special," César repeated.

"That would be my guess."

"He was protected in the SS," César ruminated, "and he's still being protected now. Why?" César closed his eyes. "Maybe it wasn't what he did but who he did it for. It could be the same man." Opened them. "A German with power who was SS on some kind of special assignment, maybe even for Himmler himself." Was it Himmler? Is he still alive? César counted to ten to clear his imagination. Some leaps just didn't work out. "A German financier," he said to Clément, "who used Francke for his errand boy." And some did! "Go back over André's notes on Oberst-Haupt, the company that owns it. See who's at the head; could be our man."

"What man?"

"Bock's partner. Bock was on Himmler's staff and now he's after gold. His partner was there too, working on getting gold. That was his special assignment. They stole some of it, hid it in the lake. Now Bock's killing off the others so the two of them could split it." César felt better already, might even try to escape. "If I can find his partner," César growled, "I'll find Bock."

After Clément left he called the Meurice.

* * *

Waking from his afternoon nap, César went for a walk. On the third floor he found a sun-room facing north, a huge box with gray support columns surrounded by endless rows of utility furniture covered in orange plaid. César sat by the window soaking up the shade.

Against the inside wall cringed a worn Ping-Pong table whose net seemed to be made of elastic stockings strung together. Two men played cards on the table. They wore blue robes and were standing up.

The only other life was a young couple in the far corner. They were dressed in street clothes and sat so entwined they looked like a single body with two heads. The Dachau dogs, César thought, straining to watch them. The girl had long black hair and talked rapidly with her hands; the blond boy kept nodding.

A man eventually entered the room and walked laboriously down the aisle to the windows. He smiled at César and flopped nearby. His face a slab of chalky white, the man began flexing his fingers, thin reeds of bone and skin that had the same skeletal pallor. He seemed startled when César moved nearer.

"Not much sun here," César announced. "They'd have done better to put it on the other side."

"Used to be a cafeteria," the man said. His eyes were pinpricks of iridescence in a pale sea. "About a year ago they shut it down for losing money. Now it's all machines, even the coffee."

"Been here that long?"

"In and out."

"How long this time?"

"Three weeks, almost four." The man glanced at César. "Chemotherapy and radiation."

César nodded and went back to staring at the flat horizon. The age was difficult, though he guessed somewhere in the early fifties. It was hard to tell without any hair.

"What about you?" the man asked. "Operation?"

"Gunshot." César took a few deep breaths to clear his head. "I'm with the police," he added by way of explanation.

"Must be exciting."

The man kneaded the fingers of one hand into the other palm, pushing with whatever strength he had. His arms bent into wings, he pressed them together. The effort seemed hardly worthwhile to César.

"Rheumatism?"

The man reversed the position of his hands. "Things always feel stiff after a session upstairs."

"How many more you have?"

"This was the last," he answered after a moment. "Tomorrow I go home for good."

There was some justice after all, César reminded himself. Sometimes people even got a break.

"Then you won."

"I lost."

* * *

"Your mother was from Stuttgart," Kussow said softly.

The hospital was a study in silence, as if pain felt somehow relieved and death had taken a holiday.

"A German Jew."

Nurses moved about less noisily and so did visitors; patients tried not to complain. France was a Christian country and to suffer silently on the Sabbath was a Christian virtue.

"I had Elsa for twelve years," Kussow reflected from his chair near the bed. "When she died I said no more; the next week I went out and got Shin Bet. Life goes on."

He sat stiffly erect, the white shirt starched and shiny under his jacket, his black shoes flat on the floor. The shadows in the room were slanted, growing longer. On his lap he clutched an envelope.

"I think you'd better go over that again," César said in a strangled voice. "Who are we talking about?"

"You," Kussow replied sadly.

"But my mother was French."

"Her maiden name was Dietrich," said the German. He shifted in his seat and a shadow reached across the envelope.

César's first thought had been senility, a sudden attack. Except senility didn't attack; it infiltrated, slowly. Lunacy? Kussow wasn't raving. Or even smiling, so it wasn't a joke. Who ever heard of Germans joking, anyway?

"She was born in Stuttgart. I have a copy of her birth certificate here." He opened the envelope.

César carefully unfolded the paper, strained to focus. A female infant—parents Magda and Stefan Dietrich—girl named Sara—hair brown, eyes blue. Her race: *Juden.*

"We've been friends a long time," César pleaded. "If this is—"

"It isn't," Kussow assured him.

"What then?"

"The truth."

César's father married Sara Dietrich in Stuttgart in 1934. He'd gone there to visit friends, met Sara and fell in love. The feeling was mutual. He soon took her back to Strasbourg. The two cities are near each other and Sara Dreyfus occasionally visited her parents. In 1937 her mother died of cancer; the next year her father was shot by the Gestapo for illegal Jewish activity. He was a Stuttgart lawyer who by law could no longer practice.

César knew none of this; his parents never talked about it. His earliest years were filled with a loving mother and father. Of course they were French. Didn't they live in France? He just naturally assumed—And now?

"When did you learn of this?" he asked Kussow in a voice that sounded to him strangely harsh.

"Only since you started the Bock investigation. You're a Jew so we checked to see what we could find."

"We?"

"Israeli Intelligence. They asked me to help out."

"And the birth certificate?" César asked.

"We found one of your mother's oldest friends still living in Strasbourg, a woman she'd known from her Stuttgart days. The rest was easy."

"How'd you find the woman?"

"In Strasbourg? Listen, finding a Jew in Strasbourg is like finding a flower in spring. Why do you think it's called the Jerusalem of France?"

César didn't understand. "Why me?" he demanded.

"You're still a Jew. We need you."

"We again."

"The same we. The Israelis, Jews, us. You."

"And Bock?"

"He's German," Kussow said. "Right now he's a danger to Jews."

"I'm trying to stop him."

"You're trying to catch him. The Israelis will stop him."

In the circumstances César thought himself surprisingly calm. He was someone else listening to his friend discuss murder.

"Why is Bock a danger?"

"I don't know," Kussow sighed.

"Or won't say."

"Will you help us?"

"And let Bock get away?"

"Let him get what he deserves."

"You should know me better than that. Oedipus, remember? Searching for truth and blinded by justice. You always said you saw that in me."

"So did your wife and look what happened. It's over."

"You mean destroyed."

"I mean help us."

"I can't, even if I wanted to. Bock killed and it's my duty to bring him to justice under the law. It's my job."

"I understand," Kussow sympathized. "You're just obeying orders, like any good German."

In the room darkness had pushed the light nearer the window, shadows filling the empty space. César wondered if his calm reaction was normal.

"What was the idea of telling me all this?"

"German Jews were the first to feel the Nazi insanity. We thought if you knew there was German blood in you, then you'd be more agreeable to working with us."

"I'll have this quickly checked, you know."

"Of course."

César, stunned, forced himself to think. "Bock's in Germany now. What can I do?"

"Originally Tel Aviv wanted you to stop the investigation. But now we need your help."

"How?"

"Tell us where he is."

"I don't know where he is."

"When you do." Kussow hesitated. "Bock's a professional, and so are you."

"Meaning?"

"We need a detective to root him out for us."

NINETEEN

He suffered from the sins of the mother.

César Dreyfus had become Dieter Bock.

His mother's sin was the wrong religion.

"You're part German," Kussow had told him, "but you're still a Jew."

Or maybe just the wrong country.

"Who am I?" the boy had asked his parents.

He wanted to be like everyone else, but the more he tried the more he failed. His kind would always fail, of course.

"A French Jew," they had said.

What's the difference between a French Jew and a German Jew?

"I'm half a Nazi," César told Nicole when she came to his room.

The French Jew was lucky to make a living and the German Jew was lucky to be alive.

Nicole didn't care.

César had a French father and he had a German mother.

They both were dead.

* * *

The corridors were crowded with hospital personnel on this Monday morning. Most wore white and never wondered how they would look in black.

Why was Bock a danger to Jews? César asked himself.

In Germany, Bock would be reaching for gold. Once rid of the rest, he'd be in the water bringing it up. Like the Nibelung rising out of the Rhine.

The orderlies brought breakfast to the rooms. Nurses hurried through the halls with silver instruments, looking very efficient. In surgery masked men with laser eyes cut away tissue as if it were paper, laying open organs reeking of abuse.

César ate his cereal wishing for wine. Grains reminded him of farm animals, a part of his youth.

Why would Kussow not tell him what Bock knew?

In the next room a man was wheeled out, his chest and legs strapped. Near the elevators in the hall's center, the reception station bristled with activity. There were phones to answer and feelings to question, patients seeking solace.

When the doctor showed a cheerful face, César told him his time was up. Stool nodded. He'd be going in the morning. Wasn't this morning? Tomorrow morning. Now! No! At least I tried, César shrugged and the doctor smiled.

"You must be a good detective," he offered.

"What makes you think so?"

"All the practice you get. They tell me you've been practicing right here."

"Best place for it, hospitals." César grimaced, squeezed off the words. "Cesspools of murder. A slip here, a needle there. Who'd know?"

"I would have made a great detective if it wasn't for my father," Stool rambled, his voice wistful. "He wanted me to think of the living instead of the dead."

"Smart man."

"Dumb. I see more dead in one day than you do in a month."

"So there's your challenge."

"What challenge?" Stool snorted. "I already know who killed them. It's all in the doctor's manual, cut and dried. Not you, though. You never know. Right?"

"Wrong. There's someone who killed a dozen people in the past year"—César could swear Stool looked envious—"and I know all about him, more than anyone."

"What will you do?" Stool asked. Fascinated, he doted on murder and mayhem.

"Nothing," César sighed, sinking the hook. "It's like you say, what good is it if you already know."

"You're just going to let him go?" The doctor couldn't believe it.

César shrugged. "When he gets to two dozen, maybe I'll give him another look." A pause, playing out the line. "You see? You and me, we're the same, after all."

Stool's jaw sprang open.

"Death holds no mystery for us anymore," César droned. "Only life."

* * *

The rush was over by nine and chenille robes drifted down the halls again. César opened his door and stepped onto a glass floor redolent of pine. He tripped to the center desk where a stern nurse admonished him for racing on floors that had just been waxed. What if he'd hurt the finish? She wanted no more of that.

Stairs were at the end of the corridor, stone steps with iron caps at the edges to prevent slipping. César took them one at a time, slowly, his hand on the metal railing. He didn't want to injure them.

The first floor was busy with people waiting. Even those who moved had an expectant air about them.

Were the Israelis already after Bock?

He strolled once around the lobby to get his bearings. No one tried to stop him, though his robe brought some looks. In street clothes he would have been invisible.

The entrance doors were constantly in use; large glass panels on both sides allowed light into the lobby. César stood by one of them and counted the cabs. Outside, people passed in groups full of smiles. Those who walked alone were lost in thought, their faces tight.

The Nazi Bock was responsible for the deaths of millions of Jews, including César's parents. Now the Jews wanted *him* dead. But César had been the first hunter. Why should he give up what kept him going?

Germans were good, Nazis were bad.

The man going home to die was twenty-nine years old.

* * *

The phone at his ear, César listened to Briand as one might hear the voice of doom. Fearful, yet unbelieving.

"The signature matches yours perfectly."

"It's mine?"

"Your signature all right. Every last one of them."

"But how could—"

"Each one a perfect match."

César felt the earth tremble.

"Too perfect."

"What's too perfect?"

"Every letter's exactly the same."

"That's bad?"

"That's good."

The tremors slowed.

"People never sign their names the same way twice," Briand said. "Not exactly the same."

César didn't understand.

"There's always slight variations in the letters. A *t* is never crossed the same way twice, or the space in an *l* or the *d*. The flourish at the ends of words is never precisely the same; neither are most capital letters. Even the spacing between names or initials varies. To have two signatures alike in formation and spacing," Briand explained, "is almost impossible, one in billions. But to have four, as I have of yours on these letters and cards, well—I think you see the odds."

"They're mine but not mine."

"Yours, yes, but you didn't sign them."

"Copied?"

"Traced."

The tremors stopped.

César understood the implications. Someone from headquarters had stolen a letter with his signature and sent it to Zurich, or sold it to someone who sent it on. Tobie Maton? The cleaning crew? He probably got the forged documents from Zurich the same way. César would not think about it. Criminal fingers stretched into the police at all levels. Everyone knew that.

"Inspector?"

Briand, still on the line.

"I'm here."

"I'd like to show these to a colleague who often helps the police. He carries a lot of weight with them."

"You're sure about the tracing?"

"You doubt my ability?"

"Only my good luck."

"When Internal Affairs sees what they're up against, they'll fold fast—"

"Not leeches like that."

"—unless they're out for blood."

César admitted the possibility.

"Someone's pushing them, as you say."

"Pushing, not forcing."

"They're feeling the pressure," Briand suggested, "so what's the difference? You know who it is yet?"

"On Monday a German named Francke flew in from Munich and stayed at the Meurice. He left a number with the hotel where he could be reached, a number I keep on a list of trouble. It was Internal Affairs."

"A German's after you?"

César struggled with his own thoughts for a moment. Nothing could change the fact of German blood in his veins. He'd already checked with Strasbourg. It all fit too well, like a suit from a good German tailor. He'd always been aware of his rigidity and obsessiveness; they were obviously minor aberrations in his critical Gallic temperament. As long as he was a French Jew, he was all French.

"I'm part German myself," he said. "It's a long story."

"At least you're not all German."

*   *   *

Durac came by to report on Marie Pinay. He first insisted on knowing of the inspector's health. Hospitals were hotbeds of disease.

"My view entirely," César revealed, "but this time I seem to have escaped the worst. It's back to the office in the morning."

"*Gott sei Dank!*"

"You know German?" César was suddenly conscious of such things.

"Grew up on it," Durac confessed. "My father used it whenever he was mad at my mother, just to spite her. He knew she hated it, thought it too guttural. She always answered him in Italian, which got him even madder because he despised the Italians."

"So how'd you learn French?"

"They fought in French, at least when it got serious. Fighting"—Durac shook his head in memory—"was their recreation. It raised the blood and didn't cost anything. Me? I don't fight. Too Italian, I guess." He laughed. "But sometimes the German comes out, which is where I got this idea about Marie Pinay. The suspect's back, by the way."

"What's he say?"

"Claims he didn't know her but I could see something's eating at him. I'm sure he just needs a little push."

"And your idea?"

"What I propose is to get an actress to become Marie Pinay, put her where he can see her and maybe he'll crack. I know someone, well, my girl friend actually—she's a professional—who'll do the part very well."

"Your first name is Alphonse?"—César was warming up to Durac, a reminder of himself a while back—"You said the idea came from the German."

"Just that my father had a mistress for a while when I was about fourteen, a former actress. Nobody ever heard of her, I suppose, but she did have a bit part in *The Blue Angel.* A walk-on, anyway."

The Blue Angel—César had seen it a dozen times—starred Marlene Dietrich at her seductive best. When César first saw it in the original German he fell in love, a lifelong devotion. Now he saw that his love should've told him more about himself. Marlene Dietrich! Same name, too. Maybe Catherine Deneuve wasn't really meant for him. But how about Marlene? César began to picture fantasies he'd never even dreamed of.

"You remember Marlene Dietrich?"

"Always loved her," Alphonse said.

* * *

Dupin announced he was being relieved of command and placed on desk duty at headquarters. "Just until this thing is settled."

"It isn't my money," César told him.

The chief inspector thought the decision a good one, give everybody time to sort things out.

"Not mine," he repeated.

"Of course not yours. But can you prove it?"

The Napoleonic Code: guilty until proven innocent.

"Time works wonders," Dupin said.

"It gets Bock away."

"There'll be other Bocks."

"Not for me," César insisted.

"Nothing you can do now."

"I can always quit."

The word had a nasty sound to it, a finality César never intended.

"You can't quit"—Dupin took a deep breath—"because you've already been relieved."

"What if I refuse to be relieved?"

"Then you could be dismissed."

"In which case I'll quit."

"Quitting is itself sufficient grounds for dismissal."

"But I haven't quit yet."

"Then you're relieved of command."

* * *

He slept until supper and afterwards got his clothes from the closet. They'd been brought by Clément, his brown suit with the sleeve button missing, a white shirt, the other pair of black shoes, too many things. Clothes were a nuisance like food, almost as bad. A trap, designed to distract.

As darkness seeped into the room, the garments on the chair assumed a grotesque shape. A dwarf with squared shoulders stood holding a white flower to his chest. The pants were pipes bent at the joints. His feet had no toes; there were four of them.

What did Bock know?

* * *

César put on his shoes and stepped into the hall and off the floor and out the hospital, just as planned. No one stopped him. He walked down the stairs and through the lobby, his suit a badge of release. At the corner he waited for a taxi to take him across town to Montparnasse, steeling himself for the task ahead. When the driver wanted to talk, he found a silent passenger unwilling to listen. A *flic* for sure. He had the eyes.

Up past the cemetery the streets became more residential as the shops and bistros of the inner ring gave way to blocks of stone steps. César bid *adieu* to the buried Captain Dreyfus; he hoped he wouldn't disgrace the family name in his hunt for Bock, as Kussow had intimated. Mouth grim, he was still feeling sorry for himself when they stopped in front of her apartment house. He quickly paid off the driver and mounted the steps to the double doors and the bell he'd pressed once years ago. Or had it just been weeks?

* * *

A stampede of animals greeted his eyes, paintings that seemed to change as he drew near. There were at least twenty on the wall, in clusters of three and four, all of them small and delicately framed in ebony. The surfaces shimmered in the light. At the room's far end the light dazzled as Jacqueline Volette greeted César with a smile.

"Prismatic art," she breathed, "is not for everyone since it changes before your eyes. That Arabian steed, for example. Did you examine it closely?" She removed the picture from the wall. "Held a certain way in the light, it's a garland of flowers. Another way"—she tilted the miniature, holding it deftly between her palms—"and it becomes the stallion. Artistic," she beamed, "and beautiful besides."

"Apparently nothing's what it seems anymore"—César looked less at the miniature than at Jacqueline—"not even the animals."

"Least of all the animals, Inspector." She returned the stallion to his stall. "One moment a lamb, the next—"

"A lioness?"

Jacqueline laughed—"A rose bouquet"—sat down. "Actually, prismatic art is an Arab form that evolved out of the Moslem proscription against depicting humans and animals. Since artists weren't allowed to paint horses, they hid them behind landscapes and still lifes. Naturally they did the same with people. Which proves, I guess, that you can hide most anything if you're clever enough."

"Even a killer's heart," César suggested.

"I am glad to see you're out of the hospital." Her hand fluttered in sympathy.

César marveled at the thoughtful concern, the hint of caring in her lowered eyes, the catch in her voice and, always, her inviting smile.

"How is Bock?" He leaned forward, intent. "Or should I ask where is he?"

"I really couldn't say," she murmured sweetly.

"More lies?"

"Have I lied?"

"Only from the beginning," César said gently. "I expected it, of course. You and Bock were lovers and so you lied, everyone does. Now I'm not so sure. In the hospital I had a lot of time to think; it's great when you have nothing else to do. I read all the reports again, too, and talked to people in Germany who knew Bock years ago. Learned a lot. Did you know, for instance, that his favorite color is black? Or that he wanted to be a pilot in the *Luftwaffe?*"

Jacqueline did not.

"Well, as I say I did some thinking, and one of the things I thought about was why Bock killed his wife. The insurance money wasn't that much and he really didn't need it with his skill in such demand. If she was a bother, he could've just walked away like most do. The truth is he had no motive for murder—unless it was passion. Mutual passion with someone standing in the way. There's your motive. And one of your lies. You and Bock were lovers *before* your sister died, and that's why she went out the window."

"You're being foolish," Jacqueline sniffed. "Why didn't we just go away if we were lovers at the time?"

"Because Bock couldn't change his identity with you along and his wife still alive, too much of a risk."

"Why would he want to?"

"For when he got the gold."

"What gold?"

"The gold in the lake," César said. "Didn't he tell you about it?"

On the walls the beasts of the field grazed quietly. More than the plains of Africa at this moment, the room was alive with animal cunning; César could sense it in his hunter's eye. He almost saw Bock hiding in the next room, ready to pounce. Or was he hiding in one of the paintings? Jacqueline had called them prismatic art; César saw only hired assassins and secret police. Was it possible? he asked himself.

"One reason I didn't see it sooner was the alleged burglary at their home. We couldn't find the thief because he didn't exist. There was no burglar"—César felt his heart slowing—"except for you. You stole your sister's eyeglasses. Bock was with his wife at the time and you were the only person close to him." Would it have made any difference if she'd loved him a little? Something more for her side?

"When you talked about your sister never having a father and wanting an older man, you were really talking about yourself. You didn't know your father, either. You were, what, four when he died? Bock became father, lover and everything else to you. Well, maybe not everything"—he was glass and about to shatter—"since there were things only you could do."

"I don't know what you mean."

"Then listen to me"—César's resolve was cracking—"because I'm going to tell you why Bock couldn't become a fighter pilot in the *Luftwaffe*. It's very simple, actually. So simple"—he saw the flicker of fear—"it changed your life." He'd never noticed how sad her eyes were, even tragic. "Bock didn't fly planes because he had a phobia, a dread of height. He couldn't go above the third floor."

"They lived on the fifth."

"Lived, yes, the rent was cheap." César spoke swiftly now. "But Bock could barely look out the windows, didn't go near them. There are witnesses who swear he wasn't able to go near anything open above ten meters. So your sister—"

"My sister was pushed," Jacqueline said fiercely. "Why would she jump?"

"She didn't jump."

"Then you agree he pushed her."

"Dieter Bock never pushed your sister out that window," César said sadly. "You did."

TWENTY

Men ran the police department and some ran over it; most who did were eventually found out.

Jobert was old and distressingly thin, his face a map of perversity, the body a bag of tricks. Grunts of pleasure seemed constantly to erupt from him as he walked or talked. This illusion of congeniality served Jobert well in his work. He headed the Internal Affairs division of the Paris police, and those who saw in him the fool quickly became fooled themselves. Everyone agreed there was something sinister about Jobert's devotion to duty.

César had accepted the division commander's invitation to ferry him from the hospital to headquarters and Jobert was pleased. Tuesday traffic was usually heavy and, after all, there was a strong bond between them. Both were police officers, superiors, men of rank who had much to talk over. César thought it best not to refuse.

"We don't ever want to condemn an innocent man," Jobert insisted, his voice dripping with integrity.

The uniformed man at the wheel kept looking in the mirror to see if Jobert was watching him.

"On the other hand we don't intend to let you get away either."

"Nothing you can do," César said.

"There's always something we can do. Always something," Jobert said with conviction, as though needing César to see his sincerity, "that we can do to you."

"Like what?"

A red light held them back and the driver hunched forward over the wheel, eyes pointed. His hand gripped the shift lever.

"An interesting gambit." Jobert twisted his body more in César's direction, prompting a succession of grunts. "Our work is much like a chess game with moves and countermoves, or even the posturing between two superpowers. One makes a move and the other has the option of direct confrontation or an oblique maneuver. You have chosen direct confrontation."

A meshing of gears announced a quick getaway. The starting gate was soon left behind in a burst of speed that swiftly took them to the next red light, where the race would begin anew.

"Did I really have a choice?" César asked.

"No."

In the flow of traffic again, the driver weaved smoothly in and out of lanes filled with recalcitrant malingerers and dedicated madmen.

"In this confrontation you apparently see yourself the winner," Jobert said. "Your signatures were obviously traced so you're not legally responsible. We see it differently. Your first signature was real, of which you kept a copy. The rest were traced by you, using your own copy."

"I forged my own signature?"

"In effect, yes," Jobert said.

César's body swerved with the car. He wondered if Jobert had always been mad. "Why would I do that?" he asked.

"Precisely for this very reason," Jobert crowed in triumph. "If caught, you could claim forgery."

"You mean my claiming forgery proves I did the forging?"

"How else would you have the original documents?" Jobert pointed out with unassailable logic. "Unless you planned it all yourself."

"But I turned them over to you."

"And we appreciate your honesty in giving us the evidence," Jobert assured his startled listener, "but that merely proves your guilt."

César felt an urge to kill. He'd long suspected that Internal Affairs used humanoids from colony planets. If he opened Jobert's skull, he knew there'd be the same silicon chips and diodes found in any computer.

"You can claim innocence of the forgery but that makes you guilty of receiving stolen property," Jobert warned. "Of course, they are presumably your own letters so theoretically your property and not stolen—if forged by you. But if you didn't forge them, they probably are not legally yours and thus are stolen. That would place you in a precarious position, don't you see?"

The Peugeot passed Place de la République, moving closer to the city's heart. Ahead lay the fabled boulevards and galleries, the tourist's Paris with the Cité at the center and on it, the vast and dismal building that housed the Prefecture of Police.

"So you think I'm guilty," César said.

"Absolutely not."

Behind the car the sun kept rising. Silver metal suddenly gleamed like gold.

When they reached the Boulevard de Sébastopol, César breathed a sigh of relief. It was a straight run all the way down to headquarters. He would be glad to get back, even relieved of command and surrounded by lunatics. Soon he'd be home, the only one he had. He was beginning to feel better already.

"We don't want any trouble from your people." Jobert squirmed in his seat amid squeals of satisfaction.

"What people?"

"The Jews, of course."

"I don't know any Jews."

"The Israelis seem to know you. We'd like to know how."

There were people drinking breakfast at the outdoor cafés; others merely ate, eternal hunger in their eyes. The waiters moving through the aisles were swift and deadly, training for the tourist season. Ahead lay Place du Châtelet and the approach to the Cité.

"Why do you think the Israelis are interested in me?" César asked.

"We believe it has something to do with the Bock case," Jobert said. "You could be selling them information, even working with them."

"I thought the bank account came from Bock himself."

"That's still a possibility."

"But losing ground, you mean. What does Francke say?"

"What do you know about Francke?"

"I know he's the anonymous source for Zurich and the one who's been putting pressure on you to get rid of me."

"Pressure only creates activity," Jobert grunted. "We go strictly by the evidence."

"What does it show?"

"That you're working with the Jews. Maybe even the Germans."

"What Germans?"

"We don't know. Are you?" Jobert asked.

"I don't think so."

"There, you see? You admit it's possible you might be violating French law that expressly forbids civil servants to work for a foreign power."

"I'll admit the possibility"—César wondered if he'd ever really understand the secret police mentality—"if you admit you have nothing to take to a departmental trial."

"We'll find out anyway."

Silence took them the last mile down the sling of Sébastopol past the shops and stalls of the quays and into headquarters across from the Palais de Justice.

"I'm glad we had this little talk," Jobert said as the Peugeot swung into the police courtyard. "It always helps to get a fresh viewpoint in these matters. If you're working with foreign agents, you must tell us what they want. If you're not working with foreign agents, you must still tell us what they want since they're obviously working with you. We see Francke's pressure as a diversionary tactic to throw us off."

"You mean his pressure to get me dismissed proves we're working together."

"How else would you know him if you're not involved?"

"But he's trying to ruin me!" César screeched.

"He knows we'd never do that."

"Then my trial is off?"

"Not if I have anything to say about it."

* * *

César's morning went so fast he forgot to eat lunch and then skipped his nap for reward. His battered old desk was a joy, his chair a delight, the couch a relief. He decided to revel in the feeling while it lasted. He walked the floor, browsed the bookcase, loitered in the office. It was all wonderful.

Too bad the rest of his life was terrible.

He was a Jew who grew up French hating Germans. He was a man obsessed with a woman who had killed. He was a hunter after a prey no one wanted him to catch. He was an inspector without a command. He was lonely.

Was he in trouble, too?

César, a true believer half the time, knew the answer was somewhere in the middle. Maybe the German would take time, his obsession might disappear, perhaps even the hunt would continue and his command be restored. He would probably always be lonely.

But like Kussow had said, life went on. Or Dupin who said things would settle. Or his barber who said he shouldn't worry.

Nobody said he couldn't use the phone.

He was on it all morning. In Germany he talked to the Munich police. A room was rented at the Vier Jahreszeiten for May 7 from 1 to 5 P.M. That's right, tomorrow. Rented to Oberst-Haupt; César spelled it. In that room would be a man wanted by the French police for a half-dozen killings. . . . Yes, a German national. His name was Dieter Bock but he'd be using another name, a new identity.

César gave them Bock's description but didn't mention his SS past; Munich would capture killers but they didn't need Nazis. He suddenly understood, having some German in him. It was all a terrible mistake. Germans didn't want to make war on anybody. Didn't they disband the *Wehrmacht?*

Switzerland wasn't much help. The money for his bank account each month came out of a drawing fund financed by Ander Dunant. A normal transaction, as César was told. He supposedly sent the cash to Dunant who deposited it in his own general account and credited the amount to César's. Done all the time in Zurich, where dozens of currencies flowed into the big banks through intermediaries, always Swiss nationals. All it took were forged letters of consent from César and his signature on official forms. Clandestine groups often kept such accounts open until one was needed for blackmail or exposure. This time he'd been lucky, maybe.

Could they tell him the dates of deposit? To check against Dunant's.

Not without authorization.

Whose authorization?

His.

He was giving it.

They couldn't accept it.

Why not?

They never gave out such information over the phone.

Then why did they want his authorization?

To tell him they never gave out such information.

César hung up. If he lived to be German he'd never understand the Swiss.

Dupin stopped by with some innocuous paper work; apparently the order relieving him of command was simply meant to absolve the brass of any responsibility. César was officially in limbo, a hunter without protection. Like his prey. Worse, Bock still had a shadow that César needed to flesh out. It was the way to his prey, but whose way? Who was Francke's boss?

Clément didn't know. Rather, he knew too much. Too many bosses owned Francke. Oberst-Haupt was run by Swiss gnomes who answered to Kaiser Systems, an Austrian outfit with bosses everywhere. Kaiser itself was ruled by a German money combine called Goethe with seven listed bosses. So who knew where the franc stopped?

"We know about Goethe." César looked at Clément's names. "That's the one, Hans Weber. Chief operations officer but not on the SCE list." Neither was Francke who had a Nazi past but wasn't a big financier. "Still"—if they couldn't go through every boss, why not go for the top?—"let's check these seven just to keep our hand in it. Start with Weber." He gave the names back to Clément. "We're after someone in the SS, preferably on Himmler's staff or at least attached to Berlin headquarters."

"Why a financier?" Clément asked.

"His job was getting gold. Trading for it, maybe even stealing it. He knows a lot about money. Once you know that"—for the first time in weeks César felt lucky—"you don't go back to selling shoes."

"Suppose he's not on the list?"

"Then he'll be on the next."

"But suppose he's not?"

All of a sudden César's luck changed. What if his name wasn't anywhere? Maybe a friend got Francke the job.

César left his office a step behind Clément. Restless, he was going to walk all thirty-five bridges connecting the Left Bank with the Right.

"In the rain?"

"It's only raining on the outside," César answered mysteriously.

Clément shook his head, hoped his boss wasn't going to get heavy now that he pretended to be part German. It had to be the Bock case; he was trying to identify with his quarry. Clément knew it wouldn't work. You could stick a frog up a rat's ass and it would still croak.

* * *

They strolled through the aviary, where birds of every feather flew freely. The administrative head, who as a boy had sold gold-painted finches for canaries, kept the umbrella open.

"The Jews, you say?"

The director nodded. "Israelis, actually."

"Whatever would they want with Dreyfus?"

"Jews always stick together, something in the blood."

"Do they?" The administrative head closed one eye, sighting his prey. "I wouldn't know."

Both men muttered silent oaths at rampaging children.

"Nasty place, here."

"Too many birds."

He picked off a great blue heron.

"It could be the Bock affair."

"What's that?"

"The Jews. They could be using Dreyfus to lead them to Bock."

"It's possible, yes."

"If he does"—the director thought it best not to bring up the matter of gold—"it could antagonize the Bonn government."

"Hardly," said the bird fancier. "Isn't Dreyfus supposed to be half a *boche* himself now?"

"His mother, actually."

"Just his mother?" The voice had a ring of disappointment.

"Which is why nothing of the German blood appears in his background file. Had they known eighteen years ago—"

"Not only a Jew," the administrator declared without emotion, "but a German too." He drew a bead on another bird. "What else?" Smashed it in his mind.

"The father's line apparently goes back generations. They're distant relatives of Captain Dreyfus, by the way. From Devil's Island?"

"*That* Dreyfus?"

"The same."

"And his mother's German?" The administrator sighed. "How strange life is."

"Is it?"

"Some lives, yes." He cocked an eye at a spoonbill. "Did you know there was a German officer who held information from the very beginning that would've proved Captain Dreyfus innocent?"

"And did he?"

"Never even spoke up."

The director smiled. "I hear our Dreyfus hates Germans."

"A true Frenchman," agreed the administrator with enthusiasm. "For a Jew, that is."

They came to the end of the aviary.

"I'm game for another try."

"Are you? The swallows, I suppose."

"There were a few mallards I missed, as well. What about you?"

* * *

Evening came, people went and César collapsed. He wasn't ready for the world yet. He'd made only seven bridges over the Seine but done a lot of thinking in cafés. It might be too late to get Bock. If the Munich police didn't stop him at the hotel, he was gone. They couldn't watch every lake in Austria. César thought of the gold waiting in the water. Who'd believe it without proof?

Leaving the office after two hours on the couch, he heard about Martel's body being found in Neuilly; shot in the back of the head. César understood. By getting rid of Junot, Martel had become a liability himself. An ambitious man, he had schemed once too often; still, he'd almost made it. The saddest words in the world. César hoped they wouldn't be said of him and Bock.

* * *

She was waiting for him in the darkened room, standing by the door with perfumed hair. "I'm your homecoming party," Nicole promised.

She kissed him, her body opening to his touch. César kept his eyes closed, wanting not to see her, knowing he would see Jacqueline

Volette. A trick of the mind, he told himself. His obsession was over. What he needed was right here, someone who needed him. He opened his eyes and saw Jacqueline.

"Gold," she gasped in his ear, "everything we want."

* * *

He was a ribbon of light. Infrared warmed him with thermal radiation, ultraviolet soothed him with short waves. Intense and reflecting, he smiled on every object he met and cast out darkness wherever he went. But each time he reached for her, she was gone.

In the morning he found himself wrapped in sheets, a hard sleeper. Nicole beamed down at him. Breakfast in bed gave way to the time of day. Confused, he kissed her.

Dupin was first with the news, waiting. Internal Affairs had shelved his departmental trial.

"Jobert?"

"He doesn't like to lose. Says it gives him headaches." Dupin was almost jovial. "You okay?"

"No."

He hadn't spent a full night with a woman since his marriage. A restless night full of fantasy. He radiated trouble.

"You're no longer relieved of command."

"In that case I might not quit."

Noises from the hall grew louder and passed by. Morning was always the busiest time for Homicide, mopping up the blood from the night before.

"Stay on Bock." The chief inspector liked theatrical exits. "Unless you get a better offer."

By the time Alphonse called in with the results of their little improvisation, César had drunk a quart of coffee.

"Couldn't reach you last night," Alphonse said. "Anyway, our fish took the bait. I made sure he saw Marie Pinay up close. She was perfect. The suspect fled into a bar and she followed, not saying anything or even looking his way. By the second stop he was screaming at her, which is when we moved in."

"Anything good?"

"Everything but a confession."

"We'll get that."

"Worked just like we figured."

A generous way to put it, César thought. The idea had been Durac's, and all the work as well. The detective was too good for a local.

"You eat lunch?" he asked.

They would go somewhere, anywhere. Alphonse didn't care much for food so it made no difference to him. César knew he'd found his man.

* * *

"We were tricked," the Mossad representative admitted in outrage. "That's clear now, after all these years."

"The Nazi?"

"Him."

Kussow closed his eyes to the truth, hoping it would disappear. It wouldn't, of course, and neither would his guest.

"A blessing now threatens to turn into a nightmare unless something is done."

"But thirty years ago the gold—"

"Twenty-nine, to be exact. Not that it matters anymore if the Nazi talks."

"Then make sure he doesn't."

"As for that, the first thing you should know . . ."

He'd been sent from Tel Aviv to apprise Kussow of the danger, political and possibly even personal. A trap had been set for the Jews soon after the war, and was only now sprung.

". . . and so we have to ask you to do something you swore you'd never do again. It will also involve this inspector friend of yours, Dreyfus."

"César?"

"Has he ever killed a man?"

Kussow made a scoffing noise. "He already told me he intends to bring Bock to trial."

"Only Bock? Then there's still a chance."

* * *

"Two names, actually." The ministry official handed the sheet to César. "They've been withheld until now."

"Withheld by whom?"

"The SCE, initially. Both have been politically helpful to Bordier and he saw no need to embarrass them."

"You said initially."

Jules let out an impatient sigh. "The ministry supported the move."

"Meaning you've had the names for a while, too."

"We've known of them, yes."

"Why?"

"Why not?" Jules snapped. "They're two of West Germany's most powerful men, both loyal supporters of the government and, I might add, of our own president's policies. Naturally we sought to protect them."

"And now?" César asked.

"Now there seems to be a matter of gold . . ."

The story had it that the bird of paradise visited each person only once. If you weren't home, he left a tail feather to show you all you'd ever get. If the wind blew away the feather, you got nothing. But at least you still had hope that someday you would be visited by the bird of paradise.

César glanced at the data sheet on two more West German financiers with Nazi pasts uncovered in the SCE sweep. The first was a Foreign Office vice-consul under Ribbentrop and now a leading banker in Düsseldorf. The other was an SS major on special assignment to Himmler's staff—César's heart skipped a beat—who now headed a group of financiers in Frankfurt. It was Goethe Associates.

Goethe—César tore into Bock's file for the report, held it in hands that shook—owned Kaiser Systems which owned Oberst-Haupt which owned Otto Francke who sat at the right hand of God who owned everything.

César slumped in his chair staring at nothing, seeing the bulletin board that wasn't there anymore. Menard's darts were gone, too. So was Menard. They'd come a long way together, not as long as him and Tobie but long enough. When your partner gets killed, César reminded himself, you should do something about it.

He dialed Clément, told him to forget the rest of Goethe. He already knew which one it was. Francke's boss, Bock's partner, the man who ultimately hired Kayser, the one who framed César, the Nazi who hid the gold, the SS officer on Himmler's staff, the brains behind the plot and the financier who owned a painting of Hitler. They were all the same man.

"Who?" Clément wanted to know.

"Who else?"

* * *

Athena, the goddess of wisdom, was said to have sprung from the head of Zeus as a fully formed thought. With Hans Weber it was money.

The German knew how to make it—and how to hide it. In the SS he was an expert at money manipulation; the SCE data sheet also had him trading in gold and precious metals for the Nazis. After the war Weber went into industrial financing, using funds from undisclosed sources. Clément's notes showed he bought up companies in a dozen different industries, forced out competitors, created cartels. It was a golden time for ruthless men with unlimited funds; Germany was rebuilding under the Marshall Plan and the opportunities were endless for empire builders like Weber. His companies now controlled billions of deutsche marks, according to César's contacts in Bonn.

"West German industry," the contact explained, "largely expands on financing put together by groups of moneymen. Goethe's one of the biggest. Frankfurt, for example, owes much of its resurgence to them. So do some politicians."

"How much real power do they have?" César asked.

"Willy Brandt was one of their early favorites and look what happened to him. Or a decade ago with the missiles for Nasser's Egypt? They showed their disapproval and the money dried up just like that."

"An Israeli deal?"

"They probably saw it as bad business. The two countries have a lot of trade agreements."

"What about Weber himself?"

"Knows everybody, can get many favors. The rest he could buy."

"That big?"

"Big enough."

"All from the SS," César fumed. "The man's got the devil's own luck."

"And a little help from the devil."

"Help?"

"His uncle was Heinrich Müller."

When Clément arrived, César was at the window staring into space. Coughing to get his attention, the detective trudged to the couch.

"Chocolate's the worst drug there is," Clément said darkly. "They have this five-foot-three addict in Robbery who ran through a dozen candy shops. Claims he used to be six-three but chocolate shrinks you."

"Must be going for temporary insanity."

"Sounds permanent to me."

"What about Weber?" César asked.

"He's in Germany now. Has a castle near Wiesbaden, and a half-dozen other homes scattered around the country." Clément was relieved that his boss was back in command. "How'd he learn about you?"

"Bordier!" César spat it out like an epithet.

"But why?"

"Politics," César said bitterly. He had found threads of gold that led to German financiers with Nazi pasts and present influence. "What else are the political police good for?"

"So the bank account came from Weber."

"So did the pressure on Internal Affairs."

Clément was impressed. "You must have him worried."

"Not me." César reached for his jacket. "If he has any sense, he's thinking about Bock."

* * *

At the Marmottan museum they found rooms full of Monets but not a single Lelouch. No one even looked like him. "Water lilies," sneered Clément who didn't like Impressionism. All that light supposedly hurt his eyes. César, more eclectic, favored anything within proximity.

"Doesn't look like a painter." He stopped in front of Renoir's portrait of Monet. "The eyes are too small."

"More like a sex fiend." Clément thought all artists were moral degenerates. His younger sister once went with an artist who painted her in the nude after they had sex. In the nude!

In the nearby park they covered the lower lake where Lelouch often spent his day off, after staring at his favorite pictures. On weekends half of Paris came to the Bois de Boulogne, a métro stop away.

A father could take his brood and scuttle them on the grass while he consorted with nature, or another woman. Mothers read or chatted or even watched muscular males row delicate girls who seldom moved. It was all very pastoral and homicide seemed far away. César described Lelouch to a vendor.

"What he do?" The vendor wiped his nose with a napkin.

"Nothing."

"You're looking for him and he did nothing? Sounds just like the government."

"Have you seen him today?" César didn't know why he bothered.

"I'm a communist." The vendor squinted at César. "Been in the Party thirty-five years next October, no, thirty-six, ever since Hitler started. You remember Hitler? The government sold him my country, that's right. And only the communists had the courage to get it back. We saved Paris, did you know that?" He showed César the scar on his arm.

"Clean wound."

"I was lucky. Got it less than a mile from here fighting the Nazis. They wanted to blow up the city. Imagine! Blow up Paris."

César studied the vendor, a true patriot or else a crackpot. The woods were full of them this time of year.

"I read about it." He shook his head. Imagine, a communist selling hot dogs.

"So you want one?"

"Have you seen him?"

"Who?"

They found Lelouch seated on a bench watching them look for him.

"Why didn't you call out?" César demanded.

"The air is a rubber band," Lelouch said mysteriously.

César sat wearily, not used to the wild outdoors. "What do you know about chocolate?" He bent down to tug at his shoelaces.

"A killer," Lelouch reported.

"How so?"

"There was this politician in Switzerland? Shot the town's mayor five times and then claimed chocolate intoxication, said he'd gorged himself until he didn't know what he was doing."

"He killed somebody because he ate too much chocolate?" Clément didn't believe it.

"What he get?" César asked.

"Three years and a letter of appreciation from the Swiss chocolatiers for all the free publicity."

César took off his shoes and squeezed his toes. "How about Heinrich Müller?"

"Another killer."

"Anything else?"

Lelouch shrugged. "They pass over the land like the wind. Who sees the wind?"

"Someone saw Müller."

"When?"

"Thirty years ago."

"He disappeared the next day," Lelouch confided. "There was talk he went over to the Russians since he admired their secret police so much. But most believed South America, where he helped set up a series of SS escape routes. In the sixties he supposedly came back with a new name."

"Back where?"

"Bavaria."

"Didn't they look for him?"

"Who wanted to look?" Lelouch sneered. "He was only head of the whole Gestapo during the Nazi terror, and Klaus Barbie's boss and the boss of Adolf Eichmann. Just the biggest SS killer still alive. Twelve million dead? Nothing to get excited about. Stalin killed more than that and nobody went after him."

The lakefront was a green garden across the water, the sun a red ball beyond the trees. In the afternoon stillness only the birds could be heard.

"What about the Israelis?" César whispered.

Lelouch tilted his head up, looked at the canopy of leaves. "After the war they had another war for a new country; when they looked again, the big-name Nazis like Müller were long gone." He jerked his head forward. "All these years there's been no bounties on his head, no Jewish businessmen spending millions to capture him, like with Mengele. Now it's too late, of course. All the emotion's gone." The waiter blew into his hands; a wisp of a man, he was chilled ten months of the year. "They say Eichmann thought Müller was the devil himself."

In the Bois de Boulogne were miles of hiking and riding trails.

César wondered if he'd ever get to any of them. He tied his laces, stood and took a few steps to loosen the legs. He glanced at Lelouch, his face a thoughtful frown. "You ever hear of *Anvil?*"

"The 'Anvil Chorus,' " Lelouch hissed, "from Verdi's *Il Trovatore*. It celebrates the sun, the gold of a new dawn."

* * *

At 5 P.M. Munich detectives entered Room 225 of the Vier Jahreszeiten hotel on the Maximilianstrasse. Since a little past noon, when they began their surveillance for a suspect answering Bock's description, no one had entered or left the suite. In the lavish bathroom they found the nudy body of Otto Francke hanging from a pipe, an overturned chair nearby. His clothes were arranged neatly on the bed, the wallet and watch in his shoes. A blank sheet of letter paper and a pen lay on the dresser. It was an apparent suicide.

César was notified within the hour.

"It wasn't suicide," he said.

"Maybe it was, maybe it wasn't." According to Munich police, there was no way to prove from the neck injury whether he was struck or strangled.

"Not suicide."

"We'll never know."

At that moment not too far from Paris headquarters, Yishay Kussow spoke to Jerusalem.

"What did he say exactly?"

Kussow repeated César's words. "Bock's important to the Israelis because of the *Anvil* gold."

"That's not much by itself."

"He'll go further."

"How much further?"

"He's very capable," Kussow warned.

"But not dangerous," declared the Mossad leader, "unless he goes to Germany after Bock."

"Shouldn't he be told?"

"Only then."

TWENTY-ONE

It had been the worst week of his life. To an obsessive like César, waiting was the ultimate torture. Not that he hadn't worked but it was all in the head. And to what end? He was here and Bock was there.

"How could Francke have been murdered?" Clément had asked. "His neck was snapped by the rope, and there were no bruises on the body and no evidence of drugs."

To Clément the murder—if it was murder—was a mystery, much like a killing in a locked room. But hadn't the inspector already solved just such a mystery? Well?

"The rope itself hid the original bruise," César explained. "Bock slammed the edge of his hand into Francke's Adam's apple and killed him instantly. Then he simply hanged the body from the pipe."

The perfect murder. As the Munich police admitted, there was no way to prove whether he was struck or strangled.

Perfect, César agreed. Just like all the others. Otto Francke was Bock's May victim and final kill. Except for his partner . . .

By the end of the work week he had completed arrangements for making Alphonse Durac his chief assistant. Clément's time would come, no doubt, but not yet. César needed someone more like him, his own kind.

Clément was disappointed but not difficult. He didn't really expect to get the job; the inspector thought him a womanizer since he was still single. Jews didn't play around unless they were married.

César spent the weekend at home—this strange place he hardly even recognized—trying to fit the final pieces of the puzzle. They all had the same shape: Jacqueline Volette. Bock and Weber and five others, including Francke, had stolen gold. Now only Bock and Weber were left and it was winner take all. On paper Weber, with his considerable power, clearly had the edge. But Bock was the professional killer, which was the whole point. And Jacqueline was working with him. If she killed her sister, she also killed Kurt Linge who died the same way in Vienna.

It was a truth César found almost unbearable.

* * *

Monday morning brought him to Dupin's office, with Jobert in the other chair. Suspicion was etched on their faces. They wanted to know about Hans Weber.

"Your reports don't even mention him," Dupin complained.

"There's no proof."

"Proof of what?"

"Complicity in murder."

"We're talking about office reports," Dupin snapped, "not fucking white papers for the ministry."

"No one seemed interested in the German murders," César protested.

"You mean accidents."

Jobert's eyebrows shot up. "What have they to do with Weber?"

"They weren't accidents. Bock killed them for the gold."

"Gold?"

"What gold?"

It was all suspicion, of course. Nothing could be proved against Weber or even Bock; the German kills were virtually a separate case from France, where some hard evidence existed. Yet César stood by his conclusions. They were in it together for the gold. Had been, anyway. Now things were different.

"In what way?"

"Kayser blew the partnership. Only one wins now."

"And the other?"

"Weber loses."

César saw the look they exchanged. He'd been working too hard, needed a rest. The death of his partner, his own close call. Even inspectors came apart sometimes.

He didn't bother to ask how they learned of Weber. The ministry knew all about playing politics.

Dupin tried again. "Hans Weber is one of the most influential men in West Germany, a millionaire many times over, and you suggest he's involved in murder?"

"Involved, yes. Bock's a hired assassin and Weber was his partner."

"He's also a favorite of the ministry here."

César was not impressed. "Money breeds power," he acknowledged.

"Damn it, the man controls billions. What would he want with Bock?"

"More."

"How much more?"

"Everything," César insisted. "Do you know they were on Himmler's staff together?"

"He was a Nazi and so was Bock. What else?"

"They stole the gold, hid it. Them and five others, all dead now."

"Killed by Bock, you claim."

"Working with Weber."

"Why would he need Weber?"

César considered the question. "He controlled the resources to get the gold out of Austria, move it to Switzerland."

"Why would Weber need him?"

"To kill the others."

"Were they killed?"

"Four accidents and a suicide in five months? All SS, friends or at least knowing of one another. What are the odds?"

"This gold," Dupin grumbled. "Where'd it come from?"

"The SS was smelting it near the Mauthausen concentration camp," César answered carefully. "Kayser suspected Bock had something to do with gold."

"He tell you that?"

"Maton told me."

"Maton?" Jobert was startled. "Did he know about the gold?"

"They were going to try for it after they killed Bock. Blackmail Francke for it."

"He was Kayser's client."

"But he worked for Weber."

"How did Maton learn of the gold?"

"Through Kayser."

"How did he learn of it?"

"He had a lot of SS contacts. Over the years he probably heard rumors and started putting things together when Francke hired him to take care of Bock."

Jobert sat there grim as a ghost. Even Dupin had lost his impassive theatrical pose. César began to believe they knew more than they were saying.

"Where's Bock now?" It was almost a whisper.

"Germany. Or Austria," César quickly added.

"After the gold?"

César hesitated.

"Or after Weber?"

"The gold," he guessed.

"Makes more sense." Dupin grimaced. "Why didn't you tell us about Maton's interest in gold before?"

"What was there to tell? He wanted to hunt for it."

"He almost gets you killed," Jobert rasped, "and you say what's there to tell?"

"That will be all for now," the chief inspector said.

Walking out, César was aware only that he'd done it again. He hadn't mentioned Jacqueline Volette. Like a lover he had kept silent, but he would've thrown Nicole to the wolves. Maybe he didn't deserve any woman. He probably didn't even deserve to live.

* * *

The office was carelessly rearranged. Painters had come and gone, frenzied arms that rolled colors onto walls and then left for darker corners, leaving behind belongings that no longer seemed to fit. Under a blazing ceiling the room gleamed like metal. César lowered the shade to find his desk.

The rest of the morning was spent in reading about Gestapo boss

Müller and Barbie, the Butcher of Lyon, and Mengele, the Auschwitz angel of death. It was like taking a trip through hell itself.

"This time," César swore afterwards. "This case."

                              * * *

Jacqueline was beautiful, her clothes a model of money.

"I wanted to see you in your natural habitat," she said by way of explanation. "Try to straighten out the misunderstanding we had."

"Is that what it was?"

She took in the room's sinister brightness. Even the smile couldn't hide her fear that she would wind up like this again someday.

"It's true about Bock and me," she admitted. "We were lovers even before Bernadette died."

"Ah."

"It was my fault." Jacqueline had felt guilty since her sister's death, as if she were responsible. In a way she was. "Bernadette killed herself," she confided.

"Your sister committed suicide?"

"She found out about us. Didn't want to live anymore."

Jacqueline went on to say that in her grief and anger she'd told the insurance company Bock had killed his wife, but of course they did nothing since it wasn't true. Then when César came along with Bock's supposed murder, she jumped at the chance to hurt him and so she told César about the picture not being Bock and how he'd killed her sister. He was guilty, too. If it hadn't been for him, her sister would still be alive.

"No," César said. "The truth is Bock dumped you when he left for good. He probably blamed you for his wife's death. He dumped you and so you had to get even. You always have to get even. Your father dumped you by dying and you got back at him by getting an older man, a father-lover. That's what you do best. You get even."

Jacqueline bowed her head, held herself rigid. Her hands were pressed into the cushions of the couch. When she looked up again, tears were in her eyes.

"It's true, what you say. He always blamed me for Bernadette. When he said he was leaving I was frantic, tried to talk him out of it but he wouldn't listen. So I decided to punish him, hurt him as I'd been hurt." She dabbed at the tears with a tissue. "Don't judge me, César, until you understand how hurt I was, try to understand."

César stared at her, his eyes empty. "You're a good actress," he granted. "Mostly I think it's how warm you look when you're lying. Blood would boil in your mouth."

"I meant every word."

"You meant nothing," César snarled, "and neither did I." Every breath was a weight pushing against the mass in his chest. "Until this moment I didn't realize how good you really are. Or how dangerous."

"Don't say that."

"You're like Dupin, another gifted actor. Who'd ever believe I told him about the gold, and Maton too? Tried to tell him—only he didn't want to hear it."

"What—"

"Doesn't matter." He hunched over the desk. "What I told you before about Bock dumping you? I just wanted to see what you'd say. Anything that works, right?"

"No!"

"Yes! I'm a man obsessed, and you counted on that. But men have been known to turn on their obsession when it becomes too painful." César stood. "Nobody dumped anyone. You and Bock are still lovers"—he walked around the desk—"I've had a look at your phone calls for the past few weeks"—pulled a chair over to the couch—"a half dozen to West Germany, always to public booths so Bock couldn't be traced." He sat down next to her. "He told you when and where to call. So now let me tell you the rest of it. You contacted the insurance company last year to see if they had any suspicions about Bock. They didn't; he was clear. And you put me on the right road with the picture because Bock wanted a police trail in case his partner double-crossed him. Bock's been directing all of it, including you and me, and behind him is Weber. You know Weber, don't you?"

"No." Barely a whisper.

"A millionaire like that? I thought beauty always went to money, a beauty like you anyway. Your interest in money, I mean. You'd do most anything for it, wouldn't you?"

"Don't, please."

César pressed on. "When you pushed your sister out the window, it gave Bock an idea. Our boy appreciates ideas, especially about accidents. He needed different ways but they had to fit the victims. Linge's office was six floors up. Bock went to see him on some excuse and took you along. While they talked you admired the view of Vienna. What was that steeple there? Linge came over to show the sights and Bock had to sit in his seat because he couldn't make it to the open balcony window. But you could, Jacqueline. You were just that determined to get your share of the gold. And after all, you'd done it before. You looked where Linge pointed and you nodded and squealed and held his arm and when he was leaning out to show you something, you just pushed. It wasn't murder like shooting someone; he probably would've fallen anyway. Except his body landed on a parked car three meters out. You push hard."

Jacqueline had her face buried in her hands, as if shielding it from the blows of César's words. Her fingers were steel claws, her shoulders stone buttresses. Instead of a frightened female he saw a sphinx, stolid and unyielding. Beyond reach.

He tried anyway. "When Kayser approached you to betray Bock for money, you pretended to agree. He needed you to call Bock, get him to come to the slaughterhouse where he'd be killed by Inspector Maton hiding in the dark. You too; Kayser wanted no witnesses. But you were really laying a trap for him, and I was caught in the middle. When I called you Bock's mistress, hoping Kayser would let you go, he just laughed. He knew you were more than that."

César paused, his face a mask of thought. Could she lead him to Weber as well as Bock?

"So what happens to you now?" he asked. "Bock will go down; we know what he looks like and the German police are checking their forgers for his new name. That leaves you nothing to show for your efforts. There's still Weber, of course, with all his money and the gold too. Maybe you could marry him. Isn't that what you said last week, you might marry a millionaire? But now you say you don't know Weber. Which is strange when you think of it"—his voice suddenly grew harsh—"since you made a call to Frankfurt the day after we had our little chat and you saw Bock was finished. That's why you called Goethe, wasn't it? To talk to Hans Weber?"

Jacqueline raised her head, the eyes red rings. Her voice was scratchy, not at all the roar of a lioness. Yet she was at her most dangerous at this moment, he thought.

"All lies," she said.

"Lies?"

"All of it."

César shuddered, hoped it was a sign of sensitivity and not cheap sentimentality.

"You made it up," she said, "trying to frighten me." She smiled, a shy hope. "You're cruel and devious."

"Don't be silly. You did everything just like I said." Her words stung him. "And I'll tell you something else. Your boyfriend's in more trouble than he knows. The Israelis are after him. He doesn't have a chance."

César didn't believe it. Bock was the best.

"Anything," she whispered, rising. Her eyes were wet with promise.

"Nothing." He remained seated.

That night César dreamed of Marlene Dietrich for the first time.

* * *

"I know nothing of her death," the suspect wailed in the airless cubicle to which they had brought him, "nothing at all."

"Nothing, everything." César took off his jacket. "Why do we always think in extremes?"

Alphonse sat on the other side of Caboche and watched him carefully.

"Most things are somewhere in the middle," César said, "because there's more room."

"I hardly knew the woman," Caboche protested.

"A matter of degree," César continued, rolling up his shirtsleeves. "For instance, you knew Marie Pinay from the bar."

"As to that, I never even—"

"You talked to her on several occasions about your work, in front of others."

"Well, yes, but—"

"And were seen to argue with her."

"Only once when—"

"See what I mean about degrees?" César asked helpfully.

"All right. In that case I will tell you the truth. I only talked to her because of Fernand."

César nodded and exchanged glances with Alphonse who quietly opened his notebook.

"He asked me to, and more than once," Caboche began.

* * *

The building was bent into a past full of neglect, its entrance gained through a crumbling archway. Beyond, a cluttered courtyard led up to the rooming house.

Inside, in a small dank room on the third floor they found Fernand. Heavyset and scowling, he cursed them for interrupting his sleep.

"Caboche told us everything," César declared.

Fernand shook his head vigorously. "Don't know any Caboche."

"No Caboche?" César raised an eyebrow. "He seems to know you well enough."

"You're looking for someone else," Fernand objected.

"He sometimes works with you on odd jobs," Alphonse reminded him.

"Lives around the corner." César smiled. "You remember now."

"Oh, that guy. Yeah, sure. What's he done?"

"Says he saw you beat up a woman last month."

"He's a liar," Fernand snarled. "I never touched her."

"Who?"

Fernand shrugged. "Whoever he said."

"Why would he lie?"

Another shrug.

"We found the woman and she confirms his story," César said. "Is she lying too?"

"They're both liars," Fernand insisted.

"She still has some of the bruises."

"And she's ready to see you charged."

"She wouldn't dare—"

"Tell us about it."

"That can be explained," Fernand assured them.

"Can you also explain your friendship with Marie Pinay?" César asked brusquely. He watched the suspect's eyes shrink to red dots. The name would mean nothing in the ear of a stranger or the mouth of a liar, but the eye reflects the truth and the truth was that Fernand had been caught.

His voice grew plaintive, the whine more evident. "I know nothing."

"So you say," César sighed, "and so we wait to hear exactly what it is you don't know."

Both men were soon booked for the murder of Marie Pinay. She had fallen asleep in a drunken stupor before satisfying them sexually, and they decided to teach her a lesson. They'd been drunk, too.

* * *

César was a leper no longer. People talked to him again; some even smiled.

"What about your cases?" Dupin asked gravely.

There were none: Pinay was found and Bock lost. Dupin promised him more. Meanwhile, César was to work on his report.

"I knew you had nothing to do with it," he told César.

"With what?"

"Anything," said the actor vaguely.

The next afternoon saw the director at César's door, a first. He stood perfectly still, his lips barely moving.

"You seem to have a gift for eliciting strong emotion, not always favorable I may say. Yet you are apparently good at what you do. So good, I am told, that sometimes you fail to keep us apprised of what it is exactly you are doing. This could be calamitous should you need assistance we might otherwise be able to offer. They tell me we would miss you. For all our sakes, then, I hope you will keep us informed. To do less would be imprudent. Survival, like the law, works better if you don't piss on it too much."

* * *

Nicole didn't see at all.

"I thought we had an understanding." Her dark eyes raked César's face.

"An understanding?"

"No strings."

"There are no strings."

"Then obviously we're not really together. So how can we be what it is you say, not right for each other?"

There were diners at every table. Sleek women in black; they all looked like Catherine Deneuve, a listless representation. The men were mostly carbons too. Craving acceptance, they sought only to please.

"If we're not together, what's there between us?" César asked.

"What's between us is the space between us," Nicole said. "That way we can be whatever we want to each other without any strings."

"We can be with each other because we're not together?"

"Not really."

"But if we were really together, that would change everything."

"Naturally. Then what you say would make sense."

"What's that?"

"That we're not right for each other."

"Do you think we are?" César asked.

"No."

"Then you agree with me," he said in surprise.

"It doesn't matter," Nicole noted, "since we're not together."

César held his pleasing smile, prepared for tearful protestations but none came; only waiters who whisked away their plates. Others brought delicacies as more wine was poured. The glasses had burnished gold stems.

"I thought you should know how I felt," César said finally. "A beautiful woman like you deserves the best."

"Every woman does."

"I wouldn't be good for you."

"Probably not."

"I could never really love you."

"Not enough."

"You'll find someone much better for you."

"And quickly."

César felt a sudden flush at the temples, a flutter of breath. Things were not going as he'd planned. There was no reason to stay with Nicole when it was Jacqueline he wanted, whose face he saw, lips he kissed, body he touched. It wasn't fair to Nicole. Or to him. Still, he didn't think she should be made to suffer. Perhaps he was too hasty.

"I suppose we could see each other sometimes," he offered.

"Not if there's talk of being together."

"I thought you needed me."

"I never said I needed you, César." Nicole smiled sweetly. "Just that I wanted you." She finished her wine, set the glass down and pushed it away. "But we don't always get what we want. Do we?"

* * *

Alphonse listened carefully to details of the Bock case.

"They might try to kill me," César warned.

His new detective sergeant didn't see why. "Everything you suspect is in your report."

"Not everything."

* * *

At night he sat in the office, a spider silently spinning, and stared at the threads he'd just spun. Bock was gone, the kiss of death to a tracker of men.

In the late hours the house leaked sounds, and footfalls in the hall thundered as cloven hooves. Evil desires lined the memory like vaults in a mausoleum.

Why didn't Bock kill Weber? Then only predator and prey would remain.

* * *

Daylight knows no darkness.

Bock needed him, for now anyway. They'd meet, each wary of the other, discuss gold that belonged to the Jews.

No wonder the Israelis—

"Perfection," César had once said to Menard, "is what police work is all about. It's everything but we never reach it."

"Will we ever?"

César had looked at the eager young detective and saw himself. "Only if we keep trying," he'd said.

Now Menard was gone, and so was César's wife. He had his work and she had his love. But it wasn't everything and so it wasn't love.

"This is no time for new cases," Dupin told César. "Something's happened."

* * *

At week's end César was ushered into an elaborate wood-paneled chamber of Louis XV and modern comfort. Behind his Boulle desk sat the avuncular Prefect of Police, the department's political boss, flanked by a pair of somber men in dark suits. Smoke ringed the room in a bluish smear.

The commissioner wasted no words. "My life is suddenly filled with your remarkable exploits as a hunter, especially your keen scent for gold. Not only my life"—the face was impassive, a leathery pouch for eyes and nose and imperious mouth—"but that of your country of birth as well." The mouth forced a smile. "I presume I have your interest, Inspector."

"*Monsieur* Commissioner."

"Good. Now because of your sensational report, and certain other, ahh, political aspects that have come to light"—he looked at his assistants—"the government has decided to take seriously some of your more, ah, esoteric allegations regarding this matter of hidden gold. For example, if extensive smelting was done at the camp in Austria"—he referred to a sheet on the desk—"Mauthausen, as you say, then the raw material for the castings most certainly came from the looting of Europe. In that event it could literally involve billions of francs, or deutsche marks or even dollars. The estimate given us by the foreign ministry is about three billion dollars at the 1945 price; today, of course, it's worth five times that. In the next decade"—the commissioner's eyes positively glowed—"the gold could easily reach ten, even twenty times its original value. We might be talking as much as fifty or sixty billion"—it was barely a whisper—"which would certainly make it the biggest treasure in history. Are you still with me, Inspector?"

"I already reached much the same conclusion."

"Did you?"

"Only that the meltings had to come from Nazi plunder, as you say," César added hurriedly, "especially of the Jews."

"I said nothing about Jews." The commissioner was not pleased. "To continue, we have contacted the Austrians and Americans. At this moment Austria is searching the lakes near the camp. I should mention"—his leonine head tilted toward César—"that both West and East Germany have indicated they will petition the International Monetary Fund for the return of any gold found."

"May I ask how they learned of the possibility?"

"Political realities," the commissioner sighed. "The government told them."

"The gold supposedly went to the SS groups after the war," César said. "Why did Austria believe some of it might still be hidden?"

"Not some of it, Inspector Dreyfus. All of it."

César didn't understand. His report made it quite clear—

"That part of your report," the commissioner interrupted, "has to do with a murder investigation and holds no interest for the governments concerned." He spoke distinctly, a sign of impatience. "Since nobody seems to know what actually happened to the gold, they're proceeding on the assumption that all of it could still be hidden.

Your report merely gives them some hope—and a locale, of course,"
he added as an afterthought. "May I go on?"

The commissioner blew his nose into a monogrammed handkerchief. "For much of the war the SS ran a small-arms plant near the
camp, itself unusual in that it was not under any political supervision. Arms plants have a smelter, as I'm sure you know. Now it
seems there were other, ah, peculiarities about the plant. For one
thing, nobody who worked in it was ever seen again. I mean even the
SS guards. For another, the shipments received were far more numerous than those sent out. And—this should interest you—the man
who handled the shipments was one of those killed, according to
you, by this Dieter Bock." The commissioner picked up the sheet
again. "Gerd Wilhelm Streicher." He replaced it on the desk, gazing
past César at the billows of smoke emanating from the assistant
commissioners.

"Other irregularities keep coming to light, enough of them to lend
weight to your suppositions, some of them anyway. Max Baur
headed the Gestapo in Linz which controlled the Mauthausen area,
Linge worked out of Linz, Von Schirrmacher was on Himmler's staff
with Bock."

"Where does Weber fit in?"

"He doesn't. There's no evidence linking *Herr* Weber to
Mauthausen."

"He was on Himmler's staff, too. His job was to get gold."

"To trade for it, not make it."

"Francke was his messenger boy and Bock killed him."

"Otto Francke hanged himself. His company was in trouble and
he feared being fired."

César saw that Weber was too powerful to be taken so easily. He
decided not to mention the Israelis.

"This is a complex matter," the commissioner noted, "that
reaches across national boundaries. What we don't need at this point
are still more complications. Bad enough one of our own men was
involved, even peripherally. I mean Inspector Maton, of course. Now
we are faced with this Volette woman. You've kept her out of your
investigation all along; you've protected and shielded her at every
turn. We don't know why, other than some sick relationship. Suddenly you say she's been with Bock from the beginning, his lover at
least. All right, we can use this to our advantage. The woman is

being sought for questioning in the death of her sister. She is missing and we want to talk to her. Now do you understand why you're being told all this?"

"Is there proof against Jacqueline Volette?" César asked.

"It's not the woman we want."

César began to see the financier's fine hand. They had made a deal, after all. "Then she's just the excuse," he suggested.

"To get you there."

"Where?"

"Your mother was German," the commissioner said softly, his voice sympathetic. "Don't you feel an urge to find your roots?"

TWENTY-TWO

He stopped in Stuttgart, a ghost wandering where his mother had lived and married. He peered in shop windows, searched passing faces. Did anyone know of . . . It was hopeless, of course. The Jews of Germany were gone.

* * *

The hotel manager was trying to be helpful.

"Not a trace," César complained.

The man had lost his own parents to Allied bombs, didn't like to dig up the past. "Some do, some don't," he said thankfully.

"Nothing."

"Nobody's perfect."

* * *

In the afternoon César went to the Nazi war crimes center in nearby Ludwigsburg to check on Bock and Weber. The former women's prison compound housed thousands of Nazi documents and a card file with more than a million entries, archives to assist in the prosecution of war criminals.

The research had been scrupulous and the hunting slim. In thirty years German courts sentenced only five thousand Nazis out of an estimated three hundred thousand suspects, and most of these came at the end of the war. Between 1970 and 1975, less than one hundred were convicted.

"Twelve million people murdered and only five thousand convictions!" César found it hard to believe.

The future would be worse, he was told. Investigations were slowing, trials winding down. In another decade it would all be over, a victim of death and remembrance; witnesses would be dead or too old to recall. So would their torturers, most of them dying peacefully in bed.

There was nothing on Bock or Weber. They didn't torture or kill anyone helpless, just stole the gold out of their teeth after others killed them.

A lot of gold was stolen for the melts at Mauthausen, as César saw from a huge wall map. In their twelve-year reign of terror, the Nazis ran seven hundred concentration camps. Auschwitz was just the pinnacle on the pyramid of death.

*   *   *

Jobert had seen César before he left, a matter of some urgency since they probably wouldn't meet again.

Why not?

Why would he come back?

"We didn't know you were half German," Jobert said. "Not that I have anything against them"—he grunted in sympathy—"in fact, my first wife was Turkish, which is almost German. And I'll tell you something else; my own son from the Greek wife is in Sweden right now and that's close enough. They're all German, those countries, all sausage eaters. I can smell a German a mile away, unless he's French. So I'll tell you what I think. This whole Bock case is a cover for a communist plot by the East Germans and you're part of it."

"Are you crazy? I broke their spy ring."

"To throw us off, yes. But that's exactly what we'd expect you to do," Jobert confided. "Bock worked for the East Germans. The Swiss Kayser also worked for them occasionally and so did Baur. Weber himself has important economic ties with the country and the woman Jacqueline Volette studied in Leipzig. Now you'll be there just when the East Germans are trying to get back billions supposedly stolen from them. And Mauthausen and all this Nazi gold isn't that far from the Czech communist border. Still think I'm crazy?"

"I'm not a communist."

"Neither was Hitler," Jobert said, "but he ran the National Socialist Party."

* * *

A ripe fetus dropped from the womb and began to spread.

César had left for Frankfurt.

Its umbilical cord stretched across Europe.

"It's Bock you're after," the commissioner had said, "but it's the gold we want."

It grew to hate before it learned to love. The boy was father to the man, as always.

"Gold is the god of the earth," they had reminded him.

The man mingled his destiny with that of his adopted country, his energy fusing the two. At first no one paid attention; people are so blind.

Which prompted César to think of the gold of the Nibelung.

How could one man change the course of history? How could he not?

"Just like the *Ring* operas," Clément had said when he saw César off. "Hitler's favorite."

Were there dreams in the womb? Age one? Two? Did it know even then what it would become? Did anyone?

He could as easily have been born in Stuttgart.

Heil César.

* * *

Frankfurt lay at their feet. Atop its tallest skyscraper sat a gold nest with walls of glass through which millionaires looked down on mortals.

Weber was even more impressive than César had imagined, his tanned aristocratic face a measure of money and the comfort and care it bought. He wore a silk suit that radiated elegance. Not a gray hair marred his polished head; even his eyebrows were bushy and black in the best Prussian tradition. The man exuded charm and good breeding but it was the ruthless drive that finally impressed. Nothing would be allowed to stand in his way.

They had their drinks in Weber's lavish suite, amidst Louis XV tables and Oriental rugs and Mondrian paintings. Strains of Wagner wafted through speakers, Siegfried and Gunther and Hagen playing out the plans of the gods. César had never heard the music so clearly.

"I understand your mother was German," Weber said. He loosened his belt, the buckle hammered out of pure gold. "You speak it well."

"I prefer French."

"So do I." Weber smiled, another gold touch in an otherwise drab world. "The language of love."

"And money?"

"Same thing."

"I was asked to see you first," César offered. "I don't know why."

"Does it matter?"

"Does that mean you're not going to tell me?" César asked. "Then it matters."

"Then it means I'll tell you what I can," Weber said smoothly, as if he wanted the inspector to see how reasonable he was. "Do you know who I am?"

"You're Bock's partner," César charged. "Why would you want to see me?"

"To help you with Bock, of course."

"That would help you."

"Only me?" Weber was surprised. "I'm told you want him for some killings in France."

"And more here."

"Then shouldn't you listen?"

The financier seemed to speak in stereo, resonant to a fault, but with each channel transmitting different signals so that nothing was defined.

"Try to imagine a country where you need a wheelbarrow full of money to buy a loaf of bread. That was Germany before Hitler came to power. It was economic chaos," Weber said, "and he put Germany back on its feet."

"With its heel on the neck of others," César protested.

"The point is the war was economic, at least until he got foolish. But some of us in the SS stuck to the original goal: order. We traded for gold, for stable currencies and raw materials."

"Traded what?"

"Whatever it took."

"What it took were millions of lives."

"It was war!"

"It was murder!"

The silence grew uncomfortable until Weber quietly said, "My job was getting gold, nothing more. Others were doing the same, acting under official orders. We were going to save Germany." He shook his head in bewilderment. "Instead, half of it went to the communists. But at least we saved the rest."

"Bock probably thinks he saved it too."

"Bock is a madman. He thinks there's gold hidden."

"Maybe he's right."

"He's wrong. At the end of the war all the gold went to the SS underground groups."

"Even the gold smelted at Mauthausen?"

"There was no gold at Mauthausen, only what we stored nearby— all of it traded from other countries." Weber's face showed concern. "That's apparently part of Bock's delusion, and now you seem to have it."

"The small-arms plant," César bristled. "Is that delusion?"

"No, that was real. It made small arms."

"And those who disappeared. Did Bock make them up?"

"Men always disappear in wartime."

"Even SS?"

"Whole squads vanished in Greece," Weber argued. "Why not a few in Austria?"

César changed the subject, startled by the financier's evasions. What good were denials in the face of facts? He didn't have to listen to lies. "What is it you want from me, Mr. Weber? You say there's no hidden gold, which means you're not Bock's partner. And you're surely not afraid of him coming after you, with all your protection. So what exactly can I do for you?"

"Let me do something for you, Inspector. I can get you Bock."

"Why would you?"

"If you're right about him killing those others—"

"As if you didn't know."

"Let me finish. If you are right, then he also killed a loyal friend in Otto Francke and for that I want him to pay."

"Don't make me laugh," César snapped. "You sent Francke to the hotel to kill or be killed. Him and Bock were the last of the group that stole some of the *Anvil* gold—except for you, of course. You wanted them both dead, hoped they'd kill each other off." His smile was grim. "Now you're stuck with Bock."

Weber's eyes were hooded, the pupils steel shot in a bottomless cannon. "I was misinformed about you, Inspector. You are a stupid man in a stupid job," he jeered. "Even your lies are stupid."

"But you? You're smart," César badgered. "You send a sparrow after a hawk. Who'll you get to go after Bock now? There's no one left."

"You're wrong." The financier leaned forward, his manner intent. "There is someone left."

"Who?"

"You."

César didn't believe it. "You had five men murdered and now you want me—"

"You will not bait me again," Weber promised. He glanced at his watch. "The police have been known to say anything to get what they want."

"I was just thinking the same about you."

"Then why not work together against Bock?" Weber settled back in the plush lounger, once more at ease. "With no gold in Austria, he'll want something for his troubles at my expense. That's how we can get him."

"We?"

"Let's say I make a deal with him," Weber explained. "His delusion didn't work out? All right, I have plenty. I would give him more than he'll ever need. He could go away, leave me alone. Good for me —and good for you."

"How so?"

"You'll get your chance at him," Weber said. "You've had some troubles of your own in Paris. Suspended, wasn't it? With Bock under your belt, you'll go back a hero. A political assassin and mass killer? They'll probably give you a medal."

"And what must I do first?" César asked belligerently.

"What you should do anyway," Weber answered. "Kill him."

César thought back to the commissioner's words. They didn't care what happened to Bock; he was expendable, a guide to the gold. They wanted it, any part of it, as payment for two hundred thousand Frenchmen. If César was in on the find, the politicians could always work something out.

"I have a plan," Weber added.

Nor did they care where it came from. The Jews of Europe were dead, so were the Slavs and Gypsies. Who was left to claim it? And if there was no gold, then Bock was just another killer. Nobody cared if a killer lived or died. Only Weber. And him?

"Where's Jacqueline Volette?" César asked.

"With Bock, of course." Weber stared at him in amusement. "They're lovers, didn't you know?"

"Except she's working for you now."

"Is she?"

In that case he was expendable too. Who cared about an inspector? A good way to get rid of him, better than dismissal or prison, and with an inspector's funeral thrown in free. The final payoff for Algeria. Tobie had been right after all: they never forget.

"Still interested?"

César felt himself slipping from grace; it was the only way he could stay close to Weber and the gold. Even more, it would get him to Bock. He had traded with Maton and Martel, and each time he'd fallen further. This was the third trade, and the last.

"Inspector Dreyfus?"

"I'm listening, Mr. Weber."

"The beauty of the free enterprise system"—the financier picked up his brandy—"is that someone profits from everything." He raised the glass in a toast. "To someone."

* * *

Hauser had a round face that smiled easily and hardly ever betrayed his thoughts.

"What do you know," he asked his guest, "about *Anvil?*"

"Only what you tell me."

In his fantasy, César saw the Ring of the Nibelung melted down for its gold. Out of it came the sun and the moon.

The inspector was in West Berlin to learn what he could of the prize, to gird himself for the battle. His host was an authority on the Nazi years.

"Anvil," Hauser said, "was strictly an SS deal, a way to get *gelt* as well as glory."

They sat in the huge main gallery of Hauser's chalet, with its own balcony of books. In the mornings, sunlight flooded the room through the great gallery windows.

"The project was closely guarded by a small cabal of ranking SS headed by Heinrich Müller. Even those others in the SS who knew about *Anvil* had no idea of its size."

For two and a half years, the plant kept spewing out bullion as the shipments of gold objects arrived from plundered towns and homes and bodies. By the end of 1944 death and destruction were everywhere, and Nazi Germany was in flames. The war was almost over, though Hitler still dreamed of victory in the ashes of defeat. In October he formed a home army for defense. In November he sent the V-2 vengeance rockets against England. In December he launched a final offensive in the west, the last great gasp of German military might. When it failed, so did he.

In January 1945, Hitler locked himself in the Reich Chancellery and slowly went mad. He would have his victory yet, and one the world would never forget. It was to be his *Götterdämmerung,* he screamed at the Nazi leaders, and that of the German nation as well. Their orders were clear. They were to destroy everything. Destroy, destroy, destroy . . .

"But, of course, you can't destroy gold," Hauser said. He pursed his lips in a thoughtful frown. "Who would want to?"

By March the end was in sight and the *Anvil* furnace was shut down, the workers killed, the compound leveled. Even the guards were slain, by an SS colonel named Schirrmacher who herded them into portable showers and locked the doors and dropped in the amethyst-blue crystals of hydrogen cyanide. Gassed like millions of others, their naked bodies burned at Mauthausen.

"By then," Hauser explained, "the gold had already been shipped to Switzerland for the secret SS accounts—"

"All of it?"

"—so the story goes."

César rubbed his hands together against the sudden chill. "There's proof?"

"No proof," Hauser sighed, "for any of it. You should remember that. Whatever we know of *Anvil* is by indirection and secondhand accounts. Most authorities don't like to think of it at all—too much mystery—or they regard it as just another small-arms plant that dabbled in gold on the side. They had one in the Lublin camp did the same."

"But there was gold stored near Mauthausen," César insisted.

"Billions, but the general opinion is that it came from trading with other countries such as Turkey. And from blackmail. The Bank of Italy, for example, was blackmailed shamelessly."

"So there's no way to tell if some of it was held back"—César's voice rang with disappointment—"or stolen from storage before it was all shipped out."

"Not really," Hauser admitted. "But for whatever it's worth, I don't think any of the *Anvil* gold ever reached Switzerland. None of it, and I'll tell you why . . ."

* * *

On the way into East Berlin, César kept going over Hauser's words, felt their grip.

". . . inconceivable that after thirty years not one scrap of paper has turned up, not one person come forward. We're talking billions disappearing without a trace. Inconceivable, yes, but not impossible. The other reason is the important one for me. From what I know of Müller and the men around him, I can't believe they'd ever let go of that kind of treasure. Remember there were no checks on Müller toward the end. As Nazi Germany fell apart, Himmler and the other leaders had more important things to worry about. Müller's crowd could've bought off those who knew, or even killed them, and kept everything for themselves. There were a lot of SS deaths in the last few months of the war that were never fully explained—the documentation is a matter of record and another unsolved mystery—especially in Berlin and Munich, mostly high-ranking officers. All they'd have needed were a few SS killers like that Von Schirrmacher and . . ."

"Bock!" César remembered saying as the room started to reel.

* * *

The city was a stone snake that slithered silently through deserted streets. Armor protected its scales and no citizen came too close. Three times a day its keepers changed positions, donning new masks, and every so often it was fed sacrificial lambs.

One kilometer east of the snake on a quiet avenue, those who watched the keepers kept their counsel. There were no guards. On the outside the massive gray blocks squatted in the sun while inside, the building burned with energy and ran full of angry ants.

On the second floor, César sat in the office of the watch captain and listened to him castigate his counterparts in the city's western sector.

"Amateurs," he announced finally. "They all piss milk and shit snow." He made a face to fit his invective. The secret police in East Berlin operated out of the Ministry for State Security and watched the people's police as well as the people. The captain's detail also included the border guards strategically stationed along the Berlin Wall. "Too easy over there, eh? Makes you soft."

He looked pointedly at César, not in the best of shape, and curved his mouth in a fierce grin. Behind him a somber face stared into the camera, dark-rimmed glasses and receding hairline giving a professorial appearance. Next to it a goateed man smiled expertly.

"A capitalist police inspector in a socialist state," the captain grinned, "is like a worm in fruit."

"Even worms," César replied, "turn to gold in the sun. Look at your First Party Secretary up there on the wall."

The two men faced each other across a desk piled high with papers. A bookcase nearby bulged with still more papers, many of them covered by colored cardboard which turned them into reports. The socialist societies survived by report.

"Last year there were 5,324 border crossings from east to west," the captain reported, "but only a dozen happened here. Twelve out of more than five thousand! Shows what organization can do."

"And a brick wall."

"That's organization, too." The captain slapped the desk for emphasis and a sheaf of documents slipped off the other side. "You're having a problem with that now or you wouldn't be here."

César bent down to retrieve the material from the floor.

"So are you."

"In what way?"

"Ten days ago"—he returned it to the desk—"one of your own border guards climbed over the wall."

"A lunatic," the captain suggested, "or else a victim. There's some evidence he was drugged, shot with a dart to make him turn traitor. Or maybe he just saw the lights of West Berlin and gave in to his escapist fantasies. Either way he doesn't count as an individual. Socialism is only interested in the masses." He reached into a pocket, came out empty, tried another, a third, looked over the sea of white in front of him, plunged in—

"You spoke of an exchange."

"That would be mutually beneficial."

—without success, began rummaging through the drawers, middle, left, right, finally found it, his pipe. "A mutual exchange with a capitalist?" He started searching for the tobacco.

"Happens often," César said.

"Who wins?"

"It's mutual."

The captain found a tin in the bottom drawer, opened the top. It was empty. "So you'll soon know where Bock is." He carefully closed the top. "Who is it you want?"

"Heinrich Müller."

"The Gestapo Müller?" Put the tin back in the drawer.

"Rumors had him going over to the Russians."

The pipe went into his pocket.

"I need to know where he is."

"Why?"

"And if he's still alive."

An orderly brought in a tray and placed it on a chair. The office was incredibly cramped. No carpet graced the floor, no curtain lined the window. César sat with his legs jammed against the desk.

"The room is temporary," the captain noted after the orderly left, "only two years so far." He poured the tea into silver mugs. "Müller's been thirty years."

"Müller for Bock," César said.

"Remind me why I care."

"Reimer was your man."

"He's still dead."

"Bock killed him."

The watch captain set the mug in front of César. On the tray, little cakes of color and cream rested on silver wrappers which were opened. Next to them lay two blue napkins with the name of a restaurant in West Berlin.

"Bock lured Reimer to Paris and killed him," César repeated.

"Why would he do that?"

"He could be working for the West Germans again."

"Really? Some cakes?" The captain reached for one—"They're marzipan and quite good"—bit into it. "No, I'm wrong. They're not marzipan at all. They're mazarin. Do you like mazarin?" He held out the tray. "Are you sure? Pity."

The captain finished the square of cake and folded the silver wrapper in half, then quarters—"Now shall I tell you, *Herr* Dreyfus, the real reason Herbert Reimer was killed?"—and placed it at the edge of the tray. "He was killed because we wanted him dead." He took up his napkin and carefully wiped his mouth before laying it on top of the wrapper. "We paid Bock for seven kills, not six. Reimer was the last; the reasons need not concern you. As for Dussap, about whom you asked, he worked for us in Strasbourg until he became a drunk who talked too much. We would've used Bock more but obviously he had other plans, which included changing identities with Reimer who resembled him. The piano wire, an old Nazi trick, made it even better. But you, I am told, discovered the switch and Bock had to buy his way out so he gave you our operation in Paris."

"Then you have reason for wanting to find him."

"At first glance, yes. You can imagine our surprise when we heard Bock was found dead. And then to be told by the West Germans that it was really our man Reimer. By the West Germans! Now, that really hurt." His eyes still blazed at the insult. "And, of course, Bock did sell out one of our units. Still"—he began rifling the desk again—"realities have a way of shifting. For example, another group could be set up in Paris, troublesome surely"—found a second pipe under a pile of papers—"but not impossible." It already was filled with tobacco and he quickly lit up in triumph—"Now let's look at the other side"—puffed a half dozen times. "Why did Bock want a new identity? He did nothing frivolous, as you must know. For him everything had a reason and a time, everything." Pungent smoke filled the room. "We think that the reason is gold, and the time—"

"Did you say gold?"

"Gold, yes, hidden gold. Nazi gold. Our gold."

Both men drank from silver mugs, their minds mired in gold.

"You see my point," the captain suggested. "The German Democratic Republic is engaged in a drive to get back billions of deutsche marks stolen from us after the war. If there's any gold hidden from the Nazi era, it rightfully belongs to us since we are the sole legitimate heir to most of the Nazi citadels." He popped the last little cake into his mouth. "If Bock finds it, we'll claim it."

"How will you know?"

"Count on it."

The captain slapped at his stomach and burped. Pipe in hand, he leaned back and smiled through the bluish haze, a creature content with the world. "Now that I've told you why we want Bock alive," he purred, "suppose you tell me why you want Müller dead."

TWENTY-THREE

The arsenic eaters of Austria began, legend has it, after the gold ran out. When all the gold was gone from the land, the ancient smelters turned to iron and in the province of Styria so many iron smelteries abounded that the sky grew dark from dawn to dusk and the smokestacks disgorged impurities in the form of a fine white powder and the country soon was covered with the white trioxide dust known as arsenic.

First the animals grazed on the powdered fields and developed greater endurance. Then the people ate of the magic bloom and their stamina increased and they grew more beautiful, with clear complexions and rich glowing hair. The practice spread until arsenic was added to the diets of infants and arsenic paste was eaten like butter. Soon the delicacy became an addiction and then there was no withdrawal except death.

And then some of the arsenic eaters turned to others with their mouths poisonous . . .

* * *

From Berlin César had come to Linz where it all began, tracking Bock's footsteps and those of Weber and the others, seeking anything that would give him an edge. He walked the Mauthausen ruins, now overrun with wild grass, stood at the top of the quarry where the trucks waited for the blocks of stone, descended the staircase of death into the pit of hell. He felt the vaporish evil even after thirty years, saw the ghosts, heard the silence. Was it all a game to the guards? A matter of logistics to their leaders? Men like SS General Oscar Dirlewanger and Willi Brenner helped set up the murder machinery at Mauthausen. All those bodies must have been troublesome, untidy. Should life be abolished for being too messy? Only here. What should they live on? Smoke. What would become of them? Smoke.

In his hotel room overlooking the town square—the very hotel from which Hitler stood on the balcony to proclaim the new and glorious *Reich*—César reread his notes on Mauthausen. Dirlewanger and Brenner had fled to Egypt after the war to escape Allied vengeance—along with Warsaw Gestapo boss Leopold Gleim, Eichmann's top lieutenant Franz Radmacher and Himmler aide Bernhard Bender. Other Nazis followed them by the hundreds in the early fifties, most working for Nasser's Egypt. César wondered if Müller was one of them. Could he resist a second chance at the annihilation of the Jews? One-third of all the Jews in the world had already been murdered.

In Linz, with its quarter of a million population, César talked to people who knew nothing of Mauthausen. Slave labor in the camp? They didn't believe it; wasn't that against the Geneva Convention? The Nazis made mistakes, *natürlich,* but they were not stupid. Some were more pessimistic. Wasn't life itself largely a matter of chance? Well then, someone had to lose. Others longed for the *gute alte Zeit,* the good old times before the Nazis. Or even after the Nazis. During? What did they know of that? They'd just lived their lives, followed orders, did what they were told. It was all a big mistake, anyway. A tragedy. *Ach,* that fool Hitler. What trouble he caused. *Gott im Himmel!* Still, he did have some good ideas—

* * *

"This won't be like two years ago in Norway," the Mossad chief warned, "where the wrong man was killed. We're still suffering from that one. There'll be no dozen-man teams here, and damn little support. The last thing we want is attention." His voice was a soft slap at the past. "To make matters worse, your man is himself a skilled assassin so don't underestimate him. As for the French inspector, we'll just have to see what develops." A pause. "I should remind you that Gestapo squad reunions are held regularly where you're going, so watch yourself." His smile was forced. "Whatever would we do without politicians to make new accommodations? What would they do without us to break them? You leave for Germany tomorrow."

"And my contact?" the Israeli agent asked.

"You'll meet him in Munich."

"He knows what he's doing?"

"Hopefully." The general was uneasy, wanted the mission over. Had the Nazi told them all he knew about this Dieter Bock?

"First time down here," the younger man said nervously.

"The Mossad Hilton."

They were in an underground bunker near the central police station, used by Israeli Intelligence for secret discussions. Jerusalem, unlike Tel Aviv, had a heavy Arab population.

"Seems soundproof enough."

"Bombproof too."

Both men smiled. Bombs were a part of Israeli daily life but that didn't make them any less fearsome.

"About this police inspector," the agent said.

"César Dreyfus."

"Anything I should know?"

"Just that he's already in Germany, was anyway. This morning we heard he'd gone from East Berlin to Austria."

"Linz?"

"And Mauthausen."

"Tracking Bock."

"Both of them, I would say."

"So it looks like he'll go along with us."

"Except you can never trust the French. Look at de Gaulle; he almost destroyed Israel all by himself."

The bunker was reinforced concrete six feet thick on all sides, two rooms. The inner room held a steel conference table. Bunk beds were stacked against a wall; near the ventilator shaft on the other side lay a cache of weapons.

"If Dreyfus doesn't cooperate—" the agent persisted.

"He'll find him."

"Then we'll kill him."

"Bock's not the problem," the general confided. "It's the other Nazi."

* * *

The grounds were a forest, the house a castle. It was hard to believe one man owned all this.

His estate sprawled northeast of Wiesbaden, in the wooded hills of Taunus. Within its folds were roe deer and wild boar, and its streams ran full of fat fish. On a rise looking out to the Rhine stood the main complex of buildings, its manor house a restored double-winged Gothic castle, towered and turreted, with tunneled walls and colossal courts. Here lived the owner, close to nature and his Learjet and private landing field.

The helicopter had whirled in from the southeast, out of Frankfurt, to deposit César in the waiting limousine which whisked him off the Tarmac toward the financier's baronial home. There, he'd been swiftly shown to the study where the lord of the manor awaited him.

"To your return," his host said affably. He poured his usual measure of kümmel into a snifter and added a touch of goldwasser. Flecks of gold leaf shimmered in the glass. "Though I must admit to a certain curiosity."

César settled for brandy in a pony, one of a pair from the court of Ludwig the Mad. His eyes followed the financier back to his desk.

"You lied to me, Mr. Weber."

"Did I?"

"Your first lie was telling me there was no gold smelting at the Mauthausen camp, when the plant ran for more than two years. Streicher and Linge kept it running, Bock and Schirrmacher kept it secret, and Baur kept it quiet. No doubt others were involved, all disposed of long ago. You and Francke handled SS headquarters."

Weber smiled a dark scowl. "That seems to account for all of us."

"Not quite," César said.

"And the second lie?"

"That the *Anvil* gold went to the SS underground. Here I was thinking your group stole some of it, a small part that wouldn't be missed, and hid it in a nearby lake. Now I see I wasn't ambitious enough. You had bigger dreams."

"What dreams?"

"You stole all of it."

Behind the sculptured desk of Italian marble, centered on a wall of superbly carved wood panels, hung a huge gold-framed portrait showing a regal figure in proud stance, confident and filled with moral purpose. A halo of reddish light glowed about the head. The face was strong, stern. A banner lined the bottom: *Ein Volk, ein Reich, ein Führer.*

Hitler!

César read it again and again, bold white letters on a black border. He'd found the portrait that commanded Himmler's office through the Nazi years, the painting that gave Kayser his excuse in Paris. Now if he could only find his darts.

"You're seriously suggesting that seven of us—"

"Not seven," César interrupted. "There were eight of you."

"Eight?"

"He was the most important."

"Who?"

"The only one who could've carried off such a scheme, your uncle Heinrich."

The rest of the room reflected the financier's passion for opera. Autographed prints of operatic greats lined the walls while stacks of records occupied every flat surface. Music played constantly, especially Wagner and Verdi. A generous contributor to companies from Wiesbaden to Vienna, Weber had been named opera's man of the year in 1971 by the newsweekly *Stern.* It was his favorite tribute.

"Like most truth seekers," he now told César, "you're more wrong than right. Yes, there was some gold smelted at Mauthausen but it was only part of the treasure. Most came from trading and other sources, largely through me." The voice rang with sincerity. "And yes, the gold was hidden in a lake but just until it could be safely channeled into Switzerland."

"Why lie about it?"

"Would the details make any difference? The war's over, the gold's gone. It kept thousands of SS free—men who merely did their duty —and helped their families survive. It even helped the German economy. You must know that ninety percent of the SS stayed right here at home."

While they talked, the supreme second act of Wagner's *Götterdämmerung*—with the maddened Brünnhilde seizing the point of

Hagen's spear and swearing an oath to Siegfried's death for false-hood—surged through the speakers.

"And Bock?" César asked.

"Like you, he got the idea we'd kept some of the gold; that we all cheated him somehow. He demanded money and I refused."

"And now you want him killed."

"If he killed the others—"

"He'll come after you."

"I'm the only one left."

"What about Müller?"

"Müller's dead."

César nodded. "The East Germans say he didn't go over to the Russians in '45. Where'd he go?"

"South America."

"Tell me about it."

"What's to tell?" His stare speared César. "He was an SS general who escaped."

The inspector put down his empty glass. "So as far as you're concerned *Anvil* is just a memory and the war—"

"The war's over," Weber repeated.

"Not yet, I'm afraid."

César suddenly felt himself one of Wagner's troubled mortals, the light and dark sides of his psyche locked in fearful battle. At least the outcome would bring order out of chaos, he told himself, forgetting that in Wagner it had also brought about the twilight of the gods.

*   *   *

Someone like that was a danger, the financier informed his startled listener. He had only one goal: to destroy whatever he could. He would say anything, and do anything. He knew too much for his own good. He couldn't be trusted, he . . .

". . . can't be trusted," the man now told the other. "He's out to get Weber."

He glanced around furtively as he spoke of César's threat. A Jew who hated Germans, wanted to kill the golden goose, maybe ruin their lives. Something had to be done about such a threat, would be done. Not yet, but soon. Very soon.

"When the time comes," the financier said to the man, "kill him."

"Kill him," said the man to his partner.

* * *

César wandered through Wiesbaden, walking off his anger. Someone was going to get away with murder, and the gold too. Weber was lying, of course, all lies. He had the gold and Bock had the gun. A stalemate, César decided, that he was supposed to break by killing Bock.

But where did the Israelis come in?

In the hotel he took the elevator to the fourth floor. The hallway had flowered wallpaper and brown carpeting with a bristly nap. TV monitors stared from ceiling fixtures at both ends of the hall. In the middle was an exit door that swung outward; someone used it as César passed. Two doors down he turned the lock and went inside.

She was standing in the dark of the room. He thought at first of a vision, then a statue. Her throat stirred.

"The clerk let me in," Jacqueline said. "Your wife arriving before you got back. I convinced him."

"You seem able to convince men of anything."

"But not you."

"Does it matter?" César asked. He heard his heart, felt his blood. It was madness, a disease. He hated her, he—

"Perhaps if we had met sooner . . ." said the siren.

She touched his face with her fingertips, warm against his skin. This is God's will, César told himself, and the only thing they had in common. Body heat pulled him forward, already out of control. She buried her head in his shoulder.

"Fantasy," she murmured. "Every man should get his fantasy once before he dies."

Her body was electric, fusing his. He stood helpless in her design.

"Am I going to die?" he asked.

* * *

Nicole was a river that carried him softly to the sea.

Jacqueline was an ocean that swept him far from shore.

"I'm not really French or German," César said. "I don't belong anywhere."

"You belong here," Jacqueline urged, her hands on his back.

"What about tomorrow?" César felt himself drowning, losing her.

"We've already had all our tomorrows," she whispered.

"Not all."

"Stay." She held him in her.

* * *

The Gestapo boss was dead, according to his nephew. A heart attack, sudden and massive, his mouth sprung open in a paroxysm of pain, his fingers bent into claws. He had died in his bed, in the bedroom of his home near Garmisch-Partenkirchen close to the Bavarian Alps, high walls of rock and ice that separate Germany and Austria.

César had flown there after Wiesbaden, to stare at the chalet in which Müller had lived and died under an assumed name after his return from South America.

In Garmisch César spoke with the police doctor, who recalled the death two years earlier. No autopsy was done since he'd been under a physician's care for heart trouble. Strictly routine.

Not routine to César, who didn't believe in coincidences or even in convenient heart attacks. Weber had him killed, and the inspector knew why. Gold!

Except Müller would've been on his guard with any man. But a woman?

"Yes, there was someone with him," the doctor remembered with a laugh. "In his bed, apparently, which is how he died. Too much"—the voice winked—"exertion for an old man."

"And the woman?"

"Young and beautiful, according to the servant. German, of course. They never found her; probably married. She couldn't have helped anyway. It was an obvious heart attack."

César saw instead succinylcholine chloride and Jacqueline Volette who spoke six languages, including perfect German.

"Was the body buried?"

"Cremated, in Munich."

César left town on the wings of paranoia.

* * *

On his way to Munich, César faced the truth of his obsession. It wasn't only Bock. Jacqueline Volette was homicidal, too; she'd killed her sister and Linge, maybe even Müller. Who else? Smiled at them and then calmly pushed them or poisoned them or whatever beautiful and cultured killers did. She'd fooled César for a long time. No, that wasn't true; he had allowed himself to be fooled, and he'd played the part well. Now he was an actor, too, pretending there was no blood on her hands as she held him, closing his eyes to the greed in hers. The money was all she saw. "Don't trust her," Weber had warned.

"Why tell me?"

Weber's face folded into a cruel mask. "You want her for yourself," he said. "A female version of Bock."

"But you bought her."

"Kill him and you can have her," Weber urged.

"Then you'll have both of us."

"And you'll have me."

César had marveled at the man's audacity. Weber was a gambler behind his slick business facade, a reckless empire builder and quite mad. If Hitler had a son, he would be Hans Weber. Both used people as pawns in a contest where lives didn't count. It was all a matter of power, and the triumph of the will. César had sat in Weber's study, with Wagner's music swelling, and stared at Hitler's portrait.

"We have to help each other," Weber was saying. "You know Bock's a killer. There are a dozen dead already, you say. Yet all you want is to bring him to trial? You can't hold a man like Bock. Only death can claim him."

"And for that you offer me fame and now the woman. But where's the money?" César asked, curious. "Isn't wealth the third part of the devil's deal?"

"All you want."

"So the hunter merges with his prey, a mating of instincts."

"It's Bock you're hunting, not me."

"It's Bock I hunt but you I see."

"Then look again. Without me you'll never see him."

"Never?" César closed his eyes, saw himself shoot Weber where he sat. Then Bock would have to come after him, for wrecking his vengeance. "You're not like Hitler after all, Mr. Weber. He would've known that all roads lead to Rome, or even here to Wiesbaden. A warrior takes only the high road, right? You should know better than that. I'll meet with Bock and kill him if I have to. Then I'll come for you."

"Then we will help each other," Weber rejoiced. "By tomorrow things should be arranged. Bock and I will meet—and you'll take my place. I'm the only one who can help you."

"You have no choice," Kussow had said. "Help us."

Who had sent Jacqueline to him, to fuel his fantasy, soften him up? César would gladly kill Weber just for that. For that alone.

No longer the hunter, he was now running with the wolves.

TWENTY-FOUR

The monument to the Madonna stood in the center of the Marien-platz. Strollers rested in rows of white chairs while shoppers scurried like nervous birds. Deep below the gray flagstones of the Munich square, steel railway cars still went to Dachau.

*　*　*

Fifteen years a hunter had given César certain survival skills that sometimes worked. Or put another way, his fifteen years had earned him only two bullet wounds, a few stabs, several concussions and a fistful of bruises. On the other hand, he was still alive.

After a quick lunch in the train station he changed money, ac-cepting a computer printout that showed what he gave, the rate of exchange, and what he received. What he'd received was five deutsche marks too much but no one believed him; he spoke German with a French accent.

On the way downtown to police headquarters, he studied the peo-ple. Only the Nazis reared up on their hind paws and devoured human flesh until they were sated.

Why had Jacqueline come to him? César asked himself. Was it just Weber?

In the business district the lunch hour brought people into the streets. They wandered and held hands and nuzzled, as if they were in Paris. Imagine!

Traffic moved slowly, a sign of prosperity. The department stores worked feverishly and clerks faced the onslaught, not all of them bravely. At selected corners, private ambulances stood ready for any emergency; sickness meant money, a growing business.

He listened to passersby. Every word was conspiracy and where more than two gathered was a plot.

At a construction site men moved earth like it was water. Other men moved the water.

His view was of gabled roofs and cathedral spires and crenelated ramparts. There was neo-Gothic stonework everywhere.

He passed an open stall filled with *Weisswurst* and *Schweinshaxen.* The white sausages or roast pork knuckles? asked the smiles of those who served. César resisted and walked on.

Here people ate joyously, greedily. In public! Open bags and puffy cheeks and heads thrown back for liquids. Grease paper and sandwich paper, with tissue paper for fruit. Fingers were licked as part of the meal. Local custom, César told himself; in Italy they broke glasses.

He watched someone impale himself on a sandwich shaped like a submarine.

Germans were thick through the middle and had barrel chests. There was a frantic conviviality about their overeating, almost a mania, as if they had to eat their weight each day or die.

What they ate was seductively simple, most of it related to other animals.

What to think of such eaters? And drinkers? Possessed, possibly. Almost two hundred liters of beer were consumed annually for each Munich resident.

At the huge Hofbräuhaus beer hall in 1920, the leader of the National Socialist Party got up a week after St. Valentine's Day to give his belated love letter to the German people. It called for mass murder and the rape of the world. Maybe Hitler was drunk, César thought, and never fully sobered up. But why did they keep serving him?

Buses carried people who didn't want to walk. Streetcars carried those who couldn't. Flowers grew between the cracks.

He neared police headquarters and the drab law-enforcement complex. As everywhere, justice was forced to work through gray bunting. Being blindfolded, César imagined, had its drawbacks.

The building boasted a guard and directory; César found the section he sought and followed his instincts. Detectives were paid to ask questions of people who didn't like to answer; they understood secrecy and never lived on the ground floor.

Jacqueline Volette had been with Bock out of passion, and was with Weber out of greed. Or were they the same thing?

Roses were red. So was blood.

* * *

The homicide commander introduced César to Max and Bernie, who would work with him. The commander had talked to César by phone, and he'd told the two detectives what little he knew of the case.

"I wish there was more"—César spread his arms—"but all we can do is wait for Bock to show himself."

"Where's he now?"

"My guess is he's still in Munich."

"How you know he was here at all?"

"He killed Otto Francke."

Max and Bernie exchanged glances as their superior cleared his throat. He had other duties so he would leave César in capable hands, which meant he had no intention of getting involved in anything that included Hans Weber. The man could pick up the phone and destroy him, ruin his career. As far as he knew, Bock was wanted for a series of French kills; no evidence existed for any murders on German soil. Luckily, police cooperation between nations was better than on the political level. The killer would be caught and packed off to Paris, along with the Frenchman. And good riddance.

"You've been told about the alleged accidents?" César asked when the commander left. "One of them happened here last month."

"You speak good German," Bernie said. He was a burly man with a florid complexion and a body that needed exercise. "I checked out Altomünster myself. Nothing strange about it. Streicher was alone when something went wrong with the baling machine. He got down to take a look and the damn thing started up. It happens."

"Happened last year over in Parsdorf." Max was small and wiry, with deep-set eyes and cropped hair. "Fell off a tractor and got chopped to nothing." He looked at Bernie. "Remember that one?"

"How could I forget?"

"It was Bock," César insisted. "All of them, but made to look like accidents."

"Let's forget them for now," Bernie told César. "You're here to get Bock for the French jobs, right? We're here to help you. That's all we're interested in. If he shows his face we take him. Terrific. Everyone's happy and you get to go home."

"With Bock," Max said. "Then if it turns out you're right about those accidents, well"—he winked at Bernie—"we'll know you already have him. What could be fairer than that?"

"But you don't believe it."

"Doesn't matter," Bernie said. "We know enough."

"Don't need to know anymore," Max added.

"Just where he is."

"What's important," Max said, "is that you understand you have no authority here, no privileges. You can't even carry a gun. Whatever you do is through us. We'll handle the heavy stuff on Bock."

"And Weber?" César asked. "Will you handle him too?"

There was an uncomfortable silence until Bernie finally said, "We feel Weber can take care of himself. In Germany our millionaires can do almost anything they want, otherwise what's the point in killing yourself to become one? Now, if someone else tries to kill them—" He let the thought hang.

"You think Bock wants to kill Mr. Weber?" Max asked.

"Right now I'm more worried," César answered truthfully, "about Weber wanting to kill Bock."

Max threw up his hands as Bernie walked around the desk, slumped in the chair. "Suppose you tell us all about it"—his face had the first flush of irritability—"this plan for bringing Bock into the open."

* * *

In the hotel César turned on the television and arranged his thoughts. Bock would have to die; the Nazi was his other obsession and he had no choice. He paced the room down the length of carpet, his feet measuring the meters. Neither did Weber; Bock knew about the gold and would always be a threat. The door had a brass bolt; the window was sealed. But so did he.

A bellboy brought the package he had sent himself from Paris. César tipped him and opened the wrapping, took out the waterproof bag. He carried it into the bathroom and put it in the toilet tank. The tub was cemented to the floor so he couldn't hide anything behind it. The pipes were placed inside the walls so he couldn't hang himself.

* * *

They sat in a corner of the squad room dismissing the things he told them about Weber, their eyes widening in apprehension. A wooden bench ran along the wall under a cork board full of neighborhood news. The chairs were kitchen castoffs with curved armrests, standard police issue. Only once had César encountered comfort, even opulence, in a police station—hunting the Bordeaux Creeper in Istanbul—but that was then and this was Max behind the mask.

"There is no gold," he argued. "We checked with the Austrians and they found nothing in the lakes. So why would Weber want Bock dead?"

"Then he moved it."

"Then Bock wouldn't know where it was. Still no problem."

"You must be crazy," Bernie told him. "A man like Weber wouldn't need to hire a cop to kill Bock. So he's good. So are others. Besides, he's no threat. If he kills the golden goose, he doesn't have a shot at the gold you say Weber's hiding. You see?"

"I'm not crazy," César said.

* * *

He tried Paris again, got through this time to Alphonse who'd checked on Müller with the Nazi hunters. Klaus Barbie was in Bolivia and Mengele in Paraguay, along with thousands of SS, but there was no word about Müller.

"But Barbie returned recently from Austria, where his daughter lives. You think he could be mixed up with Bock?"

César didn't see how, even though they'd met in Lyon in 1942. More likely Weber, with his connections, knew Barbie. Could he have sent the gold on to South America? And now enlisted Barbie's aid in getting rid of Bock? Anything was possible with that kind of money.

"Inspector?"

"Not even any rumors?"

"Nothing."

"Müller's dead," César decided. "What about Jules?"

"De Gaulle's hatchet man in Algeria," Alphonse reported. "Since then he's shuffled through several ministries, but wherever he went heads rolled."

"Now I know," César said.

Junot had been his protégé in Algeria; there was some talk the police might be involved in his death. Maybe even Homicide in the person of Inspector Dreyfus, who'd often been at odds with Junot.

"What's it mean?" Alphonse asked.

It meant César was hopefully a dead Jew, as far as Jules and the ministry were concerned. They wanted some of the gold, or at least a guarantee it wouldn't end up in East Germany—the Americans were behind that. If all went wrong, he was the perfect scapegoat.

"Should I say we spoke?"

César told him to say nothing.

* * *

The next time they came at him with even more insistent denials, and César kept repeating the connections between Bock and Weber until he saw it was useless. Then he saw something else.

"Nazis!" he gasped. "Weber was a Nazi. You think I'm trying to get him for that, so you can't see a thing I'm saying. No wonder he wasn't worried what I'd do."

Bernie and Max sat with closed mouths, their lips thin as penciled lines. Only their eyes raved.

"You really are all the same"—César couldn't help the bitter laugh—"and I'm no better."

* * *

"You should have stayed home, Inspector." The BND operations chief was disappointed. "There is no gold."

"There's no gold in Austria," César said. "That's not the same thing."

"Tell it to Bock, if you can find him."

"Bock's here somewhere, waiting to see Weber's money."

"If we can help," the agent said. He reached down to a drawer. "Care for some?"

"Can you help?"

He poured into a glass with fluted stem. "Sure?"

César watched him drink, smack his lips. He poured another, downed it, put the bottle back. "A private—celebration," he burped. Smiled, his face reddening. "No, we can't."

"But you can share in the gold if we find it."

"It would be German gold and this is Germany."

"It's Nazi gold."

"Why quibble?" His eyes were roller bearings. "What about Bock?"

"Weber wants him dead, offered me the job. Which doesn't make sense if there's no gold. He says Bock's crazy. You think he's crazy?"

"Like a fox."

"That's what I told them here. They think I'm crazy."

"They think you're dangerous." The voice was a warning. "They think you're out to get one of their heroes. Watch yourself with them."

"We're talking about police."

"You're talking about money, and money buys police."

"We're not all like you people," César snapped, surprised at his outburst.

"If we can help in any way." The operations chief pressed a button on the desk.

*　*　*

Bernie dropped by with words of conciliation—and to make sure César was comfortable.

"Very nice here, clean. The management doing their best for you? If you were a little higher"—he looked out the window—"you could almost see the Alps. Beautiful. So things are going pretty well. Some of us think you might be right about Bock. But Weber's the one in danger, now even more."

"What danger?"

"We went back over Streicher's stuff, out at his house," Bernie said. "In his album we found a photo of four men standing by a lake. Three of them are already dead, all separate accidents in the past few months. Those odds are bad enough, like you say, but the fourth man—"

"I have the same photo," César said. "It's Bock."

"It's Weber."

* * *

The sun lazied overhead, its rays painting Munich in a yellowish cast. There was activity in the hall as guests left and others arrived. The cleaning crews went from one room to the next, models of swift efficiency. César thought of himself trapped in Germany, a Jew in a Gentile *kibbutz*.

On the street, cars pulled up to curbs to discharge passengers as lights flashed in chromatic sequence at the corners. Well-dressed men walked confidently across hotel lobbies.

Where was the *Anvil* gold?

* * *

The Israeli Wrath of God hit teams used long-barreled Berettas with special Parker-Hale silencers.

Zeev gave his weapon a final check and carefully placed it in the black briefcase, as did David. Downstairs they were met by their driver. It was fifteen minutes to the hotel.

The Mossad death squads were formed in the wake of the Munich Olympics massacre of eleven Israeli athletes and the Tel Aviv airport slaughter in which Palestinian-backed terrorists gunned down twenty-six and wounded seventy-seven. When Golda Meir announced to the Israeli parliament that henceforth anti-Jewish terrorists would be eliminated wherever found, she was heralding the wrath of God.

The two Israeli agents had first worked together a year earlier, in a try for Mengele in Asunción. The villa was ten rooms on two floors with a porch in the rear, set well back from the road and protected by clumps of trees and a six-foot wall. The driveway veered to the right and ended at the house in a circular flourish of white stone; its center gate was closed and presumably locked.

They had pulled into a nearby clearing scouted earlier, the doors left open. In the dark the four Israelis looked like demented woodsmen with their green ski masks and camo flak jackets over bulletproof vests. They moved noiselessly, using hand signals. In their right pockets rested their weapons, the pockets enlarged to allow the weapons to be brought up firing. The sawed-off-shotgun technique taught in the Mossad always aimed at the belly, a much bigger target than the head and with the heavier magnums almost always fatal.

Over the wall, two teams twenty meters apart. Nearing the house they saw no one. Lights gleamed and Zeev found Mengele's room. He motioned to David: corner window left. Slowly they worked their way to the porch, one, another, three, four. Still separated, each man covering the other, point and flank.

At the windows Zeev made his final decision as team commander. Storm or stealth? On his signal they stormed into the house, guns drawn. In seconds David was up the stairs, Zeev at his heels. Mengele's door was blasted open on the run, with David working the silenced Uzi. Zeev was first in the room, tightening on the trigger. It was all trained motion and second nature, a skill raised to an art. The eye, the brain, the finger working together. Find, affirm, pull. Bang! In the belly. He'd done it a thousand times in his head, in his sleep. It was an extension of him, his arm. Nothing went wrong with his arm. Everything went wrong.

No one was in the room.

The house was empty. Not a man, nobody. The lights still burned, the clocks ran, the meters turned. Outside the trees still lifted their limbs to the heavens where the stars continued to shine. Only the earth had stopped moving, and suddenly grown cold.

The Auschwitz angel of death had been somehow warned, and was gone for good.

Now in Munich, the car pulled up to the hotel curb to discharge the two well-dressed men who strode confidently across the lobby to the elevator.

* * *

César was ready to leave when the knock came. Perfect timing, he told himself as he opened for the cleaning woman. The gun changed his mind, a Beretta at his head. The man motioned him to silence. The other, younger, closed the door. Their search was quick, thorough. Afterwards they walked through the hall—César in the middle with his hands in his jacket pockets—to the exit door and down the stairs. Crossing the lobby attracted no attention, a trio of businessmen with briefcases. The car was waiting; César sat in the back with the older man, a study in silence.

Ludwigstrasse was a wide swatch of prewar buildings that eventually turned into Leopoldstrasse and led to the heart of Schwabing, the city's bohemian quarter. As they drove north César studied his captors. The leader had small sad eyes in a narrow triangular face, a Mediterranean cast. There were no wasted movements, a professional. The other was taller, sturdier, with lighter hair and skin. His eyes were larger, too, and he flicked them more often in the rearview mirror. César saw him as less predictable, the weaker of the two, but no amateur.

A series of turns in the quarter took them to Schraudolph Street and a four-story building near the end of the block. They quickly marched César up the stairs to a second-floor apartment in the rear, darkness blanketing the hallway. David used a key to open the door and his companion followed César into the kitchen, the gun waving him forward. "Through there," Zeev said.

Upholstered furniture lined the walls, set pieces in deep pile. It was all turn of the century, as far as César could tell, a gilded age. The third room yielded beds with filigreed headboards and dressers on fluted feet. At the back was the largest of the box rooms, filled with opaline vases on delicate end tables and mirrors with gilt frames and hinged cabinets of books bound in leather, or what looked like leather to him. There was a miasma of decadence about the room, the whole apartment—César felt it—an atmosphere of decay, an emanation of death. Or was it just that everything smelled so old? In the far corner between the two sets of windows, a wild beast suddenly yowled and Yishay Kussow stroked its fur in reassurance.

"Cats," he smiled up at César, "are very jealous, would you believe? Like people, they resent intrusion."

César stood rooted in amazement.

"Shin Bet here is perfectly reasonable until his space is invaded," Kussow said. "Then he attacks, but always in defense. Does that sound familiar to you? Come, sit where I can see you better." He indicated the chair on his left. "My eyes," he sighed. "They tell me I might go blind someday and I tell them someday I won't be here. They'll see." He went back to stroking the cat. "Animals are great mimics of what we feel. Did you know that an octopus shows all our emotions? Anger, fear, jealousy—even playfulness. Shin Bet shows them all, too—but if given the chance he'd also eat the octopus."

"But this is Germany!" César had crossed the room in a daze.

"So I vowed never to return"—Kussow nodded sadly—"and here

I sit. An old man's senility, you might think. Or maybe the wandering Jew who can't break the habit. Could even be"—he shooed Shin Bet off his lap—"I'm here to talk to you." He appraised César as a jeweler would a watch. "You look better than the last time we met. The hospital didn't suit you."

"Neither do guns with silencers."

"For which I apologize." A frown. "They feared you would tell your people in Paris, without realizing the consequences. I told them a show of force wouldn't impress you."

"Mossad?"

"Let's say they are not Hashemite Bedouins."

He removed his glasses and reached for a newspaper. César had watched them being cleaned many times, always with paper products. Vegetable fibers cleaned best, according to Kussow, but the wood pulp of tabloids was the cheapest. He had long ago learned to live with the garbled letters of newsprint constantly pressed on the glass, insisting this did not distort his view of the world.

"You're helping them," César said. "Why would they want you to talk to me?"

"Maybe because you can help too."

"Why should I?"

"It's your country."

"My country is France."

"But if something went wrong, where would you go?"

César looked around helplessly.

"Not here," Kussow gasped.

"Didn't you tell me my mother was German?"

"And thirty years ago they killed her for being a Jew. Now they just don't like you. Before the war Munich had forty thousand Jews; today it's about five thousand. They don't advertise for more." Kussow rubbed the square of paper over the glasses. "But you still have Israel if things go wrong. Jews from anywhere in the world can enter Israel. It's the law."

"It's Bock, isn't it? They're here to kill him."

"More than Bock, I'm afraid. You insist on seeing this"—he folded the used paper and stuffed it in his breast pocket—"as a case of bringing a killer to justice. But it never was that simple. Is your justice so primitive it sees only the hunter and hunted? This case was

always about gold"—took up another sheet and tore off a square—
"and a people's will to survive."

"The Jews?"

"The Israelis."

Kussow held the glasses up to the light, frowned, laid the paper
aside and rubbed the lenses briskly on the lapel of his jacket. "So, I
am no longer blind." He lifted himself out of the chair. "Come, we'll
walk and continue our storytelling."

The pair was gone, the kitchen empty. César strolled past shops
and cafés with Kussow glancing around as if expecting, dreading, a
hand on his shoulder. Young people were everywhere, fluid with
conversation. The section had a vitality César quickly felt, but there
was no charm or beauty. Its streets were straight, the buildings flat,
and he began to sense his distance from home.

Toward the end of the block they entered a restaurant with a
kosher sign on the window, found a table in the rear. More men than
women were at the tables, none of them alone. César couldn't blame
the Jews of Munich for sticking together. His host recommended the
flanken or pickled *fleish* and César included some schmaltz herring.
With *flanken?* César confessed himself an adventurer, which meant
he was hungry. The drink was beer; this was Munich. Light or dark
didn't matter to César, who hated beer. He promised himself a
double dose of *vin blanc* when he got home. If he got home, he
thought moodily.

"Schwabing is a little like the Left Bank," Kussow was saying.
"The student quarter and the artist colony as well as the commercial
sex center. It's also a prized residential area, which makes for a mix.
Crazed husbands rape respectable students or the crazed students
turn respectable families into drug addicts, take your pick." César's
herring arrived. "You know what you're doing with that? So, nothing changes here. I lived in Munich as a boy, before we moved to
Berlin. I have fond memories of Schwabing; saw my first young lady
here as a matter of fact, a student, took my breath away. I told her
I'd never forget her body. She said she'd forget mine quick enough."
He laughed at the memory. "I think I was too young for her."

"What about the gold?" César asked.

"There is no gold. Didn't Hans Weber tell you that? You say you
went to see him. He should've told you."

"He did."

"Well?"

"How could the Bock case be about gold, as you claim, if there is no gold? And how could it have anything to do with the Israelis?"

"How could it not? The gold's gone and the country exists. Think about it."

Kussow's borscht disappeared in flurries of silverware as César wrestled with the final piece of the puzzle. The killings came out of men wanting gold, wanting to hide it. Or hide what happened to it? César held on to the thought as the truth began to reveal itself with stunning and cumulative logic, much like a royal flush opening in a player's hand.

"The gold is gone"—César strained as if giving birth—"because the Israelis"—*of course*—"they already have it!"

"Had it."

His face fell.

"They traded it," Kussow confided.

"For what?"

"For Israel." He dipped gingerly into the pickled *fleish*. "Do you think countries grow on trees? Like money"—Kussow smiled at his *bon mot*—"they have to be paid for. The Jews carved a nation out of nothing, fought odds of a hundred to one. And they won! They beat Goliath, not with slingshots but money for guns and people. There was no Marshall Plan for Israel, remember. In 1945 all you had in Palestine were the Haganah, which specialized in illegal immigration, and the Irgun and Stern groups. And sitting right in Jerusalem was the Grand Mufti screaming for the extermination of every Jew in the Middle East. Can you imagine what it did to the Jews coming over from Europe to hear the word *extermination* again? I remind you that in thirty years no Israeli has ever suggested exterminating Arabs. When Chaim Weizmann called for the creation of a Jewish state in Palestine, they laughed him out of London. Over our dead bodies, they told him. What they meant was he'd better get the guns."

"But how did they get the gold?" César demanded.

"You really should try this," Kussow said. "I think it's better than in Paris. No more beer? A true Frenchman. If you look at the menu" —he talked between forkfuls—"you can see this place is not kosher but kosher style, which is almost meaningless. They even serve milk products with the meat. Did you know, by the way, that all fruits and vegetables are kosher? But not all fish, only those with fins and scales. Most birds are out, too, even their eggs. As for animals, they have to chew their cud and have a split hoof, so no pigs or horses. Not only that, the animals have to be killed in a certain way and the meat specially prepared. Kosher is probably the toughest injunction man's come up with yet. Who says it's a joke being a Jew?"

Kussow reached for his coffee.

"What I mean is they have a kosher sign and no one complains." He poured in the cream. "After thirty years the Jews in Germany are still silent, even among themselves."

"No more than you," César growled.

"Not here." Kussow looked around, a stranger in a strange land. "Even tables have legs that listen."

On the way back Kussow told a story, "so you will understand what I'm going to say." It was 1918 and the British general Allenby took Palestine from the Turks in an overall desert victory made famous by Lawrence of Arabia. There were 400,000 Arabs in Palestine and 80,000 Jews. By 1939 the Jews were one-third of the population. After the war they expected the homeland promised them in the Balfour Declaration but the British, concerned over their oil supplies, wanted Palestine to remain predominantly Arab. Which was when the Jews began their illegal immigration on ships like the *Exodus,* running the British blockade. The resistance had started. By 1946 it was guerrilla warfare and by 1947 armed rebellion. In May 1948 the British finally pulled out and Ben-Gurion proclaimed the state of Israel. The next day five Arab armies attacked Israel's 650,000 Jews and the real war of independence was on.

"What's to remember," Kussow now reminded César, "is that in those three years between 1945 and 1948 the Jews came from rocks and spears to a fighting machine that defeated the combined armies of forty million Arabs. They had ten thousand rifles, six hundred machine guns and eight hundred mortars, a drop in the bucket. There were no artillery pieces or antiaircraft guns, no tanks, no planes or ships. To get them would take billions. The bravery was there, yes, but nobody gave anything for bravery; they wanted cash. There was no nation yet, no international credits, no political deals. Just some people with a foolhardy dream who needed every franc they could find."

Going up the steps Kussow tapped César's back with his finger.

"The whole world knows about the *Exodus* because it brought the Jews out of bondage. But what do you think paid for it? And for all the other ships? And the guns it took to create a new nation?" He was breathing hard by the top of the landing. "You see what I mean? Or are we both getting too old?"

César cursed the darkness of the hall. In Germany, he told himself bitterly, a displaced Jew discovers why there is no gold sought by a half-dozen countries, and a French inspector learns why six men are murdered. Kussow was right. Suddenly he felt a lot older.

"So now you want to know how the Israelis got the gold," Kussow said in the apartment. "I should think much of what I could say has already crossed your mind."

"Then my answer must have crossed yours."

"Let me try anyway," Kussow pressed. "I'd hate to think I came all this way for nothing."

He sat in the same chair, the cat again on his lap. "Hans Weber is a brilliant man," he began quietly. "Brilliant and obsessive, always a dangerous combination, as you know." The smile included César in the thought. "In 1945 he knew the Nazis could not come back. He also saw Germany had to rebuild swiftly or all of it would end up communist. The gold was no good to him; its origin would be quickly determined. One of the biggest treasures in history and he couldn't even claim a reward! The Austrians would take it in payment for what the Nazis stole; so would the Russians. Both would shoot him as well. On the Allied side he probably wouldn't get shot but there'd be nothing for him. Only one group would possibly pay for it and strangely enough, it was theirs anyway."

A door slammed nearby and eyes darted out of habit, the face a stab of fear. The voice, when it came, was even softer.

"Weber had contacts from the war and in early 1946 he met with Jewish leaders in Zurich and offered them a treasure that could help pay for their fight, about two billion dollars in gold. All he wanted for his trouble was fifty million. Can you imagine a worse pill for the Jews to swallow? Doing business with a Nazi? But they went for it; they wanted a country even more. Over the next few weeks the gold was taken secretly to Switzerland, and Weber got his bank account. The Swiss bankers could say nothing by law. The Nazi naturally wouldn't talk, and the Jews deemed it in their people's interests not to reveal anything about the gold. Weber evidently used his share to help rebuild West Germany." Kussow stroked the cat as he talked. "Now just so you don't think I'm raving, remember that in 1946 Hans Weber came out of nowhere waving millions and buying up everything in sight. No one knew where it all came from; there was talk of Russia or America. After a while he got so big the talk stopped. But that kind of money—in a country of economic collapse —had to come from somewhere." He bunched the animal's fur at the neck affectionately, then smoothed it out. "You have to ask yourself why," he urged.

"Jesus!"

"A good man but not God," Kussow sighed. "And neither are we. All we can do is pray for guidance."

In the afternoon shadows, César's eye began to see the room's mystery as well. No one lived here; it was a prop, the Munich drop for the Mossad.

"Thirty years is a long time," Kussow continued after a moment, "and Weber and the Jews soon went their separate ways. Then a few weeks ago the Nazi abruptly asked Israeli Intelligence for help. A man named Dieter Bock had somehow learned of the gold deal and was trying to blackmail Weber for half of his share to keep quiet."

"How'd Bock learn about it?"

"He was in on the original steal and supposedly stumbled onto someone who'd seen Weber with the Jews in Zurich." Kussow shrugged in disbelief. "Anyway, the Mossad wasn't particularly interested in what happened to *Herr* Weber and told him so. Which was when he told them about Heinrich Müller."

"Müller?"

"Weber's uncle, who controlled the *Anvil* gold. Or should I say stole it?"

"I told you that."

"You merely confirmed it. Weber had already confessed it." A hand gently lowered the cat to the floor. "Dieter Bock was part of the group and apparently so were those he killed."

"And the Mossad?" César asked.

"Everything suddenly changed. The Jews had been tricked in 1946, and that includes the intelligence agencies. Bad enough they had to deal with a Nazi moneyman who was returning what was rightfully theirs. Now they learned it was Müller who'd really pulled the strings. He was Weber's partner all along." Kussow looked grim.

"Heinrich Müller, who was responsible for more dead Jews than Eichmann ever dreamed of—Eichmann got his orders from Müller! —and more than anyone convicted after the Nuremberg trials. Now you begin to see the problem. Weber said this Bock threatened to tell about Müller's involvement in the gold deal. Who'd believe the Jews didn't know about Müller? They kept the gold a secret, didn't they? They needed it and so they took it. But to deal with the devil himself—?" Kussow shuddered. "You see? The world would believe the worst."

"Müller's dead," César stated flatly. "I think Weber had him killed."

"Probably. But it doesn't change the irreparable damage such a false story would do."

"You think the Jews would've taken the gold if they'd known about Müller?"

"Of course not," Kussow wheezed, "but who am I? There are political considerations, no doubt. Anyway, they want to end this threat once and for all; put Bock where he can't talk."

"They think he's in this alone?"

"What they think is with Müller dead, Weber decided to get rid of the others before they learned the truth about the deal and came after him. They were obviously told the gold went to the SS underground. Apparently nobody mentioned the fifty million that changed hands."

"So Weber got Bock to do his dirty work—"

"By telling him about Müller and promising him some of the money."

"Which he never intended to give."

"Naturally."

"And now they want me to kill Bock for them."

"No, they want you to kill Weber."

César's eyes clouded over. "That's funny, you know. Weber wants me to kill Bock. Who do you want me to kill?"

"That *is* funny. The Israelis are much better at it. What did you tell him?"

"I told him I'm listening, same as I'm telling you."

"Simply put, their men can't get near him and you can."

"What you mean is, there'd be hell to pay if anything went wrong."

"That, too, of course. Hans Weber is a very important man."

"So is Dieter Bock, at least to me."

"The hunter and the hunted," Kussow nodded. "Did you ever stop to think that all of you, even the Israelis and the Munich police, are reflections of one another, bound together in the chase? You don't really have a choice anymore, none of you." His finger wagged at César. "There is one difference, though," he urged. "Two of you were SS."

TWENTY-FIVE

Max and Bernie took César to dinner near the hotel, a rathskeller in the basement of an office building where heaping plates of German food were served.

"We hear the Israelis are interested in Bock," Max said. Knife and fork flying, he sat over mounds of meat. "You know anything about that?"

"Nothing," César lied. "Any trouble?"

"Not really," Bernie said. "It's happened before."

"Too much for my money," Max barked between bites. "Should stay where they belong." He ate, oblivious to Bernie's hard stare.

"There's been some friction between the department and the Israelis ever since the Olympics. They don't think we did enough," Bernie said, "or at least not well enough."

"What kind of friction?" César asked.

"Shit, we lost a man, too," Max snarled. "They weren't the only ones. And we killed most of the Arabs."

"Yeah, but the Israelis lost eleven," Bernie said. "Don't forget that."

"Damn Jews!"

"You mentioned friction," César prompted Bernie.

"After the massacre the Israelis started hitting back at the Black

September terrorists," Bernie explained. "Killed maybe a dozen so far. Ain't that right, Max? At least one was here. Some near misses, too, on Germans they suspect of helping the PLO." He shrugged. "We don't like anybody turning Munich into a shooting gallery."

"Especially the Jews." Max looked at César. "Nothing personal, you understand."

"He means the Israelis," Bernie said. "They all feel we owe them something. There was an incident about a year ago where they roughed up a few of our men. We had to teach them some manners and they didn't like it."

"They've been looking to make points ever since," Max added. "We figure this Bock thing might be it. Are you sure you haven't heard anything?"

"Not us exactly. It's the department. There's a special unit they got now to go after foreign agents."

"But most is with the Jews and the Arabs." Max wiped some gravy from his shirt. "More than half from what I hear. Just the Jews and Arabs," he repeated mechanically. "Makes you wonder."

"Who told you more than half?" Bernie asked.

"You know Feidler in North Homicide? He worked with them for a while."

César picked at his pork, thinking of Kussow and the two Israelis. The police probably didn't know about the apartment or they'd have knocked by now.

"I'm so hungry I could eat a boiled Italian," Max enthused.

"They're nothing special," Bernie argued. "All they can do is that spy stuff. Give them a good murder and they couldn't find their ass in a circle."

"I didn't say they were special, just that they deal with the Jews and Arabs a lot." Max eyed César suspiciously. "This Bock isn't a Jew or Arab, is he?"

"He was SS," César said.

"Not too many Jews in the SS," Max conceded.

"But if the Israelis do go after Bock," Bernie drawled, "then we got trouble."

"That's what I was saying before," Max yelped. "Suppose they go after Weber?"

"Then they got trouble."

"Trouble no matter how you look at it," Max grumbled.

"Did you tell this special unit what we're doing?" César asked.

"We're chasing a West German killer. What's to tell?"

"Maybe we should," Max said. "Just in case."

"Let them find their own," Bernie huffed. "They never give us a thing."

"That's a fact."

"Guys like that"—Bernie turned to César for support—"they're always looking for glory. Meanwhile, they'll fuck up everything in sight."

"So what about Bock?" Max asked. "It's still on for tomorrow?"

*   *   *

César wasn't sure what to expect from the two detectives. They obviously found him a nuisance, maybe even dangerous as West German Intelligence had said. At least one of them hated Jews. Trying for Bock was fine but suppose something went wrong?

What would they do?

Going up in the elevator, César kept his tongue pressed against the roof of his mouth so he couldn't scream. The rage and anxiety were taking their toll.

Something else, too. He began to sense a much bigger trap, a spider's web with himself the fly.

*   *   *

Jacqueline came to him as she had promised, in the dead of night and full of life.

When she laughed he listened to the music, when she spoke he heard only the sound of her voice. Nothing else mattered. They would never be together like this again, César was certain of that. A murderer and a fool didn't deserve anything, he told himself, not even each other. But only a fool would refuse.

In her arms he lost his rage. She'd come to him once because she had to, the fool thought, and now she came because she wanted to. Weber didn't win, not entirely, nor did Bock, and the fool filled himself with hope even as he saw how hopeless it was. He would lose, too.

"It will all be over soon"—she lay on him, whispering furiously— "and then we'll have money, gold. Enough to last a lifetime. Do anything we want, go anywhere. You and me. The gold . . ."

César listened to the siren's song, a rise of vapors. Her greed had blinded her and in her grief, inconsolable, she was luring him to his doom as well.

"There is no gold," he interrupted. "Weber lied to you. There never was any gold."

"He's got gold somewhere, he told me so."

"No. He gave it to the Israelis before you were born."

Jacqueline sat up. "To you," she said fiercely. "Weber lied to you. He lied to you," she repeated over and over.

* * *

They huddled in the bed, aliens in mind if not body. He kissed her shoulders, her breasts, her navel. His fingers traced her ribs down to the curve of her thighs, smoothed over the soft curls. Their legs touched, entwined. He rolled onto her, entered her as she raised herself to his thrust, clutching him tightly. In their frenzy neither combatant felt the other's blows, blurred motion in the heat of night.

* * *

"Now that I think of it," Jacqueline said as she propped herself against the pillow, "Hans might have mentioned something about the Israelis."

"Really?" César's head lay on the flat of her stomach. "What else did he mention?"

Jacqueline's eyes went wide. "Nothing I can remember." She paused thoughtfully. "I do seem to recall him saying he had too many partners, though. Does that mean anything?"

"I wouldn't know," César replied.

"It doesn't matter." She ran her fingers through his hair. "He has gold and I'll get some when it's over."

"You mean when I kill Bock." He raised his head. "That's why you're here, isn't it? To make sure."

"César," she squeaked, her mouth forming a perfect pout.

"Did you know the Israelis are after him?" He sat up, one foot over the side of the bed. "I'm not your only hope. Maybe you should sleep with them, too. Isn't that what Weber has you for? To sleep with those he wants something from? Who would refuse you? Look at me," he shouted, abruptly angry, "I know what you've done and here I am, like a cat lapping at cream. What does that make me? What's it make you?"

César couldn't control his sudden anger. "You dumped Bock because you figure Weber's a better bet. Or maybe the two of you were in it from the start, Weber pulling the strings and you pulling Bock. And now me."

"It wasn't like that at all," Jacqueline whined.

"Tell me how it was," César taunted. "It's always the same, isn't it? 'There was this man—' Except you were the one who always left, weren't you? No wonder you never got married. Bock's trouble was he started depending on you, a bad mistake. But maybe you made the same mistake with me now. I could kill you and squeeze gold out of Weber." His hand shot out, gripped her throat. "It would be easy" —the fingers tightened—"a release from your spell. But then I'd be the same as you, wouldn't I?" He opened his fingers, dropped his hand. "What a pair we make, and me the worst. I let you get away with it."

"He promised me gold," Jacqueline snapped. Fresh anticipation shone in her eyes. "I worked for it."

"You killed for it. Now I'm supposed to do the same."

He could barely catch his breath. Suddenly he was back on the floor of the slaughterhouse, bleeding to death, with Tobie standing over him. The friends he had, the lovers! He was forced to the window.

"It's mine and I want it." Jacqueline started to cry.

Was she sane? César was already thinking of psychiatric reasons for keeping her out of prison. Was he sane?

"I just don't want to be poor again," Jacqueline wept, "is that so bad?"

He saw the little girl on the outskirts of town, dressed in rags and living on roots, the face hollow with hunger, the body wasted. Then he saw her sister. "You didn't have to kill her," he said coldly.

"Bock made me do it."

César turned to her in the dark. "Always somebody else. Now it's Weber."

"What choice do I have?" Jacqueline asked petulantly. "He has what I need. Just this once and I'll be free." Her voice softened. "We'll be free."

"With Weber."

"Or without him."

He returned to the bed, drained of emotion and helpless in his ambivalence. Would she really kill Weber? Or would it be him?

She squirmed up to his side, her leg over his. An arm circled his waist. Her head lay at his shoulder, the hair soft against his skin, like a kiss.

He was alive to her touch and dead to the world. Through crescent eyes he watched her drift into sleep, the body losing definition. In the darkness he dreamed of death.

* * *

Later he stole out of bed into the bathroom, where he removed the waterproof bag from the tank and took out Bock's pistol. He sat on a chair next to her sleeping form, held the gun to her head.

Tomorrow he would use it.

"Let the Israelis take care of him," Kussow had said. "Bock's too good for you. When's the last time you fired a gun?" What he meant was for César to take care of Weber instead. "Jerusalem sees him as trouble, maybe even blackmail."

"For what?" César asked. "He already has everything."

"Everything's nothing to men like that?"—Kussow shook his head in dismay—"only more matters."

So it came down to murder, César realized. Spies liked to call it assassination or termination; terrorists called it execution. But he was a policeman and to him it was murder. He was paid to prevent it, not commit it. He had never murdered anyone in his life.

"God's giving you a chance to help your people," Kussow had told him. "You'll find your way."

Zeev and David would kill Bock at the meeting place before César even arrived. Afterwards he would phone Weber and insist on bringing him photos of the corpse. What could the man say? Bock was dead, the threat removed. He'd humor the inspector this one time, give him what he wanted. Not gold, of course, and not the woman either.

In the dark, César stroked Jacqueline's hair with the barrel of the gun.

How could he tell her the truth when all he saw were the metallic rings around her eyes? The gleam of gold was set deep within the iris, a mote that sparkled. There was no way to remove it; only death would release her. And him?

Bock was his responsibility. Maybe Weber, too. Who knew how

many people he'd destroyed? Nobody got that big without leaving a wake of destruction. Even the Israelis were intimidated.

In his mind, the idea grew like an evil fungus.

One was as much a killer as the other. César knew that a man born to be hanged is never drowned; neither Bock nor Weber would ever feel the bottom of the bathtub.

The financier had spent most of his life building an empire based on the *Anvil* gold and he wasn't going to give any of it away, not if he could help it. He'd also been involved in at least a half-dozen murders; Bock had called them the Anvil Chorus, according to Jacqueline, a listing of the dead. He'd already tried to have Bock killed, and now had called on the Israelis and even César. He would also want Jacqueline dead.

In sleep, her face was soft with innocence. The sleep of the dead, César thought. He pulled back the pistol and walked into the bathroom. Soon he lay down beside her, his eyes closed, his head oozing plots. In his dream he was on the autobahn headed west out of Munich when he met Weber in a clearing.

"Where are you going?" Weber asked.

"Home to Stuttgart," César answered.

Weber glared at him. "You are lying to me, César. You say you're going to Stuttgart to make me think you're going to Paris, when all along you really are going to Stuttgart. You're a liar, César!"

By the side of the road he stood silent in the stare of accusation, his life a conviction of lies, as Weber's hand slowly unraveled from its sleeve and turned into a golden gun.

* * *

"How far is it?" César asked on the way down to the monastery at Benediktbeuern.

"About fifty-five kilometers." Max was driving.

"It's near Bad Tölz," Bernie said. "Less than an hour."

The meeting place was Bock's pick. A twelve-hundred-year-old Benedictine monastery with woods and cloisters, away from Munich and Weber's money. It was an inspired choice.

"We hear you're an Israeli agent," Max said.

"At least he didn't say Jew," Bernie clucked in approval.

"A Jew general."

* * *

It was raining lightly, a steady misting that kept windshield wipers wet and the air soggy.

"This won't last," Max assured them.

"No problem," Bernie said. "We have plenty of time."

The meeting was for noon. A good hour for Bock, César thought. High noon was no place for snipers.

"I don't like this weather," Max complained.

"Change it."

Everything fit so far, which usually meant it was wrong. Jacqueline had left early, full of fright. Would it go all right? He had told her not to worry. What else could he say? She saw gold and he heard death.

César settled back into the soft cushion, the gun hard against his ribs. He closed his eyes. The Israelis would already be there, waiting for Bock. To even a score, pay a debt, kill him. Try to kill him. After that it would be his turn.

They drove past the wooded valley of the Isar river. Patches of fog hung low along the embankment.

"What about the Volette woman?" Max asked. "Where does she fit in?"

"How do you know about her?" César asked in return.

"We know you're screwing her, right?"

"Max is so tactful it's a pleasure working with him," Bernie said and turned to Max. "You're always so fucking tactful."

Bernie sat in back with César, who wished he were in front. Backseats were for the condemned and their executioners. He sloughed off the thought as more paranoia.

Maybe he should have told Jacqueline she was doomed, but truth often wore the robes of cruelty. Besides, he wasn't sure of anything. Weber could easily give her some gold and let her go, about as easily as he could give up Bock. Delusion always came disguised as truth.

She would be with Weber at the Munich opera that evening, his victory celebration. A big backer, he had a private box next to the stage.

The valley fell behind as the car raced down the concrete ribbon, a loud drizzle splashing over curved glass. The sound was rhythmic, a rain forest of the mind. César felt himself devoid of thought, an organic mass of spiraling tissue and helical codes and gaseous fluids. A river of motion in a dead sea. When the bottle surfaced he saw the face of the devil—inside the bottle, imprinted on the glass. He reached out to touch the devil's face and brushed his own; his hand jerked, his eyes flew open.

"So what are our chances?" Bernie asked after a while.

"He'll show," César said.

"I mean taking him alive."

"Is that what we're doing?"

The car kept a good pace, a machine for eating up kilometers.

"Let's get a plan," Max said eventually.

"What plan?" Bernie growled in annoyance. "We let him meet Bock, then we show our guns."

"That simple?"

"Why complicate it? Bock's one gun, we're two."

Max looked in the mirror. "He's killed some people."

"So have we."

"Suppose he brought help?"

Bernie turned to César. "Would he?"

"He doesn't need any."

"See?" Bernie said into the mirror.

Except for Jacqueline Volette, César thought. Bock got her to do what he couldn't.

Max lowered the window. "Real air," he exulted. "We're almost there."

"Already?"

"Bad Tölz. We have to check in with the local police."

At the station César stretched his legs while the others went inside. Marktstrasse had a curved sweep and slope to it. At the head of the street stood a warrior with raised lance. Gabled roofs formed a broken skyline.

He began to feel like the fly again. Max and Bernie were too calm about confronting a hired assassin of Bock's caliber. Didn't they have any imagination? Was Gerd Streicher calm when Bock walked into his field?

Someone was in for a surprise.

"All set," Max mumbled into the car.

"Just a formality," Bernie grunted.

"Won't bother us." Max pulled away smoothly.

Nobody followed them. César watched Max's eyes in the mirror. They never looked back.

Outside of town the road narrowed as deep country set in. Trees formed canopies of darkness; field fences ran to the road. The chalets became larger, more distant.

"A few minutes more," Max said cheerfully.

"We got time."

They passed through the hamlet of Bichl due south.

"Nice country," Bernie said. "Might settle here someday."

Max snickered.

"Somebody searched my room last night," César said, "while we were in the restaurant."

"Find anything?" Max asked.

"There's a gang working the hotels in the area. Ain't that right, Max?" He didn't wait for a reply. "What'd they take?"

"Nothing," César said. "Not a thing."

"Now that's strange." Max pumped his head up and down. "Isn't that strange, Bernie?"

The rain had dropped to a drizzle that steamed down only in spots. Was that good or bad? All César knew was the Munich police hadn't found Bock's pistol. He should've practiced over the years. Was the safety off? His hands were already sweating.

Max drove around to the side of the monastery, slowed to a stop. The motor died. They sat in silence, ten minutes early.

César closed his eyes and saw the death's head grinning at him. Weber had played him for the fool right from the start; he wanted Jacqueline dead, and now César as well. He had no choice. César was after him too. It was survival of the fittest, as with any hunt. The Israelis would kill Bock and then someone would kill him. Which one? Max hated Jews. Afterwards Jacqueline would be easy.

He should've figured it sooner; Weber's kind of money bought even the police.

They listened to a replay of a soccer match in Hamburg. There were winners and losers.

Outside, insects snapped up other insects as fast as pincers could close, mandibles crush.

César sat upright in the seat, thinking furiously. They'd known about the Israelis all along, were counting on them to finish Bock. Then they'd shoot him with Bock's gun, which was why they didn't want the local police around. But how far did the conspiracy exist? The Munich superiors? The Israelis? Paris?

His breath came soft as a caterpillar's cry.

Nothing mattered now—not the Israelis or even Bernie and Max —only Bock and himself, as he'd always known it would be. Even with the pistol he could do little against both of them. He had one chance, something he alone knew. The Israelis were no match for Bock; they were to him as seeds blowing in a strong wind. Now had come the time for falling by the wayside.

Bernie kicked open his door. "Let's go."

They walked through the monastery gate, César in the lead. To the left a long driveway led to the buildings, great slabs of gray stone forming massive religious monuments whose spires stretched to the sky, as if importuning the heavens for entrance. Behind them rose the first spurs of the Bavarian Alps in the distance. The church was double-towered, a Gothic holdover festooned with Bavarian Baroque. Nearby were the cloisters with their colonnade opening to a courtyard. The trio kept to the right at the tree line; beyond the buildings the path led farther into the woods, past manicured groves of lindenbaum. In small circular clearings, as if they had sprouted there from seedlings, were religious statues.

Max and Bernie had dropped behind César. Visions of flight danced in his head to funereal music; he wouldn't stand a chance. Gradually the brush became less dense and the sky more visible. Rounding a bend César saw the described meeting place some forty meters ahead. In a clearing gouged out of the forest stood a chapel, focal point for those on retreat. Momentarily unseen, he pulled out the pistol and threw it into the brush by a big scrub tree without breaking his stride. Soon he approached the chapel. There were benches on both sides, green pine planks bolted with cedar ties. On one of the benches sprawled Yishay Kussow.

He stared at César, the eyes wide and opaque. A red smear stained the front of his shirt, ran down his trousers to the ground at his feet. Propped under his chin was a branch whose other end had been wedged into the plank between his knees; the branch held his head high. His throat was slashed from ear to ear, jagged folds of flesh still wet with blood. Kussow's hands were flat on the bench, the palms down. He appeared to be rising, a body caught in motion.

César stood over his friend, his own fears forgotten. Kussow had come along anyway, made himself part of the death squad. His way of trying to even the score with those who destroyed his whole family. César had tried to warn him.

Max and Bernie came running up, thinking it was Bock. They seemed pleased with themselves until they saw the body.

"What the fuck!" Bernie exploded. "Who's this?"

"Someone who died a long time ago." César freed the branch, let Kussow's head fall onto his chest. "A ghost."

"You dumb Jew bastard," Max screamed. "You were supposed to—"

"Shut up, Max."

César saw the truth steal over Bernie's face. Bock wasn't dead. He licked his lips, hesitated. Now he knew, César thought. Now he realized what he was up against.

The click of the gun came from the doorway. They watched transfixed as the gun passed into the light, a silencer on the end of its snout. "In here," rasped the voice. The weapon waved them forward.

"You butchered him like an animal," César said as he filed past.

"Isn't that what you do to prey?"

The chapel was small, a dozen benches facing a tiny altar with a triptych of saints. On the red satin rug, a statue of Christ stretched out its arms; frescoes of the Last Judgment decorated the barrel vaulting.

Dieter Bock faced them on the altar. He wore a monk's habit, the sash corded on the left and the sleeves flapped over to form balloon cuffs. In his hand was a long-barreled .22-caliber Beretta automatic with a Parker-Hale silencer. César had seen it before. There still was hope.

Bock caught César's stare. "Israeli," he said. "They redesigned it for ammunition that fires only fifteen meters so they don't kill bystanders." He seemed amused.

"We're police officers," Bernie said, indicating himself and Max, "from Munich."

Bock kept his eye on César. "You've been tracking me." It wasn't a question.

"He came here to kill you," Bernie said. "Like his friend out there."

The eyes tightened. "What about that?"

"I told him you were too good but he wouldn't listen."

"Israeli?"

"Just a Jew from Dachau."

"I never went near Dachau," Bock hissed. "What about the Israelis?"

"I told them the same thing."

"They should've listened. One's still out there."

"He's after you," Bernie insisted, pointing at César.

"That's the truth," Max said to Bock. "Nothing we want you for —no warrants on you in Germany."

"Then why are you here?"

"To take care of him," Max admitted. "He was causing trouble for Mr. Weber."

"He wanted to get Weber," Bernie added, "arrest him for murder."

They still didn't understand, César thought.

"So he'd kill me if the Israelis didn't," Bock said, "and then you'd kill him."

"Oh no," Bernie assured him, "it ain't like that. We were all set to finish him off when he found the body. We have no reason to want you dead."

"No reason," Max emphasized. "We saved your life coming here."

"How was he going to kill me?"

"He's got a gun," Bernie said quickly. "A Walther PPK."

"Our men found it last night in his room," Max added. "In the toilet tank."

The Beretta shifted to César. "Take off your jacket."

"I have no gun," César said.

"He's lying," Max snarled.

"It won't work," Bernie shouted at César.

"I only came in Weber's place to talk to you," César said to Bock, "but I didn't know he'd already bought the police too. Looks like we both were fooled."

"Search him," Max screamed.

César removed his jacket and handed it to Bock, pulled out his pockets, rolled up his trousers. There was no gun.

"He's got to have it!" someone shrieked.

"Got to!" said the echo.

They faced each other, two hunters tracking the same scent all the way from Mauthausen to Munich, from Paris to Frankfurt and Wiesbaden. Only they had known the struggle, or could share the resolution. César held Bock's gaze, fed it his thoughts—not his thoughts, his instincts. Felt the other's in return, the wolf's desperation. They had that in common, too.

Bock's eyes flickered as Bernie and Max dissolved in a blur of motion, their hands clawing at survival.

Bernie was dead when his body hit the floor, shot between the eyes; falling, his head struck Christ's feet and rolled onto the rug. Max's fingers actually touched his gun before he crumpled to the altar's steps, a bullet in his brain. Bock's gun swerved back to César. Not a hair moved on his hand, not a finger trembled. Only the eyes had changed, the pupils dilated; César saw the excitement of the kill. It was what he lacked, would never have. Bock would always beat him.

"Where'd you dump my gun?" Bock demanded. "I know you brought it."

"In the woods. It wouldn't have helped against both of them."

"So you left it up to me." Bock bent down, scooped Max's pistol from its holster. "You're just like Weber," he growled. "Always depending on others to do your killing." He snapped out the magazine, ejected the round in the chamber.

They exchanged jackets and shirts. "Now we're going to flush your other friend," Bock said, handing César the empty pistol.

They exited the chapel with Bock in front in the hostage position, his hands behind his back as if tied. In them he held his own small automatic against César's stomach. The Israeli agent wouldn't come close enough to distinguish faces, but he'd see the pistol pointed by the gunman at the hostage's back.

Twenty meters out César felt the silent bullet rip through his arm above the elbow; the distance was too great for the special ammunition to be more accurate, César's one hope. He grunted and dropped to the ground as if dead, the empty pistol flying out of his hand. There was a flurry in the brush to their right and Bock raced for it. When he'd gone César pushed himself up and stumbled along the path, holding his bleeding arm. He ran until he came to the bend where he'd thrown the PPK. He searched frantically, finally found it in a tangle of roots. With his good hand he fashioned his belt into a tourniquet, gripping it in his teeth as he tightened. Finished, he moved deeper into the woods toward the buildings in the distance. Ahead a misshapen log turned into David's body, his throat cut like

Kussow's. Bock had wanted no noise that would bring the monks running.

A moment later César heard shouts in the direction of the chapel —then a single shot.

Bock!

With his left hand he worked off the safety on the PPK. He was no match for the Nazi in a gunfight, as good as dead. His one chance was other people. He shot into the air—seven cracks of thunder in the quiet countryside—until the magazine was empty. Bock would understand, weigh the odds of coming after César against escape. He still had Weber to go.

* * *

The local police were sympathetic. César was one of them, after all. He'd been wounded in a gun battle with an assassin who worked for East Germany. The arm was treated, put in a sling. César asked the doctor to extend the sling to his hand.

They found Zeev's body behind the chapel. Inside were Bernie and Max. The assassin Dieter Bock had vanished.

César quickly told the locals all he could. They had come to arrest Bock, wanted for seven slayings in France. César did not know the two men killed in the woods. The third was a former concentration camp victim who was also trailing Bock. The Munich police knew about his assignment; so did Paris, of course.

Back in Munich, César was asked not to leave West Germany until things were sorted out. He had no intention of leaving without Bock. Weber, too, if possible.

This time he knew where to find both of them.

TWENTY-SIX

On the Max-Joseph-Platz the Munich State Opera House was aglow with a dazzle of lights. Under its stuccoed ceiling and single massive chandelier, seated in a half-dozen semicircular tiers, two thousand Wagnerians awaited the opening of the red and gold curtain. Flanking the vast stage were huge Corinthian columns supporting five tiers of boxes. In one of them, a gilded enclosure set slightly above the stage, sat Hans Weber and Jacqueline Volette.

At the colonnaded entrance César stood with the supervisor of the National Theater security section and watched a young couple search frantically for their tickets. There were still fifteen minutes to curtain.

"Wagner." The supervisor shuddered. "When he's on nobody gets any peace." He smiled to show he wasn't really complaining; Wagner and Mozart were the two repertory stars. "I guess I've seen more Wagner than most people. Nine years now."

He popped a candy in his mouth while an aide reported, a two-way radio at his belt. As he left the radio began to squawk.

"You know of course that a French inspector doesn't mean anything here," the supervisor told César. "Nothing."

"Just professional courtesy," César said. "I didn't want to make a fuss by dragging in the local police."

A group arrived, splendidly dressed, and moved smoothly up the main promenade hall. There large mirrors reflected a galaxy of crystal candelabra, early-nineteenth-century elegance.

"Hard to believe this building's only twelve years old," said the supervisor, "instead of two hundred. The whole thing was destroyed in the war, you know. When they rebuilt it they went back to the original plans. Good job, too. Why do you think your man's here?"

"He likes Wagner."

"Who doesn't? Some of that music makes my skin shiver." The supervisor answered his own radio for a moment. "Hate these damn things."

"Useful, though." César fought an impulse to ask for one in case he spotted Bock.

"Not everyone can take him. Wagner, I mean. Had a man here a few years back quit on me; the music was actually painful for him. It reaches too deep into people, if you ask me. Makes you feel things best left alone. Now, I wouldn't want to feel that an inspector from France was trying to get backstage by making up stories."

"Neither would I." César returned the smile.

"Just so we understand each other." The supervisor reached into his jacket pocket. "I'll give you one of these security passes, take you everywhere but the women's washroom. For that you'd need an operation."

* * *

Still ten minutes to go. César walked the length of the auditorium, past the state box, two balconies high and supported by Grecian caryatids, to Weber's private loge. Two men stood by the entrance, bodyguards. Weber came out immediately, all smiles and polish, and led him to a side room at the end of the red-carpeted hallway, the bodyguards following.

"I'm pleased to see you," Weber said, closing the door on them.

"You mean you're surprised to see me."

"Not at all, Inspector. I have absolute faith in your abilities." He chose a gold-pillowed chair. "Now, why do you want to see me?"

"Aren't you afraid of Bock?" César asked.

"Should I be?"

"You've tried twice to have him killed. He'll come after you for that. It's not the money anymore; he knows you won't stop until he's dead."

"Let me tell you something about the German police." Weber crossed his legs, seemingly at ease. "Ordinarily they're very good, but when one of their own is killed they become wounded tigers. Remember the Olympics? Now two are dead. Bock doesn't have a chance. Knowing him—and the police—I don't think he'll be captured alive. Do you?"

"And until then?"

"Until then I'm wrapped in a cocoon of guards and my home is a fortress." He didn't sound unhappy. "Also, I leave for London in the morning on business. Two weeks at least. By then . . ."

César recalled Kussow's words that the Israelis couldn't get to Weber. But he had. They were in a closed room, alone. He could kill the bastard, even if he died for it. With his bad arm he could still kill the man. I should be strangling the life out of him, César thought.

"I'm sorry about your arm," Weber said, as if reading César's mind. "I understand the Israelis did it."

"You sent them."

"I asked them."

"Like you asked me?"

"Killing Bock would've been a public service. The man's a cold-blooded murderer."

"So are you," César snapped. "Bock was the instrument but you directed the Anvil Chorus."

"You're distraught, Inspector. Obsessional love is often worse than the real thing. I was merely trying to help."

"You were trying to help me get killed."

"I was trying to help you kill Bock."

"Five people died today because of you."

The financier bristled. "And Bock escaped because of you."

César saw it was useless. The man was a model of rectitude. He'd never killed anyone, just talked about the possibilities.

Weber glanced at his watch. "It's true I had some misgivings about you," he conceded, "but I see now they were unfounded. There's no proof of anything. The *Anvil* gold? With the others gone I'm safe and when Bock dies it will be over."

"They all had to die," César said reflectively, "but it was Müller you were really after. That's where his share of the gold went after the war, didn't it? Heinrich Müller was your silent partner all these years."

"Heinrich Müller was a dangerous man," Weber said simply, "with dangerous friends."

"He was also getting old, probably wanted to do things with his half of the empire. You didn't like that, decided to take everything for yourself." César nodded sadly. "You're still a Nazi, Mr. Weber, even dressed up in a business suit. You have no class."

"And you have no proof." He checked his watch again. "It's time."

"There's still the woman," César warned. "If she dies—"

"Jacqueline?" Weber gaped in astonishment. "You really are a marvel of paranoia, as bad as Bock. Why would I want her dead?"

"She was with him, remember."

"Which has nothing to do with me. Besides, she's involved too."

"I know about Linge."

"Do you know about Müller?" Weber stood. "You see? She can't talk without cutting her own throat." At the door he turned. "I assure you, Inspector, I mean Jacqueline no harm. I'm actually quite fond of her, even intend to give her some gold." He laughed. "Don't you think she's earned it?"

With the overture to *Siegfried* ringing in his ears, César made his way backstage, seeing Bock everywhere. Did Weber underestimate him? César wondered. Did he really believe Bock would disappear without exacting revenge? Weber was protected but Bock was remorseless. It was his last chance at Weber—and César's last at him. For both, their days in Germany were over.

Backstage was a cavernous quadrangle, and unimaginably cluttered. Ropes dangled from pulleys and hoists; an overhead steel track ran from end to end, used in moving heavy scenery. Electric throw switches for the lighting were grouped on control panels against the far wall, with circuit breakers lining the edges. At the rear a corridor led to the dressing rooms, where waiting performers busied themselves with last-minute magic. The rooms were small and filled with theatrical pursuits. Beyond them was the wardrobe enclosure with its endless rows of costumes. Through a connecting passage César found the set department, a barn that housed painted clouds and stretches of forest alongside rubber rocks and lovers' balconies. Nearby rested a waterfall that had run dry. A waterfall in Munich!

On stage, Siegfried tested the sword forged by his sly Nibelung foster-father Mime, striking it with all his strength on the anvil. To his dismay the sword shattered.

How would Bock get a shot at Weber? César asked himself. He couldn't get into the loge with the bodyguards there.

Unless he were invisible. Then he'd just walk in and stand behind the financier with his silenced Beretta. The police had found only one in the woods.

In the dressing rooms Fafner and the other performers primed for their eventual entrance. Workers in rubber-soled shoes waited for set changes. There was a quiet competence in everyone, a gathering of experience.

César followed a stairway down to the heating and maintenance levels, asked about unusual activity. No one had seen anything.

Why would Bock take the Beretta if he didn't intend to use it in public?

He checked basement rooms and tried locked doors, peered at the faces of those who passed. The underground passage connecting the opera house with the 450-car garage beneath the Max-Joseph-Platz was empty.

What was more public than a performance?

Upstairs again, César wove his way round to the orchestra pit, wooden-floored and resting on beams for better acoustics. From the rear of the pit he listened to the music: the marvelous motives, the elemental brooding and confident elation. He found it impossible to remain indifferent to the music or the composer. Wagner was Hitler's favorite.

With *Die Walküre* riding through the German skies and the Rhine Maidens racing the seas, César managed to feel elated and depressed at the same time. Power, even in music, was an aphrodisiac. But so was the lack of power.

Above him, Wotan leaves the stage as flames spring out at Mime, who fears that Fafner the giant dragon is coming to get him.

At the right of the stage a door opened to the hallway leading up to the various tiers. Weber's loge was on the first level; anyone from backstage could go unseen up the stairs. César stationed himself by the door. Bock might try to surprise the guards that way.

The surroundings became animated. Muscular men warmed up for shifting scenery at the end of Act One. Stagehands shuttled back and forth. At his post César smoothed out the sling. His arm felt like someone was walking on it.

He noticed costumed performers in the wings. They could observe the drama without the audience seeing them.

There was no way Bock could chance a shot from the auditorium. And the Beretta could fire only fifteen meters, which ruled out a sniper's bullet. It began to look like an impossibility.

The costumes seemed peculiarly colorless, as if the force of the music had drained the life out of them.

What to think of people who spent their lives running around stages singing of mystical love and magical acts? Deviants? Fantasy mongers? César had never known anyone in show business.

Wagner told of a race of dwarfs who lived in the depths of the earth and produced gold, and of a race of giants who lived on the earth's surface and won the dwarfs' treasure, and of a race of gods who lived in the lofty skies and interfered. And which am I? César mused.

Bock would have to be crazy or magical to try anything from the rear of the stage; everyone would see him. Unless no one saw him.

César began pacing by the door, his head spinning tales of its own. All of them dealt with a race of Nazis who lived in hell and ended with the last two killing each other. With no one interfering.

There were many ways to be invisible. Repetition was one—mailmen were never noticed—and another was to blend in with the scenery as actors did.

He couldn't stay where he was; something gnawed at him. Instinct, perhaps. He was in the wrong place. Bock wouldn't go for the stairs because there'd be no retreat. It had to be the stage or the wings. The performers!

César hurried across the back wall and down the corridor to the dressing rooms, looked in each again. All were empty. He tried different doors, searching for something amiss, anything.

Jacqueline had killed, yes, but she knew that Weber had ordered the deaths. She could be made to talk, now, someday. Even without proof it would raise suspicion, especially among Müller's dangerous friends. Weber would not allow such a threat to hang over him. Why would he let her live? Or give her gold?

Gray-green walls stared at him, empty space mocked him.

Bock was here. Weber was there, with Jacqueline seated next to him, both of them prominently displayed. Yet she had no reason to be there, a Lorelei combing her golden hair on the Rhine. She was as much a target as him.

A target!

César stopped, startled. Jacqueline had crossed Bock, betrayed him. He would have to kill her as well. And he'd kill her first so Weber could see her dead, know what was coming in those few seconds before he, too, felt the bullet's warm rush. It was part of Germanic legend—betrayal before business—the heritage of both men.

He found the wardrobe mistress face down by her desk; the small round hole in her forehead hardly bled. Costumes were scattered everywhere.

He raced for the wings, his heart pounding insanely. Weber had Jacqueline there for Bock to kill! After the first shot he'd duck to the floor, let his bodyguards take care of Bock. He would be safe, finally, the two of them dead. The last trap.

It was madness. César felt himself floating in cotton.

On the great stage, Mime is brewing a sleeping potion for Siegfried, planning to kill him later with the sword Siegfried has just forged—

In the nearer wing were a half-dozen silent observers in costume. César furiously whirled them around: all were women. Helpless, he gazed across the stage at the opposite wing beneath Weber's box, saw one of the performers, hooded and robed, raise his arm.

—while on stage Siegfried raises his sword to test it on the anvil, bringing it down with a deafening crash.

"Bock-k-k-k!"

César's agonizing cry splintered the air as the anvil split in two, a miracle of steel on iron.

In the box on the first tier, Jacqueline Volette slumped silently to the floor. Weber was already under the railing, his bodyguards reaching for their weapons as the curtain came down on Siegfried's exaltation and César's despair.

Dieter Bock was gone.

César burst across the stage past startled performers—a madman with a broken arm!—to the other wing. The cumbersome sling slowed him down and he threw off his jacket. Barreling through the horrified onlookers, he spotted a gray garment on the ground by the back wall. It was the hooded robe; Bock had rid himself of it on the run, César supposed. He covered the distance on flying feet, past the robe and into the corridor.

César heard only his own steps in the stone passageway, stretching straight back from the stage. Overhead lights in black bulb-shields threw strange shapes on the walls. At the next turn, César caught sight of someone rounding a curve in the corridor. When he got there Bock was scooting down a flight of iron steps. At the bottom a series of tunnels led to the storage bins; the other way ran to the north wall and the truck bays used for deliveries. César darted from one tunnel to the next. None of them, he quickly realized, would take Bock out of the building; as long as he could track his prey he had a chance. If he could only get close enough. He wheezed as he flew, already out of breath. He could feel Bock's presence, furious, trying to escape his ardent pursuer.

Passing the bins he pounded on the doors, examined the padlocks. None was open. He headed toward the north wall and the transport doors. At the tunnel's end was a second, shorter stairway. Bock was descending into the bowels of the earth. Like the Nibelungs, César thought, but without the gold. His arm hurt; he felt fresh blood trickling down his skin, staining his shirt. He refused to look; it would disappear if he didn't look. What mothers told their children, some mothers. He stopped, listened, heard rattling noises nearby. He hurried ahead, came out on an open area. There were three truck bays feeding into a concrete platform, with overhead doors for each; they must have been what Bock was trying. All were padlocked, which meant he'd doubled back.

César started across the platform, felt the sting as the bullet sliced through his leg. He stumbled, fell, rolled off the concrete ledge into the bay next to one of the parked trucks. Bock was too good for a flesh wound; he'd picked off a shot at more than fifteen meters, the bullet spent. The other end of the platform, César supposed. He straightened the sling, pushed himself up and hobbled around the front of the two trucks to the steps on the far side. Looked over the top, cautiously. In the office squeezed into the building's corner, Bock was searching for keys to unlock the transport doors. César slowly approached from the blind side, trailing blood. He ducked under the windows until he got to the opened door. He would take Bock by surprise.

Shouts were heard in the distance, a swelling of voices. César turned toward the sound just as Bock whirled around, saw him standing in the doorway.

"You!"

César's head snapped back; their eyes locked in combat.

Bock grabbed his gun from the desk, ordered César inside. "It will be your vault," he promised.

"And yours," César said.

The Nazi held out a set of keys—"Not just yet"—screwed his face into a quizzical frown. "Why do you chase me?"

"Why do you run?"

"We are the same," Bock snarled, "partners in the hunt. Who's to say which of us is the prey?"

"We may be hunters," César granted, "but we're not the same."

Sounds reverberated again, still distant.

Bock's hand closed over the keys; in the other was the long-nosed Beretta. "You came to me once today without a gun, and I let you live," he reminded César. "Now there's nowhere left for you to run."

"Or you."

The Beretta came up in Bock's hand as César fired the concealed PPK in his sling. The bullet smashed into Bock's side. Bock lurched, tried to level his gun at César. The sling jumped as the next two slugs slammed Bock in the shoulder and neck; the Beretta flew out of his grasp. The fourth shot creased his scalp on the way down. A tongue of flame licked at the edges of the burned bandage.

César eased the fold of the sling up over his head and off. The arm fell to his side and he almost fainted from the pain. Bock was lying on his back, breathing in angry gasps. His eyes were open. César saw the SS killer standing over his victims, solicitous to the end, making certain they were dead. César's parents and Yishay Kussow and all the murdered millions. Jacqueline Volette, too. César knelt next to Bock. He pried the pistol out of his cramped fingers with his other hand and forced the barrel into Bock's mouth and pulled the trigger. Bock's head jolted off the floor as tissue exploded through the crown of his skull. This time nothing will save you, César raged. He pulled the trigger again, and then again until the gun was empty.

The hunt was over.

César placed Bock's pistol on the body, where it belonged.

He had committed murder. He'd killed someone who might have survived. He had murdered.

Now they were the same. Now he was one of them.

Bock had won, after all.

The sounds were coming closer.

Weber had won as well.

* * *

The inspector's letter eventually reached La Paz, Bolivia, where it was routed on to leaders of the *Kameradenwerk,* the Nazi underground organization that evolved out of the network of SS clandestine groups formed after the war.

While convalescing, César had written a brief account of Weber's activities concerning the *Anvil* gold, ending with the financier's plan that led to the murder of a half-dozen SS officers, including Major General Heinrich Müller, Gestapo boss of bosses.

Through a friendly source, César's account was given to someone with contacts in the underground. Its leaders knew of Müller's death in 1973. A tragedy, one of the greatest Nazi heroes! Now they read of Müller's murder.

Within days a team from "Spider," the discipline squad of the *Kameradenwerk,* was enroute to Frankfurt and Wiesbaden. Unlike the Israelis, they were German and would be on their own hunting ground. They would track down the final name in the Anvil Chorus.

As César had known from the beginning, the Nazis were always there. It was the reason for everything.

EPILOGUE

Spain. César looked out onto the morning street of the quiet sea-coast town. The buildings were bleached white in the sun, hundreds of years of sun burning down on brick and mortar, cement and sand. Almost as white as the white of Algiers, he thought. Here he liked mornings best, with the sun a constant companion. A hat was an easy price to pay.

He had put on a few pounds, learned to like food a little more. Castilian specialties even looked good! And the grape was still drunk. If not of French vintage, it was yet pleasing and good for the stomach. God surely wouldn't have made the Spanish grape if He hadn't meant it to be pressed. Drinking it, the locals believed, was honoring God's work. And César was a devout believer.

It had been five years since his retirement from the Paris Police Department, seven since the deaths of Dieter Bock and Hans Weber.

In that time he'd remarried—a Spanish woman of honesty and spirit—and begun to raise a family. He had found a new life, one that brought him much satisfaction. Yet the shadow remained.

Now maybe it was time to lay the demons to rest.

He would tell his story of murder. Tell it just as it happened, through the eyes of an inspector of police.

Who, after all, knew more about such things?

He would call it a novel.

And all would pretend it wasn't the truth.

He'd even include the possibility of hidden treasure, of gold still missing. The Israelis received two billion dollars, but estimates placed the *Anvil* gold at three billion. What happened to the other billion in gold?

It would be still another mystery to add to all the others.

César sat at the typewriter, his hands already sweating, the resolve weakening. A murderer in the confessional.

Where to begin?

In the beginning. In Paris. In April.

*   *   *

Everything is so easy for the young, who are not hampered by wisdom or experience.

"Suicide," said the youthful detective from headquarters, "plain and simple."

The two of them stood off to one side of the room, their words pointed, their eyes narrowed in that careful look all policemen seem to share. They had watched the corpse removed, the noose unwound; on the floor a chalk outline marked where the body had fallen. All the pictures were taken, the information noted. What more could be done with suicide?

"Not so simple," suggested the tall spare inspector. He was older and wiser and had seen a few things in his day. . . .